320

MW00757832

BISHOP   Bishop, Anne.

Wild country.

MAR - - 2019   32026030031386

$27.00

DATE			

WITHDRAWN

FOREST PARK PUBLIC LIBRARY

BAKER & TAYLOR

WILD
COUNTRY

BOOKS BY ANNE BISHOP

The Others Series

Written in Red
Murder of Crows
Vision in Silver
Marked in Flesh
Etched in Bone

The World of the Others

Lake Silence
Wild Country

The Black Jewels Series

Daughter of the Blood
Heir to the Shadows
Queen of the Darkness
The Invisible Ring
Dreams Made Flesh
Tangled Webs
The Shadow Queen
Shalador's Lady
Twilight's Dawn

The Ephemera Series

Sebastian
Belladonna
Bridge of Dreams

The Tir Alainn Trilogy

The Pillars of the World
Shadows and Light
The House of Gaian

WILD COUNTRY

THE WORLD OF THE OTHERS

ANNE BISHOP

FOREST PARK PUBLIC LIBRARY

MAR - - 2019

FOREST PARK, IL

ACE
NEW YORK

ACE
Published by Berkley
An imprint of Penguin Random House LLC
1745 Broadway, New York, NY 10019

Copyright © 2019 by Anne Bishop
Penguin Random House supports copyright. Copyright fuels creativity, encourages diverse voices,
promotes free speech, and creates a vibrant culture. Thank you for buying an authorized edition
of this book and for complying with copyright laws by not reproducing, scanning, or distributing
any part of it in any form without permission. You are supporting writers and allowing
Penguin Random House to continue to publish books for every reader.

ACE is a registered trademark and the A colophon is a trademark of Penguin Random House LLC.

Library of Congress Cataloging-in-Publication Data

Names: Bishop, Anne, author.
Title: Wild country / Anne Bishop.
Description: First edition. | New York: Ace, 2019. | Series: [World of the others; 2]
Identifiers: LCCN 2018041885 | ISBN 9780399587276 (hardback) |
ISBN 9780399587283 (ebook)
Subjects: | BISAC: FICTION/Fantasy/Contemporary. | FICTION/Romance/Fantasy. |
GSAFD: Fantasy fiction.
Classification: LCC PS3552.I7594 W55 2019 | DDC 813/.54—dc23
LC record available at https://lccn.loc.gov/2018041885

First Edition: March 2019

Printed in the United States of America
1   3   5   7   9   10   8   6   4   2

Jacket art by Robert Jones/Arcangel Images
Jacket design by Adam Auerbach
Book design by Laura K. Corless
Interior art: Cedar tree forest © Anna Om/Shutterstock.com

This is a work of fiction. Names, characters, places, and incidents either are the product of
the author's imagination or are used fictitiously, and any resemblance to actual persons,
living or dead, business establishments, events, or locales is entirely coincidental.

For

Janet Chase

and

Jana Paniccia

ACKNOWLEDGMENTS

My thanks to Blair Boone for continuing to be my first reader and for all the information about animals, weapons, and many other things that I absorbed and transformed to suit the Others' world; to Debra Dixon for being second reader; to Doranna Durgin for maintaining the Web site and for all the information she shared with me about dogs and horses; to Patricia Briggs for her contribution toward my knowledge about horses; to Janet Chase for showing me around Reno and the surrounding area and helping me find inspiration for my frontier town; to Adrienne Roehrich for running the official fan page on Facebook; to Nadine Fallacaro for information about things medical; to Ann Hergott for her help with the map; to Jennifer Crow for being a sounding board for the story during our dinner-and-book-binge evenings; to Anne Sowards and Jennifer Jackson for the feedback that helps me write a better story; and to Pat Feidner for always being supportive and encouraging.

A special thanks to the following people who loaned their names to characters, knowing that the name would be the only connection between reality and fiction: Kelley Burch, Douglas Burke, Candice Cavanaugh, Janet Chase, Jennifer Crow, Roger Czerneda, Merri Lee Debany, Michael Debany, Nadine Fallacaro, James Alan Gardner, Mantovani "Monty" Gay, Lois Gresh, Jana Paniccia, Craig Werner, Dawn Werner, and John Wulf.

BENNETT TOWN SQUARE

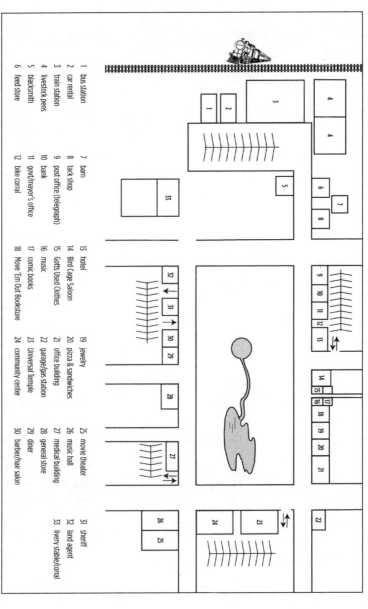

1	bus station	7	barn	13	hotel
2	car rental	8	tack shop	14	Bird Cage Saloon
3	train station	9	post office (telegraph)	15	Gotts Used Clothes
4	livestock pens	10	bank	16	music
5	blacksmith	11	govt/mayor's office	17	comic books
6	feed store	12	bike corral	18	Move 'Em Out Bookstore

19	jewelry	25	movie theater	31	sheriff
20	pizza & sandwiches	26	music hall	32	land agent
21	office building	27	medical building	33	livery stable/corral
22	garage/gas station	28	general store	
23	Universal Temple	29	diner	
24	community center	30	barber/hair salon	

Note: This map was created by a geographically challenged author.

© 2019 by Anne Bishop

AUTHOR'S NOTE
ABOUT THE STORY'S TIMELINE

If you've read *Etched in Bone*, some of the events in *Wild Country* will be familiar to you. That's because the timelines of the two stories are intertwined and take place shortly after the war between humans and the *terra indigene*.

WILD COUNTRY

A year from now, it would be called the Great Predation—those terrifying days when the Elementals and the Elders, the *terra indigene* who are Namid's teeth and claws, came out of the wild country and brutally thinned the human herds in Thaisia. In some cases, they wiped out the entire population of human towns in the Northwest and Midwest in retaliation for the slaughter of the Wolfgard and other forms of shifters who had kept watch over the human places.

Now, with death still fresh in everyone's minds, *terra indigene* and humans alike want to claim those empty places, especially the places of strategic importance.

Bennett is one of those places—and the Elders are staying nearby, waiting for the humans to make another mistake.

Waiting for them to make the last mistake.

CHAPTER 1

Windsday, Sumor 25

Jana Paniccia followed the gravel paths through the memorial park. There were no cemeteries on the continent of Thaisia, no individual gravestones, no family mausoleums unless you were very rich. Cities couldn't afford to waste land on the dead when the living needed every acre that they were grudgingly permitted to lease from the *terra indigene* who ruled the continent.

Who ruled the world. They had smashed and torn that harsh truth into humans around the world, and only fools or the blindly optimistic thought there was any chance of things going back to the way they had been before the Humans First and Last movement had started the war against the *terra indigene* here in Thaisia and in Cel-Romano on the other side of the Atlantik Ocean.

Instead of gaining anything from the war, humans had lost ground—literally. Cities had been destroyed or were no longer under human control. People were running to anyplace they thought could provide safety, thinking that the larger cities were less vulnerable to what the Others could do.

In that, too, humans were wrong. The destruction of so much of

Toland, a large human-controlled city on the East Coast, should have taught people that much.

But this wasn't a day to think about those things.

Jana found the large flower bed with the tall granite marker in the center.

There were no graveyards, no gravestones, in Thaisia, but there were memorial parks full of flower beds and small ponds, with benches positioned so the living could visit with the dead. She looked down the double column of names carved into the granite until she found the two she'd come to see. Martha Chase. Wilbur Chase. The foster parents who had taken her from the foundling home and raised her as their own. There hadn't been even a birth certificate left with her when the Universal Temple priests had found her on the temple doorstep. Just a printed note with her name and birth date.

All bodies were cremated and the ashes mixed with the soil in these flower beds, the names carved in the granite the only acknowledgment of who was there. Martha had loved growing flowers, and Pops had always tended a small vegetable garden in their backyard. Jana was the one who had no skill with the soil, no matter how hard she tried. She knew a rose from a daisy, understood the difference between annual and perennial, and, most of the time, had dug up weeds instead of flowers when she tried to help Martha tidy the beds.

You have other talents, Pops used to say with a laugh.

Other talents. Gods, she hoped so.

They had died in a car accident just a week after she'd been accepted into the police academy—one of only three women to be accepted. She'd spent the first few months struggling with her classwork and the hostility of her classmates while traveling from Hubb NE to a village near the Addirondak Mountains to meet with the Chases' attorney and take care of her foster parents' estate. There wasn't much. Martha and Pops had never been interested in things, but the sale of the house and furnishings was enough to pay off the school loans she'd taken out to attend a community college while she tried to get accepted into the police academy. It was enough to pay for the academy and living expenses. She'd been frugal, but if she didn't get a job soon . . .

"Hey, Martha," Jana said softly after looking around to make sure she was alone. "Hey, Pops." She sat on the bench, her hands folded in her lap. "I graduated from the academy. The only woman who stuck it out. Martha, you always said I was stubborn, and I guess you were right. I have a meeting with the academy administrator next week. Hopefully it will be about a job offer. The gods know, every human community needs cops right now, and everyone else in my class has already been hired by towns in the Northeast Region, which lost officers last month because of the war. But I know there are positions that haven't been filled yet because no one wants to take a job in a village stuck in the middle of the wild country. They say that's just delayed suicide. Maybe they're right, but I'd take that chance."

She looked at the flowers growing in the bed and wished she could remember the names of some of them. "I came to say good-bye. It's getting harder and harder to purchase a bus ticket, and I'm not sure I'll be able to get back here again. And if I'm hired—*when* I'm hired—I may be leaving in a hurry." She paused. "Thanks for everything. When I get to wherever I'm going, I'll light a candle in remembrance."

Jana hurried through the park, gauging that she had just enough time to reach the bus stop near the park gates and catch the bus back to Hubb NE. She hoped that by this time next week she'd be heading to another town to do the only job she'd ever wanted to do.

CHAPTER 2

Windsday, Sumor 25

"I quit."

Tolya Sanguinati studied Jesse Walker as they faced each other over the counter in Bennett's general store. The look in her eyes made him think of the lightning that sometimes filled the sky in this part of Thaisia. Despite being a dangerous predator—far more dangerous than the humans here appreciated—that look made him wary. "You can't quit."

"Oh, yes, I can."

He took a step back and considered. It was tempting to point out that, since she didn't actually work for him, she couldn't, technically, quit. But Jesse Walker was the unofficial leader of Prairie Gold, a small Intuit town located at the southern end of the Elder Hills. As such, she was his most important human ally. He couldn't afford to lose her knowledge or cooperation, so it probably wasn't a good idea to point out anything.

Erebus Sanguinati, the leader of all the Sanguinati on the continent of Thaisia, had told him to take over Bennett after all the humans had been slaughtered by Namid's teeth and claws. The town had a train station that serviced all the ranches in the area, as well as Prairie Gold. That made it an important place that the Elders would no longer allow humans to control because, under human control, the trains that traveled back and forth across the land had brought enemies to this part of Thaisia. Had brought death to the Wolfgard and other shifters.

Every place inhabited by humans was in turmoil right now because no one knew how many of those places had survived. With quick communication between regions severed by the Elders' destroying the telephone lines and tearing down the mobile phone towers all along the regional boundaries, e-mail and phones of any kind were useful only within a region. But even within a region, no one really knew whether a phone went unanswered because someone wasn't in the office at that moment or because there was no one left in that town to answer it.

But the rest of the Midwest Region wasn't his problem. Right now, his problem was the slim, middle-aged, gray-haired woman who had been helping him prioritize the tasks necessary to keep the train station open and to deal with urgent things like spoiling food and pets that had been left in residences.

Until he traveled to Prairie Gold to be Grandfather Erebus's eyes and ears, Tolya had lived his whole life in Toland, one of the largest cities on the entire continent. He'd had the most extensive human-centric education available to the *terra indigene* and had been among the Sanguinati who monitored the television newscasts and the newspapers as a way of keeping an eye on what the duplicitous humans might be planning. And he'd been among the Sanguinati who had actual contact and dealings with government officials and businessmen. But those meetings had been formal, official, devoid of personal contact and feelings beyond the loathing each side felt for the other.

Nothing in his education or years of experience had prepared him to deal with messy, daily interaction with humans who had no interest in being formal, official, or devoid of personal contact. Even his previous interactions with this woman while he helped her and the other residents of Prairie Gold prepare to hold out against humans trying to cut them off from supplies hadn't prepared him to deal with her now.

"Why?" he finally asked.

"Because you're not listening," Jesse Walker snapped.

"I listen to everything you say," Tolya countered.

Her right hand clamped around her left wrist.

Jesse Walker was an Intuit, a kind of human who had a heightened sensitivity to the world, and her people had feelings about everything from animals to weather to sensing if someone was lying. Each Intuit didn't have feelings about everything—their minds would break under that kind of strain—but each developed a sensitivity that matched who they were or the work they did. For Jesse Walker, it was people, and an aching left wrist was her tell that something about a situation made her uneasy—and the more severe the ache, the more dire the situation.

"I have listened," Tolya said again. "But perhaps I'm not under-standing?"

He watched her anger fade. Her right hand still cuffed her left wrist, but the hold was looser now. He wondered if her wrist would be bruised.

"What are we doing here?" Jesse Walker asked. "Are we just cleaning up what will become a ghost town with a few people manning the train station or are we doing something more?"

An important question. Looking at her, Tolya realized his answer would do more than decide the fate of this town. It would ripple through-out Thaisia in the same way that Simon Wolfgard's decision to hire Meg Corbyn had started ripples that were part of the reason he was here in this town trying to figure out this woman.

If Simon were standing here right now, Tolya would cheerfully snap the Wolf's neck. Then again, if he tried to be fair, Simon hadn't known that taking in one stray human female would end up with the *terra indigene* trying to help—and even protect—packs of humans.

"Not a ghost town," he said carefully. "Bennett is no longer a human-controlled town, but that doesn't mean it has to decay."

"Or that its workers are transient?"

"They aren't meant to be transient. Some of the young humans who have come here don't feel this is the right place. They came for adven-ture . . . or something."

"They came for opportunities," Jesse Walker countered. "They came because their home communities in the Northeast Region are crowded and it's hard to find work, hard to learn a skill. And many of them left home for the adventure. But they also left what they knew because, sud-denly, there are a lot of empty human places in the Midwest and North-west. I have the feeling that there won't be any new human places. Not for a long time. Not in Thaisia. Humans made too many mistakes over the past few months for the *terra indigene* to tolerate us anyplace we aren't already established. So if the empty places aren't reinhabited now, they'll fade away."

"I don't think the Elders will allow humans to move back into those empty places," Tolya said.

"Not alone, no. But there are *terra indigene* and Intuits working together here to take care of animals and make decisions about the food in the houses. And there's a lot more that needs to be done. Decisions have to be made about every single thing in every single residence."

"I can't do that," he protested.

"Neither can I. That's why you need more than strong young men who will happily eat all the ice cream and cookies they find in the empty residences but don't know what to do with the medicines. And whether those Elders of yours were justified in killing everyone in Bennett, those people may still have family somewhere who would appreciate having the personal effects. Having young men with a lot of energy and strong backs is great, but you also need skilled labor and professionals if you want this to be a viable town. Why can't we create a place where *terra indigene* and Intuits and Simple Life folk and other kinds of humans can live and work together? Learn from each other. I got the impression that the Lakeside Courtyard and the Intuits in Ferryman's Landing were trying to do exactly that—build a new community that had room for everyone."

"Dangerous." Tolya looked out the big front window of Bennett's general store. "If the wrong kind of human comes here . . ."

"I know. No one can afford to make a mistake."

"Then how do you suggest we get these new citizens?"

They heard the clip-clop of a horse coming down the street. Barbara Ellen Debany, their pet caretaker and almost-vet, waved at them as she passed the store.

"Same way you got her," Jesse Walker said, smiling as she released her left wrist long enough to return the wave. "Have someone else screen the candidates before they get here, and then you make the final decision about who you want living in this town." She took a folded piece of paper out of the back pocket of her jeans and handed it to him. "Ideally, those are the professions and skills you should have in Bennett for starters."

Tolya unfolded the paper. His eyebrows rose as he studied the list. Then he looked at Jesse Walker. "Anyone from Prairie Gold who might want to fill a position?"

"Kelley Burch. His skills are wasted in Prairie Gold, and there is a jewelry store here that needs someone to run it—and Kelley would have a better chance of selling some of his own designs, whether he sells them in Bennett or sends them on to someplace back east to sell on consignment. I'm going down to Prairie Gold tomorrow. I'll talk to him then."

"You want to spend time in your own store."

She nodded. "I need to be home for a couple of days."

"I'll get this list out as quickly as I can." The Elders weren't allowing the telephone and telegraph lines between the regions to be restored except under special circumstances. He could call or e-mail Jackson Wolfgard, who lived in Sweetwater, a settlement in the Northwest, but reaching Lakeside in the Northeast Region required extra time and effort.

As he left the store, he looked at the Intuit woman and wondered if Jesse Walker would come back and continue to help him. Then he noticed that she was no longer holding her left wrist—and he breathed a sigh of relief.

Virgil Wolfgard stood next to a tree near the south end of the town square and watched the human female and the blue horse walk toward him. The wind was in the wrong direction to carry his scent to the horse, which was meandering across the paved street toward the grass in the square, and the female seemed too preoccupied with something that wasn't right in front of her to control the horse or notice the predator who was watching her.

Not noticing was dangerous, something the female should have learned while she was still a puppy.

He stepped away from the tree, putting himself right in front of the horse.

The horse snorted and planted its feet, causing the female to grab the saddle horn for balance.

"Easy, Rowan, easy," she said. Then she gave Virgil a wary look. "Sheriff."

"Barbara Ellen." Virgil looked at her companion. "Horse."

His brother, Kane, who was in Wolf form, joined them, causing Rowan to snort again.

Barbara Ellen gave Kane a wobbly smile. "Deputy Wolfgard."

Virgil held up a small red collar. She took it and read the tag attached to the collar. "Fluffy," she said sadly. "She was a nice cat."

"We didn't eat it," Virgil said, anticipating the question she didn't dare ask. "Too much fur and not enough meat."

"Not much of an epitaph for poor Fluffy."

Maybe not, but that wasn't important. He and Kane hadn't killed the cat, but *something* had torn the animal apart. Not for food. For fun.

And that *something* wasn't any form of *terra indigene*.

"The horse was paying attention," Virgil said. All right, the horse was more interested in reaching the grass, but it did notice him first. "You were not. Why?"

"I was thinking about some stuff," she replied.

He didn't ask what she was thinking about. He just stared.

"But I should pay attention when I'm riding," she added.

"Yes." Virgil stepped aside. So did Kane.

Barbara Ellen pressed her legs against Rowan's sides—and grabbed the saddle horn when the gelding bolted out of reach of the two Wolves.

Virgil shook his head as he watched her reestablish dominance and slow the horse to a walk. <Follow her,> he told Kane, using the *terra indigene* form of communication. <Make sure she doesn't fall off.>

The only good human was a dead human. He hadn't thought much of that species before the Humans First and Last movement had attacked the Wolfgard. He thought far less of them after those humans slaughtered his pack, leaving him and Kane the only survivors because they'd been ranging ahead of the pack, looking for game. They'd come running back when they heard the guns, but by the time they arrived, the pack was dead or dying, and the humans were gone.

They'd followed the trail of the trucks until scent markers made by Namid's teeth and claws crossed the trail. Not willing to tangle with the

Elders, he and Kane had returned to the small wooden den the pack had used to store items useful to those who could take human form. After packing the little they could carry in Wolf form, they had headed away from what had been their home territory, looking for humans to kill.

Instead, they ended up in Bennett, where the Elders had erased the enemy and yet were allowing those *creatures* to return.

He'd never seen one of the Sanguinati until he'd met Tolya, who had been given the task of making sure the wrong kind of humans didn't try to reclaim the place. But for that, Tolya needed humans as well as many forms of *terra indigene*. And he needed enforcers who were strong enough and feared enough that humans would follow rules and not become troublesome.

That was how Virgil ended up the town's dominant enforcer, with Kane being the second enforcer. He didn't know anything about human law, hadn't spent much time around actual humans until now. But if one of the two-legged threats caused trouble, he knew how to stop them dead in their tracks. And blood in the street would be a good reminder to the rest of them of why they should behave.

And then there were the two-legs like Barbara Ellen he felt reluctantly compelled to protect.

He walked along the edge of the town square, which served as a park surrounded by the town's original business district. A natural spring was the reason for the grass and trees—was the reason the town had been built there. The spring had been semicontained by human-made barriers, but the water still bubbled out of the ground, providing drinking water for everything with fur or feathers—and humans too.

When he came abreast of the general store, he stopped and waited for Tolya to cross the street and join him.

"Was there a problem with Barbara Ellen?" Tolya asked.

Virgil cocked his head. "Why do we call her that? The humans call her Barb."

"Barbara Ellen sounds dignified. I'm hoping she'll grow into the name, like a puppy grows into its big feet."

"Huh." That made sense, except . . . "She's young but she's an adult, not a pup. Do you really think she'll grow into a dignified name?"

"I am hopeful."

Tolya's dry tone made Virgil smile. Barbara Ellen Debany had ties to the Lakeside Courtyard because her brother was a police officer who worked directly with Simon Wolfgard. That made her special among the humans who were in Bennett. And being special meant he had the task of trying to keep her out of trouble. Which made him think of the way she tended to want to befriend any and every critter.

"Are there any Snakegard here?" he asked.

"A couple of Rattlers arrived last week. Why?"

"Someone should explain to her about staying away from things that could kill her." Virgil thought for a moment, then added, "Things that aren't us."

"Speaking of things that are not us, Jesse Walker feels we need to bring in more humans to become permanent residents and take over the businesses."

"More." Virgil's lips pulled back in a snarl. "More of *them?*"

"And more of us. Enough *terra indigene* to maintain control of this place." Tolya met Virgil's eyes. "How would you feel about that? Being around them at all is difficult for you and Kane."

"I don't know human law," Virgil growled. "I know how to kill." Too often after a day around humans, he wanted to shed this terrible form and howl out his rage before he tore into throats and bellies and left bodies in pieces like . . . like . . .

"There is too much human bounty here for us to abandon this town," Tolya said quietly. "If we don't hold on to it, humans will flood in to claim what they can."

"Just because we hold on to it, you think the enemy *won't* find this place?"

"Find it? Yes. Even with the travel restrictions that limit humans migrating between regions, they will find a way to reach this place. Control it?" Tolya shook his head. "The Elders won't allow that. If the Northwest, Southwest, and Midwest Regions are purged of humans, they'll be held to the coasts and the towns available to them there."

"And we'll have back what was ours in the first place," Virgil snapped.

"Should a human like Jesse Walker die? She protected the young in the Prairie Gold pack. She's teaching a young Wolf human skills."

He liked Jesse Walker, as much as he could like any human. "There will be enough of us to stand against the humans if they turn rabid?"

Tolya nodded. "Enough of us who can work in the shops alongside the humans and be ever watchful—and kill what cannot be allowed to remain among us."

"We need to find someone who knows human law."

"Another deputy. I'll add that request to the list of professionals I'll send to Lakeside. We'll see what help Simon and Vlad can provide in the way of humans while we send a message among our own for any who are willing to live near humans."

They walked up the street together, parting at the building that held the sheriff's office.

Going into the back, Virgil studied the three cells. Not a lot of space for wrongdoers, but it would have to be enough.

Humans. Couldn't live with them; couldn't eat them all.

CHAPTER 3

Thaisday, Sumor 26

"Did I do something wrong?" Rachel Wolfgard asked, an anxious whine beneath the words.

"No, honey, you did a great job," Jesse replied. "I just need time in my own place for a few days."

"Familiar smells are good." Rachel's hands gathered up the skirt of her summer dress and tightened into fists that would, most likely, crease the lightweight material. "I didn't mark territory in your store, even though it is my store too."

"Appreciate that. Urine smell in a store selling fresh food tends to put people off their feed."

"Why? One of the men came in yesterday and made a fart that smelled so bad Shelley Bookman left her shopping and went outside, and when she came back, she asked me to smell the food to make sure it still smelled fresh."

It took effort not to smile. "Smelled that bad, did it?"

Rachel nodded. "My eyes watered."

"Which man?" It hadn't escaped her notice that the juvenile Wolf had not named the bad-mannered lout. "It wasn't Tobias, was it?" If it *was* her son, she'd be having a few words with him.

"No," Rachel replied quickly. "Tobias wouldn't do anything that smelled that bad."

No longer able to hide her smile, Jesse turned toward the canned goods that filled the shelves along one wall. It sounded like Rachel had a little crush on Tobias. She was too young for him, of course, just as he was too old for her—not to mention her being a *terra indigene* Wolf and him being a human.

Then her boy walked into the store.

"Howdy, Rachel," Tobias said. "That dress looks nice on you."

"Thank you, Tobias. I am wearing the underpants and undershirt too because that is what females should wear beneath the clothing that is seen." Rachel looked at Jesse. "And I have learned how to wash them. Ellen Garcia taught me while you were away."

"That's good," Jesse replied, studying the way Tobias blushed but gave no other sign that underclothes weren't something usually discussed with the other gender.

Not a crush on her son, Jesse decided as she watched the two of them. This was a very innocent younger sister revealing things to her older brother.

It made sense. With the exception of the nanny, all the adults in the Prairie Gold pack had been slaughtered by members of the Humans First and Last movement. Heeding Tolya Sanguinati's warning, she and the rest of the women in Prairie Gold had gathered up the children, human and Other, and headed into the Elder Hills to a spot where they would be safe from human killers.

Now the *terra indigene* settlement had a new leader, Morgan Wolf-gard, and a new enforcer, Chase Wolfgard. Along with the Grizzly Wyatt Beargard they were the main contacts between the Intuits and the *terra indigene*—including the Elders who lived in, and protected, the hills.

Rachel continued to travel from the *terra indigene* settlement and work in Walker's General Store, under Jesse's supervision and on her own during the days when Jesse was in Bennett helping to sort things out there. Morgan and Chase weren't happy about their lone juvenile female being surrounded by humans, but their allowing Rachel to be in town was the strongest indication that they were trying to get along with the humans who lived in their territory.

And Morgan and Chase didn't scare her half as much as Virgil Wolfgard, Bennett's new sheriff.

They needed workers in Bennett. They needed people to resettle the town. More than that, they needed someone Virgil would trust enough that he wouldn't look at every human as the enemy.

"Did you come in for supplies?" Rachel asked. "I could make up a box of supplies like cans of beans and coffee and—"

Jesse watched the back of Rachel's dress swish as the young Wolf lost control of the human form enough to regain her tail, which was wagging to indicate her eagerness to help. Fortunately, the girl was facing Tobias so he didn't notice.

"Ellen is coming in for supplies tomorrow. I'm here to talk to my mother," Tobias replied.

"Okay."

When he didn't say anything, Jesse looked at Rachel. "Honey, why don't you finish stocking the shelves. Tobias, you come on to the back room with me."

A little whine, followed by a human-sounding sigh. Understandable that Rachel felt anxious anytime she was excluded, but the girl needed to learn that sometimes other people needed privacy and not everything was shared by the whole pack, however "pack" was defined.

"You look tired, son." Jesse pressed her hand against one side of Tobias's face.

"We're all putting in longer hours." Tobias leaned against the wall. "Too few men for the amount of land we're trying to cover and the cattle we're trying to keep track of."

"There might be relief coming."

"If they can sit a horse, I'll hire them. Gods, even if they can't sit a horse, I'll hire them."

"Don't set your sights too low. I think I've convinced Tolya Sanguinati that we need more people if he doesn't want Bennett to turn into a ghost town."

"You think he'll agree?"

"I think he will. But we'll need to be careful, watchful." Her right hand closed over her left wrist. "We need the people. We need to keep the town alive. But what is good for us won't be the only thing getting off the train."

CHAPTER 4

Thaisday, Sumor 26

Parlan Blackstone sat at one of the tables in the executive car, playing solitaire and ignoring the looks from the men who were playing poker at another table. He wasn't sure they knew who he was when they'd invited him to join them, but he'd had a bad feeling about two of the men and had declined, claiming he didn't have much of a head for cards.

They hadn't believed him, but no one was drunk enough—yet—to call him a liar.

At the next stop, he'd leave the executive car and retreat to his private car. He'd hoped to play a few games during this stage of the trip to balance the rising cost of train fares, but the men in the car . . . They wore expensive suits, but they were still thugs.

The Blackstone Clan might be gamblers and swindlers, but they weren't thugs. Not that he was opposed to hiring muscle who liked the sort of work that required brass knuckles—or guns—but the Blackstone name was never associated with those activities.

Parlan didn't look over at the other men, but he sensed a change in their intentions. There was no one else in the executive car. From the perfume scents in the washroom at the back of the car, he knew there had been one or more women with the men before the last stop. Since the women weren't in the executive car now, they'd fulfilled their purpose and were no longer wanted.

He wondered briefly if they'd been left at the last station or had been tossed off the train. He had a feeling at least one of those men would find tossing a woman off a moving train amusing. Or expedient. And he had a strong feeling that they were considering doing the same to him after relieving him of his wallet and a few of his teeth.

Not that they would have a chance to relieve him of anything.

One of the men shifted on the padded bench seat. Parlan ignored him; didn't reach for the derringer or the knife he carried because at the same moment the man stood up, the door of the executive car opened and two men walked in from the regular passenger car.

The first man didn't look at the four men, but Parlan knew he saw all of them. Those men might be thugs, but this man was a stone-cold killer who truly enjoyed his work.

The man nodded to Parlan before taking one of the leather seats behind Parlan's bench seat. He chose the aisle seat, where he could see the other men, who no longer found Parlan interesting.

The second man stopped at Parlan's table. "Not your usual game."

Parlan looked up and smiled. "Hello, Henry. Have a seat." After Henry Hollis settled in the bench seat opposite him, he gathered the cards and shuffled. "I wasn't in the mood for my usual game. What about you?"

Henry took out his wallet and laid a hundred-dollar bill on the table. "A farewell game."

That was all Hollis was going to wager? Parlan looked at the bill and wondered if Henry had fallen on hard times. "Farewell? You going somewhere?"

"I'm giving up the life."

He looked at Henry in surprise. "What's this?"

"It's time to quit."

Parlan was aware that the four men had noticed the bill Henry had put on the table and sensed they were wondering how much Henry might be carrying. Then they looked at Judd McCall sitting quietly behind Parlan.

As long as those men were the first ones off the train, Henry would be safe. No one but a fool tangled with Judd.

"Why quit?" Parlan asked. He dealt two hands of blackjack. Henry hit and busted. Parlan deliberately took a card that also put him over twenty-one.

"Have you tried to do much traveling in the past month?" Henry glanced at the cards. "Stay."

Parlan took a card and won that hand.

"The Northeast and Southeast didn't get hit as hard as other places, but the bigger cities in those places surely did," Henry continued. "I've heard at least one-third of Toland is nothing but rubble and corpses. A couple of the big cities in the Southeast aren't much better. The people who used to look for a big game aren't looking to play cards these days. They're looking to buy food and repair their homes. They're looking to restore their businesses. They're hiding in their houses when the sun goes down." He sighed. "The travel bans are strictly enforced, at least for the trains. And anyone foolish enough to drive at night carries a loaded gun on the seat beside him, figuring that if he's caught, a bullet in the brain will be more merciful than whatever will be done to him by what's out there in the dark."

"That's what you've heard?" Parlan dealt a couple more hands, not asking if Henry wanted to hit or stay. Didn't matter. It was just something to do with his hands.

"I was in a Southeast city playing in a high-stakes game when the news reports showed all the dead shifters that were killed by followers of the Humans First and Last movement. And I was still in that city when the Others retaliated." Henry's voice remained calm, conversational, but when he looked at Parlan there was fear in his eyes. "Traveling from town to town for games? Not the way I want to live anymore—mostly because I realized that I wanted to live."

"Then what are you going to do?"

Henry laughed quietly. "My sister and her husband live in a small town on the western side of Lake Honon. They own an old-fashioned general store—the kind of place where you can buy basic groceries and a bottle of wine or a six-pack of beer along with a coloring book or a toy for the kids, and the wife can look through a box of patterns to make a new dress. They even have bolts of cloth and needles and thread and whatnot for sewing. A year ago they wanted to expand but couldn't get a loan from a bank. So I put in the money and became a silent partner." He smiled. "I figured I was tossing money out the window, but she's my sister. Anyway, they got the building renovations done and purchased the merchandise they wanted to add. And now? They and their old-fashioned store survived when the Others ripped through all the human towns. Now they're an important fixture in that part of their town and need help running the place."

Parlan didn't scoff, but it took effort to keep his voice politely interested. "You're going to give up being a gambler to become a grocer?"

Henry nodded. "I'd made the decision before all of . . . this . . . happened. I'm glad I did. I had my sister's reply in my pocket when I bought my ticket, showing that I was returning to family and a job. Wouldn't have been able to cross back into the Northeast without that letter. The old life is gone, Parlan. The days of being able to cross the continent on a whim aren't coming back anytime soon, if ever."

It rippled through him, that same feeling that told him a game was going sour and it was time to walk away from the table.

Henry Hollis was right. It would take years for Toland to recover, if it ever came back to what it had been. From the things he'd heard, Hubb NE was a quagmire of displaced people pouring into that city, looking for food and shelter. Desperate people and professional gamblers did not mix. Lakeside? Something about Lakeside and the other towns in that area had always made him uneasy. Not because of the Others. He'd always successfully avoided contact with *them*. But he'd had the feeling there were other kinds of hunters in Lakeside who couldn't be discouraged or bribed—and just might twig to why the Blackstones were such successful gamblers and swindlers.

That left Shikago. And once he'd worn out his welcome there? Then what?

"Where do you get off?" Parlan asked.

"Shikago is the closest station to the town where my sister lives. From there I'll take a boat." Henry laughed softly. "I'm told it's a common way to reach the towns along the lakes. You just have to get used to some of the travelers being a bit . . . furry."

Parlan shuddered. He didn't want to think about having to deal with the Others. "Well, Henry, I wish you luck."

We need to get out of this car. When he felt this strongly that a game was going to go wrong, he didn't ignore the feelings that came from being an Intuit.

Parlan gathered the cards and put the deck in his pocket. He nudged the hundred-dollar bill toward Henry. "You keep it." He smiled. "We'll be at the next station in a few minutes. You can buy me lunch."

He saw Henry open his mouth, ready to remind Parlan that the executive car provided food as part of the cost of the ticket. Then Henry moved his eyes to look toward the four men at the other table. Parlan gave the tiniest nod.

Thugs dressed in suits were still thugs.

When the train pulled into the station, Parlan rose swiftly and headed toward the door with Henry right behind him. He didn't look back, but he knew Judd had also moved, and whatever was said—or done—would encourage the men not to follow.

"Come with me," Parlan said, going down the steps so fast he almost slipped. They were on the wrong side of the train to be seen by the four men or anyone at the station, but he still crouched low as he hurried to his private car. Once they were inside, he lifted the side of one of the window blinds just enough to see Judd walk off the train and go into the station.

He didn't see the four men who had been in the executive car.

Just before the train began to pull out of the station, Parlan heard a quiet knock on the door of his private car before Judd walked in, holding a paper bag.

"The best they had," Judd said, pulling sandwiches and bottles of beer out of the bag. He took a sandwich and a bottle of beer, then retreated to the chair farthest from the table where Parlan and Henry sat.

"I always admired how you knew when to avoid a game," Henry said.

Parlan got up and locked the door before returning to the table and unwrapping his sandwich. "I'm just good at reading other people's tells."

"Your daughter was good at reading those fortune-telling cards."

That wasn't the bitch's only skill, but reading those cards was an ability seen at every harvest fair and was, therefore, nothing extraordinary, nothing that would call undo attention to the family.

"Sweet girl," Henry continued. "Is she still traveling with you?"

"No, she hasn't traveled with us for a while now," he replied quietly.

"Too bad. I could have asked her to read the cards and tell me my future."

Parlan stared at Henry with cold eyes. "She lost the knack for seeing the future."

"Sorry," Henry said. "I didn't realize . . ."

He waved away the apology. "All families have their troubles. We'll work it out." He asked Henry about the town where the sister and brother-in-law lived and deflected any more talk about his own family—especially any talk about his ungrateful daughter.

CHAPTER 5

Firesday, Sumor 27

Already out of sorts because Prairie Gold's post office was still closed, Abigail Burch returned to her little shop and felt a dissonance so severe she began to shake.

Where had *that* come from? She had to find it before it unraveled the protections that had kept her safe for the past three years.

She approached the bison-scented jar candles on the display table. What had sounded like a good idea, using *free* bison fat instead of buying tallow from Floyd Tanner, had turned out to be a spectacular failure. Even the Wolves didn't want to use the darn candles and they *liked* the smell of bison! And now that nothing could be wasted, she had to keep trying to unload the things on Prairie Gold citizens who took pity on her. At least there weren't that many candles to sell.

A chill ran through her. There had been a dozen jars on the table when she'd left. Now there were six more.

Abigail stepped away from the table. This shouldn't be happening. *Couldn't* be happening. Nothing she'd done when she'd gone through the steps to turn bison fat into candles could account for this dissonance. Except . . .

She hadn't counted the number of jars. She'd *thought* she'd made more than a dozen, but when she came back from a lunch break and didn't find any more, she figured she'd been mistaken. Now six more candles were on the display table and they . . .

Damn you, Kelley. What have you done?

It was possible that Kelley had found the other candles stashed in the workroom they shared and put them out on the table before going to his meeting with Jesse Walker. It was possible he hadn't noticed anything wrong with them.

Kelley was pretty clueless about a lot of things, taking everything and everyone at face value. How else could she have played him so well for the past three years?

She'd needed a patsy to help her get farther away from her father and the plans he'd made for her, and she had found the perfect mark. When Kelley had found her drunk in an alleyway and had paid for a room at an inn and then stayed with her through the night, listening to her tearful story about the abusive father she had run from when she was seventeen, and how she'd been on the run for the past two years, she knew she had him. He wanted to help a damsel in distress, was ready to fall in love with a sweet, simple girl who just wanted a happy life with him.

She was many things. Simple and sweet weren't among them, but it was a persona she had perfected for her part of the cons she had played with her uncle. At fairs or outdoor markets, they would have a booth where he would swap genuine stones and replace them with glass while doing a minor repair on a piece while she distracted the mark with her sweet patter about lucky stones and how she could choose just the right one for that person. And she could choose exactly the right stone for a person. That was her particular ability. But she could, and usually did, choose a stone that created a dissonance that would bring that person just enough bad luck when they gave in to an impulse and sat down for a game of cards with her father, whose persona was a frontier gambler.

Finding out that Kelley was a goldsmith and worked around gemstones was an unexpected and unpleasant hitch in her plans since she needed to avoid any stones that might dilute the energy of the stones she kept with her to deflect bad luck and create prosperity, but when he said he loved her and wanted to get married, she'd agreed—with some conditions.

They had moved three times in the three years they were married, finally settling in Prairie Gold last summer. She'd worried about living in an Intuit town, but everyone bought into her persona because Kelley had bought into it. Sometimes she was so bored with Kelley and this life she wanted to scream, but her father would never come to a small Intuit town in the middle of nowhere, and that meant she was safe from him—and safe from the other one. So she wore the old-fashioned dresses and read tarot cards and made candles and soaps that her neighbors bought out of kindness—and avoided getting close to the stones Kelley kept in his half of their shared workroom.

But now there were these candles, this *dissonance.*

The door to her little shop opened.

Abigail forced herself to smile at Rachel Wolfgard. "Good morning, Rachel."

"Good morning." Rachel eased into the shop, each cautious step bringing her closer to the table with the defective candles. "Jesse is having a meeting at the store. She told me to take a break and visit a store I haven't seen yet. I have not been in your store. You sell candles and soap. The *terra indigene* use those things when we are in human form." She reached for one of the jar candles.

"No!" Abigail shouted, certain everything would be ruined if those candles left the shop.

Rachel leaped away, startled. "I wasn't going to steal. I have money—wages—to buy human things."

As soon as Rachel moved away from the display, Abigail felt she could breathe again. She raised one hand in a placating gesture. "I knew you weren't going to just take it. But those candles are defective. They shouldn't have been put out for anyone to buy. I can show you other candles."

Rachel backed toward the door. "No. I don't need one."

Shelley Bookman, the town's librarian, walked in. Rachel turned and fled, dashing into the street. Shouts and the squeal of brakes.

"Gods!" Shelley said, standing in the doorway. "Phil Mailer almost hit her. Jesse should talk to her about the proper way to cross the street."

If she'd taken one of the candles, Phil wouldn't have stopped in time.

Shelley closed the door and walked over to the display table.

Abigail found it hard to breathe. A dissonance in someone else's life wouldn't have produced this effect. This only happened when a dissonance threatened to bring something dark into *her* life.

"You still have some of those bison candles?" Shelley said the words with the same forced enthusiasm as someone being fed marginally edible leftovers for the third night in a row.

"Don't!" Abigail shouted when Shelley picked up one of the jars. She grabbed the jar and threw it on the floor with enough force to break the thick glass. "You can't have that one. It's not right for you! It's not right!" She grabbed another candle and smashed it on the floor. "They're not right!"

The third jar didn't break, so she went into her workroom, rummaged through her box of tools, and returned to the display table with a hammer. Air burned her lungs as she picked up each jar and set it on the floor. Then she swung the hammer hard enough to break the jars. Swung the hammer over and over and over.

Had to stop the dissonance, had to protect herself. Had to . . .

The hammer mashed through the candle, revealing something inside besides the wick. Using the hem of her dress, Abigail dug it out. A tumbled stone no bigger than her thumbnail. Quartz.

Heedless of the glass, she mashed the other broken candles and found more tumbled stones. Agate. Jet. Carnelian. Hematite. Turquoise. They could have been good stones for someone else, but they were bad stones to be around her.

"Gods above and below, Abby." Kelley stood in the doorway that connected his shop with hers, staring at her. "What are you doing?"

She twisted to face him, felt a shard of glass slice her knee. But she didn't feel pain. Not from the glass. She felt rage at this boring fool who had torn a hole in her defenses.

"How could you do this? *How could you?*"

"I thought . . . Just something extra. A little surprise when someone burned the candle. You didn't have to touch the stones. You dislike my work so much, I'm surprised you even realized there were a few tumbled stones missing from the bowl in my shop."

I knew they were in the candles. I could feel them.

Kelley hesitated, then walked over to her. He took the hammer and helped her to her feet.

"You're bleeding." He sounded sad—and there was something else in his voice she didn't recognize. Something she didn't like.

"I'll help Abigail clean those cuts," Jesse said as she stepped into the shop. "You clean up the glass."

Kelley nodded.

Remembering who she was supposed to be, Abigail didn't protest when Jesse took her arm and led her to the washroom at the back of her shop. It didn't surprise her that Jesse would show up, but she asked the question anyway. "Why are you here?"

"Because Rachel came running back to my store, too scared to make much sense, followed by Shelley, who said you were having some kind of fit," Jesse replied sharply.

When had Shelley left? When she'd gone into the workroom to find the hammer? Or had Shelley fled after she started smashing the candles? She hadn't noticed, couldn't remember.

"Sit." Jesse pointed to the closed toilet. Opening the daypack that was now so much a standard part of Jesse's attire that people barely noticed it, she pulled out the first-aid kit and a bottle of whiskey. Pouring two fingers into the water glass Abigail kept on a ledge above the sink, Jesse held it out. "Down in one."

"I'm not supposed to drink," Abigail whispered. "I promised Kelley I wouldn't drink." Of course, Kelley had believed she'd been drinking hard for two years before he found her and doing some bad things to pay for the drink, so her giving him that promise had meant a lot to him.

"We'll call this medicine. If he has a problem with that, he can talk to me."

She downed the whiskey. Funny how it didn't taste as good as the sips she took on the sly when Kelley was gone for an afternoon and wouldn't notice.

Jesse said nothing while she washed the cuts and applied antiseptic ointment and bandages. She put everything back in her daypack before she leaned against the doorframe. "You scared Rachel so much she ran into the street and almost got hit by a car. That was unkind."

Stupid Wolf should have been run over. No, don't think that way. Sweet, simple Abigail wouldn't think that way.

"I'm sorry," she whispered.

"I sense people. It's how my Intuit abilities manifest themselves. But I've never been able to get a good feel for you. We've always thought you were a sweet girl and a bit simple, dressing up in those long dresses women wore in my grandmother's day and making your soaps and candles. But you're not simple, are you, Abigail? That's how you've chosen to hide and is as much of a costume as the clothes."

Bitch. She'd always known one mistake around Jesse would end the game, but she had to keep trying to work the con until she found a way out. "I'm not bright. Never was. Everyone said so."

"When you and Kelley showed up last summer, looking for a place to live and a place to work, we made room for you. Intuits have always tried to make room for their own, since we often can't survive in towns run by humans who see our gifts as threats. I couldn't figure out why he wanted to live in such a small place. He's a goldsmith with a lot of talent for creating beautiful pieces of jewelry. He wasn't going to get much work from the rest of us. Nobody here is rich enough to buy what he creates. But he wasn't the one who wanted to live in an isolated place like Prairie Gold, was he? You're the one who wanted—or needed—to live in a place where no one would think to look for you." Jesse smiled grimly. "I never got a sense of you, Abigail. Until now."

It sounded like a threat.

Jesse pushed away from the doorframe. "You and Kelley have some things to talk about. Then you and I will talk."

"About what?" Abigail asked, pretending she didn't know.

Jesse walked out of the washroom, letting the question hang in the air.

Abigail sat in the washroom for a minute—or maybe an hour. She didn't know. Her body remembered the feel of a strap across her back when she'd messed up somehow and given a mark a stone that would bring good fortune. And she remembered the fear that had filled her just before she made the decision to run. She couldn't go back to that. She wouldn't.

But today Kelley had seen a moment of who she really was—and so had Jesse.

* * *

Jesse reached the sidewalk in front of her own store when Phil Mailer, who was not only the editor of the *Prairie Gold Reporter* but also ran the combination post office, telegraph office, and business center, called to her and ran across the street.

"Is Rachel all right?" Phil looked pale. "Gods, Jesse. She ran right in front of me. I almost didn't stop in time."

"But you did stop in time," Jesse said. "She didn't come to any harm." *Not physically, anyway.*

"Thought she knew enough not to run into the street like that."

"I'll talk to her." She'd be talking to a lot of people today.

"Don't want Morgan or Chase to think I was careless with one of their own. Especially . . . Well, you know."

She did know. Rachel wasn't old enough yet to be looking for a mate, but she was the *only* surviving female of the Wolfgard pack who would be old enough in the next year or two to mate and have young. The two dominant Wolves would never forgive the humans in this town if one of them injured—or may the gods help them, killed—the young Wolf. "I'll explain it to them."

She walked into the general store. Rachel turned away from the shelf where she'd been stocking dry cereal, her amber eyes still full of fear.

"Does Abigail have rabies?" Rachel asked. "We know about rabies. It's a dangerous sickness."

"She doesn't have rabies." Jesse kept her voice matter-of-fact. "Her body isn't sick. But something upset her and she behaved badly."

"She didn't want me to touch the candles she made."

"She didn't want Shelley touching the candles either." She knew they were alone, but she made a show of looking around the store. "Where is Shelley?"

"She said she was going home to change into clean underpants, but I didn't smell any pee or poop."

So hard to keep a straight face when the girl said things like that. "That was an excuse to go home for a bit until she calmed down. Abigail scared her too."

"It's better to be around pack when you're scared."

Setting her daypack on the floor, Jesse gave Rachel a hug. "You're right about that." She stepped back and picked up her pack. "Can you look after things out here? I need to make some calls and handle some paperwork."

"You need to call Tolya Sanguinati," Rachel said. "He said I didn't need to fetch you, but you should call him as soon as you were done with Abigail."

Jesse went to her office, which wasn't more than a corner of the back room that had been sectioned off with partitions and a long curtain that was usually tied back but took the place of a door when she needed some privacy. She turned on the lamp and stared at the phone.

Part of her wished she could send a direct e-mail to Steve Ferryman, the mayor of an Intuit village located on Great Island. But there wasn't direct access to anyone in the Northeast Region. Probably just as well. She wasn't in charge of Bennett, wasn't the leader. Whether Tolya Sanguinati chose to resettle the town was his choice, not hers.

Tolya had taken over the mayor's office as his workplace, so she dialed that number.

"Tolya Sanguinati."

How many people felt a chill when they heard "Sanguinati"? "It's Jesse. Rachel said you called."

"Yes." A beat of silence. "We have been fortunate that the young humans who have come to Bennett to assist in sorting the possessions of the former residents have been cautious around the *terra indigene*. Adding too many humans too quickly might cause . . . tension."

"Might provoke your new sheriff or his deputy into biting first and asking questions later?"

"That too, but I was more concerned about the Elders and whether they would see a town full of humans as an . . . invasion."

Jesse braced her head in one hand. The Elders had killed every man, woman, and child in Bennett a few weeks ago. They could, and would, do it again if the humans weren't careful. "We still need more people to sort through possessions; we need people to try to find the heirs of anyone who left a last will and testament. There's a need for people to work the ranches."

"I don't disagree, Jesse Walker, but I have discussed the possibility with Virgil Wolfgard of more humans settling in Bennett, and we agree that the Elders will not react well to there being more humans than *terra indigene* living in the town."

"More Wolves working in the stores?"

"No." Tolya's voice held regret, reminding Jesse that he had known Joe Wolfgard, the previous leader of the *terra indigene* settlement near Prairie Gold. "No, there aren't enough Wolves left who are willing to work around humans. Virgil and Kane are here because the rest of their pack was lost. There was no reason for them to remain in their old territory. Other forms of *terra indigene* would come to fill the empty spaces, learn human kinds of work."

"Forms as deadly as the Wolves and the Sanguinati?"

"Yes." Tolya waited, then asked, "Do you still want me to inquire about arranging for more humans to come to Bennett?"

Did she? Bennett's population had been contained by the boundaries of the land leased to humans and, equally, by the amount of water the *terra indigene* had been willing to include as part of that lease.

"Let me review my list again. I truly believe we need to populate Bennett, but doing it in stages might be a wiser way to go about it."

"Very well. I will wait to hear from you." Tolya hung up.

Jesse set the receiver in the cradle and leaned back. She felt strongly that she was making the right choice for Prairie Gold, but she didn't know if she was making a choice that the people coming to Bennett could survive.

When Abigail came out of the washroom, the glass had been swept up and the floor cleaned of any residue left by the candles she'd mashed. Kelley stood in the doorway between their two shops. When they'd first arrived in Prairie Gold, they'd taken whatever had been available for work space and a place to live. They couldn't afford to pay for two shops, so they'd divided the display space of one by putting up a wall and doorway. The back room, which was a common workroom, hadn't been separated. Didn't need to be. She'd stayed away from his half of the room.

"I'm sorry I upset you," Kelley said, staying in the doorway. "That wasn't my intention."

"I know that. Kelley—"

He held up a hand, cutting off her words. "When I asked you to marry me, you had conditions, one of them being that we live in a small town, the smaller the better. So we ended up here. Can't get much smaller than Prairie Gold. This place suits you. You make your soaps and candles and don't think about how we're barely getting by."

"We're doing okay." She ignored the way her heart started pounding in her chest.

"Because I repair jewelry people already own and make a few inexpensive pieces people can buy for gifts. Mostly we get by because I do odd jobs for anyone who needs an extra pair of hands and pick up enough money to pay our bills and buy the food."

Abigail blinked as if blinking back tears. "Do we need more?"

"I do." Kelley looked away. "Yeah, Abby, I do. I'm a goldsmith. I love working with gemstones and metals. I don't mind giving my neighbors a hand when it's needed, but I do mind that I can't do the work I love. Especially now."

Why now? She knew why. That moment when she'd stopped playing sweet Abigail and lashed out at him had shattered the illusion, had been the moment when his Intuit abilities had kicked in and he realized he'd been played.

"They need someone to take over the jewelry store in Bennett," Kelley said. "They need someone to evaluate all the jewelry from the houses, do an inventory. In exchange for doing that work, I'll be given the store, which has a workshop in the back where I can make my own designs again. I told Jesse I'd take the job."

"What? How could she offer that to you? How could you accept without talking to me?" *Play the part. If you don't let the persona crack, you might still convince him it was just a flash of anger and not a revelation.* "When did you tell her?"

"I called her while you were in the washroom."

Damn it! If she hadn't lingered in the washroom she could have stopped him from calling, or at least delayed his decision until she could figure out what to do. What she couldn't do was stay here on her own. Now that Jesse had twigged to her not being what she pretended to be, she couldn't play sad, sweet Abigail who was bewildered by Kelley leaving her.

For a moment, she considered whether she could hook Tobias Walker and live on the ranch, but making that play would give Jesse even more of a reason to examine everything she said and did from now on. No, she needed to get as far away from Jesse Walker as she could, and now that meant leaving Prairie Gold.

"Can I come with you?" she asked in a small voice.

He hesitated. That wasn't good. Finally he said, "It's Bennett, and there will be all kinds of folks there. It's the sort of place you wanted to avoid before."

"But everything is different now. A new start for both of us." She took a step toward him. "An adventure."

Another hesitation. "I think you should do what's best for you now, and I'll do the same."

Kelley stepped back into his own side of the building and closed the door.

Abigail ran back to the washroom. Clutching the sink, she let the angry tears fall.

Damn Kelley for putting those stones in the candles! If he hadn't done that, there wouldn't have been that one revealing moment.

No choice now except to go with him to Bennett. Maybe, once they were away from Prairie Gold, she could reverse the effects of the dissonance at least until she figured out what to do.

CHAPTER 6

Earthday, Sumor 29

Abigail washed the dishes from the evening meal, her mind spinning. Kelley had barely spoken to her since Firesday, hadn't touched her when they went to bed, despite her trying to encourage him in the shy way typical of sweet Abigail. He'd spent yesterday packing. Phil Mailer and Shelley Bookman had helped him pack up his shop, which didn't take long. He had some loose gems as well as the semiprecious stones that were mostly in the bowl he'd kept on the counter near the cash register. He had some gold and silver to create his own pieces. And he had his tools.

In the afternoon, he'd filled a box with the books he enjoyed that didn't appeal to her. He packed his clothes; even washed what was in the laundry instead of asking her to do it. Not that he didn't often do the laundry, but every task he did for himself seemed to take him farther away from her.

He wasn't taking any furniture. Not that they had arrived with much—a bed and dresser, a round kitchen table and two chairs, a bookcase. The pots and pans and box of mismatched dishes they'd used since arriving in Prairie Gold had been purchased at the used-goods store. The loveseat, rocking chair, coffee table, and lamps in the living room had been purchased at house and yard sales in Bennett and carted back to Prairie Gold in Tobias Walker's pickup truck.

They hadn't bought anything new except a few books and clothing they had needed to replace when things wore out or they needed to purchase to suit the weather. Sweet Abigail wouldn't have cared about possessions. Besides, despite the marriage license and the plain gold band she'd tolerated because he was a goldsmith and she'd had to wear *something*, she'd known this was temporary. That it had lasted three years was the big surprise. She'd been on the run for a week when she'd found Kelley, not the two years she'd told him, so she'd been seventeen when they'd married—under the age to marry without parental consent. So they might not be legally married anyway.

Not something she intended to admit unless it worked in her favor.

She finished the dishes and went into the living room. Kelley sat in the rocking chair, reading. Was it significant that he had chosen the rocker instead of the loveseat, where she could have cuddled up against him?

Perching on the edge of the loveseat, she said, "I'd like to come with you, if you're still agreeable with me doing that."

Kelley closed the book but kept his finger between the pages, a sign that this would be a temporary interruption.

Taking care of her was still a habit, but if she didn't convince him soon that she was still the girl he had rescued, whatever he'd felt for her would break altogether.

"All right," he finally said. "Tobias is picking me up in the morning, so you'll need to be ready then if you're coming with me."

"So soon?" He'd packed all his possessions and was clearly ready to leave. She just hadn't expected it to happen so quickly. She hadn't expected him to want to leave *her* so quickly.

He nodded. "If you're not ready then, you can come along the next time someone makes a trip up to Bennett and has the room."

He wasn't offering to wait an extra day, wasn't offering any kind of help. Not good.

"Did you tell them you wanted a house?" she asked. He had mentioned that housing came with the job, either an actual house where they would have to pay for utilities and taxes, or an apartment that included utilities where they would pay rent and telephone.

"Didn't give them a decision yet. I'll be staying at the hotel for a few days. I'm told everyone does. The people working to clear out the places have an apartment building clear of goods—or have the goods shoved into a couple of the apartments in order to let residents move in to the rest of the units. And houses are being cleared, but it's a lot of work. Everyone coming in is expected to help some with the clearing. An hour or two each day, along with whatever job you take." He paused. "Anyone with a house might have to take in a boarder."

"Oh, I wouldn't want a stranger in my house," Abigail said quickly.

"That's part of the deal."

Strangers at every turn. Danger at every turn. And Kelley sounding so distant instead of protective.

"I'd better get my packing done." She went into the bedroom and closed the door as quietly as she could. Then she pulled out the box that held two decks of tarot cards. She'd told Jesse that one deck had belonged to her grandmother. She'd had a grandmother. Everyone did. She'd never met her old granny, but the kindly woman who had taught her a bit about reading the cards had been old enough to be someone's grandmother.

She'd stolen the cards because the woman had refused to read the cards for Abigail the night before the Blackstone Clan was leaving town, had claimed she'd done a reading about Abigail earlier in the day and the cards had revealed that Abigail wasn't interested in giving an honest reading, only in knowing enough to make people believe what she was telling them was true.

The bitch had deserved to have her precious deck of cards stolen.

She set the cards aside and opened the velvet bag. She poured the stones out on the bed, then picked them up, one by one. Agates and jasper. Onyx and jet. Stones for power and opportunity. Stones for prosperity and luck. Stones for protection. She'd spent a year gathering this combination of stones that resonated in exactly the right way with her and with each other, forming a veil of safety. The stones had given her that thin window of opportunity to run away before her father gave her to Judd McCall as a "wife," had brought her the luck of crossing paths with Kelley on the night she'd stupidly gotten shitfaced drunk, had helped things fall into place to bring her to Prairie Gold—a place her father would never think to look for her.

But those dissonant stones Kelley had put into some of the jar candles had torn the veil of safety her stones had created around her. Oh, her stones were still working, were still in resonance with her, but there would be that tear now, that bit of dark energy that would cling to her, that would attract other kinds of darkness.

She handled each stone before putting it back in the bag. Then she picked up her deck of tarot cards. But she didn't unwrap the silk scarf she kept around them.

What if the cards indicated that she shouldn't leave? What if they indicated she should go but danger would be waiting?

Of course it would be waiting. Sooner or later, her father would find her—and kill her if he couldn't bring her back under his control. The Blackstone Clan didn't tolerate anyone whispering its secrets, especially one of its own.

No choice. Not really. She would go with Kelley and hope she wasn't found for a long, long time.

Sighing, she tucked the decks of cards and the bag of stones back in the box, fetched her suitcase, and packed what she didn't want to leave behind.

CHAPTER 7

Windsday, Messis 1

Jana Paniccia opened the bottle of wine and filled a water glass. Getting drunk wasn't the answer. Wasting money on wine instead of buying food wasn't the answer.

But what *was* the . . . *frigging* . . . answer?

"Insufferable bastards." She swallowed too much wine and choked a little. "'Too much turmoil in the world right now, Ms. Paniccia.'" She perfectly mimicked the prissy voice and smug attitude of the administrator who ran the Hubb NE police academy. "'Can't be rocking the boat now and upsetting the status quo.' Status quo, my butt." Jana waved the glass in a sweeping gesture. "You should be grateful to have anyone want to be a cop right now. Uphold law and order? You and my great-aunt Fanny." That had been one of Martha's sayings. Jana had never known what it meant, but it fit the occasion.

The academy had taken the tuition and fees quick enough. The instructors had let her take the classes—and take the bruises, both physical and emotional, that the other cadets dished out because she had *dared* to want to work in a field that was exclusively male.

Smaller didn't mean incompetent. Not as muscular? So what? She had brains, and *she wanted this*. Hadn't wanted to be anything else but a cop for as long as she could remember.

"*You're romanticizing the job, honey,*" Pops had told her. "*You've read too many stories about the frontier and a kind of law that didn't exist even then.*"

"*So I should be a waitress or a secretary?*"

"*I didn't say that. You're choosing a hard road, and there's no certainty that you'll succeed. But if that's what you want, you give it everything you've got. If spunk and attitude can make up for you being a girl in a male-dominated field, then, by gosh, you'll make it and you'll wear that badge with honor.*"

She had survived the loss of people she loved. She had survived the academy. But she'd used up her savings, and there was almost nothing left. No hope of a job as a police officer, despite her qualifications. And with everyone in Thaisia reeling from the *terra indigene*'s slaughter of humans across the continent, she wasn't sure there was much hope for anything.

She was feeling a little light-headed from the wine and lack of food when her mobile phone rang. She didn't recognize the number, but it was a Northeast Region area code. Had to be since calls couldn't cross regional boundaries anymore.

"Hello?"

"I have a message for the person at this phone number." A male voice.

"You found her."

"Do you have something to do with law enforcement?" he asked.

"Is this a joke?"

"No. This is . . . The message was cryptic, but I believe an opportunity to work in law enforcement will be coming up soon. A badge. A six-gun. Hills. If this means something to you, get to Lakeside as soon as you can."

"And do what? Go to every police station asking if I can have a job?" Jana's hand tightened around the phone. "Who put you up to this?"

"Not the police stations. Go to the Courtyard. That was the message."

"Who gave you this message?"

"That's confidential and, as I said, cryptic. But the last piece of information was this phone number. That's all I can tell you, except . . . If you're going, go tomorrow. By bus. If you take the train, you won't get there in time."

In time for what? "Wait. *Wait.* Who are you?"

He'd already hung up.

Jana's hand shook as she ended the call. Had to be a prank, someone setting her up. Her classmates most likely. The gods only knew, she didn't have much to take with her. A bus ticket to Lakeside, with the extra charge for baggage, would leave her with barely enough money to rent a room for a week, and she'd be able to do that only if she scrimped on food. If she went, she'd be stranded in an unfamiliar city, and her classmates, who should have been her colleagues, would be laughing their butts off at gullible Jana.

But what if it wasn't a prank?

She checked the recent call log on her phone, wrote down the number of that last call, then tried calling it. No answer. That didn't surprise her.

Jana put the phone on the tiny table in the kitchenette of her rented room, then went to one of the boxes that held the books she didn't want to part with, the ones that were her favorites, her comfort reads. She looked at the covers of the frontier stories that had belonged to Pops or that Martha and Pops had given her over the years. She lifted a few out of the box, then stared at the cover of the next one—the frontier story that Pops had returned to over and over.

The background was a landscape of rugged hills unlike anything she knew. The main focus of the cover was a sheriff's badge and a six-gun.

Jana shivered.

After the compounds where the blood prophets lived were exposed as being little more than prisons where the girls were trained and then exploited for their ability to speak prophecy when their skin was cut, officials in government and law enforcement had scrambled to find out more about these girls. That wasn't an easy task because the *terra indigene* had scooped up the girls who had survived being thrown out of the compounds in order to hide the worst of what was being done to them. So the instructor who had talked to her class about the *cassandra sangue* hadn't been able to tell them all that much except to say that prophecy could be cryptic, often revealed in images that didn't make sense.

The caller said he'd been given a cryptic message that had included her phone number.

What if the phone call wasn't a prank?

She had spunk, and she had enough attitude to hold her own and be a cop. And she didn't have anything to lose.

Jana poured the rest of the wine down the sink, washed the glass, then hauled out her two suitcases and packed so that she could get to the bus station at first light.

To: Tolya Sanguinati, Urgent

Received your request for workers who are willing to migrate to Bennett. The Lakeside Courtyard will hold a job fair and will interview Simple Life folk and Intuits for the positions you indicated were the most urgent to fill. There may be some *terra indigene* who will also travel to Bennett. The fair will be held from Messis 6 through Messis 8. We will send you the list of potential employees so you will know what humans to expect and what jobs they can do.

—Vlad

CHAPTER 8

Firesday, Messis 3

Relief filled Tolya as he read Vlad Sanguinati's e-mail. He didn't know how many humans would be arriving or what professions they would fill, but this would prove to Jesse Walker that he had taken her concerns seriously. And it would balance the invitation he'd asked the Elementals to send to the *terra indigene* living in the Midwest to come to Bennett and participate in a mixed community. There were already several shifter gards here, along with the five Sanguinati who had joined him from Toland, but more *terra indigene* would be needed to keep the Elders from reacting harshly to an influx of humans.

He placed a call to Jesse Walker, doodling on a message pad while he listened to the phone ringing. Doodling was a new human activity, one he found surprisingly enjoyable. He filled the top part of the paper with crosshatching before a female voice said, "Walker's General Store."

"Good afternoon, Rachel. This is Tolya Sanguinati. May I speak to Jesse Walker?"

"Are you sure you want to?"

Not anymore. "Is there a reason why I wouldn't want to speak with her?"

"She's growling at paper. I don't know why. Well, a piece of paper cut her finger and she said words I'm not supposed to learn. I offered to bite the paper because I have better teeth, but she said she didn't need help. I was on a ladder, dusting the top shelves in the store. That's why the phone rang and rang."

That made sense, except he was fairly sure Jesse Walker also had a phone in the back room, where, presumably, her desk for paperwork was located. Could she be so injured she couldn't answer the phone? Or was she ignoring the thing?

Some background noise, then Rachel said, "It's Tolya Sanguinati. He wants to talk to you."

"Mr. Sanguinati," Jesse said once the phone exchanged hands.

She sounded cornered. No. Stressed? Prey was so difficult to gauge by just a voice coming over wires.

Not prey. Not edible. But the courtesy he *didn't* hear in her voice suggested he should skip the back-and-forth words that usually began conversations with humans. "The Lakeside Courtyard is holding a job fair next week. Hopefully the new citizens will start arriving by the end of next week and early the following week. I don't know how many they will find that they consider suitable, but they will try to find the humans—"

<Tolya,> Virgil called. <You're needed outside. Now.>

"—you indicated were a priority," he finished.

A beat of silence. "Thank you." Jesse sighed. "Thank you."

Her relief sounded excessive and he wanted to ask what was wrong, but Stazia Sanguinati, who was the manager of the bank, said, <Tolya! What should we do?>

"I have to go. I'll call with more information when I have it." He hung up and hurried out of his office. <Virgil? Where . . . ?>

<Town square, at the spring. Barbara Ellen is also there.>

<Who else is there?>

Instead of answering the question, Virgil said, <Hurry.>

The mayor's office looked out over the square, but trees blocked his view of the spring. He opened the window, shifted to his smoke form, and flowed down the side of the building and across the street, moving at a speed he couldn't match in his human form.

As soon as he was in sight of the spring—and the two females, one of them being Barbara Ellen—he stopped to assess the danger. Virgil was there in human form, Kane in Wolf form. Stazia was in human form. Isobel, who was in charge of the post office, was a column of smoke partially hidden by one of the trees.

"Do you need help?" Barbara Ellen asked the female who was drinking spring water out of cupped hands. "Have you had anything to eat?" A hesitation. "Do you understand my words?"

That was a good question. The female was *terra indigene*. That much Tolya sensed. But the form? Something dangerous. Something lethal, even to the rest of them. Something even Virgil had hesitated to confront, despite another Wolf and two Sanguinati supporting him.

Tolya shifted to his human form, the movement drawing the female's attention. When she straightened and turned to face him—and streaks of black suddenly appeared in her gold, blue, and red hair—he felt the unpleasant sensation of being genuinely afraid.

Harvester. Plague Rider. A rare form of *terra indigene* that, for the most part, were solitary because they were so deadly. When a Harvester's hair turned solid black, he or she could kill another creature with just a look. The Sanguinati mostly lived on blood taken fresh from their prey. A Harvester took the prey's life energy, turning organs into black sludge.

She looked human enough to pass for human at a distance, if her hair wasn't coiling and changing color at the moment she was seen. But her eyes were black or so dark a brown to make no difference. That and a feral quality no human could match meant that, up close, she would never pass for human.

How many humans had she killed before she had learned the form this well? She wore a mishmash of clothes that looked more like layers of rags—and she looked half starved.

He moved toward the Harvester, giving her a reason to focus on him. He knew Virgil was tensed, waiting for the moment he could dash over to Barbara Ellen and pull her out of immediate danger.

The Harvester must have sensed the tension in the Wolf, because she turned to face Virgil—and her hair changed to broad streaks of red and black with threads of gold and blue.

"Stay away from her," the Harvester said.

Protective? Barbara Ellen was an adult female, but there was something bouncy and puppyish about her that tugged at protective instincts. He just hadn't considered that *this* female would respond the same way.

"He means her no harm," Tolya said. "He is the sheriff. That means she is under his protection. And mine." He flicked a look past the Harvester. "Barbara Ellen, please go with Isobel."

"No." More of the Harvester's hair turned black.

Tolya swallowed his frustration. If they all survived this day, he was going to say some sharp words to Barbara Ellen Debany about approaching strangers who were, quite obviously, more than a little strange.

"Mr. Sanguinati is the leader of the town, and my boss," Barbara Ellen said. "I should do what he asks."

Her expression said she didn't understand why he was acting like such a . . . Well, he didn't know what the human term would be that matched her expression, but he was sure it wouldn't be flattering.

"If you'd like one of the canaries, I could bring one over to wherever you're staying," Barbara Ellen said.

The Harvester turned to face the girl. "This is food?"

Barbara Ellen's eyes widened. "No. A canary is a yellow bird that sings. I thought you might like one for company while you're here."

"Company."

The word was spoken softly, but Tolya suddenly knew what had brought this female to Bennett. How much courage had Simon Wolfgard, the leader of the Lakeside Courtyard, needed when Tess had shown up looking for company, for a place to belong? And did he, Tolya, have that much courage? There were no Plague Riders in Toland. Or there hadn't been before the Elders and Elementals had unleashed their fury on the human-controlled cities.

"Are you looking for work?" Tolya asked.

"Yes," she replied. "I heard . . . words. I followed the words here."

Just how far had the Elementals flung his request for *terra indigene* to come to Bennett? Obviously far enough for a Harvester to have heard and responded.

"Let's go up to my office and we'll discuss what kind of work you would like to do," Tolya said.

The Harvester took a step toward him, then turned back to Barbara Ellen. "I would like a yellow bird that sings. For company."

Barbara Ellen smiled. "I'll select one for you and bring it . . ." She hesitated.

"I will let you know where to bring the bird," Tolya said. He extended his arm in the direction of the government building. "My office is this way."

The Harvester followed him, the black streaks changing to mere threads in the gold he assumed was her base color. She looked over her shoulder and bared her teeth. "The Wolf will bite the Barbara Ellen human."

Tolya looked back. Virgil had closed the distance and now stood with his back to them, blocking their view of Barbara Ellen—and her view of one of Namid's most ferocious predators.

"No, he won't," Tolya said. He suspected Virgil would do a lot of snarling that would display his teeth, but he wouldn't *use* them. Not on Barbara Ellen.

Still, there was no reason to take chances. <Isobel, stay with Barbara Ellen until I'm available to talk to her.>

<I will. Virgil is angry.>

He hadn't expected anything different.

"I'm Tolya Sanguinati," he said as he and the Harvester crossed the street. "What is your name?"

"Scythe."

Blessed Thaisia. "Welcome to Bennett." He opened the door of the government building. "Let's see what we can do about finding you some work."

Virgil waited until Tolya had gotten the Plague Rider out of sight. Then he grabbed one of Barbara Ellen's arms and hauled her over to the jail. She tugged and pulled, *finally* realizing she had done something wrong. She yipped and yapped at him. He ignored the yipping and yapping, glad to see Kane racing ahead of him and shifting to a human form to open various doors in the sheriff's office.

"He shouldn't be naked in public," Barbara Ellen said, taking a break from the yipping and yapping about Virgil hauling her to the jail.

"Virgil," Isobel warned.

He ignored Isobel too. Barbara Ellen had too many ties to the Lakeside Courtyard for him to do what he should do, which was force her down until she showed her belly in submission. He figured, for a human, this would be the closest thing.

He grabbed her other arm and lifted her until she was trotting on her toes and too unbalanced to realize what he intended until he put her in one of the cells and locked the door.

She stared at him, shocked. "You're arresting me? For what? Being polite?"

"You're like a puppy trying to befriend a rattlesnake!"

She blinked. "She's one of the Snakegard?"

"No, she's not Snakegard."

"Then why did you say—"

"She's dangerous!" The words came out as an angry howl. It was good she was in the cell. The bars kept him from biting her.

"I thought she was someone like Tess," Barbara Ellen said. "Her kind of *terra indigene*, I mean. And Tess isn't dangerous." Her forehead wrinkled. "Unless someone makes her angry. My brother told me several times to get gone if Tess got angry."

What was he supposed to do with a human who could recognize a Harvester and still didn't understand she was dealing with a deadly predator?

Keep her here and let Tolya deal with her, that's what he could do.

Virgil looked at Isobel, who had followed him to the cellblock. <Can you find something that will keep her busy while she's here?>

<I'll find something,> Isobel said.

He walked out with the Sanguinati, closing the cellblock door to muffle the renewed yapping.

Tolya stared at Scythe. "You want to run a saloon? The kind that would have been here when Bennett was a frontier town?"

"Yes."

"Why? How do you know about such a place?"

"My . . . kind . . . have hunted in such places since humans first came to this part of Thaisia. I like the stories about the olden times. I thought this place might . . ." She looked around, disappointed.

Even among the rest of the *terra indigene*, so little was known about Harvesters. Scythe looked to be in her late twenties but she could have been a hundred. From what she'd said, she'd had no formal human-centric education, but she'd learned to read and do sums and had listened to the teaching stories that were the accumulated knowledge of her kind. And she had learned to take the human form to mask her true form, whatever it was.

He didn't doubt for a second that nothing but another Harvester could look at that true form and survive—the possible exceptions being the Elementals and Elders, and he wasn't sure about the Elders.

Leaning forward, Tolya rested his hands on the desk. "So you want to run an old-fashioned saloon. With . . . girls?"

"Yes."

"For . . . mating?" Human mating practices were much different from those of the *terra indigene*, but he found the idea of bringing human fe-males to Bennett and permitting them to be . . . used . . . extremely dis-tasteful. Perhaps some females enjoyed mating with several males, but if the males weren't a united pack of some kind, they wouldn't work to-gether to raise the young that came from such mating, so he didn't see the point of that kind of behavior on the female's part. It wasn't practical.

"No," Scythe said coldly. "I want to run a saloon, not a brothel. The girls would dance and talk with customers. They would sing to entertain. Any male who tried to have more than that . . ."

She smiled, and something in her black eyes told Tolya that males who tried to have more suddenly wouldn't have enough energy to make it out the door on their own, let alone do anything else.

A hunting ground, and not just for Scythe, who would be able to take a little sip of life energy from many people instead of draining—and killing—one person. The Sanguinati could also help keep things calm. They didn't have to bite to feed. In their smoke form, they could draw blood through their prey's skin.

"I have not read stories about frontier towns," Tolya said. It was a hole in his education that he would have to remedy quickly. He would ask Jesse Walker to recommend books. He should be able to find her sugges-tions among the books in the houses or in the bookstore or library, which were still closed because they couldn't spare anyone to work in those places. "What else did humans do in such a saloon?"

"They played games involving cards. Usually for money. Sometimes a human cheated and there was fighting. That I will not allow."

Which meant Scythe's saloon could be a place where the Simple Life folk who would be working on the ranches could come and socialize and not become prey for other kinds of humans.

"I think I know a place that would suit you," Tolya said. "There is even a suite on the second floor for the owner and a small office on the ground floor."

She watched him.

"I would suggest that you use a stage name for your business dealings with humans." He smiled, showing a hint of fang. "With humans, there is such a thing as too much honesty."

She thought about that for a moment, then nodded. "I will be called Madam Scythe."

He'd been thinking of something more benign, but maybe having a saloon run by someone named Scythe would encourage good behavior.

"Madam Scythe it is." Tolya wrote the name on the pad of paper. "While you journeyed here, did you consider a name for your saloon?"

There was warmth and a little bafflement in her smile. "No, I didn't. Tell me about the yellow bird the Barbara Ellen female will bring me."

Not sure what one thing had to do with the other, he said, "It is a kind of bird that humans call a pet. It lives in a cage. I don't think it could survive here if it were released outside." He didn't know if that would be true under other circumstances, but with the number of predators in the area, he doubted a small bird that wasn't native to this part of Thaisia would survive long.

"Rather like the humans themselves, living in a place that is surrounded by Elders." Scythe smiled again. "I will call my place the Bird Cage Saloon."

Tolya pushed back from the desk. "Let's take a look at the building and see what needs to be done to get your business up and running."

CHAPTER 9

Watersday, Messis 4

Tolya walked around the town square, appreciating the park that made up the center of the business district—a park made possible because of the spring that bubbled up out of the earth, defying its manmade containment to spill over into a narrow channel that ended at a small pond. The spring had originally been a natural watering hole for everything that lived around here, but when humans reached the northern edge of the Elder Hills and negotiated with the *terra indigene* to settle in the area, they made the spring the center of their territory, corralling the water and siphoning it off to supply water to all the businesses. Trees and grass grew in the square. Birds and small mammals lived in the square, but none of the larger "normal" animals that lived in the area made it in far enough to reach this source of water.

There were other sources of water in the wild country. Or so he'd been told. During frontier days, he imagined the square would have been used as a place for horses to drink and graze while humans bought supplies in the stores. Now?

Tolya stopped and watched two ponies—one black and one brown—grazing near the pond.

Now the square provided a shady place for a different kind of steed.

He continued his walk, past the Universal Temple and the community center, then up the other long side of the square, heading toward his office.

Hundreds of humans had lived in and around Bennett. Maybe a few thousand. Tolya didn't know, didn't care. The task of clearing out all the homes was daunting. He wasn't sure they ever would—and with everyone feeling pressured to provide living spaces for the humans migrating to Bennett next week, he wasn't sure they should. Teams of human males were still going through the houses and collecting the food that could be salvaged. Other teams were going through an office building that had small offices that could be used by a variety of professions. Jesse Walker recommended letting the newcomers sort through the business files or box them up and put them in the basement storage area, but she emphasized the need to clean the offices and hire people for janitorial services for the whole building.

If the people who were going to run the businesses were expected to sort through the files in their new offices, why couldn't they sort through the belongings in their new homes? And how upset would he make Jesse Walker when he announced his decision to stop the cleanup as it was currently being done?

And how was a species that seemed to need so much going to be able to survive on so little? Bennett would not be allowed to swell to its original population, and life would be simpler because of that.

Tolya stopped in front of the Bird Cage Saloon, which was a hive of activity. For a form of *terra indigene* that lived on the outskirts of almost everything, Scythe had recognized the one business that had galvanized all the humans who were already in Bennett. And not just because it was a saloon and a place that provided the alcoholic beverages humans liked to drink. It was a *frontier* saloon, with bartenders and girls dressed as they had dressed decades ago. Madam Scythe even hired an Intuit who would be the saloon's professional gambler. Jesse Walker said there was *romance* to the idea—a concept he didn't understand but accepted.

He felt another predator silently moving toward him but gave no sign of knowing until Saul Panthergard said, "Tolya."

He dipped his head to acknowledge the Panther. "Saul. Are you settling in?" It had surprised him that one of the Panthergard had wanted to be this close to humans—until he'd been introduced to Joshua Painter, a human who had been raised by Saul's kin and was, in human terms, considered Saul's younger brother.

The Panthergard weren't as solitary as the cougars whose form they had absorbed many generations ago. They had learned how to hunt as that cat hunted—in fact, they could hunt far better than the animal. But regardless of whatever form the *terra indigene* absorbed to keep them the dominant predators in the world, regardless of whether they took the shape of Ravens or Wolves or Panthers—or humans—they were still *terra indigene* and lived solitary or in packs according to the ways of their particular kind of *terra indigene* and not the shape they could wear over their true form.

"The cub needs to be socialized with his own kind, but I can't teach him how to be around humans or even talk to humans," Saul said. "He needs a task so that he can fit in, and he needs a teacher."

Movement in the square made Tolya turn. Barbara Ellen, riding the blue horse named Rowan, cantered toward the sheriff's office, her face scrunched up in anger—an expression so unusual for the usually bouncy almost-vet that Tolya realized she must have been brooding about yesterday's clash with the sheriff and had finally worked up to being mad enough for a confrontation.

"Follow me," he told Saul. "I have a teacher for Joshua." *If Virgil doesn't eat her,* he added silently as he shifted to his smoke form and raced toward the sheriff's office.

He arrived just ahead of Barbara Ellen—and just in time to shift back to human form before Virgil walked out of the office. There were flickers of red in the Wolf's amber eyes, a clear warning that Barbara Ellen wasn't the only one who was angry.

Barbara Ellen's blue eyes didn't change to provide such a warning, but the horse reacted to her emotions. Or maybe Rowan reacted to Kane's sudden, and silent, appearance in Wolf form as the deputy came around the side of the building.

Barbara Ellen dismounted and said, "Hold this," as she flicked one of the reins at Kane. He snapped at the leather and then looked surprised that he was now a horse holder.

Exploding fluffball, Tolya thought, remembering Vlad's phrase for uppity human females as Barbara Ellen stomped up to Virgil.

"Look!" She pushed up the sleeve of her shirt to reveal dark bruises. "Look! That's police brutality!"

Virgil leaned toward her, bringing his face closer to hers before he pulled back his lips and revealed teeth that were too long and sharp to be human. "You were resisting arrest."

Her mouth dropped open. "I wasn't arrested. You didn't arrest me!" She looked at Tolya, who wondered what he was supposed to do.

"If you howl 'police brutality' for a bruise you got because you fought me, then I'll write up your stay in the cell as an arrest for disturbing the peace," Virgil growled. "Or we can just say you spent a few hours in jail because you needed some 'me time' to help you remember that many predators who will be in this town don't know much about humans and need to be approached with some measure of caution and sense. Which way do you want me to report this to your brother the cop?"

Her mouth opened and closed, making Tolya think of a fish out of water—a comparison he was sure should not be shared with any female within a day's travel of this town.

"Barbara Ellen and I have business to discuss," Tolya said to Virgil. "Do you need to continue this discussion?"

"I wasn't interested in this discussion in the first place." Virgil stared at Barbara Ellen and growled, "The next time, the bruise you get as discipline will be from my teeth."

Barbara Ellen lowered her head and muttered a word quietly enough that a human wouldn't have heard what she'd said. Unfortunately, the four males standing around her heard the word just fine.

Virgil showed his teeth.

<Let it go,> Tolya said. <I have something that will keep Barbara Ellen from chewing your tail for the rest of the day.>

Virgil eyed him, clearly torn between wanting to establish dominance over the fluffball and getting her out of his fur. <Fine. Take her.>

More gently than Virgil had grabbed her yesterday, Tolya closed his hand over Barbara Ellen's wrist in an inescapable hold. "Come with me."

"What about Rowan?" she protested. "I should take him back to the stables if I'm going to be a while."

"Kane can do that for you."

<I can?> Kane didn't sound interested in being a horse walker. <I have to sniff around the town and do deputy things.>

Tolya didn't respond to the Wolf. Instead he reached out to the Panther. <Bring your cub to the government building.>

"Are all the pet animals fed and watered?" he asked. Since she was an almost-vet, this was her primary task right now—caring for the small animals that had survived until she could convince other humans to take them.

"Yes, but—"

"Good. I need you for a special task."

"We're all supposed to help sort things from the houses for a couple of hours each day."

Tolya nodded. "You'll be sorting books." No one had asked why he'd designated a room in the government building as the place to store the books that had been removed from houses and now would have to be sorted into some kind of order. The truth was, he'd wanted to keep that task for himself instead of handling other, less interesting, human possessions. But to keep the peace, and to help Saul, he would give up some of the pleasure of looking through the books.

"You'll also be showing another member of our community how to do this sorting," he continued. "In return, you may select a bag of books as a bonus for being a mentor. I would also appreciate you setting aside any books you find about the frontier days. Those would be for me."

"Okay. Who am I helping?" she asked, almost pulling ahead of him now that the task sounded interesting.

"Joshua Painter."

"Oh."

What did "oh" mean? Good? Bad? He guessed it meant something good since her blue eyes now had a sparkle to them that had nothing to do with being angry with Virgil.

"Saul feels Joshua is ready to interact with humans," Tolya said. "I thought sorting the books would help the cub reinforce his reading skills, and you, having experience with shifters because you lived in Lakeside, could help Joshua bridge the gap between his old life and this new one, as well as answer any questions he has about human things."

"I can do that."

Barbara Ellen had not shown this level of excitement when she'd met other young males who were staying in Bennett. She had been friendly, and being one of the few human females currently living in the town, her company was sought after by many. But this . . . giddiness . . . for a male she hadn't met? Well, he would assess her emotions at the end of the day. If there was no change, he would preempt receiving another message of alarm from Officer Debany in Lakeside by writing to Vlad and telling *him* about Joshua Painter. After all, if Barbara Ellen's brother was going to get excited about her living with a parakeet named Buddy, he could imagine the man's reaction to a male who had grown up among the Panthergard—a male who was a few years younger than Barbara Ellen, although just old enough to be considered an adult. He wasn't sure that mattered or should be a concern, but it was another thing to keep in mind.

"What are you going to do with the books?" Barbara Ellen asked. "Sell them? Give them away?"

"Jesse Walker indicated that we might find many copies of some books and only one or two copies of other titles. She also said some books are more valuable than others. First editions and uncommon texts."

Barbara Ellen nodded. "That makes sense. We'll probably find a lot of copies of last year's bestsellers."

"Jesse Walker's suggestion was to make the popular books available for free and set aside the valuable books to be sold in the bookstore as a special category."

Once they reached the government building, he led her to the room he had set aside for this sorting task. Boxes of books were piled along the edges of the room and under the big U-shaped table in the center, as well as on the folding tables that filled the space under the windows.

"Do you want me to stay and introduce you?" Tolya asked.

"No, I'm sure we'll get along just fine." She gave him the same bright smile she'd given him the day she'd stepped off the train. Barbara Ellen Debany was ready for another adventure.

He wasn't sure *he* was ready for her to have another adventure. "I'll be in my office if you need anything. The office is on the second floor."

"I know." She was already pulling boxes from under the table. "Oh! Is there a drinking fountain in the building? We might get thirsty."

"I'll arrange for water and glasses to be brought in."

"Thanks." Bright smile. Dismissive smile?

He wasn't used to feeling superfluous.

He didn't like it.

And he wondered if sending the Debany parents a card expressing sympathy for the work involved in raising a young human would be inappropriate.

Two minutes after entering his office, Tolya shifted into his smoke form, flowed down the stairs, then up to the ceiling, and . . . snuck . . . past the door to the book room before flowing down to the floor and shifting into human form. Then he waited near the building's front door for Joshua Painter to arrive.

He was being cautious. That was all. Joshua might be human, but he had no knowledge of human behavior and what might be appropriate when a male and female were together. Alone. But not *together*. Barbara Ellen had a friendly manner that human males found attractive, but it might be misinterpreted as something more by someone who was in Bennett to learn about his own kind.

But maybe Joshua also needed protection from their almost-vet, who seemed a little too interested in this one particular male? The Sanguinati took advantage of humans' casual mating practices, using seduction to lure their prey, but that knowledge didn't help Tolya now when trying to anticipate a human's potential interest in another human and how swiftly mating might occur once interest was indicated.

Mating was *not* part of this instruction. He would make that clear to *both* humans.

The door opened and Joshua stepped inside, stopping when he saw the Sanguinati.

Tolya took a moment to study the young male. A supple, lean body. Dark brown hair with a hint of gold and red—sun highlights, those hints were called. Unusual eyes—green with an outer ring of gray. At least, he hadn't seen any other human with eyes like that. The boy's short-sleeved shirt fit his body, but the trousers were a size too big and had those storage pockets on the outer thighs.

"Mr. Sanguinati."

"Mr. Painter."

"Saul said you wanted to see me."

"Yes, I wanted . . ." Tolya breathed in and the words vanished.

He had seen Joshua and Saul walking around the town square, giving themselves a chance to become acquainted with their new territory. Tiny houses lined both sides of one of the streets off the square—houses that might have been built by the original settlers and didn't look like they had more than one room and maybe a bathroom. When Saul decided the cabin he'd originally chosen as their den was too far from the town square and the activity he wanted Joshua to experience, he had claimed two of those tiny places, side by side, so that the boy would have his own den but would still have the security of his older brother nearby.

It had been a good decision since some of the young men who seemed intent on settling in Bennett also chose houses on that street. Tolya wanted to ask if humans formed bachelor packs the way some other animals did, but he hadn't been sure if the question would be considered rude.

Yes, he'd seen Joshua Painter walking around the square, looking at the stores. He'd even spoken to the boy a couple of times. But they had been outside, and the wind had not been in his favor. Now, standing inside the building . . .

He doesn't smell like prey. He's human. I know he's human. Why doesn't he smell like prey?

He knew the answer. It just wasn't a realistic answer because the only other person he'd met who didn't smell like prey was Meg Corbyn, the Lakeside Courtyard's Human Liaison. The blood prophet.

"You wanted . . . ?" Joshua prompted.

"Barbara Ellen is going to teach you how to sort the books."

"Barbara Ellen." Joshua took a step back. "How can *she* teach me? She's not very smart."

He bristled. "Why do you say that?"

"She tangled with Virgil. How smart can she be?"

Tolya sighed. The boy had a point. "Humans have a saying about having book smarts and street smarts. Barbara Ellen has book smarts, but her previous dealings with the Wolfgard were less . . . exciting . . . and may have given her a false understanding of what a dominant Wolf will tolerate."

Joshua thought about this and finally nodded. "Street smarts are about knowing how to move in the world, yes? Recognizing what is safe and what is dangerous."

Tolya nodded. "That is a good description."

"So I will learn book smarts from her, and maybe she can learn some street smarts from me." The boy looked like he was bracing himself for some kind of conflict. "But I don't want to have sex with her. Saul thinks it would be better to avoid mating with females until I have learned more about what is expected from a mate."

"I agree with Saul. It would be better to refrain until you understand more about human females. They have feelings about such things, and are, in their way, more like us in not seeing much, if any, difference between sex and mating when they are truly interested in a male." He would find a pair of pliers and pull out his own fangs before admitting he felt insulted by Joshua's lack of interest in the girl, especially since he didn't want either of them to have that kind of interest in each other. And he realized he needed to stop trying to explain human sex before he got both of them confused.

"Come," Tolya said. "I'll introduce you to Barbara Ellen."

Joshua followed him into the book room, and he made the introductions.

"Barb," she said, giving Joshua a big smile, almost bouncing with puppyish enthusiasm. "My human friends call me Barb."

Tolya left the room but stayed near the door, out of sight, as he listened to Barbara Ellen explain her sorting method. And then . . .

"What do you like to read? What was it like living with the Panthergard? I used to live in Lakeside and was studying to be a veterinarian because I wanted to take care of animals. I didn't get all that far in the classes, but I did work as a vet's assistant for a while. That's how I ended up coming to Bennett. They needed someone to take care of the pets, and I was chosen. Mr. Sanguinati calls me an almost-vet. Do you like mysteries? I love mysteries, especially the Crowgard cozies, which aren't cozy at all. And the Wolf Team books."

He didn't hear any of Joshua's answers. Wasn't sure the boy had a chance to answer as Barbara Ellen pelted him with questions. But Tolya felt reasonably sure the two of them were safe with each other. For now.

Back in his office, he stared out the window and thought about Joshua Painter. Why hadn't other *terra indigene* noticed that the boy didn't smell like prey? Or had they noticed but didn't understand the significance? Had any of the shifters who had helped find and release the *cassandra sangue* relocated to Bennett? Or was he the only one here who had been close enough to a blood prophet to know what it meant for a human to be not prey?

He could be mistaken. Maybe Joshua's scent was different because he had lived with the Panthergard. The boy was already different enough from the rest of the young human males. Why complicate his life by suggesting he wasn't like them in other ways?

He didn't have to say anything. He could wait and see if someone else noticed a difference in the boy.

After all, if Joshua Painter did come from a line of blood prophets, they would all know soon enough.

Jesse entered the general store in Bennett and sighed.

"Mom?" Tobias laid a hand on her shoulder. "You all right?"

She patted his hand. "I'm tired. I'm glad tomorrow is Earthday and we can stay home and rest."

"You don't have to do this."

"Yes, I do." Her right hand reached for her left wrist. She stopped the movement, but she knew Tobias had seen her tell. "If for no other reason, I need to figure out the most sensible way to stock the shelves in my own store."

"You're meeting Tolya Sanguinati?" Tobias asked. "Do you want me to stay with you?"

Surprised, she turned to look at him. Tobias's intuitive gift primarily had to do with animals and with people only in relation to animals. It made him a good rancher—and it helped him deal with the *terra indigene*.

"I'm not looking forward to discussing what I strongly feel we need to discuss, but I'm not worried about being alone with him if that's what you're asking under the offer to stay."

Tobias studied her. "Okay. But I'd like to talk to him too about how to distribute the new hands, assuming the Lakeside Courtyard finds any to hire, and who should be the foreman of each ranch we're going to try to keep going."

"I'll tell him. Where will you be?"

"The livery stable. I want to look at the horses there, want to make sure the people working there actually know something about horses." He hesitated. "And then I thought I'd take a look at the saloon. It's not open for business yet, but people are welcome to come in and take a look."

It didn't surprise her that the first business in Bennett to be fully staffed and truly operational would be the saloon. There had been more than one "watering hole" in the town, and someone might eventually open one of the other ones, but for now the Bird Cage Saloon would be an important gathering place.

"Go on, then." When he turned to leave, she added, "Tobias? I'd like to know about the people working there—and the person Tolya Sanguinati chose to run the place."

"You think that will be important?"

"Yes, I do."

They studied each other. Intuits did not dismiss the feelings that had helped them escape the persecution of humans who feared their gifts and had helped them bargain with the *terra indigene* to establish communities that were well hidden in the wild country.

"Anything in particular I should look for?" Tobias asked.

Jesse shook her head.

The door opened and Tolya walked in with a long roll of papers. "Mr. Walker."

"Mr. Sanguinati." Tobias touched the brim of his hat and left.

Jesse went behind the counter. No reason to except she felt easier.

"We can't keep doing this." She hadn't meant to say it so bluntly, but she was tired—and she was scared for herself, for her son, for the people of Prairie Gold, and for the newcomers, who, she was sure, weren't prepared for the daunting truth about Bennett no matter what pictures they had seen on the TV or in newspapers. Picking through the lives of so many people, realizing that what had eliminated the entire population was out there, watching, waiting . . .

Bennett was a carcass. Sooner or later, the scavengers would start arriving to pick at the spoils. And then more people would die.

She jerked when Tolya's hand closed over her right hand, which had a tight hold on her left wrist.

"I know your tell, Jesse Walker, and I know the scent of fear. Why are you afraid?"

"Outlaws, scavengers, squatters," she whispered. "They'll be coming too. Maybe not on the same trains that bring the people we want, but they'll be coming close behind. They'll find a way to get here because this place is ripe for the picking, and there's nothing we can do."

She felt surprised when a tear rolled down her cheek. Felt even more surprised when Tolya gently brushed it aside.

"We can't keep doing this," she said again.

"'Doing this' being clearing out the houses? I know. That's why I brought these maps of the streets. I had some thoughts about . . . prioritizing."

She moved her hands to indicate she wanted to be released. Tolya immediately raised his hand.

Taking a tissue from the open box she had placed near the cash register, she blew her nose and considered priorities.

"Jewelry, money, bank information, and legal documents are the important items that might be in each home, yes?" Tolya asked. "Those are the things that should be set aside for any potential heirs, if the attorneys who settle here can find anyone. These items are more important than clothing, books, furniture, and the food in jars and cans."

"All the alcohol should be collected," Jesse said, tossing the tissue in the little wastebasket she'd also tucked behind the counter. "I think . . . I *feel* the task of clearing out the houses is taking a toll on the young people doing the work. Some of them may come to depend on alcohol to numb their minds and hearts in order to face the work. And drugs. The houses should be cleared of all the drugs. Let the doctors who come here figure out what to do with prescriptions and such."

"You fear for the young humans. But humans keep alcohol in their homes. There is a store here that sells nothing but alcohol."

"Which isn't open because there is no one to run it yet." Jesse frowned. If access to the free alcohol was stopped, would some of the young men resort to breaking into the liquor store? "The saloon could sell bottles and act as the liquor store for the time being as well as being a place to buy a drink and socialize."

"I will mention this additional requirement to Scythe," Tolya said.

A chill ran through her. "Scythe?"

"Madam Scythe as she will be known at the saloon."

"Is she a shifter?"

"She can take human form."

Evasive. She didn't expect Tolya to tell her everything. She didn't live in Bennett, wasn't a part of the governing body here. But Prairie Gold would have a hard time surviving if Bennett disappeared completely, so she did have a stake in what was happening here. "What is she?"

Tolya studied her. "A rare form. A ferocious predator, even by the standards of other *terra indigene*. Understand that knowledge about her cannot be disseminated without great risk to your species."

Gods above and below. Did she want the burden of that kind of knowledge? Was there really a choice? "Tell me."

"She is a Harvester, a Plague Rider. The Sanguinati drink blood as their preferred sustenance. Her kind harvest life. It can range from a sip of life energy from many different prey to killing her prey. Her hair indicates her mood. Red is anger. If her hair turns solid black, she can kill with a look."

"Why . . ." Jesse struggled to speak. "Why let her stay here if she is so dangerous?"

"Would you have her on the outside, where she is alone and sees all of you as prey?" Tolya countered. "The Lakeside Courtyard has a Harvester running the coffee shop, and the arrangement has worked well for them. They are careful around her, as we must be around Scythe, but it is safer for everyone to have her among us at this point." He paused, then added, "Besides, she is enthusiastic about running a frontier saloon."

"She'll kill people."

"Yes. She will protect the beings who work with her." Tolya unrolled the papers he'd brought in. "I think we should establish residential territories so that humans with the same customs can live together if that is what they desire. Also, by designating neighborhoods open to habitation, we can reduce the pickup of garbage and other government services."

"You'll still need to have someone drive around the streets with unoccupied houses to keep an eye on things."

He smiled, showing a hint of fang. "Why drive a vehicle and waste gasoline? If the Ravens, Eagles, or Hawks see something, they'll tell us."

Jesse looked at the street map of Bennett and *knew* that, while Tolya's point about services wasn't a lie, that wasn't the reason for designating particular areas as approved housing. "These are boundaries."

His smile faded. "As you pointed out, there will be scavengers and squatters. Humans who are not suited to be here. There are no real boundaries, Jesse Walker. Not anymore. But there can be acknowledged areas where humans will be considered not edible as long as they don't provoke the *terra indigene* into attacking them."

"And if someone decides to live in one of the houses outside those areas?"

"They might survive."

But it wasn't likely. Suddenly she realized why Tolya wasn't that concerned about scavengers and squatters. Every kind of *terra indigene* would look at those people and see meat.

There was no mercy in the wild country, no safety in the dark. She knew that. But she wondered if the people coming to Bennett fully appreciated what that meant.

And she wondered what else Tolya wanted to talk about but shied away from.

She took a deep breath and blew it out. "Could we drive around these areas you designated? I think I could get a feel for whether or not they would do what you have in mind."

"Of course. I welcome your input. I will locate someone with a vehicle to drive us."

"Tobias can drive us. He was going to take a look at the saloon, so we could meet him there." And she'd like to take a look at the madam running the place.

Kelley didn't want a house, was adamant about not wanting the work of taking care of a house and whatever yard was attached to it. Abigail didn't want an apartment, was certain being in an apartment complex would expose her to danger and leave her vulnerable in a way that living in a house wouldn't.

A month ago, Kelley would have given in. But a month ago he'd still believed the story she had spun about her life before meeting him, had still believed she was the sweet woman he'd loved and married. Now they were two people who were living in the same room at the hotel but not even sharing a bed while they wrangled about where to live.

She had a feeling the wrangling wasn't going to go on much longer. *Couldn't* go on much longer. Her new neighbors had to see her as sweetly odd Abigail Burch who had sold soaps and candles when she'd lived in Prairie Gold.

Maybe it would be better to arrange things so that Kelley would leave and she could be the sad, brave wife he'd walked out on. That could work—as long as she chose the right kind of neighbors.

Abigail wandered one of the residential streets, making sure she looked adrift, homeless.

In order to eat free food and have a free place to stay, everyone coming into Bennett was expected to put in forty hours a week in some kind of work—and part of that work included helping to sort and clear out houses and businesses. She had tried to help sort and clear out the clothing, but she couldn't stand being in the bedrooms, especially the ones that had belonged to the children. So she volunteered to clean the offices, scrubbing windows and floors, dusting furniture, cleaning the bathrooms. Even that work wasn't without its unpleasant surprises. One person had kept a small bowl of tumbled stones on a desk, and those stones created another dissonance, another tear in the protections she had created around herself with her own collection of stones.

Abigail closed her eyes. She needed . . . She needed . . .

"Hey!"

A hand grabbed her arm. She gasped, pulled away, staggered. The hand grabbed her arm again.

"Easy. Wow. Have you been out in the sun too long? I live across the street. Come over. I'll give you some water."

Abigail looked at the young woman—at the gullible mark—with the blue eyes and freckles sprinkled across her nose and cheeks. Perfect. "Thank you."

"I'm Barb. I'm just moving in over there." She pointed to a house. "You're pretty wobbly. I'd say you should see a doctor, but we don't have one yet. I'm what Mr. Sanguinati calls an almost-vet since I've been taking care of all the pets who were left behind when . . . they were left behind."

She wasn't really listening. She was staring at the house next to Barb's. "Who lives there?"

"It's currently unoccupied." Barb hesitated. "It hasn't been cleared out. I've heard they aren't going to do that anymore. If you want a place that hasn't been cleared and is in one of the approved zones, you have to pack up all the stuff you don't want—and pack up the things that are on the list of items that *have* to be turned in. Do you want to see inside? I was given the keys to the houses on either side of mine so that I could show them if anyone was interested. The house on the other side of mine was cleared out, so you'd have to go around to the storage areas and select furniture and all the other things you'll need. That might be easier if you're on your own. But some people think just removing what they don't want is easier than lugging out furniture in order to lug in different furniture that does the same thing."

Abigail barely glanced at the empty house to the left of Barb's. The places that still held the footprint of the people who had lived there were hard to endure, but somehow that empty house felt worse.

"I'd like to take a look at that one." She pointed to the house on the right.

"I'll fetch the keys—and some water. I'll just be a minute." Barb ran into her own house, leaving Abigail alone to study the house next door.

Bennett was haunted by the echoes of the dead. That might never change. But on this residential street, she wouldn't be exposed to anyone coming into town.

And even if Kelley didn't come with her, or moved in with her but didn't stay long, that might work out for the best.

Messis 6
To: Tolya Sanguinati, Urgent

We have selected twenty-four Simple Life males to work on the farms and ranches around Bennett. We also selected five Simple Life females to work on the farms and ranches. Four of those females will do cooking and whatever is needed to take care of the human dens. The fifth female wants to herd things. She knows how to ride a horse and says she can lasso animals. None of the males mentioned this ability. Vlad and I agreed that, if we had to deal with her, we would give her cows to herd to keep her from herding other things—like us. But it's your decision.

The ranch humans will take a train to Bennett on Windsday, which is the same day we will interview the humans who are doctors and attorneys and other professions that work out of offices.

—Simon

Messis 6
To: Simon Wolfgard

Instead of biting her, I put Barbara Ellen in jail for a while on Firesday. When she yapped about it, I told her she needed "me time," something I heard a cop in the TV box say to a human male before putting him in a cell.

This is a useful thing to say to females since it makes them too annoyed to continue yapping, but what, exactly, is "me time"?

—Virgil

Messis 7

To: Tolya Sanguinati

We have found some humans to work in the stores. With this new group of humans coming in, you will need to figure out how to pay them so that everyone can buy the goods that will need to be replenished and that you will need to purchase from suppliers, like gasoline, milk, and toilet paper. You may not have experienced this yet, but human females turn predatory when there is a noticeable lack of toilet paper.

Some of the humans who are qualified to work in the stores will start their migration tomorrow, traveling with the Simple Life humans. The humans who said they needed extra time will go with the group leaving on Firesday.

Also, Steve Ferryman told us that news of job openings has traveled past Lakeside, and even though all the humans are supposed to see Simon and me first, several Intuits on Great Island feel that humans we haven't seen and approved will be arriving and looking for work. You should be wary of any humans who don't have a letter from us.

—Vlad

CHAPTER 10

Thaisday, Messis 9

Apparently, Captain Douglas Burke wasn't big on small talk. Or maybe this was part of the test. Some people were comfortable with silence; others had to fill a space with the sound of their own voice. Or maybe he was waiting to see if she'd ask questions that would reveal her ignorance.

Or maybe the big man with the fierce-friendly smile didn't have any agenda to make her look bad and spoil her chances of getting this job.

"Were there many applicants for the deputy position?" she finally asked. It would be good to know how many other people were being tested. It would be good to know if she had any chance at all.

"Just you," Burke replied. "Don't get cocky about not having any competition. If you're not qualified, I'll do everything I can to make sure you're not on that train tomorrow."

Jana bristled. "If you bothered to look at my transcript, you would know I'm qualified."

"Haven't reviewed the transcript yet; I assume you brought a copy of it with you?"

"Yes, I did."

Burke nodded. "I did look at the résumé you provided to Simon Wolfgard. Read it twice, in fact. You look good on paper, Ms. Paniccia, but a lot of cadets who graduate from the academy look good on paper." He turned into the parking lot of the Lakeside Shooting Range. He pulled into a space, shut off the car, and looked at her. "Looking good on paper doesn't mean a damn thing in the wild country. You being a woman isn't the issue. You being a baby cop about to head out for a job that most experienced men wouldn't touch? That's an issue. Today is about finding out what you can do, about finding out if you have enough grit and backbone—and common sense—to survive what you'll be facing every single day."

She felt her temper heat and struggled to keep it controlled. "I survived the academy. I can survive whatever is out there."

Burke studied her for a long time. "Let's find out."

Not having a service weapon of her own, she had accepted Captain Burke's when he offered to let her use it. He'd made no comment about that except to say that he didn't think she would have a problem acquiring a weapon in Bennett and it probably was best not to have one with her on the train.

After the shooting range, Burke drove her to a gym where Officers Karl Kowalski and Michael Debany tested her hand-to-hand and self-defense skills. It wasn't textbook academy. Some of the moves they threw at her were down and dirty, the kind of moves a person used to survive. They didn't spare her from getting bruises, but she sensed that they weren't trying to inflict an injury that would prevent her from taking the job.

"You'll do," Kowalski said after one of her moves ended with Debany landing on the mat. "You have any questions?"

"Is there anyplace where I can take a shower or at least wash up a bit?" she asked. The place didn't say it was a men's-only gym; it just didn't make any accommodation for women—not in terms of locker rooms, showers, or toilets.

Kowalski grinned. "Captain took care of that." He waved a hand toward the locker room. "Ladies first."

"Well, after me," Debany said. He walked into the locker room, then came back out in a minute. "Clear."

When they'd gone in to change into workout clothes, Kowalski had waved her to a different aisle of lockers while he and Debany changed in the next one over. They had stuffed her daypack into a locker with Debany's things and didn't explain why. They didn't have to. She'd seen the look on the men's faces who had waited to go in—and she'd seen them slide a look at Captain Burke, who seemed to be paying no attention but, most likely, could give someone an accurate description of every man who was there. If her clothes had been by themselves in a guest locker, she might have found them torn—or fouled. But none of the men who had come in after them would touch a cop's locker, no matter what they thought of her presence. It was equally clear, at least to her, that no one on the right side of sanity messed with Douglas Burke.

She took a quick shower, then dressed in clean underclothes, a tank top, and a shirt that she tucked into her good pair of jeans. She pulled her hair back in a low ponytail and went out to wait with Captain Burke while Kowalski and Debany showered.

As they walked back to the car, with Burke in the lead, Debany said, "My sister lives in Bennett now. She can give you the skinny about the town and everyone she's met."

"You have any questions for us?" Kowalski asked again, slowing down and keeping an eye on his captain.

Dozens. But there was one she'd like answered before she got on that train. Jana pulled out a slip of paper from the back pocket of her jeans. Then she hesitated.

"I'm not like the rest of the people who applied for jobs in Bennett, am I?" she asked.

Kowalski shook his head. "Everyone else was Simple Life or Intuit."

"Intuit?" She'd heard stories about people who could "sense" things, but she'd had the impression from things she'd overheard at the academy that most cops thought that people who claimed to have feelings about things were just grifters who cheated gullible people out of money or goods.

"Intuit communities are usually tucked away in the wild country and aren't human controlled," Debany said. "But a few of those communities have been hiding in plain sight for years. Like Ferryman's Landing on Great Island."

"What about towns in the Finger Lakes?" she asked.

"Ever heard anyone at the academy refer to a town as a woo-woo community?" Kowalski asked in turn.

"Yes."

"Odds are good the place is an Intuit town."

Was she being foolish to trust these men? She'd trusted a few fellow cadets when she'd first arrived at the academy, thinking their overture of friendship had been real. That had been a harsh lesson, the first of many. But now, what did she have to lose? "I got a phone call telling me to come to Lakeside if I wanted a job in law enforcement. The caller said he'd been given a cryptic message and my phone number. This is his phone number."

Kowalski took the paper and slipped it into his pocket. "You tried calling back?"

"No answer." She hesitated. "I'd like to know if I'm being set up."

"I'll see what I can find out on the QT and get the information to you before you go."

"Assuming I get the job."

Kowalski smiled. "Assuming."

Jana sat in A Little Bite with Lieutenant Crispin James Montgomery while Captain Burke and Simon Wolfgard decided her fate, at least as far as this job was concerned.

She'd told Montgomery about her love of frontier stories and how she'd imagined herself as the sheriff squaring off against the villains. She didn't know why she'd told him that. Maybe it was because, sitting with him, she thought he was a man who could have worked with her, *would* have worked with her, if society's ideas about certain kinds of jobs had been a little more flexible.

Then Simon Wolfgard and Captain Burke were standing next to the table and Simon was handing her the travel letter and pass for the train fare, along with a letter addressed to Tolya Sanguinati, the leader in Ben-

nett. Simon Wolfgard also said that Officer Debany's sister, Barbara Ellen, would be her housemate.

Despite her best efforts to maintain her feelings, emotions welled up
inside her and leaked out a little.

No comments about women being too emotional to be on the job—
except from Wolfgard, but that was a concern about whether watery eyes
and a runny nose indicated illness.

Within minutes of being offered congratulations and best wishes, she
acquired a Crowgard pen pal and was told by the coffee shop's manager
that a ride was waiting for her in the access way.

Jana hurried toward the back door of the coffee shop, then retraced
her steps, wanting to thank Burke and Montgomery one last time for
their part in her having a chance to be a deputy. And she wanted to ask
where she could find Merri Lee. When she'd come to the Courtyard a
few days ago to ask about law enforcement work, Merri Lee had told her
about the job fair and which day to return to fill out an application. Jana
had promised that if she got a job in Bennett, she would write and let
Merri Lee know how she was getting on.

"The job fair is over." The manager of the coffee shop sounded . . .
different. Almost threatening.

Staying in the back hallway, Jana looked into the main room and
stared at the woman's hair as it changed to red-streaked green and began
coiling.

Oh, that couldn't be good. She'd figured the woman was *terra indigene*, but the hair changing color and coiling like that made her feel . . .
uneasy. No. It made her feel a little sick—and very afraid.

She withdrew enough not to see or be seen, but, darn it, she was a
cop—or about to become one officially. Burke and Montgomery were in
the coffee shop and might need backup. Not that there was much she
could do since she didn't have a weapon.

"Didn't come for a job. Came to see family. Was told there was a place
we could stay." A pause. "Hey, CJ."

Burke said something in response to the other man, but Burke's voice
was so low Jana couldn't make out the words. Then she heard Montgomery's answer. "My brother. Cyrus James Montgomery."

A car horn honked. Remembering there was someone waiting to take her to the hotel, Jana hurried to the back door and out, waving a hand to let the minivan's driver know she was coming.

A family drama. None of her business. But . . .

Cyrus James Montgomery. If she had access to a police database and looked him up, she wondered what she would find.

Messis 8

To: Tolya Sanguinati and Virgil Wolfgard

We are sending doctors, lawyers, a toother, and a vet who is trained to work with large animals like horses and cows. And we found a human female deputy to work with Virgil. She knows how to shoot a gun and fight with her hands. She wants to ride a horse, and she has agreed to live with Barbara Ellen Debany.

These humans will be leaving Lakeside on Firesday. John Wolfgard will also be on the train. He worked with us at Howling Good Reads, so he can run the bookstore and has experience with humans, both as customers and employees.

—Simon and Vlad

Messis 9

To: Tolya Sanguinati, Urgent

The Hope pup drew the attached picture. I don't know what it means, except that it is a warning meant for you and Virgil.

—Jackson Wolfgard

CHAPTER 11

Thaisday, Messis 9

Abigail made her voice and hands shake a little as she set the plate of scrambled eggs and toast in front of Kelley. She'd spent two days pleading with him to look at the house she wanted, and when he finally did go with her, all he'd said was "If that's what you want."

He still loved her—or his memory of her—enough to move into the house. But she'd read the tarot cards last night and they indicated that he wouldn't be staying very long.

"Do you want me to pack you a lunch?" she asked after fetching him a glass of orange juice.

He watched her, the food on his plate untouched. "Why are you doing this, Abby? Why do we need a house this size?"

They didn't need a house this size. *She* didn't need a house this size. But she did need her friendly neighbor who would unwittingly help her solidify her sweet Abigail persona, regardless of what Kelley might tell people.

"Why are you volunteering to sort through other people's things? You always claimed you were extrasensitive to the residue other people left on objects, and that was the reason everything we owned, even stuff that was brand-new, had to be washed and set out in the sun before you could stand having it in the house. Books you got out of the Prairie Gold library were 'aired' before you could read them. And now you're going to put in forty hours a week pawing through things owned by strangers who were killed by the *terra indigene*?"

"It has to be done."

"A few days ago, you were willing to clean any kind of commercial building in order *not* to clear out private residences, and suddenly you're okay with it?" Kelley pushed aside the plate of food. "I can't tell if you're lying to yourself as well as to me, but I'm pretty sure you're lying to me, if not now, then before when you made such a fuss about things."

"I've never lied to you." Well, he hadn't caught her in a lie until now.

"Fine. You're not lying; you're just being less than truthful. Does that sound better?" His voice had an edge it had never had before. "The point is, I'm not sure I want to live with less than truthful anymore."

"We were happy in Prairie Gold!" she cried.

"You were." He pushed away from the table. "I have to get to work."

"But you haven't eaten anything!"

He didn't reply—and he didn't kiss her before he left the house.

Abigail stared at the eggs and toast a full minute before she sat down, pulled the plate over to her place at the table, and began to eat with a gusto she couldn't have shown if Kelley were still there.

Fetching the jar of strawberry jam that she'd opened the other day, she slathered jam generously over one piece of toast.

She had used her real name when she and Kelley had married, just in case she needed the marriage to be legitimate, and when she'd realized the name had meant nothing to him, she'd felt staggering relief. He'd seen himself as the hero rescuing the maiden from her abusive father. He would have started questioning things a lot sooner if he'd known her father was the leader of a clan of Intuits who gambled and swindled and conned everyone they met. They would roll into a town, pluck all the prey they could, and then move on before the law got a little too interested in them and their deals. And they always had a feeling about when it was time to move on, just like one or another of them knew who to play for the biggest score.

No one knew they were Intuits, because they had avoided Intuit towns. But anyone who did learn that little secret . . .

She never found out how her father had arranged the evidence to finger a man addled by drink as the person who killed a deputy in a small West Coast town. The man was a drunk who could barely hold a knife to cut his own dinner and certainly didn't have the skill to do . . . what the newspapers said had been done to the deputy. The lawman had died because he was sweet on her—and she'd told him the family's secret in exchange for his help in escaping from her father's control.

She had escaped, but two men had died—the deputy and the man accused of killing him. That was typical of how the Blackstones dealt with problems before they moved on. Her father called it "taking out the trash."

It was just a matter of time before someone from her family would arrive in Bennett—and then someone else would die. She just had to make sure the someone wasn't her.

Tolya reviewed the e-mails from Lakeside, as he had since the first one arrived on Sunday. Because there was no longer direct communication between the regions that made up the continent of Thaisia, e-mails and telegrams had to go through Intuit communications cabins that had been set up near the borders. Letters and business correspondence sent by anyone who wasn't Intuit or *terra indigene* traveled by train and eventually reached the destination cities and the recipients who lived there. So even "fast" communication between regions could take up to twenty-four hours before being received.

The single exception was the connection between Sweetwater, which was in the Northwest, and Bennett and Prairie Gold, which were in the Midwest. Tolya and Jackson Wolfgard had pleaded with the Elders to allow them to have direct communication with each other because there was a connection between Jesse Walker in Prairie Gold and the blood prophet pup living with Jackson in the *terra indigene* settlement at Sweetwater.

Jackson and his mate, Grace, had discovered that Hope Wolfsong had the ability to draw the visions that came to her and didn't need to cut her skin. Drawing didn't release the visions for most of the girls, but Hope's ability encouraged other girls' caretakers to explore different ways that these girls could reveal prophecy without the cutting that would eventually kill them.

Like Meg Corbyn, the blood prophet who lived in the Lakeside Courtyard, Hope Wolfsong was highly gifted, and while those who received the drawings of her visions weren't always able to interpret the pictures correctly, she and Meg had been instrumental in saving many of the Wolfgard from the slaughter organized by the Humans First and Last movement. The warning hadn't come in time to save the adults in the Prairie Gold pack, but it had come in time to save the pups as well as the Intuit town.

What all of that meant to him was a picture from Hope Wolfsong couldn't be ignored.

Tolya still hesitated to download the file. Jackson had called the picture a warning. Vlad had told him unauthorized humans most likely would be arriving in Bennett along with the humans selected during the Lakeside job fair. That meant he and Virgil should be at the station to assess the humans as they arrived—starting today, since they couldn't be certain that the strangers wouldn't arrive before the Lakeside migration.

He hesitated a moment longer before downloading the file and printing two copies. Then he studied the picture.

<Virgil?> he called. <Where are you?>

<Kane and I are sniffing around one of the designated territories for human dens,> Virgil replied. <We want to know who is supposed to live there. Then we can drive out intruders.>

<We need to meet the train when it comes in this afternoon.>

<The humans are arriving that fast?> Virgil didn't sound happy about that.

<Not the ones we're expecting.>

Silence. <I'll meet you.>

Tolya almost pitied the humans who might be viewed as intruders. Almost. He understood Virgil's rage against humans. He just wasn't sure what he would—or should—do if the Wolf couldn't contain that rage and started killing the useful humans who wanted to live in Bennett.

Not something he needed to deal with today. Slipping the copies of the picture into a slim briefcase, Tolya left his office, then stopped at the book room to check on Barbara Ellen and Joshua Painter—who were doing fine. Too fine? No, they *were* fine, still getting acquainted. No reason for alarm or to send any messages that would cause undo excitement in Lakeside.

Even so, he'd remain vigilant until the new deputy arrived. Then *she* could keep watch over Barbara Ellen Debany.

Leaving the two humans to their book sorting, he walked to the jewelry store and was pleased to see the Open sign on the door.

"Mr. Sanguinati," Kelley Burch said.

The human looked tired, strained. Whispers had reached Tolya that something wasn't right between Kelley and his mate—something serious enough that Jesse Walker was concerned. Not that she had *said* anything, but every time he mentioned Kelley or Abigail, her right hand closed over her left wrist. Trouble between human mates wasn't his business, but Kelley was the only person qualified to assess the jewelry and run this shop, and having someone in town to do that work *was* Tolya's business.

"What can you tell me about black stones?" Tolya asked.

"Was there anything in particular you wanted to see?" Kelley asked in turn. "I have jewelry here that has onyx or hematite stones. I have a jet necklace. I even have a ring with a couple of black diamonds as part of the setting. There are probably more stones in the back, including some tumbled stones that I haven't sorted yet."

"Are any of them significant? Preferred by a certain kind of human?"

Kelley thought for a moment, then shook his head. "The diamonds are valuable stones. The others are considered semiprecious, so by themselves they aren't worth a lot of money. I might be more help if I knew what you were looking for. Loose stones? Something in a silver or gold setting?"

"I don't know yet," Tolya replied. "But I want to know about anyone showing interest in black stones."

Kelley looked uneasy. "All right. There's nothing sinister about liking those stones. Black doesn't mean bad."

Tolya didn't respond to that. Instead, he returned to his office and called Jesse Walker's mobile phone, since he knew Rachel Wolfgard wouldn't answer Jesse's personal phone.

"I'm in town," she said.

"Virgil Wolfgard and I will be meeting the train. I'd like you to be there."

A hesitation. "Is there a problem?"

"Maybe. Before that, there is something I want to show you. Can you come to my office?"

"I'll be there soon."

While he waited, Tolya sent an e-mail to Vlad, asking if Tess knew anyone named Scythe. Vlad would understand that he was asking for information about another Harvester.

Jesse walked in a few minutes later and settled in one of the visitors' chairs. "Tobias wanted to bring a couple of horses to the livery stable here. They're younger animals and well trained, but he didn't feel anyone at the Prairie Gold ranch was the right match for either of them."

"He felt they might suit one of the newcomers?" Tolya asked.

She nodded. "You think there's a problem heading our way?"

"It's heading our way or it's already here. Virgil and I received a warning. I'm showing this to you because you have seen such warnings before. I'm not sharing this information with anyone else. Not yet."

He waited for her to nod again before he removed one of the copies of the picture from his briefcase and set it on the desk—and he watched Jesse Walker pale.

"I'd say Hope Wolfsong was a genius if her drawings weren't so disturbing," Jesse said quietly. "People made of black stones rendered so well you can see they're made up of many stones and aren't statues made from a block of stone."

The drawing was the street outside the Bird Cage Saloon. Rendered as ordinary humans were Barbara Ellen and an unknown female with brown hair pulled back in a tail. Both were laughing as they headed toward the saloon, although there was something in the unknown female's expression that made Tolya think she wasn't as unaware of the people around her as she first appeared. Standing at the doorway of the saloon was a human shape made of black stones, with two more of the stone humans nearby. Stazia Sanguinati was also in the picture, looking angry as she started to shift to her smoke form. And Virgil, standing upright and still dressed in jeans and a checked shirt, looked like a snarling Wolf.

But it was the woman taking up the bottom right corner that was the main reason Tolya had wanted Jesse to see the picture.

"I've only seen her a couple of times since she and her mate arrived, but isn't that Abigail Burch?" Tolya said.

"Yes." Jesse said nothing else for a minute. "She's dead. In the picture, she's dead."

"Yes." The staring eyes told him that much.

"Why . . . ?" Jesse swallowed hard. "Why is blood trickling out of her mouth?"

"I don't know."

"Are you wondering if Kelley is going to kill her? Something happened in Prairie Gold that put a crack in their marriage. Abigail has secrets. She acts sweet and a bit simple, and she acted the part so well that no one in Prairie Gold realized it was deliberate until the scene with Kelley a couple of weeks ago. To be honest, I'm surprised she went with him, and I'm surprised he's still living with her. But I'm not feeling any indication that he would kill her for any reason."

"We've been warned that unauthorized humans will be arriving in Bennett looking for work, looking for . . . opportunities," Tolya said. "That's why I want you to join me and Virgil when the train gets in. Your instincts are different from ours. I'm not opposed to additional workers, but we need to be careful."

Jesse sat back and looked away from the picture. "Yes, we do." She ran a hand over her hair. "I'll let Tobias know we'll be here for a while."

"I was about to walk up to the train station, but I can arrange for a ride if you prefer," Tolya said.

She let out a little snort that sounded equally amused and annoyed. "The train station is just up the street, and I'm not infirm. A walk will suit me just fine." She looked troubled. "I'm not happy with Abigail at the moment, but I don't want her to come to any harm."

"Then let's try to keep that from happening." Tolya slipped the picture back into his briefcase, led Jesse out of the office, and locked up. "And let us both remember that a warning is intended to help prevent something from happening."

Virgil didn't like having a human behind him, even if it was an older female who didn't meet his eyes or challenge him in any way. But she was *there*, standing in the space Tolya Sanguinati had left between the two males.

<Why is she here?> he growled at Tolya.

<She is an Intuit. She is sensitive to other people. You and I will know different things about each human getting off the train. Jesse Walker will know something else. We have a better chance of recognizing an enemy together than if we are separate.>

All right. He couldn't argue with that, because *all* humans were the enemy but some were also a threat to the *terra indigene* and the humans who were, regrettably, considered not edible.

Humans who were threats to the *terra indigene* or broke human laws would be bitten. Savagely. Maybe lethally. But he was going to get Tolya to agree that nipping the nonedibles was permitted by the sheriff and his deputy—just in case he had another reason to haul Barbara Ellen to jail for some "me time."

The baggage door opened at the same time Nicolai Sanguinati walked out of the delivery area of the train station, pulling a cart that had webbing on two sides that could be raised and lowered for loading.

"You expecting anything in particular?" Nicolai asked, looking from Tolya to Virgil.

Some meaty bones would be nice, but Virgil figured he and Kane would have to hunt those down for themselves.

"Passengers," Tolya replied.

A man wearing a shirt with the railway's logo on the pocket and across the back stepped down from the baggage car while another man tossed him the mailbags, which he and Nicolai loaded into the cart. Next came the luggage and packages that were designated for the Bennett station. The railway men moved quickly, efficiently. Nervous, but not afraid. Bennett might be controlled by the *terra indigene*, but the men understood they were safe at the station—or as safe as any human could be in Thaisia.

"That's the last of the cargo," the man on the platform said as he held out a clipboard for Nicolai to sign. "Anything to go out?"

"One bag of mail to the Northeast Region," Nicolai replied. "I'll bring it out."

Virgil caught Kane's scent before he heard Jesse Walker's quick intake of breath. The Wolfgard were significantly bigger than regular wolves and could take down prey a wolf couldn't. He looked back at Jesse Walker. "You've never seen one of the Wolfgard in that form?"

"Haven't seen an adult in a while," Jesse replied. "Rachel is a juvenile Wolf, so she's not nearly as big as your friend. I guess she still has some growing to do."

Virgil knew Morgan and Chase had taken over the Prairie Gold pack, but if Jesse Walker hadn't seen them in Wolf form, it sounded like they weren't inviting the humans to howl with them and weren't expected to be that friendly.

He envied them.

Then the first humans stepped off the train.

A pack of five young males, all dressed in dark trousers, white shirts, and the straps that held up clothing instead of using a belt. And hats.

The wind conveniently changed direction, bringing their scent to him and Kane. They smelled of clean soap and animals—and nerves.

"Simple Life," Tolya said quietly. "It is their custom for the males to dress that way."

Virgil studied the clothing carefully. Other males might try to disguise themselves by wearing that kind of clothing, but he didn't think any other male would be able to reproduce their particular scent.

The males looked at Nicolai as he came out of the station with a mailbag. Nicolai pointed to Virgil and Tolya.

Hesitation. A flash of fear when they noticed Kane and understood what he was. But they came forward, removing their hats.

"Good afternoon, gentlemen." The male Virgil considered the dominant one among them nodded to Jesse Walker. "Ma'am."

"What brings you to Bennett?" Tolya asked, giving the men a smile that showed a hint of fang.

Another hesitation. It was one thing to be told the *terra indigene* were in control of a town; it was another thing to look that truth in the eyes and hope it didn't eat you.

The man looked at Jesse Walker, then must have realized she wasn't the one he needed to convince, because he focused on Tolya. "My sister married a man who lives on Great Island. Have you heard of that place?"

"It's near Talulah Falls—and Lakeside."

"Yes." His relief was almost a taste in the air. "My sister sent a message that there was work here."

"Did your sister tell you this is a mixed community and what that means?"

"It means we must accept the customs of those who are not like us," another man said. He stood apart from the others just enough to make Virgil think he might be the same kind of human but he hadn't come from the same pack as the other four.

Kane growled—and Virgil agreed. It wasn't what the man had said but the way he'd said it. Virgil didn't smell anything *wrong* about the man, but . . .

<I don't like him,> he said to Tolya.

<Agreed.>

"Don't fuss," Jesse whispered. "I have a feeling he won't be here long."

<The Jesse female is looking at her feet and not meeting any males' eyes,> Kane said. <I don't think the humans heard what she said.>

<There are other humans waiting,> Tolya said. <We'll continue this discussion later.>

"Collect your baggage and put it in the van that's waiting in the park-ing lot," Virgil said. "Then walk down to the Bird Cage Saloon. We'll meet you there to sort out the paperwork." Not that he would do any sorting. He was the sheriff. He got to bite wrongdoers. Tolya had to deal with paperwork because he was the town's leader.

The thought of being able to give that one Simple Life male a hard bite or two cheered him up, so he smiled, showing his teeth.

The one with the stick up his tail had opened his mouth—probably to yap about going to the saloon—but one look at Virgil's smile and he hurried away to fetch his luggage.

The next group was a family pack made up of an adult female, a younger adult female, a boy, and . . .

Virgil cocked his head to one side, trying to figure out the third fe-male. She didn't look like the others. She was short and blocky and her face wasn't shaped like any human he'd ever seen. She had to be a juve-nile, but that didn't feel right.

She gave Kane the sweetest smile and hurried toward the Wolf.

"Doggy!"

"Becky, *no*," the dominant female said sharply, grabbing for the girl and missing.

Virgil leaned toward the girl, just enough to draw her attention from Kane. "Not a dog. A Wolf."

She stared at Virgil. "Wollllff." Her hand suddenly rose and came down, as if she was going to clobber Kane. Then she stopped the movement and said, "Gentle, gentle."

<She's a skippy,> Kane said as she petted his head. <I didn't know humans had skippies.>

Sometimes Wolf pups were born with a skippy brain that made it hard for them to learn how to hunt—made it hard for them to survive. If they managed to reach adulthood, many of them outgrew the skippiness but most didn't live that long in the wild country.

"She doesn't mean any harm," the dominant female said. "She's a good girl and a good worker."

"Will her brain get better?" Virgil asked.

The female's mouth tightened and she looked like she'd been driven out of more than one pack because of the girl. "No. She'll always be this way."

Huh. Virgil glanced at Tolya.

"Your name?" Tolya asked.

"Hannah Gott. I'm Simple Life." She gestured to the long dress and white apron. All three females wore white caps over their hair, although the skippy's hat had food stains on the tie strings. Virgil smelled some kind of fruit and gravy made from beef.

Hannah Gott introduced her sister, Sarah, then her niece, Becky, and finally her nephew, Jacob.

"I'm guessing you have clothing here," she said. "Lots of it that needs to be sorted into what is good and what just hasn't been cut up into rags yet. There are plenty of people now who need clothes but can't afford to buy new. I think it's possible to find communities that are in need and sell them the excess goods that are here for a reasonable price." She looked at Virgil but didn't quite meet his eyes. "I'm guessing your people might appreciate a little help when it comes to buying human garments. Especially if it's a new experience."

"Because we have Intuits, Simple Life, and humans living here as well as *terra indigene*, we are establishing communities so that people can live among their own," Tolya said.

"That's not necessary for us." Hannah Gott sounded sharp. "We would prefer to live among people who are tolerant of differences."

Her response made Virgil wonder what usually happened to skippy-brained humans.

The two railway men offered to haul the Gotts' luggage to the van, and Kane was assigned to lead them to the saloon.

And that left the last human who was waiting for their notice and permission to enter Bennett.

"Not another one," Tolya said under his breath, causing Jesse Walker to huff in a way that sounded like laughter.

The smile and the look in the female's eyes were things Virgil also recognized from his dealings with Barbara Ellen. Here was another bouncy fluffball.

"I'm Lila Gold." Her arms were full of books and folders with papers sticking out the tops. "I heard you say there's a saloon. Is it wonderful? I bet it's wonderful."

"You want to work in a saloon?" Tolya asked.

"Uh-huh. I've studied frontier towns since I was a little girl. It's kind of my hobby. Or passion. Or vocation. Something like that. And I always thought working in a saloon would be fun. Not the more carnal things that used to go on, but the dancing and singing and talking to people. I worked as a waitress while I went to school, so I know how to wait on customers. And I took a self-defense class, so I know what to do with my knee if I need to. You know?"

Virgil didn't know. Was sure he didn't want to know. She was like a puppy who couldn't resist grabbing his tail.

"You went to school," Tolya said. "What did you study?"

The smile dimmed a bit. "I took secretarial classes but I don't really—"

"So you can type and file and answer phones?" Tolya interrupted.

The smile dimmed a bit more. "I wanted to do something different."

"You're an Intuit," Jesse Walker said. "You had a feeling that if you came here, you could have something different, something that would make you happy."

"Yes!" Now Lila Gold focused on Jesse. "I was good at my job. I really was. But I'd come home at night and . . ." She waved a hand to indicate Bennett—and almost dropped all the books and folders. "A couple of weeks ago, I thought why shouldn't I give it a try? No, it was more than that. I *knew* I should give it a try. So I quit my job and packed up my belongings and bought train fare to Bennett because this is the only frontier town that still has a train station. Well, not the only one, but it was the first one on the list because the name starts with the letter *B*." She smiled at them.

She didn't have freckles on her face but she did have yellow hair and blue eyes like Barbara Ellen. What were they supposed to do with a pack of bouncy fluffballs? Could two fluffballs be considered a pack?

"We need secretaries," Tolya said. He held up a hand. "We need people who can do that work. However, if you're willing to use your skills in that area for part of your required work hours, I'll talk to Madam Scythe about giving you a chance to work in her saloon."

"Her name is Madam Scythe? Really?" The bounce was back. "That would be awesome!"

"Then let's go up to the saloon and go over all the requirements for residency in Bennett." Tolya looked past Lila Gold. "Nicolai?"

"Should we take these belongings to the van?" Nicolai asked.

"Yes. It looks like everyone will be staying," Tolya replied.

"Then I'll tell the conductor the train can go on to the next stop. He's been waiting to make sure no one needed to board. They want to leave soon to make all their stops before dark."

"Tell them we appreciate their waiting."

Jesse Walker took some of the books Lila Gold was carrying, and the two women headed for the Bird Cage Saloon.

"We have to do this for every train from now on?" Virgil asked.

"The humans migrating from Lakeside will have papers. We'll send them on to the saloon," Tolya said. "It's the ones without papers that we need to look at carefully. There is something I need to show you and Kane. Will you be back at the sheriff's office later this afternoon?"

"I'll be there."

But first he was going to go back to the office and strip off the human clothes and shift out of this human skin, and he was going to run and run in order to feel like who, and what, he was.

*   *   *

Standing in her office doorway, Scythe brushed a hand over the sapphire dress, enjoying the feel of the material. Not quite like the pictures of dresses worn in a frontier saloon, but close enough for now. Garnet Ravengard and Pearl Owlgard had found a shop where humans had had their pictures taken wearing frontier costumes and had found some clothing that looked appropriate for a saloon. They brought back all the costumes they could find and chose two outfits each. They also brought back dresses they thought might suit the owner of a saloon.

Did they know what she was, know what she could do to any of them? All of them?

The desire to belong had to be stronger than the compulsion to feast. Most of her kind didn't have enough control. Better to feed and feed until there was nothing left and then move on. But sometimes one of them wanted more—and showed others among their kind that it was possible. Not easy. Never easy. But possible.

It took years to learn how to have that control. Years and mistakes. Villages devastated by a mysterious illness, where there might be a single survivor who ended up with a dead eye after glimpsing a black-haired stranger heading away from the village—a stranger who was too sated on the lives already consumed to take one more.

Or a crop bursting with life and ready for harvest—and the whole field changed to dead and rotting plants overnight.

It took years to learn how to sip a little life energy from many and even eat food the way a human would.

She might have settled in one of the little towns that had been emptied of humans—towns the *terra indigene* had reclaimed—and lived on whatever she could find until fresh prey arrived in the form of two-legged scavengers. She had been heading toward one of them when she came across the strange girl bleeding out on the side of the road. The girl should have been prey but wasn't.

She hadn't known about the sweet bloods, the humans who weren't prey because they were Namid's creation, both wondrous and terrible.

That day, Scythe had felt the life force flickering in the girl and knew there wasn't much left to harvest, even if she hadn't felt uneasy. But she'd crouched beside the girl, careful not to touch the blood.

"*You live in Bennett,*" *the girl had said.* "*You wear pretty dresses and run a saloon. You have friends. Yellow bird.*"

"*I'm a Harvester. A Plague Rider. You think I'll be wanted in a town?*"

"*You help protect the town.*" *The girl breathed out the words* "*black stones*" *and died.*

Scythe picked up the girl and carried her away from the road. Hid the body under stones and brush. And then she found her way to Bennett.

The Sanguinati who ran the town and the Wolves who were the enforcers didn't trust her but they had agreed to let her stay, let her run this place. Eventually they might even accept her living among them—as long as she could resist the compulsion to devour all the life force of a being that mattered to the Sanguinati and Wolves.

Yuri Sanguinati, one of the saloon's two bartenders and the only one working today, turned toward her when she stepped out of the office to join him behind the bar.

"Tolya is sending some humans our way," Yuri said. "Potential workers and residents."

"From Lakeside?" Barbara Ellen had stopped in a couple of times to say hello and show her how to take care of Yellow Bird, and had told her about the humans who were migrating to Bennett from Lakeside. The girl had also told her about meeting Tess, which explained a lot about why Barbara Ellen had approached a Harvester in the first place. The friendliness was genuine, but the girl also seemed to be making a point that she would choose her own friends, regardless of Tolya's concern or Virgil's growling.

"No," Yuri replied. "Those humans should arrive on Watersday, if the train stays on schedule. These humans heard there was work here." He picked up a stack of papers off the bar. "Don Miller worked on the computer yesterday and made up these forms for potential employees. He said he had a feeling you would find them useful, and they might be useful now for dealing with these strangers."

Don Miller, her other bartender, was an Intuit who had a sense of what people needed. Freddie Kaye was another Intuit, but he had a feel for numbers and wanted to work as the house gambler.

"Are there enough forms?" she asked.

"Won't know until the humans walk through the door, but I won't be surprised if there is exactly the number of copies that we need today."

"We're going to have customers?" Garnet Ravengard sauntered over to the bar and smiled at Yuri. She had the dark eyes and black hair typical of her form of *terra indigene*. Except for a couple of black feathers mixed in with her hair, she looked human—and had more of a bosom than she'd had yesterday.

Had the Raven been able to alter her human appearance or had she achieved that effect by using some kind of clothing beneath the garnet red dress?

"The dress looks good on you," Yuri said.

"And you look like a frontier bartender, right down to the little black tie," Garnet replied.

The Sanguinati did look the part in the white shirt and black vest and trousers—and the black string tie.

No telling if the humans would appreciate the costumes and the rest of what had been done to give the saloon a particular flavor, but Scythe realized that everyone who worked there would have fun. And that pleased her.

A minute later her pleasure faded and her gold hair suddenly had streaks of blue and red—and a warning thread of black—and began to curl as five human males walked into the saloon.

"I'm Madam Scythe," she said. "Welcome to the Bird Cage Saloon."

Four of the men removed their hats in what she assumed was a gesture of courtesy. The fifth man did not.

Something in his eyes. Something that scratched at her instincts to feed. She moved toward him slowly as her hair changed to red with streaks of black and threads of gold and blue—and it coiled.

"We should not be required to be in this house of fornication," the fifth man said loudly.

Yuri vaulted over the bar one-handed, drawing everyone's attention, including hers. A movement, a reminder to be careful.

"We sell a variety of drinks," Yuri said, showing a hint of fang when he smiled at the men. "Our girls are here to talk to customers, even do a little singing and dancing. But Madam Scythe does not allow fornication in this establishment."

The man looked pointedly at the stairs that led to Scythe's suite and the rooms the employees could use during breaks or as dressing rooms.

"As you can see," Yuri said with a nod toward the stairs and the red velvet rope that was attached to the wall and newel-post, "the rooms are for employees only—and that rule is strictly enforced."

There was enough bite and warning in the words that Scythe understood that Yuri was also uneasy about that particular human. Adding to her own sense of wrongness was the way the other four men were looking at their companion, as if they, too, recognized something odd about his behavior.

"Now, if you gentlemen will fill out these forms, that will assist everyone when the mayor comes in to talk to you about what work you might do here." Yuri handed out the forms. "On the second page, where it says 'Miscellaneous'? Please provide the reason you left your previous place of residence."

Garnet went into Scythe's office, then reappeared with two pens and a pencil. "Here are writing implements if you need them."

One man approached Garnet but glanced at Scythe as he accepted the pens and pencils. "I don't know why he is saying these things," he said quietly.

"He's your friend?" Scythe asked just as quietly.

"No. He joined us at the border station. He said he was coming here and asked if he could travel with us. We thought, because of some of the things he said on the journey, that he was from a community that lives by stricter rules than our own, but that doesn't explain his rudeness."

Scythe nodded. "I'm sure Mr. Sanguinati is already aware of your companion's difference."

He returned to the table and handed out the pens and pencil just as the next group arrived, led by Kane in Wolf form. Two adult females, a boy, and . . .

<The Becky girl is a kind of skippy,> Kane said as the girl grabbed his tail. <Their pack name is Gott.>

A look of loathing aimed at the skippy girl filled the fifth man's face before he looked at the younger of the adult females and his face filled with something else. Then he noticed Scythe watching him and became busy filling out the form.

Garnet led the Gott pack to another table, taking some of the forms from Yuri as she passed him, leaving him—and Scythe—free to keep an eye on the males.

They'd barely settled the Gott pack at a table when Tolya, Virgil, Jesse Walker, and a bouncy female entered, followed by Barbara Ellen and Joshua Painter.

"All right if we come in for a drink?" Barbara Ellen asked.

"Just belly up to the bar and I'll fix whatever you like," Yuri said, hesitating for a heartbeat as he met Joshua Painter's eyes.

"Oh, this is *wonderful*," the bouncy female said, turning in a circle as she clutched folders to her chest. She focused on Garnet. "Are those feathers *real*?"

Tolya looked at Scythe. <She wants to work for you.> The look became a predatory stare. <Something wrong?>

As an answer, she looked toward the table with the five men—and frowned. What was that odd male among them staring at now? She followed the line of his focus right to Barbara Ellen, who was dressed in shorts and a T-shirt.

"A woman should not expose her limbs and incite a man to lust," he said loudly. Then he licked his bottom lip.

"This is not a Simple Life community," one of his companions said. "The other people here are not bound to live by our rules. And *we* are here because we want to explore other possibilities while holding on to our core values."

Scythe watched Joshua Painter turn toward the voice at the same time he slipped his right hand into one of the pockets in his trousers. As he withdrew his hand—a hand now wearing a leather glove that had Panther claws at the ends of the fingers—he bared his teeth and stepped in front of Barbara Ellen.

"Joshua," Virgil warned, moving toward the male.

"The marsh," Joshua snarled. "It's the *marsh*. It looks safe but it kills. I told Saul. Ask Saul."

The words made no sense to her. They didn't make sense to Tolya or Virgil either. But Jesse Walker swayed and looked like bleached bones.

Scythe didn't know who had contacted Saul Panthergard or what was said, but suddenly Tolya, Virgil, and Yuri were converging on the table where the five men sat. The odd man leaped up, knocking over his chair as he bolted away from all the males and ran straight toward her, mistakenly thinking he could get past her.

Turning squarely to face him with her back to the rest of the beings in the room she said, <Don't look.>

She heard the *terra indigene* scrambling to pull the humans to the floor or shield them in some way. Those seconds gave the odd man time to grab her arms and try to shove her aside. And in those seconds, her hair turned black with streaks of red—not revealing so much of her true nature that just looking at her would kill her prey, but sufficient for her to consume enough of his life force to make his heart flutter, to make his limbs weak.

One heartbeat. Two. Three. He collapsed and Scythe ran into her office and closed the door to protect the rest of them.

<Scythe?> Tolya called.

She'd been here just long enough to want to stay. <Do you want me to leave?>

<No. I would prefer if you stayed in your office until you feel calmer. We'll deal with things out here.>

<I meant . . . >

<I know what you meant. I would have snapped his neck. Virgil would have torn out his throat. No one understands why he collapsed, so your solution was less obvious than ours would have been.>

Scythe sank into the chair behind her desk. She didn't have to leave. Then another thought as she remembered Barbara Ellen was in the saloon. <Was anyone else hurt?>

<No. Everyone else is fine.> He sighed. <Although Barbara Ellen is a bit too fascinated with Joshua's accessory.>

That made her smile. <If the female who wants to work here wasn't scared off, have her talk to Yuri and Garnet. If they think she'll fit in with them, I'll talk to her when I'm . . . calmer.>

<Lila Gold has books and folders full of papers about frontier towns.>

She felt her hair relax from coils to loose curls, knew the black and red were changing to mostly gold and blue.

Feeling calmer but not quite calm enough to go out among the rest of them, Scythe reviewed the inventory of alcohol that had been brought in from the uninhabited houses.

Tolya guided Jesse Walker to the sofa in his office. He wasn't sure if the previous occupant of the office had used the sofa for informal talks or to take a nap—or to mate with one of the females working for him, which was something human males who held a position of authority often did. At least that was something the Sanguinati had heard about human males.

If he asked Virgil to sniff the sofa, he would find out all kinds of things he didn't want to know, so he hadn't asked.

"Are you sure you don't want to lie down?" he asked for the third time. Jesse Walker had downed two whiskeys before leaving the Bird Cage Saloon and had insisted that they needed to talk in private.

"Are you concerned about Madam Scythe?" he asked.

Jesse shook her head. "She's dangerous."

"Yes."

"More dangerous than you."

"Yes. She is a Harvester." He'd already told her about Scythe. "It's not Scythe who troubles you."

"No." Jesse pushed her hair back with a trembling hand. "What do you know about Joshua Painter, about how he came to live with the Panthergard?"

"Almost nothing. He was found and a Panther chose to raise him, help him survive. He wasn't taken, if that's what you're asking."

"No, that's not what I'm asking." She hesitated, then turned to face him. "Tolya, we need to know about Joshua Painter."

"Do we? Why?" He waited, wondering if she was about to confirm what he suspected about the boy. When she hesitated again, he added, "This will stay between us until we both agree to tell others."

Her body sagged with relief.

"You think he's an Intuit?" he asked. It was a reasonable question. Saul had said the boy had a strong sense of the world.

"He's an Intuit, but not quite in the same way that I am. I think . . ." Jesse hesitated again before saying quickly, "I think his mother was a blood prophet."

CHAPTER 12

Firesday, Messis 10

Jana stowed the cheap carryall in the overhead rack and took a window seat, setting her daypack on the seat beside hers to discourage anyone from joining her until she had time to think. The carryall, which she'd purchased yesterday at a store near her hotel, held the clothes and toiletries she'd need during the trip. Her two suitcases and three boxes of belongings were in the baggage car, along with the possessions her fellow travelers were bringing with them to Bennett.

Karl Kowalski hadn't been there to see her off, but Michael Debany had been waiting for her. Or maybe he had been assigned as the police presence that morning to make sure no one caused trouble for any *terra indigene* who might be boarding the train that day. Either way, she'd spotted him scanning the crowd and realized he'd been looking for her.

"Karl did a little digging on that phone number you gave him. The captain shut him down fast when a name popped up."

"Why?"

"This guy is out of bounds. You don't ask questions about him unless you want some powerful people paying you a call. And by powerful, I don't mean human."

"Gods, I'm sorry. I just wanted to be sure someone at the academy wasn't screwing with me. I didn't mean . . ."

Debany took a step closer—almost close enough to feel uncomfortably intimate. "Man out of bounds. A cryptic message. Karl and I figure he's getting some girls to safe houses. You know what I'm saying?"

She nodded. Blood prophets. There had been a lot of talk at the academy about those girls. At least, there had been a lot of talk about them until the war between humans and the Others eclipsed every other topic.

But . . . Didn't someone have to ask a question before a girl spoke prophecy? Why would someone ask a question about her? Or had the girl seen something moments before an accidental cut that had ended with that phone call?

"I looked up the name last night," Debany said. "On my own time. Public records. Your caller is an ex-cop. Was involved in some sort of scandal before he fell off the grid. The newspaper reports were suspiciously lean on information and totally devoid of speculation. That means everyone wanted this to go away. Even at the academy no one was telling stories, which should tell you something. But the call was legit, and this job is legit." He stepped back and held out his hand. "Good luck, Deputy." After she shook his hand, he stepped in close again. "If you come across one of those girls . . ."

Information hurriedly offered before Debany stepped aside so that she could board with the rest of the passengers going to Bennett. Even then, despite having the travel papers that proved she was part of the group, it had taken John Wolfgard's intervention to convince the conductor that she was supposed to be seated in the car reserved for the *terra indigene*.

When the train began to pull out of the station, John Wolfgard held up a list and said, "Simon Wolfgard asked me to be the liaison for the people traveling to Bennett. Before we get too far away from Lakeside, I need to check the papers of everyone in this car."

Jana opened the daypack, which held her traveling papers, a notebook and pen, and a couple of books, among other things she wanted within easy reach. John barely glanced at her papers, since he'd already seen them a few minutes ago, but he gave everyone else's papers a thorough look before he checked their names off his list.

The conductor walked in and conferred with John, who then signed off on the passenger list of people riding in the earth native car.

Once the train picked up speed and they were really on their way, Jana sat back and watched the land roll by—and wondered where they would be when the train pulled in to observe the "no travel after dark" curfew.

Before entering the government building for this early morning meeting with Tolya Sanguinati, Jesse stopped and looked around. People were up and about, heading for their jobs. How much would change over the next few days as the new residents arrived?

The dining room had been buzzing with speculation about the new arrivals. Most of the young Intuit men who had been doing the sorting and moving furniture talked about apprenticeships and which professions might be filled as different businesses opened again. Would there be a doctor and a dentist? What about a garage mechanic? What about . . . ? What about . . . ? What about . . . ?

She hoped there would be enough trained adults who stayed after they realized what they were facing, enough diversity in professions to fill the basic requirements of a community. The gods knew, Prairie Gold had one doctor and a nurse practitioner who doubled as a midwife, and she was grateful to have them in her town, but there was no one here in Bennett.

Nothing she could do about that. Besides, this meeting wasn't about the newcomers. This meeting was about Joshua Painter. Or more to the point, what he represented.

"Thank you for joining us, Jesse Walker," Tolya said when she entered the conference room across from his office.

As she said hello, Jesse realized she was looking at the town council—looking at who really ran this town. And she wondered if there ever would be a human included in the group.

The six Sanguinati were present. So were Virgil and Kane Wolfgard. They were all strong predators and were in control of the government and law, as well as the vital businesses like the bank, post office, and train station. The surprise attendee was Garnet Ravengard, who worked in the saloon and wasn't what Jesse would have considered a dominant predator.

The last individual in the room, standing apart from the others, was Saul Panthergard.

Saul fixed on her and snarled, "You think we stole a human cub?"

Surprised by his anger, Jesse took a step back.

"An orphaned cub isn't stolen," Tolya said soothingly. "Jesse Walker knows that."

"This isn't about Joshua." Jesse tried—and failed—to keep her right hand from closing over her left wrist as the feeling that she was standing on a precipice almost overwhelmed her. "Not about him alone."

Tolya guided her to a chair. "Sit down. Saul has agreed to tell us what he remembers of Joshua coming to live with the Panthergard."

Jesse sat. So did all the Sanguinati. Virgil and Kane remained standing, along with Saul, whose hands shifted into paws.

"I was young," Saul said. "Not a cub, but still young enough that I was living with my mother, still learning how to hunt. My mother's sister had an overlapping territory and they often hunted together. Unlike the cats whose shape we can take, the *terra indigene* are not as solitary."

Jesse nodded to indicate she understood. No matter what shape they took, the *terra indigene* were first, and always, *terra indigene*. They might mate based on the animal shape they could assume, thus reinforcing that form, and that shape might have some influence on their nature over decades or centuries, but that didn't change the basic fact that they were a species that had been the dominant predators since the first creatures began to walk or fly or swim and had branched out to wear the shapes of other predators in order to remain dominant throughout the world.

"My . . . aunt . . . had lost her cub," Saul continued. "She was wandering, grieving, not really hunting, when a human cub suddenly ran toward her and scrambled under her belly just like a Panther cub who was frightened. She led him to a place where he could hide, and somehow he knew to remain hidden, just like a Panther cub.

"She retraced his trail and heard humans. Angry voices. Harsh voices. Searching for the cub. Then one of the males said, 'Forget it. He won't survive out here.'

"She followed them to a place filled with death. Male cubs about the same age as the cub who had found her. That's what she guessed since she'd never seen human young before. All those cubs had been clubbed to death and left for the carrion eaters.

"The humans would kill the cub if they found him. She'd lost her own cub. My aunt returned to the human cub and led him to her den, then asked my mother for help. The Panthergard didn't spend time around humans. They didn't know how to care for a human who was so young. They asked for help from *terra indigene* who could assume human form and did sometimes go to a trading post. I don't think my aunt ever told anyone beyond the Panthergard about the dead human cubs. What was the point? She was interested in the living cub.

"My family learned how to shift to human form, learned how to speak human words so that Joshua could learn. We learned what foods were safe for humans and how to cook meat so that he would not get sick. And we taught him how to be Panther. And he . . ." Now Saul hesitated.

"And he knew things," Jesse said softly. "What happened when Joshua got cut? A human boy was bound to get cuts and scrapes growing up. My boy certainly did."

Saul thought for a moment, then shrugged. "My aunt licked the wound clean. It healed. When he got older, Joshua would take pieces of plants and sometimes mash them up with water and put the mess on a wound to help it heal better and faster. He knew things about our territory that we didn't know, just as we knew things he couldn't know since he was human and not *terra indigene*."

"What difference does it make?" Virgil growled. "Joshua is grown. He survived because the Panthergard helped him."

Jesse looked at all the *terra indigene* in the room. "What does he smell like to you? Why would a Panther, seeing a human, not see prey? Why did none of your kind make use of the . . . meat . . . left in that place of death?"

Noticing the sharp way Tolya looked at her, Jesse thought, *He knows why I'm asking about the boy's smell. And he suspects the same thing I do.*

"If Joshua survived, could there have been other boys in other places who survived because they were raised by someone other than the humans who had been their original keepers?" she asked.

"You're wondering if other male offspring who were at the breeding farms somehow escaped when they were taken away to be slaughtered," Tolya said.

"Yes," Jesse replied.

"Why kill the males?" Stazia Sanguinati asked. "Wouldn't you want them to breed with the sweet bloods?"

"One stallion with the traits and bloodlines you want can cover a lot of mares," Jesse said. "And based on what I saw yesterday at the saloon, Joshua has too dominant and aggressive a personality to be easy to handle and would have caused too much trouble at a breeding farm. I have a feeling that was true of any male toddler who managed to escape."

Silence. She felt their anger crawling over her skin like bugs she couldn't see. So many of their forms mated for life or raised the dominant pair's young as a pack effort. She'd heard about the abandoned *cassandra sangue*, had even entertained the idea of fostering one or two of the girls who had been rescued. And everyone had heard about the callous treatment of the infant boys.

"You think Joshua is an Intuit," Tolya said. "And yet you've seen him many times in town with Saul and said nothing about this until now."

Neither did you. "I didn't get a feeling about him until yesterday when he said that Simple Life man was a marsh. I knew what he meant. Treacherous. Dangerous. And I had the feeling that women of a certain age and look wouldn't be safe around that man."

"Like Barbara Ellen and Lila Gold?" Tolya asked.

She nodded. "Joshua sensed it moments before I did. But I hadn't sensed Joshua's nature, which is why I think he's not Intuit in the same way that I am."

"Does it matter?" Virgil asked. "He sort of smells like you under the scent of Panther. Well, smells more like you than us."

Jesse studied the Wolf. "Smells like me?"

Virgil thought for a moment. "Not quite like you. You smell like prey. He . . . doesn't." He looked at Saul.

Saul shrugged. "He didn't smell the same as the humans at the trading post, but we just figured it was because he was ours."

"The *cassandra sangue* don't smell like prey," Tolya said. "The *terra indigene* don't drink their blood or eat their flesh because they are Namid's creation, both wondrous and terrible. Their blood was used to create drugs a few months ago; drugs that could make someone so passive they were helpless or make someone so aggressive they would attack and kill without provocation."

"I remember hearing about gone over wolf and feel-good," Jesse said. "I hadn't realized those drugs were made from the blood prophets' blood."

"They were—and they affect humans and *terra indigene* alike." Tolya looked at the rest of the *terra indigene* gathered in the room. "I met Meg Corbyn, who lives in the Lakeside Courtyard. Her scent is unlike any other kind of human. She is not prey, despite the allure of her blood. Joshua doesn't have the same allure, but . . ." He turned to Saul. "Did your aunt react to Joshua's blood when she licked a cut or scrape?"

"Not that I remember." Saul frowned. "I remember her being happy that she had a cub again, even if he wasn't Panther." He focused on Jesse. "Why does it matter?"

Jesse's right hand tightened on her left wrist until it hurt, until she knew there would be a bruise, as she struggled to explain what she was feeling. She usually didn't have feelings about people she hadn't met. "If one boy was saved, maybe there were others who escaped, who were found, who were saved by *terra indigene* who could make room for a young human in their family. Maybe an Intuit family or a Simple Life family found a lost boy and raised him as their own. Maybe someone has found boys like that in the past few months."

Tolya suddenly tensed, and she knew she'd finally said what she needed him to understand.

"Saul's family accepted that Joshua sensed things about the world that they could not, and that acceptance may be true for any *terra indigene* who finds a child like him," Jesse said. "But it might help them to know that these boys might be the children of *cassandra sangue*, might claim to see things that make no sense. And I think Intuit and Simple Life communities should be told as well. An Intuit boy adopted by someone in an Intuit village? His abilities won't be unusual."

"But an isolated Simple Life community might feel threatened by a child who senses things, who warns of danger before it happens," Tolya finished. "The humans might think it's a sign of illness or madness if they don't know it's normal."

Or they might think the child is evil and kill him, she thought. "It could still be a sign of illness or madness, but it might not be. And it might give comfort to the people who found the dead children, who found the blood prophets who had been left to die, that not all of the unwanted children died. They just followed their instincts to a better place." Jesse looked at Saul and smiled.

He studied her and nodded, finally satisfied that she posed no threat to his human kin.

"I will send word to the *terra indigene*," Tolya said. "Can you contact the Intuit communities?"

Jesse nodded. She was part of a group of Intuits who received information about the *cassandra sangue* through Steve Ferryman, who lived on Great Island. She would send an e-mail to everyone on the list. The people in the Midwest would receive her message. So would the Intuits manning the communications cabin that could transfer messages to the cabin that was just across the Northeast border. They would send it on to Steve.

"Speaking of Simple Life, what do we do with the howler I put in jail yesterday?" Virgil asked.

"The other men insist they only know what he told them, that he asked to join them at the border station so he wouldn't have to travel alone," Garnet said.

"He had a ticket and clothes in a carryall," Virgil said. "The clothes smelled like him and matched what he and the other Simple Life males were wearing. So he is what he says he is."

"Being Simple Life doesn't mean he's a good man," Jesse said.

"I'll call the train station closest to the border and see if anything happened near there recently," Nicolai said.

"Ask if there was a news report involving women of a certain age and look," Jesse said. "The man might have needed to disappear quickly if he had behaved badly." A lame way of talking about assault . . . or worse . . . but she didn't know what the *terra indigene* thought about such things.

Virgil snarled. "Well, I'm not calling human law and asking about this human."

"Then what should we do with him?" Yuri asked.

"We could just eat him," Virgil replied. When Tolya said nothing, the

Wolf growled, "Fine. We don't eat him, but I'm still not calling any humans. When is that deputy going to show up?"

"She'll be arriving on Sunday," Tolya said.

"I'm going to have to deal with that human until then?"

"Why don't we put him on the northbound train?" Nicolai said. "The westbound train coming in this afternoon follows a route up to the border of the High North regions."

"That's just passing along the problem to someone else," Jesse protested.

Nicolai smiled, showing a hint of fang. "Not really passing along a problem."

It took her a moment to realize what he meant. Not passing along a problem; passing along a meal.

Bennett's town council didn't want to start a panic among the new arrivals by killing a man when they didn't have a better reason than that they didn't like him. But they also knew it wasn't likely that he would survive long enough to reach another human settlement where he might pose a threat to the females living there.

The meeting ended with the agreement to send the Simple Life man north, and the *terra indigene* headed off to their various businesses and tasks. Only Tolya remained, watching her.

"Your distress is a scent in the air," he said quietly. "Predators are attracted by scents like that because they signal prey that is, perhaps, easier to bring down."

Jesse opened her right hand and stared at the bruise on her left wrist. "Are you going to have a token human on the town council?"

"No. The *terra indigene* reclaimed Bennett. We run this town. The Elders won't tolerate this place continuing to exist if we don't." Tolya leaned toward her. "And if you, who should know you are safe when dealing with us here, feel distressed by our ways, then how would a human who hasn't earned our trust going to survive being in a room with us?"

"I wasn't distressed about being in the room with all of you. I was distressed by the subjects we were discussing."

"The reason doesn't change the scent or our reaction to it," he said gently. "But I will keep your question in mind, and if we find one or two humans who can earn our trust as you have, we will consider having them speak to us about human concerns in an official capacity."

That was more of a concession than she'd expected—until Tolya added, "And you could attend such meetings as Prairie Gold's representative. As you've pointed out many times, your town and your people have a stake in Bennett's survival."

Now, *that* was more like what she'd expected.

CHAPTER 13

Earthday, Messis 12

Jana repacked her toiletry kit and left the public showers in the train station. She handed the attendant the washcloth and towel, along with the ticket that confirmed how many items she had received, so that she could get back the deposit she'd had to put on the darn things—as if someone would want to take a threadbare washcloth and scratchy towel.

Then again, those things might be a luxury for some people at this point. At least she'd thought to bring some of her own soap in a waterproof container and didn't have to use the bar soap that was supplied for everyone's use.

She was grateful that she didn't have to spend money on a hotel room in order to take a shower, which some of her more fastidious fellow passengers had done, but this hadn't been something she had considered about the reality of traveling a long distance. Their car had toilets and small sinks to wash your hands and splash water on your face, but that didn't alter the fact that after two days of travel, everyone was starting to smell a bit ripe.

Part of the adventure. But it made her wonder about the personal side of her new life. She'd thought plenty about the professional side, imagining different scenarios of meeting her boss, the Wolf, for the first time.

What about the woman who would be her housemate? What kind of house would they be living in? There had to be indoor plumbing, right? Right?

Which was a harder way to travel—four straight days with the nightly stopovers or breaking up the journey and being stuck in a small town for a full day because trains didn't run on Earthday anymore? More experienced travelers probably used the day to take in a movie or eat a decent meal or rent a room at the hotel. Some of the people going to Bennett had done enough traveling in the Northeast to feel confident that they could navigate through an unfamiliar town and believe the train wouldn't pull out of the station when they were still a couple of blocks away. For the rest of them, the thought of being stranded in a border town, without luggage, without the papers that proved you had the *terra indigene*'s permission to cross the border, without anything to go back to even if you had enough money on you to pay for a ticket . . . Those were the reasons most of the passengers who had traveled from Lakeside were staying close to the station, making use of a sandwich shop or the diner that was open. And even those businesses would close an hour before dark, leaving passengers to spend another night on the train or in the train station.

Part of the adventure, Jana reminded herself as she wandered over to the station's shop. The small space held everything from bottles of aspirin and toiletries to coloring books and decks of cards. There were a few postcards, but nothing that appealed to her.

Turning away from the postcards, Jana focused on the paperbacks in a spin rack. She'd found out the hard way that she couldn't read when the train was in motion. She hadn't embarrassed herself or caused her fellow passengers any discomfort, but she didn't want to gamble with nausea again. Still, she'd have plenty of time to read this evening, just like the other evenings when the train pulled into a station for the night.

She looked at each book that was available. Some of the books held no interest for her and others she'd already read. But it was something to do, a reason to linger away from the train a little while longer.

No authors with last names ending in "gard." Was that because the station didn't want to stock anything written by a *terra indigene* or was it because the person who ordered the books didn't know such books existed? Would the bookstore in Bennett carry books written by the Others as well as books written by Intuits? She'd have to ask John Wolfgard, since he'd told her he was going to manage the bookstore.

She selected a thriller, then put it back when she realized the gun for hire was a human and the villains in the story were *terra indigene*. That was when she noticed the woman sitting in a dark corner, half hidden by the spin rack. The body language made her think *runaway*, but the woman was an adult. Short brown hair. The corner was too dark to tell the color of the woman's eyes. Jana guessed her age to be late twenties or early thirties. Definitely adult. And yet . . . runaway.

"Excuse me." The woman had a husky voice.

Jana offered a smile but kept her distance. "You need some help?"

"Are you boarding the train in the morning?"

"Actually, I'm returning to the car in a few minutes."

"The regular car?"

"No, the earth native car. I'm heading for Bennett."

"Oh."

"Are you in some kind of trouble?" Was she officially an officer of the law yet?

The woman stood and came closer to the spin rack, closer to the light. Jana noted the way she favored her left side, particularly her left shoulder. The top she wore was oversize—the kind that could be worn off one shoulder. The woman pushed it off her left shoulder, revealing a dark, fist-sized bruise.

"Have you ever dated someone you thought was really great until you learned his being really great was an act and you saw the real man? I was fast enough that he missed hitting my face." She hesitated. "I need to disappear. He went off to meet up with some friends or cousins or something. I need to be far away before he returns and starts looking for me."

"I don't have much . . ." Jana reached for the back pocket of her jeans and the few bills she'd tucked there.

"I don't need money. I have money. A couple of nights ago, he wanted a 'loan' to play a few hands of poker, and when I wouldn't give it to him, he hit me. So I closed out my savings account, packed my clothes and personal papers, and I caught the first bus out of town. Got off here. I was hoping to cross the border, find some work. But border crossings aren't easy, or safe, without the right papers."

From a few comments she'd heard from passengers in the regular car, you could cross the border if you put enough money in the right hand—unless one of the Others observed the exchange. If that happened, you'd end up in someone's belly and your skin would be nailed to the station wall as a warning.

She wasn't sure if that was only a story told to scare people into behaving, or if it had started because someone had seen a skin nailed to the outer wall of a train station. She just hoped she didn't see any evidence that the story was more than a story.

"What's your name?" Jana asked.

"Candice Caravelli."

"You in any trouble with the law, Candice Caravelli?"

"No, but Charlie might be. Charlie Webb. He's the man I was dating."

The spin rack suddenly started spinning. Coloring book pages riffled. Then . . . nothing.

"What . . . ?" Candice's brown eyes widened with fright.

Before Jana could think of a reply—or even a way to voice her suspicion of what had just happened—John Wolfgard walked into the station.

"Air says this female is running away from a bad mate," John said.

Oh gods, oh gods. She hadn't considered that an Elemental might be listening to her conversation.

Air was not the only Elemental, but Jana was not, was not, so was not going to think about what that might mean when she took a shower.

"Yes, she is," Jana said. "She needs to get far away from here, and she's willing to work. Right?" She looked at Candice.

"Absolutely. I'll do anything." Candice thought for a moment. "Almost anything. I'll do any kind of work that's legal."

John cocked his head. "You have money for a ticket to Bennett? If I allow you to cross the border with us, you have to come all the way with us. No getting off at one of the stops and leaving."

"Okay. Why?"

"Because the *terra indigene* don't know you."

There was no mercy in the wild country, no safety in the dark. She had heard that over and over again from Karl Kowalski and Michael Debany while they had tested her skills. They hadn't been trying to scare her off; they'd wanted her to use caution and common sense because there would be no boundaries between the humans living in her new town and the most dangerous forms of *terra indigene*.

Candice took a deep breath and let it out slowly. "Okay. Are there jobs in Bennett?"

"There is a lot of work," John replied. "Tolya Sanguinati is the town leader. He will decide if you can stay and what work you should do."

"Sanguin . . . Okay."

"Would you rather stay here?" Jana asked.

Candice shook her head.

Jana helped by hauling the big suitcase. She was stronger than she looked, but she was glad the suitcase had wheels. Even with wheels, she couldn't imagine Candice pulling it down the street while carrying a soft weekend bag and a purse over the uninjured shoulder. The woman probably had the essentials in the weekend bag so that she could abandon the large suitcase and run if she had to.

John stood beside Candice while she bought the ticket to Bennett. The man in the ticket booth seemed a little too keen for Candice to give him her name, which wasn't necessary since she was buying a ticket at the station, but John gave the man a toothy smile and said he would take care of the personal information at his end.

They left in a hurry, getting Candice's large suitcase stowed in the baggage car before climbing the steps into the earth native car.

Jana said nothing when Candice sat beside her. The woman was understandably spooked. Besides, once the train started moving again, people changed seats to chat and get to know the people who would be their neighbors. Hopefully by then, Candice would feel comfortable enough to take a pair of empty seats and they could both stretch out and get some sleep.

"When I first met him, Charlie was so sweet," Candice said. "Then sweet morphed into sly. He used to take me out to dinner or pay for the tickets when we went to a movie. Then he'd show up and say he was short of cash and would I mind picking up the tab. And then he started showing up, expecting me to give him sex before he 'borrowed' some money and went out to play cards or do something with somebody else. By then, he'd said some things that made me realize he was part of some kind of gang and the work that was the reason he had to travel probably was borderline legal at best. But you get hooked, you know? First you get hooked because he acts sweet and then you stay hooked because you're scared of what he'll do if you start saying *no*."

"You got out," Jana said, wondering if she'd have to deal with many domestic disputes. "You got out, and now you're on your way to a fresh start just like the rest of us."

Candice nodded. Then she sighed. "Men. You can't live with them; you can't feed them to the Wolves."

Jana's breath caught. She looked around. Nobody listening that she could see. "I don't think that's something you want to say once we reach Bennett."

"Nobody means anything by it," Candice protested. "Who would take it seriously?" She stared at Jana. "Oh."

"Yeah," Jana agreed. She closed her eyes and pretended to sleep, but she couldn't stop thinking about all the ways things could go wrong once more humans arrived in Bennett.

Alone in his hotel room in Shikago, Parlan dealt four hands, all the cards faceup. He studied the cards, much as he studied marks who bought a seat at his table. Whose hand would he bust? Whose hand would he help just enough to *almost* win the pot? And whom would he help win because the player wasn't bold enough to bet big, thereby ensuring that Parlan would still be ahead at the end of the night?

A signal knock on the door. "Come in."

Parlan watched Judd McCall enter the room. A handsome man in a rough sort of way, he had light eyes that didn't betray his taste for spilling blood when the spilling was needed—or even when it wasn't needed.

Judd took a couple of glasses and a bottle of whiskey from a tray on the dresser and poured two stiff drinks before sitting at one of the seats at the table. He studied the cards. "You finished up early."

"Half the people who used to come to play aren't alive, and I had a feeling that half the people I played with tonight were hoping I wouldn't realize any IOUs they wanted to put on the table to bankroll their play weren't worth anything." Parlan dealt more cards. "Of course, anyone putting in a worthless IOU had a string of bad luck tonight."

"Of course they did," Judd agreed. "Do I need to persuade any of them to make a payment?"

"No. Not worth it." Parlan gathered the cards. "Want to play some blackjack to pass the time while we're waiting for the others to arrive?"

Judd laughed, a soft, jagged sound. "I know better than to place a bet when you're the one holding the cards."

"No bets. Just practice."

Judd swallowed the whiskey and poured himself another glass. "All right, then."

Parlan shuffled the cards. "It's time to move on. Time to get back to the West Coast and pay a visit to Sparkletown. Those are the only people who can afford high-stakes poker right now."

"Not easy crossing borders, and we'd have to cross three of them to get to the West Coast."

They'd been on the wrong side of the continent, providing lucrative entertainment in his private railroad car and in private rooms at select hotels, when the whole damn civilized world was torn apart. Toland was useless to him. Henry Hollis had been right. Too much destruction there and travel so limited in that part of the Northeast there was the bad chance of getting stuck. And Shikago? Tonight had shown him he'd already wrung the gamblers who could afford to play with him out of everything he could. They had to move on and find another rich vein of fools, and that meant getting out of the Northeast Region.

After a few hands, Judd pulled some papers out of his inside jacket pocket and tossed them on the table. He smiled. "Couldn't get us over all the borders to get back to home territory, but there are the papers that will get all of us on a train that will cross into the Midwest. It leaves tomorrow. Also arranged for your private car to be added to the train."

Parlan didn't ask how Judd persuaded the men responsible for border crossings to provide the papers for them and the private car. Judd always knew just how to apply the right kind of pressure to the right person to smooth their travel arrangements.

"Destination?" he asked. Not that it mattered.

"For now, we have passage on a train running along the High North border," Judd replied. "Can't say if there's anything left beyond the towns with the stations." He studied the whiskey in his glass. "Sweeney Cooke slipped across the border, picked up a car once he was across. He said the previous owner wouldn't need it anymore, so the cops aren't going to be looking. What cops are left, that is."

"What's he doing on his own?" Parlan asked. Sweeney wasn't family and wasn't sharp enough for most of the cons and games the clan played. But he had a talent with his fists, much like Charlie Webb. Those two were hammers and useful when needed. Judd, on the other hand, was a knife.

"He heard rumors about abandoned towns and decided to take a look. First one he came to wasn't completely abandoned. The survivors made him uneasy, so he headed back out. The next town he came to was empty. Nobody and nothing living there, but the stores and houses were full of things for the taking—money, jewelry, liquor. He had plenty of loot in the car when I slipped across the border and found him." Judd leaned his forearms on the table. "Might want to think of setting up a headquarters, a place where we can hold our acquisitions. We can take over a couple of houses. There's food available, not to mention cars and gasoline. Once we strip the carcass of one town, and sell off everything worth selling, we can move on to the next."

"And if the next one is inhabited?"

Judd shrugged. "If the odds are against us and the saloon is open, you can play a few hands of poker to liven up the evening. If there's only a handful of squatters or survivors, well, who would be surprised to discover they didn't survive after all?"

Parlan studied the other man. "Sweeney would have fixed on easy pickings, and he's good at finding such people and places, but he wouldn't have thought about setting up headquarters and all the rest." Ever since that talk with Henry Hollis, he'd been thinking about the need for some kind of base of operations.

"Nope. He would have gone around in that car, filling up the trunk with money, the backseat with jewelry, and the front passenger side with bottles of liquor to keep them within easy reach. And sooner or later, if someone he feared didn't insist that he deposit the loot at headquarters, he'd drive into a town that still had a sheriff, and the sheriff would notice all that appropriated jewelry, and things would turn sour for all of us."

"So we keep him close enough to control but let him off the leash often enough to satisfy his acquisition fever," Parlan said. And other base needs.

"That was my feeling," Judd agreed.

"Did you appropriate all the loot and put it in a safe place?"

"Of course. Sweeney wasn't happy about that, but he didn't argue long. I gave him enough money that he could buy a couple of hours with a whore and take his disappointment out on her."

"He thinks with his cock too much of the time. He's going to screw up a job one of these days."

Judd smiled. "He does that, I'll screw him."

Parlan frowned at something Judd had said. "You slipped across the border and came back?" Since phones didn't work between regions, that was the only way Judd could have found out about what Sweeney was doing.

"Pick a back road and do it quick and quiet. One man can do it if he can reach an inhabited place and blend in. The clan wouldn't be able to get across that way. We'd draw too much attention. Each on his own, some of us would make it back to the West Coast, but not all of us."

Parlan understood that "all of us" didn't include anyone but the Blackstone family and Judd. "No checkpoints on the roads?"

"Might be on the highways used by trucks hauling freight, but not the smaller roads. Then again, the only time I didn't feel like I was being watched was when I found Sweeney in that little hole-in-the-wall town. Made sure it looked like an exchange of goods, and came back."

One by one, the men arrived at the hotel room to report any information of interest. The first ones were Parlan's son, Dalton, and his brother, Lawry. Sweeney Cooke, having successfully snuck across the border into the Midwest, was staying there and awaiting instructions from Judd.

The last man to arrive was Charlie Webb, who was baffled and furious that the piece he'd been screwing had run off before he could squeeze the last dollar out of her, and all because he'd given her a little needed discipline.

"Charlie," Judd said, "once we cross the border you can buy all the company you want."

Charlie looked like he wanted to argue, but nobody argued with Judd.

At Parlan's signal, Judd explained about the abandoned towns and how Sweeney had already scouted out a couple of them. Dalton didn't say much, but Lawry thought having a headquarters would be a fine idea. And Charlie, fixated on the woman who had run out on him, thought having a place so far out of the way that women would have to stay put and be agreeable was just what they needed.

"Then we're agreed that we should look for such a place?" Parlan asked.

It wasn't really a question. He was the leader, the front man, with his quaint manners and clothing that made him look like a successful gambler from the frontier days. The fact that he and his family were Intuits made being successful so much easier.

The men agreed, as he'd known they would.

Parlan smiled. "Then tomorrow morning, the Blackstone Clan will board our private car and head to the Midwest."

CHAPTER 14

Moonsday, Messis 13

"I appreciate you putting in a good word for me," Truman Skye said.

Tobias Walker glanced at his companion and smiled. "I'm going to miss having you around, but I'm happy you'll have this chance. You deserve the job of foreman."

"It's going to be strange working with men who aren't like us."

"Yep. But from what I've been hearing, Simple Life folk and Intuits work together in a lot of other places and get along just fine. Still, having a foreman who is an Intuit, has experience with ranching, and grew up around this land will help everyone."

"It's okay to call you if I have questions? And Ellen will help me keep the accounts straight?"

Tobias grinned. You'd think Truman was heading for the other end of the continent instead of taking over the neighboring ranch. "You can call me. You can call Ellen. If you ask her, my mom will help you choose the men who will best fit you and that particular ranch. Besides, we'll meet up here in Bennett and have a drink at the saloon and play a few hands of cards and flirt with women."

"They have women?"

Now he laughed. "They do. Of course, 'women' is a slippery word.

Let's say there are females at the saloon who talk and flirt with the customers."

"And each ranch will have a cook?"

There were priorities. A man enjoyed flirting with women when he could, but he wanted to fill his belly every day. "You won't have to rustle up your own grub when you get back to the bunkhouse. Or in your case, the main house since you're in charge."

Truman blew out a breath. "Big step."

"Just take it one day at a time."

Tobias slowed the pickup as he drove past the Universal Temple that was at the southern end of the town square. It didn't surprise him that the place to renew the spirit was at the opposite end of the square from the train station, livestock pens, and livery stable, as well as the post office / telegraph office, hotel, and saloon. After all, Bennett had its start in the days when ranch hands had come into town to blow off steam when they needed supplies or brought in cattle to ship to market.

Slowing the pickup to a crawl, he rolled his window all the way down and turned off the fan that hadn't done much except blow around hot air.

"Tobias?"

An ache along his right ribs—his own tell and warning that something was going on and he needed to pay attention. "I'll drop you off at the saloon. My mother should already be there to help choose who is working where."

"Where will you be?"

"I need to check on the horses I brought up the other day. Then I'll be along."

"You sensing trouble?"

"I just want to check on the horses, especially the buckskin."

"That one has more courage than sense," Truman said.

Tobias shook his head. "No, what he's got is heart." *And brains.*

He parked the truck and waited for Truman to walk into the saloon. Then he got out and removed the shotgun from the gun rack attached to the back of the cab. He loaded two shells in the gun. After a brief hesitation, he laid the shotgun on the seat and pulled out the under-the-seat box where he kept his revolver and gun belt when he had a passenger.

These days, carrying a gun in Bennett wasn't just a bad idea; it was suicide. The Others had made it clear that they wouldn't tolerate humans carrying weapons—especially the kind of weapons that had killed so many of the Wolfgard. And the ones called the Elders wouldn't give a man time to explain before they ripped him to pieces. But the ache in his ribs was getting worse, and that meant something was going to happen, so . . .

Tobias fastened the gun belt around his hips, then drew the revolver out of the holster and opened the cylinder to confirm the gun was loaded. He didn't usually drive around with a loaded six-gun under the seat when he was traveling from the ranch to Prairie Gold. There was no need for that. But lately, when making the drive to Bennett, he'd taken to keeping the loaded, holstered weapon on the seat beside him when he was alone.

By now he was sure some of the *terra indigene* had spotted him and knew he was armed, but he couldn't think about that because the ache along his ribs had turned into pressure. Had to get moving. Had to check on the horses.

As he reached for the shotgun, he hesitated. Something was going to happen, and he needed . . . the rifle.

Tobias broke open the shotgun, removed the shells, replaced the gun on the rack, and took the loaded rifle. After chambering a round, he locked the truck and headed across the square toward the livery stable.

He heard dogs but ignored the sound since it was coming from the wrong direction. Then he heard something that wasn't animal but wasn't quite human—a sound loud enough to be heard from a distance.

One of the Others in a fight with some dogs?

Spinning around, he ran toward the sound. As he turned down the side street next to the diner, Tobias saw the youth surrounded by three large dogs. Not pets he'd helped free and feed. Not animals that were looked after by the woman Tolya called the almost-vet.

They're wrong ones. There must have been an arena for dogfights hidden somewhere in the town. Dogs raised and trained to fight and kill. Loose in the town. Feral packs will form around them and then . . .

His ribs hurt so much it was hard to breathe.

The dogs harried the youth, snapping and snarling, but even trained killers weren't brave enough to close in. When the youth swiped at them with something that looked like claws and made that not-quite-human sound again, Tobias realized who the boy was and why the dogs hadn't brought down their prey yet. They weren't sure what to do with someone who looked human and smelled a little like Panther.

"I'm coming up behind you," Tobias said quietly, not wanting to break Joshua Painter's focus and give the dogs an opening to attack. Then loudly, "Hey! Dogs! Get out of here!"

Two of the dogs hesitated. Joshua didn't turn at the sound of Tobias's voice, didn't lose his focus on the largest of the three dogs since that one was still trying to close in.

Tobias raised the rifle.

"Saul's here too," Joshua said moments before Tobias heard the angry growl.

Three against three. Two of the dogs ran off. The last dog hesitated a moment longer before turning to run—and Tobias made his choice. He shot the dog as soon as it was clear of everyone else. Then he ran for the livery stable, the pressure on his ribs telling him the threat to livestock wasn't over.

A split pack of snarling dogs. Panicked horses trying to break out of one of the corrals. A Simple Life man with a pitchfork trying to drive away the dogs without getting trampled. And the buckskin gelding, alone in the other corral and smart enough to know he had no room to run, stood his ground as several dogs moved in.

Working the lever to chamber a new round, Tobias raised his rifle but didn't have a clear shot. More men shouting, running. More panic among the horses, who could hurt themselves if they broke through the corral.

Then two huge Wolves leaped over the top rail of the buckskin's corral and charged the dogs. One Wolf grabbed the leg of a dog that turned to run, and Tobias heard the bone snap in those unforgiving jaws. Another dog yelped as the other Wolf grabbed it behind the head and shook it until the neck snapped.

The rest of the dogs turned and ran. The Wolves didn't pursue them. Instead, they turned to look at the buckskin, who snorted and pawed the ground. The Wolves cocked their heads, then rose on their hind legs and shifted into humans who still had the Wolf pelt covering their shoulders, torso, and backs.

The rest of the horses were bunched at the far end of the other corral. The humans now gathered to watch the standoff between the buckskin and Wolves, hardly daring to breathe.

The wind shifted, bringing the Wolves' scent to the gelding—a scent that must have meant something to the buckskin, because he relaxed and took a step toward the Wolves.

"We are allies," Virgil Wolfgard said, the words a little slurred.

Tobias guessed that the Wolf's mouth wasn't completely shaped for human speech.

"We are allies," Kane Wolfgard said.

Wondering if the Wolves knew the buckskin was just a horse and not something like them in some way, Tobias watched the gelding and felt sure the horse would know these two Wolfgard from now on, regardless of their shape.

Satisfied for the moment, Tobias looked around for any sign of Elders before handing the rifle to Truman when his friend joined him. Not that anyone could see an Elder until it was too late, but better to chance leaving the rifle with someone he trusted than to leave it unattended. "Hold on to that for a moment."

He ducked between the rails and approached the buckskin. "Easy now, Mel. Easy. You did good."

The buckskin turned toward him, nudging him as it looked for a treat.

"Don't have any on me, but you do deserve a treat for being so brave, and I'll make sure you get one." With a firm grip on the halter, Tobias led the gelding to the gate. As one of the other men opened it, he said, "Let's get the rest of the horses into their stalls."

"Tobias Walker," Virgil said. "When you are finished with the horses, come to the sheriff's office. We need to talk."

"I'll be there." Taking the rifle from Truman, he led Mel into the stable.

Since he'd violated one of the town's strictest rules by carrying a gun, he was certain he wasn't going to like the topic of discussion.

*   *   *

Virgil shifted back to Wolf form, passed the dog whose neck he'd snapped, and went to look at an injured dog lying under the rails at the far end of the corral while Kane followed the scent of the dog with the broken leg. He looked up and watched the Eagle soaring high above the land beyond the train station, watched the Ravens flying ahead of Kane to keep track of the dog pack, allowing Kane to focus on the dog he needed to kill.

The injured dog saw Virgil and moved its front legs as if it could still stand and run, but Virgil knew it wasn't going to run anywhere. The horse that was not meat must have kicked this one, breaking bone and damaging the dog's insides. That was good. Humans couldn't whine about him finishing what the horse had started. Not that he cared if humans whined about dead dogs.

Well, there was one human who was going to whine a lot, and he was *not* going to be the only one who had to listen to Barbara Ellen.

He killed the dog, then left the carcass for the humans to move once they denned the horses that would be meat if they weren't with humans when they left the boundaries of the town. Then he trotted over to the sheriff's office, where he shifted to human form and put on clothes in order to do sheriff growling instead of Wolf growling.

<Tolya,> Virgil called. <I need you here.> He didn't really, but the Sanguinati dealt with many humans during the day, leaving him to walk around the town to remind the humans that there were rules that were backed by sharp teeth and strong jaws. So it would be better to have Tolya here to agree with what he wanted to do about Tobias Walker and the human weapons.

Tolya arrived moments before Tobias Walker, who smelled of fear and was still wearing a forbidden weapon. It took effort, but Virgil ignored the fear smell. That was easier when Saul Panthergard and Joshua Painter walked into the office, because the Panther's anger overpowered every other scent.

The Sanguinati didn't live in the wild country, so Tolya and the others living in Bennett were Virgil's first experience with this form of *terra indigene*. So far they'd figured out how to work together, mostly because Tolya had had experience working with Wolves when he'd first arrived in Prairie Gold, and there had been some Wolves in the Courtyard back east that had been Tolya's home territory. But Virgil was still learning how to read the town's leader.

Tolya's face and body provided no clues, so Virgil couldn't decide if the Sanguinati was angry or sad.

"You are carrying a forbidden weapon, Tobias Walker," Tolya said, his voice revealing nothing.

"Where is the long weapon?" Virgil asked.

"I took it back to the truck and put it in the gun rack," Tobias Walker replied. "The truck is locked, and there's a big Eagle perched on the tailgate, so I guess one of your people is keeping an eye on things."

"This human killed a dog that was attacking Joshua," Saul said.

"Why did you bring a weapon?" Tolya asked, looking at Tobias Walker.

"I usually carry a shotgun and rifle in the truck's gun rack. I usually have the revolver in a case under the driver's seat. I work on a ranch. It's a long drive to this town for supplies or when my mother comes up here to help you."

"You think such weapons will protect you from what lives in the wild country?" Tolya asked.

"Your kind, you mean?" Tobias Walker shook his head. "But there are rumors lately of men stopping people on the road and stealing from them. Even hurting them. There have always been people like that. I guess there always will be people like that. So I have weapons in my truck when I drive up here, just like I've got them on the ranch."

"Have you seen these humans?" Virgil asked.

"No, but when it comes to sensing people, my mother is the best there is in Prairie Gold, and she's been feeling uneasy about being away from home so much." Tobias Walker looked at Tolya. "Not that she isn't willing to help out, but it's not just the people coming in here that have been pushing at what she's feeling."

"Jesse Walker is concerned for her safety?" Tolya asked sharply. "She has said nothing to me."

"Maybe she thought you already had enough on your mind and didn't need to know about something on the horizon that might never reach here."

"If she didn't think it was going to reach here, she wouldn't feel concerned."

To Virgil's ears, Tolya sounded ready to nip someone. But Tobias Walker was right—a storm on the horizon was a maybe threat. They had a problem right here, right now.

"I want to give Tobias Walker special permission to wear a human weapon when he is in Bennett," Virgil said.

They all stared at him.

"Why?" Tolya finally asked.

Virgil focused on the Sanguinati. "Because we need to kill the dogs."

Tolya stared at Virgil, not knowing, or caring, if he was somehow issuing a challenge for dominance. "You want to kill all the dogs after we went through the trouble of releasing them from the houses and feeding them and arranging for Barbara Ellen to come to Bennett to care for them?"

"Yes," Virgil said. "They are predators. They are forming packs, which is their way, but today one pack attacked Joshua Painter and another pack attacked the horses that couldn't run away. There is a human pup in the town now, and there is a human female with a skippy brain. The Elders won't attack those humans. The rest of the *terra indigene* won't attack those humans. But the dogs will. Those humans are easy prey."

"You don't need to kill all the dogs," Tobias Walker said. "Most of the dogs are still good dogs. They aren't going to attack people or livestock. But I have a feeling that some of the dogs that are out there now were raised and trained to fight and to kill, and that's what they're going to do. It isn't going to matter if the prey is another dog or a human or one of the *terra indigene*. Those dogs are going to hunt and kill, and the packs forming around them are going to be just as savage."

"So you agree with Virgil that these animals need to be killed?" Tolya asked.

"Yes, I do. The ranches we're restoring will be bringing cattle up to send to market, and the surviving ranches north of here will be bringing cattle down. We can't have dogs attacking penned cattle or causing a stampede."

Tolya looked at the Panther. "Saul? What do you say?"

"When I find the other two dogs that attacked Joshua, I will kill them."

"Then we're agreed?" Tolya met each of their eyes.

"There's a vet's office here," Tobias said. "Maybe there's a kennel too? Someplace that boarded animals when people went out of town? Even a place with a fenced-in yard would work for the time being."

Tolya didn't remind the human that animals had been freed from fenced-in places as well as houses because that had been the only way to care for all of them. As it was, Barbara Ellen spent many hours each day taking care of the birds in cages, as well as putting out food and water for the animals that were wandering about in the town. Had she considered what would happen to these creatures when the stores in Bennett ran out of their particular food?

That was a problem for another day. But it reminded him of the problem someone would have to deal with as soon as—

Barbara Ellen slammed into the sheriff's office, rushed past him, Tobias, Saul, and Joshua, and stopped in front of Virgil.

"I want to report a crime!" she said, her eyes bright with tears. "Someone shot a dog!"

Barb sat on the cot and stared at the plastic bucket and roll of toilet paper that the mean, mangy excuse for a sheriff put in her cell as "emergency facilities" in case she needed to squat before the next designated potty break. That's what he'd said—in case she needed to squat.

Forelock! She should have remembered that she couldn't argue with a dominant Wolf the way she could have argued with her brother, Michael. And she *hadn't* been arguing. Not really. An impassioned plea to save the dogs was *not* arguing! But did the big, bad Wolf take that into account? No, he did not. He just hauled her into one of the cells, came back long enough to drop the bucket and toilet paper into the cell, and then left!

And to think she'd written sort of nice things about him in her first letter back home. All right, her only letter back home. But that was only a couple of weeks ago. Okay, maybe a little longer, but not *that* much longer.

Long enough for Michael to have received reports from the big bad without getting her side of the story? She'd write to her parents and her brother tonight—if she was out of jail by then.

Hearing the door to the cellblock open, Barb sprang to her feet and waited at the bars. She wasn't argumentative by nature, but Virgil seemed to bring out the worst in her. But she wouldn't argue with him. She'd be polite and ask if her "me time" could be done now.

Joshua walked over to her cell. "Virgil said it was all right to bring you some things and visit with you for a while. He said your me time will be done at four o'clock unless you start yapping at him again." He sat on the floor on the other side of the bars and opened the daypack he'd brought in with him. "You shouldn't yap at Virgil. He's the dominant Wolf—and the sheriff."

The way Joshua said it, being the sheriff—a human occupation—was an afterthought. The dominant Wolf part was the part that meant something to the *terra indigene*.

Barb wasn't thrilled with sitting on the floor, but it looked clean enough and she sure didn't want to spread the blanket on the floor if she was going to have to sleep with it later.

Joshua passed her a sandwich wrapped in wax paper, followed by an apple and a container of cookies that just fit between the bars. The bottle of water didn't fit between the bars, so Joshua rummaged in the pack until he found the cup he'd brought. They made sure it fit before he filled it and passed it to her. Then he unwrapped a sandwich for himself.

"Someone shot a dog," Barb said, wanting *someone* to understand why that was wrong.

"Tobias Walker shot one of the three dogs that attacked me." Joshua's unusual green eyes focused on her. "I would have killed it if it had gotten close enough for me to rake it with my claws or choke it." He reached through the bars and caught most of her sandwich before it plopped on the floor.

"Dogs attacked you? Why?"

He shrugged. "Guess I smell more like Panther than human to them. Or maybe I don't smell enough like Panther. If three of them had attacked Saul, none of them would have survived. As it was, Tobias Walker and Saul coming to help me scared them off. Two of them ran away. Tobias Walker shot the third."

"Then I can find the other two and—"

"Barb, the *terra indigene* will find those dogs and kill them. They will keep watch for the rest of the dogs that attacked the horses."

"Attacked . . . ?" Appetite gone, Barb rewrapped the sandwich in the wax paper, then set it on the cot with the apple and cookies. "Are the horses all right?"

"Most of them. I heard one of them was too hurt to save. Not sure if the injuries were made by the dogs or by the horse trying to get out of the corral and run away." Joshua took a big bite out of his sandwich and chewed. He swallowed and licked his lips clean before adding, "I don't think your blue horse was in the corral when it happened."

"He wasn't. I was at the house where I'm keeping the birds. Rowan was tied up out back." What would have happened if the dogs had found Rowan? "The sheriff could have told me, could have explained about the dogs."

"He would have," Joshua replied. "Tolya would have too. But you yapped at Virgil and got him riled, so . . ." He looked around to indicate that this is what happened when subordinate human females yapped at dominant *terra indigene* males.

Barb almost asked him if *he* considered her a subordinate female, then decided she didn't want to know. But this was a reminder that the Others didn't operate on the human idea of everyone being equal. With them, there was a hierarchy and everyone had a place within that hierarchy.

Joshua leaned forward, his expression fierce and sincere. "I can defend myself, but there's a cub . . . a boy . . . living with a group of females, and there's a female with a skippy brain. They aren't safe from a dog pack."

"I haven't had any trouble with the dogs!" Barb protested.

"Have you seen all of them? Tobias Walker said these dogs had been trained to fight and kill."

"Of course I've seen . . ." She stopped. Thought. *Had* she seen all the dogs lately? The food was gone at each of the feeding stations. So was the water. And some of the dogs that were sheltering near the feeding areas were always there to greet her, always seemed glad to have human company. But some had been missing these past few days. Smaller dogs, mostly, but she hadn't seen some of the larger dogs either. Then she remembered the cat collar Virgil had given her the other day and wondered what had killed Fluffy.

"I'll help you round up the good dogs," Joshua said.

"Okay. Thanks." What else could she say? Despite her collisions with Virgil, she wasn't stupid. A pack of savage dogs, *big* dogs, posed a danger to everyone, and posed a special danger to someone like Becky Gott, who would just see a doggy and want to pet it.

Joshua finished his sandwich, then dug into the pack again. "I brought you books. I'm supposed to do more sorting after I'm done visiting you, but I stopped and picked up books so you could read while you're waiting for Virgil to let you out."

Barb accepted the books. One was a cozy mystery she'd read before. The other was by Alan Wolfgard and looked scary. Well, maybe reading a story written by a Wolf would give her a few pointers on how to avoid annoying the sheriff.

Thank the gods the human deputy arrived tomorrow. Maybe then she could voice an opinion to someone in authority without ending up in jail.

CHAPTER 15

Sunday, Messis 14

"Next stop, Bennett."

Jana looked out the window, wanting to see the town that would be her new home as soon as it came into view.

"Maybe this wasn't such a good idea." Candice Caravelli flopped into the seat beside Jana and pressed a hand to her stomach.

"Unless you're going to try to find a human-controlled city, this is as good a place as any for a fresh start." Jana didn't add that she wasn't sure there were any human-controlled cities left in the Midwest Region.

"You're right. Besides, if I decide to try for the West Coast or some other place, I still need to find work and save some money before I can do that."

Before she could reply, Jana saw the sign next to the tracks and felt a chill run through her.

WE LERNED FROM YU.

"Oh gods, oh gods, I hadn't realized we were going to *that* town," Candice whispered.

Jana sat back, feeling queasy. She'd known why Bennett was being resettled. Of course she'd known. She'd read everything in the news-papers, watched news reports on the TV—and saw the pictures that were suppressed after that first shocked day of reports. But the truth had, somehow, been sterilized by her rush to get to Lakeside and get through the interview and subsequent tests. She had known but had thought, when she'd given it any thought over the past few days, that everything in the town would be clean and tidy and ready for the newcomers to move in. A totally unrealistic idea.

WE LERNED FROM YU.

That sign was a harsh reminder that the *terra indigene* had slaugh-tered the entire town, had mounded the bodies for reporters to find, as the Wolves had been mounded by the Humans First and Last movement after being slaughtered. What had been done with the human bodies? Should she ask? Or did you survive in such a place by leaving some ques-tions unasked?

She had chosen to come here, to work and live here. There was noth-ing she could do about what had happened. She could only do her best to prevent it from happening again.

John Wolfgard, acting as their group leader, stood up and made a sound like an abbreviated howl. It wasn't particularly loud, but it stopped all conversation in the car.

"Since all of you have travel papers issued from Lakeside, we're sup-posed to wait until any of the strangers in the other passenger car disem-bark and are dealt with."

Dealt with? Jana watched the Wolf. He'd been friendly during the trip, had talked enthusiastically about being the manager of the town's bookstore. In fact, he'd been so friendly, she'd almost forgotten he wasn't human. But something of the predator now showed in his amber eyes—a sharp reminder of what he was.

"What does that mean?" she asked.

"The town leaders want to know why the humans are here and how long they're staying." John shrugged. "Some of the humans might just want to walk to the places where there is food, like we did at other stops."

"Is looking over the passengers standard procedure?" Was that going to be part of her duties?

John shrugged again. "It's standard for now."

Jana felt Candice tense. The other woman didn't have to remind anyone that she didn't have any travel papers from Lakeside.

Not many people disembarked from the other passenger car, so it wasn't long before John was telling them to collect their bags from the overhead racks and to have their papers in easy reach. Figuring she would have to talk to someone about Candice traveling with them, since she had initiated the other woman joining their group, Jana waited while the doctors, dentist, attorneys, vet, and other professional people left the car. Finally she and Candice walked down the steps and reached the platform, with John right behind them.

She wasn't sure what she'd expected from John saying the town leaders were meeting the train. Enough individuals to control a group of people coming into town? Didn't need a group. The two men—males?—standing on the platform were sufficiently intimidating in completely different ways. The one dressed in a black suit with a gray shirt had the sleek look of a ruthless politician—or a high-priced assassin, if she went with the description of such men in the thrillers she read. The other one . . .

Shaggy hair that was a mix of gray and black, the gray not due to age, since he looked to be in his early thirties. Amber eyes that didn't hold a hint of tolerance let alone friendliness. Attractive in a rough-and-ready sort of way. Not someone she would choose to be around, because everything about him warned her he was dangerous. The man in the black suit might be more lethal in the balance, but the man dressed in jeans and a red-checked shirt was the one you'd find in the middle of bar fights and other physical altercations.

He was also the one wearing a sheriff's badge pinned to the pocket of his shirt.

This was her boss? Crap.

"Wait here," John said as he walked past the two women.

He didn't talk to the other two men for more than a minute—surely not long enough to explain Candice's situation—when he gestured for her and Candice to join the men. Males. She'd have to ask someone about the correct word to use.

"Virgil, this is your new deputy, Jana Paniccia," John said. "Deputy Jana, this is Sheriff Virgil Wolfgard."

"Pleased to meet you." Jana held out her hand.

Virgil grabbed her wrist, leaned over her hand, and sniffed it.

Her hand closed into a fist before she had time to consciously make a choice, but she retained enough control not to bop him in the nose.

Virgil released her wrist, then studied her. "She's kind of small."

She bared her teeth. That wasn't a conscious choice either. "I'm stronger than I look."

"We'll see." Dismissive, as if he'd already decided she wasn't worth his time.

Don't punch him in the face. Don't punch him in the face. Do not punch him in the face. And don't even think about a knee to the groin, no matter how satisfying the action would be in the short term.

"Ms. Paniccia, I'm Tolya Sanguinati, the town's leader." He held out his hand.

Jana shook it. "I met Vlad Sanguinati when I interviewed for the deputy position."

"I know." Tolya smiled, showing a hint of fang.

Oh, definitely tall, dark, and lethal.

"This is Candice Caravelli," Jana said, bringing the other woman to their attention.

"John explained that you are looking for work," Tolya said.

"Yes," Candice said, then amended her reply. "Yes, sir."

"What kind of work do you do?"

"I was a dance instructor. All kinds of dances. Some formal but I also taught country dances and square dances."

"Those are traditional frontier kinds of dances and would be useful for social events," Jana said.

"I also taught Quiet Mind classes," Candice said.

"Very useful for helping to relieve stress," Jana added.

"Are you one of those high-strung females?" Virgil asked.

"Compared to what?" Reminding herself that she shouldn't start challenging her boss before she'd had a chance to see the town, Jana gave Virgil a tight-lipped smile. "I find exercise and Quiet Mind stretches keep me from feeling overly stressed." And if she'd had the occasional crying jag during her time at the police academy to relieve the pressure of dealing with classmates who had made a daily effort to remind her of why she wasn't suited to be a serving police officer, that was her business.

"Let's proceed to the Bird Cage Saloon, where newcomers receive their information about housing and the town's rules," Tolya said. "Newcomers will be housed in the hotel temporarily. Ms. Paniccia, you will be housemate to Barbara Ellen Debany, who will meet you at the saloon. Are your possessions marked with your name?" He gestured to the boxes and luggage being offloaded from the baggage car.

"Yes," Jana replied.

"Then Nicolai will have everything delivered to the house except the items you have with you now. The possessions for the rest of the new residents will be dropped off at the hotel or the designated storage area."

After four days on the train, she didn't have a clean set of clothes left in the carryall, but she said nothing since she figured that caring about clothes, even for practical reasons, would give Sheriff Virgil Wolfgard another reason to claim that a female wasn't suited for the job.

Not that he'd actually *said* a female wasn't suitable, but the look he'd given her had said plenty.

"This way," Tolya said. He and Virgil turned and walked away, leaving Jana, Candice, and John to follow.

"It looks empty," Candice whispered as they left the train station and walked down the street past a feed store and tack store.

"Most likely everyone is working," Jana replied. She hoped that was the reason she hadn't seen any humans. There were some cars parked on the street, but she couldn't tell if they'd been parked there for an hour, for a day, or since the *terra indigene* had wiped out the humans who had originally lived in Bennett.

Couldn't think about that—and couldn't afford to forget it happened.

Then she stopped thinking about cars and people and looked at the buildings that ran along one side of the street. It was like stepping back in time to a real frontier town. Wide wooden sidewalks. Buildings that were cheek by jowl, with a feel of age both in their design and in the way they seemed to lean on each other for support. And every one of the buildings had some kind of supported covering over the sidewalk to protect residents from the sun and weather. It was like entering one of the stories she and Pops had loved to read. And there were even . . .

Jana stopped and stared at the two ponies grazing across the street. Chubby-legged, barrel-shaped ponies. One was black. Nothing unusual about that. The other was brown, with black legs and a mane and tail that were a stormy gray.

Despite her enthusiasm for being a mounted deputy—a desire based on girlhood fantasies—she didn't know much about horses beyond the things she remembered from books she'd read when she was a girl. But she was pretty sure it wasn't natural for a brown pony to have that color mane and tail. So if those critters weren't ponies set loose to graze, what were they?

"Umm . . . ," Candice said.

"Yeah." Wouldn't do to keep everyone waiting. Especially her boss.

She and Candice passed the hotel, crossed a side street, and walked into the Bird Cage Saloon.

"Wow," Candice said.

"Wow is right," Jana agreed. Outside, the stores looked like a real frontier town, a little tired and worn. This looked like a freshly painted movie set. There was a bartender with sharp eyes and a friendly smile and two women dressed as saloon girls. And the woman who came around to the front of the bar . . .

Oh gods.

"Look at that hair," Candice whispered.

Jana *was* looking at the hair. Mostly gold, with wide blue streaks, narrower red streaks, and a few threads of black that made Jana shiver. Not the same colors, but the manager of the coffee shop in the Lakeside Courtyard had hair like that.

Tolya gestured for them to come forward. "Ms. Paniccia, Ms. Caravelli, this is Madam Scythe, the proprietor of the Bird Cage Saloon."

Scythe eyed Candice. "Tolya says you know dances that would have been danced in a saloon."

"Some," Candice replied, sounding wary.

"You know how to work in a saloon?"

"I could learn."

Wondering if "work in a saloon" was a euphemism for a kind of work Candice wouldn't want, Jana debated the wisdom of saying something about Candice's situation. Better not. The woman needed a job and could speak for herself. And if she couldn't—or wouldn't—Jana would be in a better position to help her once she was herself gainfully employed as a deputy.

Madam Scythe raised a hand. "Garnet, take the human girl to that table over there and explain the rules."

The black feathers in Garnet's hair told Jana she was one of the Others. "Crow?"

"Raven." Garnet gave Candice a smile that was sharp but not unfriendly. "This way."

Scythe focused on Jana. "Is this the one who's going to work with Virgil?"

"Maybe," Virgil growled. Now *he* focused on Jana. "You got your papers?"

She pulled them out of her daypack, and he pulled them out of her hand.

"Sheriff's office is on the other side of the square," he said, still growling. "Show up at eight o'clock tomorrow morning." Virgil walked out of the saloon.

"I'm confused," Jana said. "Am I hired or not?"

"Talk to Virgil in the morning," Tolya said. "In the meantime, here is Barbara Ellen Debany, your housemate."

Blond hair, blue eyes, some freckles across the nose and cheeks. Early to mid-twenties, so they were close to the same age.

"I'm so glad to meet you," Barbara Ellen said with more enthusiasm than seemed warranted. "My friends call me Barb." She glanced at Tolya. "My human friends call me Barb."

"I'm glad to meet you too."

"There are papers you need to fill out," Tolya said. "Then you should go to the hotel and get the key for your room."

"But you just said . . ." Jana looked at Barb.

"You'll be more comfortable in the hotel until you have a chance to pick out furniture for your bedroom," Barb said.

That made sense. Jana filled out the paperwork and had barely written in the final answer before Barb handed the papers to someone named Yuri and hustled her over to the hotel.

"What's the hurry?" Jana asked.

"Our house was one of the few that was cleared out, so we have to replace *everything* we want, right down to the kind of hangers you prefer."

That sounded daunting.

"The thing is, we all get to pick from whatever is available, but it's first come, first served, and even though things are jumbled, it's easier to select things from a place that looks like a warehouse yard sale than going into houses that . . ." Barb blew out a breath. "That look like someone still lives there. Depending on where they choose to live within the new town boundaries, some of the folks coming in today will have to clear out the houses by themselves. Everyone is expected to put in at least a couple of hours of sorting a day, but I think it's harder when other people's clothes are still in the closet, and there are photographs on the walls. You know?"

Jana didn't know but could imagine it quite well. "I'd like to swap out some clothes so I have what I need for a couple of days."

"We'll go to the house next so you can do that and also choose your bedroom and take a look at what I've already selected for the living room, dining room, and kitchen," Barb said. "And you might want to choose a bicycle. There's a 'bike corral' next to the hotel and guests can borrow a bicycle to get around or just for fun. But it's also the place where bicycles retrieved from emptied houses are being stored and can be claimed."

"Oh." Jana tried to hide her disappointment. "I thought I would be getting a horse."

"Not enough room in the yard to keep two horses—or even one horse, for that matter, which is why my horse, Rowan, is at the livery stable. I have a bicycle as an alternate way to travel from home to stable. Or just to get around for shopping if I don't want to take Rowan out. You can choose a car—people are mostly keeping whatever was parked in their driveway, but almost every parking lot around the square is stuffed with unclaimed vehicles. The catch is that residents are limited to one tank of gas each month to make sure the government vehicles, medical vehicles, and public transportation have enough fuel. That's why most people use the buses or walk or ride a bicycle."

A different way of life. An *active* way of life.

"Oh, and go easy the first couple of days," Barb added. "A few people felt a bit sick because of the difference in altitude and drier air. Don't push too hard and drink lots of water."

The water she could do. Pushing too hard? That would depend on her boss.

For the rest of the day, Jana viewed her new home and made a sketch of her bedroom, as well as the third bedroom she and Barb wanted to turn into a shared office. They went to one of the buildings that was stuffed with furniture and selected everything they wanted for her bedroom and the office. From there, they went to household storage and packed a box with linens, hangers, curtains, and everything else they could think of needing to set up their house.

"Do you like dogs?" Barb asked suddenly when she turned a corner made by a wall of boxes and stopped.

"Sure, I like dogs," Jana replied. "Haven't had one since I was a kid, but I like them."

"Want one?"

Jana blinked. "They have dogs back there?"

Barb laughed. "No, pet supplies. Dog beds and leashes and other stuff."

"Not much point adding that stuff to what we already have until there's a dog."

"Oh, there are plenty of dogs. Being the almost-vet, I've been taking care of all of them until I can find homes for them."

Jana heard an undercurrent of emotion and wondered if Barb had been given a time limit on finding homes for the pets that had been left behind.

"Horse first, since being a mounted deputy is part of my work." And part of the reason she wanted this job. "Then we can look at the dogs and go from there."

Barb smiled. "Horse first."

They finished up all the "moving to a new place" insanity with a quick look at the free books.

Barb handed her a paper shopping bag. "Each new resident is allowed to take a bag full of books."

Jana eyed the piles of books and hoped she didn't look greedy. "Are you kidding?"

"Nope."

"Why didn't we come here first?"

"I know. I'm one of the book sorters. I already have my bag of freebies, so it's probably good that there is always more than one person here. Otherwise, I'd be too tempted to walk off with a paperback a day."

"Are we sharing books?"

"We can, unless there's one we both really want as a keeper."

"Then let's fill my bag with things you don't have yet—unless I really want a copy for myself."

"Deal. And you can take a couple with you to the hotel and I'll take the rest of them with me and put them in your bedroom."

"We need to pick up more bookcases," Jana said, eyeing the books.

"Definitely."

They finished up and Barb headed for the house they would soon share, saying it was still recommended that the humans reach their homes before full dark. Jana walked to the hotel and went into the gift shop. She had a couple of note cards in her daypack from her stash of stationary, but she bought a few postcards that were photos of the surrounding land and the native wildlife.

The last thing she did before going to bed that night was write a quick note to Jenni Crowgard in Lakeside, using a postcard with a picture of a bison on the front.

CHAPTER 16

Windsday, Messis 15

At seven o'clock, Jana found the breakfast buffet in the hotel's dining room and filled a plate with a balance of carefully selected food. Claiming a seat at a table, she went back for juice and coffee. Then she sat down and tucked in, despite her stomach having first-day-of-work jitters. Those would settle—she hoped. Even if they didn't, she would not throw up on her boss and give him the satisfaction of firing her before he officially hired her. And if he did fire her, all bets were off about the condition of his shoes after *that* discussion.

Finding the visual perversely amusing, Jana also found her appetite.

No one had talked about pay, but Anya Sanguinati, who was the hotel's manager, had told the new residents that while they were guests at the hotel their meals were free as a way of using up food that would spoil. People staying at the boardinghouse were also given their meals. She would have thought the Others would want the humans to prepare food in their own homes, but Barb had explained that the people who had initially come to Bennett had been considered a transitory work force. With the arrival of the people hired at the Lakeside job fair, the transitory work force was evolving into permanent residents. Eventually, new food supplies would be needed and people would have to pay for groceries or for a dinner out, but for now, everyone could focus on settling into their new homes and new places of work and not give a thought about cooking dinner.

The fact that the majority of that transitory work force had been male, single, and in their late teens or early twenties might have been a factor in that decision. Or not. Hard to tell since the *terra indigene* were making up the rules.

Speaking of *terra indigene* . . .

Jana hurried back to her room to brush her teeth and give herself a last chance to change her mind about what to wear for her first day on the job. That was another thing that hadn't been mentioned. The sheriff could wear whatever he wanted, but were deputies supposed to dress in a uniform? Wearing jeans made sense to her if she was spending part of her day on horseback, but was there a specific shirt or color that would be identified as the law? And was there anyplace in town that sold uniforms?

She'd figure it out. She had to. Most likely, this was the only chance she would have to be a serving police officer, and Virgil Wolfgard was already against having her on his staff. Typical male. But she wasn't going to buckle or back down. She'd stood up for herself against every man at the academy, and she would stand up for herself now. Besides, once she got her horse, she could do her work and avoid the sheriff much of the time.

She put a few personal items in her daypack, double-checked that she had her room key, and headed for the sheriff's office.

"Here she comes," Kane said from his post in the open doorway of the sheriff's office.

Virgil pounded a nail into the last corner of the sign he'd attached to the cellblock wall, then stepped back to admire his work.

Tolya had wanted a human deputy, saying humans would be more inclined to ask for help from someone who wouldn't bite them. What was understood and not said was that Virgil wasn't interested in helping humans; he was interested in protecting the *terra indigene* by eliminating two-legged problems with swift, bloody efficiency. But leashing him to a small female? What good would that do? He'd listened to what some of the humans had said yesterday. They thought it was a joke. A female deputy? Ha ha.

If anyone except Simon Wolfgard had chosen her, Jana Paniccia wouldn't be reporting to work this morning. At least, not reporting to work with him. But he knew Simon. More important, he trusted Simon—and Simon had seen some potential in this female.

Time to find out if she still showed potential now that she was here.

Jana smiled at the man lounging in the doorway of the sheriff's office. It was a professional smile—friendly enough that men wouldn't mutter "bitch" after she walked by but not warm enough to be in any way mistaken for an invitation to be *friendly*. When he removed the sunglasses and she saw the amber eyes, she hoped he wouldn't be interested in finding out if she was *friendly*.

"I'm Kane Wolfgard. The other deputy."

Oh good. She got to work with two snarlies instead of just the one she'd met yesterday.

"I'm Jana Paniccia."

Giving her a brisk nod, he went into the office and disappeared through a doorway that had to lead to rooms in the back, leaving her to come in and look around the open area on her own.

Would one of the desks be her workstation? Who took the calls, or did they have a dispatcher? Each desk had a telephone, but there was only one computer and printer set up at its own workstation against the wall.

"Deputy Jana." Virgil walked through the doorway where Kane had disappeared a minute ago.

"Sheriff Wolfgard."

Virgil pointed to the desk closest to the computer workstation. "That one is yours." He stared at the computer for a moment. "You know how to work that?"

"Yes."

"Then that one is yours too. Tolya set up the e-mail thing for the sheriff's office. You will watch for those."

"One e-mail for the whole office? Don't you want a private one?"

Now he stared at her. "Why?"

Okay, e-mail wasn't private. Good to know. Not that it mattered since e-mails, like the phones, were limited to within a region.

"You can also sort mail."

Desk work. If she'd wanted to work at a desk, she wouldn't have gone to the police academy, wouldn't have taken extra classes in order to prove she could do the job.

Virgil opened a drawer, took out a badge, and set it on the desk.

"You're not getting someone to run the office?" she asked.

"We have you."

She clenched her teeth to stop herself from saying something she might regret. Before she could come up with *anything* safe to say in response to that statement, a big Wolf trotted out of the back rooms, came up to her, and stuck his nose in her crotch.

"What the dickens are you doing?" Jana demanded.

"Kane is getting your scent," Virgil replied.

"If you need to do that, you sniff an arm or a leg, but you don't stick your nose *there*," she snapped. "It's crude and it's rude and . . . How would you like it if I sniffed your penis?"

Virgil and Kane cocked their heads. The fact that one looked human and the other was furry made the identical move kind of creepy.

"Humans do that?" Virgil sounded like she had *finally* said something interesting.

"No."

"Oh." They sighed in unison.

"You will need human weapons," Virgil said. "They are back there with other human things. When you have chosen the ones you will use, I will show you the vehicle you will drive."

Jana blinked. "I thought I was going to be a mounted deputy and have a horse."

"The horse is for inside the town boundaries. The vehicle is for outside." Virgil walked over to a map on the wall, then turned and stared at her until she joined him. "This is Bennett. The red line shows the new boundaries. This is where humans can live. This is where they will work."

The new boundaries shrunk the town to half its previous size. "Do the *terra indigene* live on the other side of the boundaries?" That kind of division was bound to keep the residents divided in other kinds of ways.

"Some of us live away from the humans, and some forms of *terra indigene* have chosen houses on the streets where humans are living."

Jana wasn't surprised to hear that Virgil was one of the Others who didn't want to live around humans.

"So I do horse patrol within the new boundaries?" she asked, wanting to be certain.

"Yes. We protect the territory within the red line, but if we need to sniff out something beyond that line, you will drive us."

Ah, so she was driver as well as secretary. This was getting better and better. "Who protects the property beyond the boundaries?"

"Namid's teeth and claws."

Jana swallowed hard. Maybe being the designated driver wouldn't be a bad thing after all.

"You should select your weapons now," Virgil said. "As deputy, you are allowed to have weapons so that you can do your job and protect the citizens of Bennett. The Elders agreed to this."

The Elders. Namid's teeth and claws. The forms of *terra indigene* who had wiped out the original population of Bennett.

"When I'm considering weapons, is there any particular danger I should keep in mind?"

"There is a pack of bad dogs that were raised to fight and kill. They attacked a human and attacked the horses in the corral. They are dangerous."

Jana tucked her daypack in the bottom drawer of her desk before going into the back rooms to explore and find her weapons. When she walked into the storeroom, her mouth dropped open as she eyed all the handguns carelessly piled on one set of metal shelves. The metal shelves on the opposite side of the room mostly held office supplies, but one shelf had been cleared and was now packed with an assortment of knives—everything from combination knives with all kinds of gizmos to switchblades to hunting knives that could do some serious damage to almost anything smaller than a grizzly. Rifles and shotguns were stacked on the floor or leaned against the shelves.

Whoever was in charge of clearing out the houses must have had the workers collect the weapons and bring them here, and whoever was do-ing the work had little or no knowledge of gun safety.

She broke open a shotgun and muttered her worst swearword as she checked two more.

Gods above and below, not only were the weapons carelessly stacked; the darn things were still loaded! The Wolves were lucky they hadn't knocked something over and gotten a foot blown off—or worse.

After removing the shells, she set the three shotguns aside and con-sidered her immediate needs.

She slipped a combination knife into one front pocket of her jeans and a switchblade into the other pocket. After a little hesitation, she selected a big hunting knife that was still in its sheath.

Stepping to the other side of the room, she found a six-shot, police-issue service revolver and its holster, as well as two boxes of cartridges and a couple of speed loaders that fit the revolver. She had to try on a few of the duty belts stuffed on another shelf before she found one small enough to fit her. After attaching the holster and the speed-loader pouch to the belt, she figured she'd have to look for the rest of her gear later—including a kit to clean the revolver. But for now, this was enough, and she didn't want the sheriff to think she was hiding out in the back to avoid doing her job.

After tucking the sheathed hunting knife into her waistband, Jana picked up the two boxes of cartridges and left the storage room. She'd have to talk to Virgil about keeping that door locked until someone—probably her, since it sounded like her job description included everything Virgil and Kane didn't want to do—examined all those weapons and made them safe to store.

A quick exploration of the other rooms back there showed her a bath-room complete with a shower stall and a kitchen with a coffeemaker, a wave-cooker, and an under-the-counter fridge, as well as a square wooden table and four chairs. Mugs, glasses, and plates in the cupboards. Silver-ware in the drawers.

On the other end of that hallway, just past the half-closed door of what she assumed was Virgil's office, was another door. Jana opened that one and found three basic cells with nothing but a cot in each. Not even a toilet, which she'd thought was pretty standard these days.

Then she noticed the sign printed with large black letters and an arrow pointing to the last cell. THE ME TIME CELL. And she knew, just *knew*, which gender was being targeted.

Mad enough to spit, Jana spun around and almost plowed into Virgil.

"What the dickens is that?" she yelled, jabbing a finger in the direction of the sign.

"It's a sign."

"The Me Time cell? Really? And who ends up in there?"

"Females who need time to figure out why they shouldn't yap at me."

"Females." She snarled the word. "Females who challenge you get put in a cage. What happens to the men? Huh? What happens to them?"

Virgil stepped forward. His shoes bumped hers. She had to crane her neck to look up at him without taking a step back. That would be a submissive act, and she would *not* be submissive. Her time at the academy had shown her that she had to stand up for herself and fight for everything she wanted. She'd thought it was harassment and bullying; she hadn't appreciated that it was a necessary part of her training.

"What happens to them?" she said again.

He brought his face close to hers and she saw odd flickers of red in his amber eyes. Baring his teeth and revealing fangs too long to be human, he snarled, "I. Bite. Them."

Stay focused on the job. Stay focused—and don't start a pissing contest you can't win.

Jana took a step back. She would stay focused and show the darn snarlies that she could do the job. "Most, if not all, of the weapons you've shoved into that storeroom are still loaded. That's dangerous. That room should be locked at all times, and the weapons unloaded. Sir."

Virgil stared at her. "You know how to do this?"

"Yes, sir, I do. Should I add it to the rest of my duties?"

"Yes." He walked away.

Yes. Just yes.

She stayed in the holding area a full minute before she felt she could see him again without launching herself at him. If she did that, she'd end up in one of those cells for assaulting a superior officer—assuming she didn't end up seriously hurt. Virgil was bigger, he was stronger, and he had meaner teeth. And he'd have Kane throwing in with him.

"You can get through this shift," she whispered. "Just get through your first shift."

Virgil reappeared in the doorway to the holding area. "Why are you still there? You have to see the car and find a horse. You can sniff around the cells later."

She paused long enough to put the hunting knife and boxes of cartridges into a middle desk drawer—and found a gun-cleaning kit already there. Then she went outside and followed Virgil and Kane, who was still furry, to the back of the building. The only vehicle in the spaces designated for the sheriff's office was a shiny black utility vehicle that had "Bennett Police" painted along the sides.

Wasn't a patrol car like she was used to seeing in the Northeast. In fact, except for the lights, it didn't have any of the accoutrements usually associated with police cars. It did have a sizable cargo area, which made her think the backseats had been folded down to accommodate the snarlies.

Could Wolves be backseat drivers? She didn't relish the idea of Virgil breathing on her neck and growling opinions while she chauffeured him around town.

"The humans who take care of cars made sure this one could travel," Virgil said. "You make sure you can drive it and know how to make it light up and howl."

"Yes, sir."

Kane lifted a leg and peed on one of the tires. Since he went around to the other side, she figured he was peeing on one of the tires over there too.

Either he was letting other predators know that this was a Wolf-approved vehicle, or he was providing the Wolves with an easy way to track the human deputy.

"Are we going to have a dispatcher?" she asked.

"Dispatcher?" Virgil frowned. "What for?"

"So that someone can call in if they need help, or for one of us to call in if we need backup."

Kane raised his head and howled. Jana felt a shiver run down her spine.

Suddenly there were Crows—Ravens?—flying toward them. When Virgil looked up, Jana noticed a large brown bird now circling overhead.

Then he looked at her and said, "If any *terra indigene* spots trouble, we'll know. But you should talk to Tolya Sanguinati and Jesse Walker about a phone you can carry with you since you can't howl loud enough to be heard. Then humans who need help can call you."

Because you won't help them.

She was getting the message loud and clear. Had the town leaders known about the animosity Wolfgard felt toward humans, or didn't they care? Was she not just fighting to earn some respect for herself as a police officer but also fighting to maintain some kind of balance between humans and Others?

She had wanted this job. Still wanted this job. But she was starting to appreciate how daunting being a cop in this town was going to be when she had the double strike against her of being female and human.

"You should go to the livery stable and find your horse now," Virgil said. "Then you will eat the midday meal humans need to avoid becoming weak. Then you will come back to the office and I will walk with you around the square so that many humans will see that you are a deputy. Then you can return and do office things until it is time for you to go home."

"And when, exactly, is that?" Jana asked.

A growly silence. "Ask Tolya. He will explain about human work hours."

Virgil and Kane looked at her.

"I guess I'll go find a horse." Jana felt them watching her all the way up the street.

It wasn't easy admitting to the two Simple Life men who were at the stable that she'd never actually ridden a horse since the pony rides of her childhood, despite having been hired to be a mounted deputy. And since sitting on a pony's back and being led around a ring wasn't the same as knowing how to ride . . .

They admitted that they'd arrived in town a few days ago and weren't familiar enough with the available horses to know which one might suit her the best, but they recognized a few that would not suit a beginner.

After some discussion, the men presented her with a bay gelding that they deemed was docile enough for her. They saddled the bay, led her to the empty corral, and gave her a basic riding lesson. For an hour she circled the corral with one of the men keeping watch and offering advice. She and the bay walked in one direction, then the other. They circled the corral a couple of times at a trot, and Jana was sure her pelvis would never be the same. But when the bay lifted into a canter, she felt invincible and free and able to take on the world—including a boss with big teeth.

Riding the bay gelding was the high point of her first day of work. Being walked around the town square like she was Virgil's pet was demeaning. The Crowgard and Ravengard rushed out of each shop as they passed by, wanting to know who she was and then staring at her with those bright dark eyes. Same with the Eagles and Hawks. But when they encountered the big golden cat that Virgil introduced as Saul Panthergard, she was glad the Wolf was with her—until they continued the walk and he made snarky comments about her not yipping at Saul for sniffing her.

Something that size with those teeth and claws? He could sniff anything he darn well wanted to sniff!

After talking to Tolya Sanguinati about mobile phones and the *terra indigene*'s idea of a workday and workweek, she finally headed home to help Barb with whatever furniture and supplies had arrived before they hurried back to the hotel for dinner. If the bed she'd selected arrived, she could move out of the hotel tomorrow.

Barb had a bright smile when Jana walked into the house. The smile quickly faded.

"How was your first day on the job?" Barb asked.

"I didn't shoot my boss," Jana growled. "I thought about it, but I didn't do it."

Barb nodded. "Virgil can be difficult." Then she brightened again. "Did you find a horse?"

Jana grinned. "I did."

"If you've got a horse, you can put up with a lot of things." Barb paused. "Your bed didn't arrive, but the bookcases did."

Now Jana laughed. "Well, there are priorities."

"Let's skip the sorting and unpacking tonight and go eat dinner. I'm starving, and we've both worked hard enough today."

"You know something, Barb Debany? I like the way you think."

CHAPTER 17

Thaisday, Messis 16

Virgil shook out his fur before trotting over to the town square to take a sniff around the spring. He hadn't seen any of the bad dogs for a couple of days, but he'd caught the scent of dogs around some of the inhabited houses where dogs weren't living with humans. He and Kane had followed some of the scents to a house on the edge of the new town boundaries—a house that had a small swinging door for animals. How foolish was that? If a dog or cat could get through the door, so could a lot of other animals. And they had. The Wolves were too big to squeeze through the door, but one of the Coyotegard easily fit and had ventured far enough into the house to confirm that quite a few animals besides dogs had entered. Besides scat, there were torn bags of dry animal food and spoiling human food that had been in the cupboards, as well as the bones of a couple of partially eaten critters.

Tomorrow Tobias Walker would help the ranch humans select some of the still-tame dogs to go live with them on the ranches. If the dogs couldn't herd properly, they would be left at the house to guard the human females and bark a warning if strangers—two-legged or four—approached. Tobias Walker had also promised to take some of the cats that had potential to live in the barns and eat the mice.

Not many of the new humans in Bennett wanted pets, despite Barbara Ellen's renewed efforts to find homes for the dogs and cats and birds.

He would deal with the pets—and her—when he had to. Right now, he had to keep the bad dogs out of his territory.

Virgil lapped some water from the spring, then headed for the livery stable. Deputy Jana's first job each day was to ride the horse for an hour so that she would learn how to do the mounted deputy tasks. He didn't understand why she didn't already know these things, but everyone assured him that having horse and rider get acquainted in the corral was smart.

He listened to the words but also paid attention to the way the humans held their bodies and the way their smell changed while they were explaining, and he was sure they were doing something sneaky. Then again, if riding the horse kept Deputy Jana from yapping at him for the rest of the day, he'd pretend he didn't know the humans were being sneaky until he figured out *why* they were being sneaky. And then he would decide who would feel his teeth.

The horse in the corral with Jana caught his scent and charged around the corral with the female wobbling in the saddle and hanging on to whatever she could grab.

That was not the correct way to ride the horse. Even he knew that.

Losing interest in the saddled horse, and wondering about the intelligence of the humans standing around the corral since they couldn't figure out that this particular horse wasn't smart enough to tell the difference between predators that would eat it and predators that would not, Virgil continued on to the other corral.

Most of the horses in that corral also started running and fussing, but the horse that was not meat pricked its ears after catching his scent, then walked over to the rails to greet him.

Virgil stood on his hind legs and extended his neck over the top rail. Horse and Wolf sniffed each other, confirming recognition.

<Have you seen the bad dogs?> Virgil didn't expect an answer. The horse wasn't any form of *terra indigene* and couldn't reply. Still, he felt he should acknowledge the difference between the horse that was not meat and the rest of the animals in the corral.

Dropping to all four legs, he gave the ground around the corral a thorough sniff, then expanded his search area when he caught a scent. Two of the dogs had come close, but the scent of humans must have scared them off.

Virgil sniffed at a tuft of fur that had a trace of skin and blood.

Or maybe the dogs had run away because the Owlgard had been hunting around the stable and had flown in on those silent wings and used talons to encourage the dogs to leave the horses alone.

He marked a few of the posts as another way to warn off the dogs, then did a quick turn around the town square. One of the two small buses now in operation disgorged workers in front of the hotel so that they could eat some food before starting their work.

Every resident was allowed to have a car, but gasoline was another matter. Eventually the humans would start grumbling about restrictions and rules and all the things they couldn't do or have, and then flesh would be torn and blood would flow.

He looked forward to that day. Until then, he'd do his job as the dominant enforcer in Bennett.

"Becky!"

Virgil moved toward the sound of Hannah Gott's voice, then veered when he spotted the skippy girl heading for the spring bubbling into the human-made pool that held some of the water before flowing down a channel that had been made to look like a creek ending at the small pond near the southern end of the square. The skippy girl liked playing in the water, but Hannah Gott didn't want the girl to be wet during the working time.

Easy enough to distract her. All it usually took was for him or Kane to show up in Wolf form. Then she was more interested in giving them hugs and pats than getting wet or digging in the dirt. Not that he found anything wrong with doing either of those things, but humans had rules about when the skippy girl could play.

Getting between her and the water, Virgil play-growled and licked and nudged her until she gave him a choking hug and followed him back to where Hannah Gott waited with the other adult female in her pack and the male pup.

"I appreciate you being so kind to Becky," Hannah Gott said when he and the girl reached the sidewalk opposite the square. "Come along now, Becky. It's time for breakfast."

"Bye-bye, Virgil," the skippy girl said, moving the fingers of one hand as Hannah Gott took the other hand and led her away.

As he trotted back to the sheriff's office to wash up and put on human clothes, Virgil thought it was interesting that the Gott pack had arrived in Bennett a week ago, but only the girl with the skippy brain could tell the difference between him and Kane when they were in Wolf form.

Jesse Walker smiled at Lila Gold and Candice Caravelli, who were waiting for her outside Bennett's general store.

"You're my helpers today?"

"Yes, ma'am," Lila said. "Is this like an old-fashioned store?"

Jesse paused to consider the question. "I don't know. It looks pretty much like mine. More small town than old-fashioned since there are the refrigerated units along one wall, and the store is set up to have a little bit of a lot of things."

She wondered when someone would ask about the empty lot next to the general store—or suggest clearing out the debris so that people didn't mistake the plot of land for a dump. It wasn't completely empty, and it wasn't a place to discard anything unwanted since the only human thing left on that land was a rusting woodstove.

No, that plot of land wasn't empty, and it wasn't a dump. It was a daily reminder that the original residents of Bennett had ignored—a warning decades old of what can happen if you clash with the *terra indigene*. Why the people had been smart enough to keep the warning but not smart enough to heed it was a question that would never be answered.

"I believe this store was built when the town was first settled," Jesse continued.

"Handy for travelers or people working in the buildings around the square," Candice said, looking around. She stared at the wall behind the cash register. "Why do so many places around here decorate with animal skulls?"

Lila studied the skull. "Are we going to have to hang animal skulls in our apartments in order to fit in? Is that a standard frontier motif?"

Jesse couldn't tell if Lila was hoping it was or hoping it wasn't. "My family has lived in Prairie Gold since the town was created, and we've never decorated with skulls."

"Hmm. Maybe a frontier version of a rock garden, but with skulls."

"We live in apartments," Candice said.

Wondering if she should warn Tolya that Lila Gold might start a fad for using bleached animal skulls as garden art or let him find out for himself, Jesse handed lists to the two women, then pointed to the heavy cardboard boxes she'd piled in front of the counter. "You have the lists for the Prairie Gold ranch, the dairy farm, and the vegetable farm. Check the expiration dates on everything I've listed and take what isn't going to keep much longer. We'll use those jars and cans of food first."

They looked at the shelves in the general store and hesitated.

"You two settled into your own places?" Jesse asked, correctly guessing the reason for the hesitation.

Lila nodded. "First thing Candice and I did after taking two of the one-bedroom apartments was select furniture and household goods. It will take a few days before our stuff is delivered, but once we're moved in, it sure would be nice to heat up a can of soup at home if we're working late at the saloon and don't finish up before the hotel dining room stops serving meals."

Jesse nodded. Give it a few more days and the hotel wouldn't be serving free meals to anyone who wasn't staying at the hotel, so wanting to stock up was sensible. "Take a couple more of those boxes to fill up for yourselves."

"Thanks, Jesse," Candice said.

Lila Gold had the same confident bounce as Barb Debany, but Jesse had a feeling that Candice Caravelli had known some dark times and felt other people's kindness more deeply because of it.

Lila and Candice were already busy filling up boxes when the four Simple Life women who were heading out to the ranches came in to select supplies for each ranch. While there was nothing wrong with any of the women—Jesse admired their courage in taking on a new life in an unfamiliar part of Thaisia—only one of them felt adaptable enough to not only embrace a different life but also be able to live comfortably with men who didn't share her beliefs and traditions. That was the woman she'd insisted go to the ranch that would be run by Truman Skye. Truman would have enough challenges without being undermined by the person who was supposed to be the cook and housekeeper.

She didn't get a feeling about whether the other women would succeed or fail, but she was certain she didn't want them working for Truman.

"We're trying to find out what companies are still in business and what kinds of foods are available," she said. "Until we find out, we don't want to waste what is here. When you get to the ranches, you might find a pantry full of moldy food or a pantry full of canned goods you can use. Because we don't know, you're each welcome to fill up four of those cardboard boxes with supplies free of charge. All we ask is that you take only what you will use. Keep in mind that each ranch will have a foreman and six to ten men who will be looking to you to provide their meals. Also, if any of you want to have a dog at the house to keep you company and warn you when something approaches the house, we have plenty of food in bags and cans, and someone will fetch those for you from the feed store."

Two of the women looked sour, as if they anticipated working hard enough to feed whatever had to be fed and didn't need something else depending on them. The housekeeper for the Skye Ranch, however, looked happy about the possibility of having a dog or two for company. Jesse would ask Tobias to go with the woman to look at the available dogs.

Once the Simple Life women started making their selections, Jesse stepped away from the counter, intending to fetch a few more boxes from the back room. Instead, she grabbed her suddenly throbbing wrist and turned toward the door as a group of strangers walked in.

There was nothing obvious about the two men, but Jesse felt certain that they were lovers at the very least. That shouldn't have produced a strong feeling of impending danger. No, what confused her—and scared her—and caused that fierce ache in her wrist, were the four children who were with them, two boys and two girls, all under the age of ten.

One man was slender, had almond-shaped eyes and straight black hair cut very short. The other man was burly and dark-skinned, with curly black hair.

"Can I help you?" Jesse asked.

"Please," the slender man said with a gentle smile. "The man at the train station said we should come here and talk to Jesse Walker."

Nicolai had sent them to the store? "I'm Jesse."

He looked at the wrist she still held. "You are Intuit?"

"Yes."

The man's smile warmed with relief, a response typical of someone who was also an Intuit—especially someone who had had reason to keep some things hidden because he'd lived among people who would not have welcomed an Intuit's abilities. "We arrived on the train and are hoping to become citizens of your fine town."

Then why didn't Nicolai direct you to the mayor's office to talk to Tolya?

She knew why. Nicolai had sent them to her for the same reason someone had relaxed the travel restrictions as soon as those men said they were coming to Bennett. Because of the children. Knowing that her Intuit ability was sensing other people, Nicolai had sent these people to the store so that she could get a feel for who they were before he contacted the *terra indigene* who would make a decision about whether the men lived or died.

Out of the corner of her eye, Jesse saw the tight-lipped, disapproving stiffness in two of the Simple Life women who stared at the newcomers. She also noticed Lila step up, ready to give a bouncy welcome. The men didn't bother Jesse, but the children did, especially the girl who had a disturbingly vacant stare.

Before she could frame a question about why two men had four young children, Joshua Painter walked into the store, swung around the men, and focused on the children. His right hand was covered in that leather glove with the Panther claws, and the look in his eyes made Jesse's skin crawl.

Eyes. Jesse looked at the girl who was Joshua's main focus, then looked back at him. Gods above and below, they both had green eyes with an outer ring of gray.

Virgil Wolfgard and Tolya Sanguinati walked into the store, forcing the strangers to move forward, caught between them and Joshua.

Virgil sniffed the air and growled, "That little female. She's . . ." He looked at Tolya, whose lips pulled back, revealing fangs.

The men put their arms around the children, protective. And the children clung to the men, although one of the boys growled at Virgil before turning away and pressing his face against the man who held him.

"We don't want any trouble," the burly man said, sounding nervous.

"Then explain why you came here with a Wolf, a Hawk, a Coyote . . . and a sweet blood," Tolya snarled.

Jesse swayed. The girl with the vacant stare was a *cassandra sangue*, a blood prophet?

Joshua lowered himself to his heels and balanced on the balls of his feet. He stared at the green-eyed girl, and his face took on an expression that wasn't as disturbingly blank as the girl's but was too similar for comfort, as if he had fallen into some kind of trance. "Sees too much, knows too much."

"She's mute," the slender man said, looking at Jesse in a silent appeal for understanding. "We think the cause is emotional trauma."

"Tell the truth, feel the belt," Joshua whispered.

Virgil snarled—a sound filled with hate.

"Why did you come to Bennett?" she asked quickly.

"We are a mixed family," the slender man said. "We had hoped that, in a town where *terra indigene* and humans lived together, we might be accepted. We hoped our children would find others of their kind to help them, teach them the things that we cannot."

Jesse focused on the men. They were parents by heart if not by blood, but if the men didn't give the right answers, they wouldn't get out of the store alive.

Then a woman hurried into the store wearing a deputy's star pinned to her shirt. Thank the gods, the human deputy had arrived. Jesse felt fear and hope rise in equal measure along with the certainty that this woman would be the deciding factor in what happened to these men and children. But she could do her part to help. After all, Nicolai had sent them here to talk to her.

"The children?" she asked.

The slender man brushed a hand over the brown feathers that covered the other girl's head—a head that had been covered with neatly combed and braided brown hair when they'd walked into the store. "Orphans. Abandoned chicks who had been taken from their own kind when they were so young they couldn't remember who they were or where they came from. How could we walk away when we were needed?"

Jesse gave him a nod of encouragement, then glanced at Virgil and Tolya. *Tell them more.*

"I am Evan Hua. This is my partner, Kenneth Stone." He smiled at the feathered girl. "This is Charlee Hawk."

"Hawkgard," Jesse corrected. "Her correct last name would be Hawk-gard.

"Charlee Hawkgard," Evan said. "Our growling boy is Mason Wolf . . . Wolfgard."

"Mace," the boy muttered, turning his head to give Virgil a quick look before hiding his face again.

"Our mischief-maker is Zane Coyotegard."

The Coyote grinned at Jesse, revealing a missing tooth.

"And this is Maddie," Kenneth Stone said, his hand on the blood prophet's shoulder.

"That one was a stray too?" Virgil's amber eyes held flickers of red.

The men hesitated. Jesse sucked in a breath.

"What we did was wrong in the eyes of the law but right in terms of the heart," Kenneth said.

"I helped her hide," Mace said.

"We all helped," Charlee said, reaching for Maddie's hand.

"The young man wasn't wrong about the belt," Evan said. "The child was reported missing. The whole neighborhood was searching for her. When we found her hiding with our children . . . The welts and bruises told a different story from the tearful parents pleading for help in finding her."

Kenneth took up their story. "We began to wonder when they didn't have a single photograph of her to put on TV. The people claiming to be her parents weren't Intuits, and she's . . ."

"We know what she is." Tolya gave the men a smile that bordered on terrifying. "We can tell by her scent. Unlike the rest of you humans, her kind doesn't smell like prey."

Kenneth swallowed hard. "We'd already been planning to leave. It was a human town, and the children couldn't always hide their true natures. When we left, we smuggled Maddie out and took her with us."

"I did not believe the parents' tears," Evan said. "I did believe the child's desperation not to be found. I felt, and still believe, Maddie would not have survived much longer in that house."

Silence. No one spoke. No one moved.

Finally, Tolya said, "What work can you do?"

"I am a priest," Evan said. "I have worked in several Universal Temples. Kenneth is a teacher."

A sound of disgust came from one of the Simple Life women.

Virgil bared his teeth at the woman, effectively discouraging her from making another sound. Then he studied Mace. "You know how to shift, pup?"

Mace nodded.

"You remember living with a pack?"

Mace gave Virgil a defiant look. "This is my pack."

Throughout the whole exchange, Joshua's focus never left Maddie. "A place with no memories, no stain of darkness. In a clean place, birds return to sing."

Strange boy, Jesse thought. She wasn't sure Joshua could speak prophecy the way the girls who were blood prophets could, but she had a feeling he was more than an Intuit if he was seeing images rather than having feelings about his surroundings.

"Can you recognize this stain of darkness?" Tolya asked.

Joshua stood, then blinked as if coming out of a light nap. "Yes."

Tolya looked at Virgil, then turned to the two men. "We don't have a priest yet or a teacher."

Jesse saw Kenneth hesitate and knew the reason. "You don't have to open the whole school building for the handful of children currently living in Bennett. There is a community center next door to the Universal Temple. One of the rooms in that building could be turned into a classroom for now. In fact, it would be good to open the center so that everyone could use it for a number of activities like a quilting circle and . . . and . . ." She fumbled. What did she know about such activities? She preferred target practice and reading to handcrafts.

"Candice taught Quiet Mind classes," Lila said. "She's interested in doing that here too. And she can teach frontier dancing."

"I . . . uh . . ." Candice glanced around, then nodded. "I could do that."

Lila beamed. Virgil grunted.

"Did you bring luggage?" Tolya asked the men.

"We left everything at the train station," Evan said.

Tolya nodded. "Nicolai will look after it. Sheriff Wolfgard and Deputy Paniccia will escort you to the hotel. Afterward, you'll come to my office and review what is required to be a resident of Bennett. If you want to stay after knowing our rules, we'll take a look at houses tomorrow and see what can be done about moving you into one quickly."

The men looked hopeful and stunned at the acceptance. Jesse felt stunned too because she had a very bad feeling that Tolya had just lied. Whatever the *terra indigene* were feeling about these men, acceptance had no part of it.

Jana would have been all right with Virgil putting the men in one hotel room and the children in another if there had been a connecting door between the rooms. But there wasn't, and she didn't have to be an Intuit or a blood prophet or anything else to know what that meant.

She kept a chokehold on her temper and her heart until Virgil closed the door to the children's room.

"You can't separate those children from their parents. They're a family." She kept her voice low to avoid being overheard, but her anger came through loud and clear.

"They're not family," Virgil growled. "They're human males who have taken—"

"They didn't take those children in the way you mean. They gave those children a home, gave them love, protection. Taught them. That's what parents do." She looked at the anger on his face, in his eyes. "What? A Panther can raise a human boy and that's all right, but a human can't love a child who is *terra indigene*?"

"There were reasons Joshua ended up with the Panthergard."

"And there are reasons those children ended up with Evan and Kenneth. Who are you to judge?"

Virgil leaned toward her. She leaned toward him, balancing her weight and balling her hands into fists.

"You know nothing about it," Virgil snarled.

"I know you don't have to give birth to a child to love it," Jana snarled back. "I was raised by foster parents. I loved them and they loved me, and we were *family*. Those men love those children, and the children love them. I can see it, even if you don't. Or won't."

Virgil stepped back and studied her.

She hoped by all the gods that she could find the right words to get through to him. "Kenneth and Evan brought those children here because they knew there would be *terra indigene* here. Wolves and Coyotes and Hawks and so many more. They brought those children here to learn to be who they are, where they *could* be who they are. This is Bennett. Who will care if a boy can shift into a Wolf? Here they don't need to be a secret in order to be protected."

We learned from you.

A chill went through her as she remembered the sign and gave a fleeting thought to how those children had ended up with two human men in the first place. Orphans, Evan had called the children. But not because of the recent killings. Lost or abandoned by their original family—or stolen from their families—they had been taken in by Evan and Kenneth a few years ago. Except Maddie.

"Maybe you should talk to the children before you make any decisions about their futures," Jana said.

Virgil released a gusty exhale that sufficiently expressed his annoyance. "Fine. We'll talk to them." He went to the hotel door, wrapped his hand around the knob, and then looked at her. "Come on. It's your idea."

The moment they walked into the room, Mace and Zane leaped toward them, growling.

"What did you do with our dads?" Mace demanded.

"Give 'em back," Zane said.

"They're in the next room," Virgil said, giving no indication if he was annoyed or pleased by the youngsters' challenge. "They have to talk to the mayor about work and finding a house for all of you."

Mace cocked his head. Since he hadn't seen Virgil do that, Jana figured it was something Wolves did.

"All of us?" Mace sounded like he didn't quite trust the sheriff.

Virgil gave the boy a curt nod. "All of you." He looked at the girls, who were on the floor near one of the beds.

The girl Tolya Sanguinati had said didn't smell like prey stared at nothing. Vacant eyes that Jana found unnerving.

If the Others refer to a girl as a sweet blood or say she doesn't smell like prey, they're talking about a blood prophet. That was one of the things Michael Debany had hurriedly told her about blood prophets before she got on the train.

Gods. What were they supposed to do with a blood prophet in their midst?

The other girl, the Hawk . . . Well the other girl *was* a young Hawk who had her wings caught in the armholes of a sleeveless shirt and the rest of her clothes bunched under her taloned feet.

Zane looked back at the girls and sighed. "Charlee does that when she's scared. That's how Dad Evan found her. The humans thought a girl had gone missing at the orphan place, and Dad Evan was there that day and was helping them search. When he saw the Hawk beating at a window, trying to escape, he knew she was the missing girl and couldn't stay in that place, so he opened the window, thinking she would fly away. Then he realized she was too young to be alone, so he went outside and found her and took her home."

Jana wondered if Zane's and Mace's stories would be similar. They'd already been told that the blood prophet had been taken from the people claiming to be her parents. Had run away, with Mace's help, and was hidden by Evan and Kenneth.

"Deputy Jana will ask Anya Sanguinati to bring up food for you," Virgil said.

"Meat?" Mace asked hopefully.

"Meat."

Mace looked at the girls. "Charlee likes meat too, but maybe you have fruit for Maddie?"

"She doesn't eat meat?"

"She does, but she likes fruit better."

Virgil walked out of the room, leaving Jana to follow. He rapped on the next door, which was immediately opened by Evan Hua, who looked frightened—and resigned.

"I'll take you to the mayor's office now to talk to Tolya."

"The children?" Evan asked as Kenneth joined him at the door.

"Deputy Jana will arrange to have food brought to their room. They will be safe there."

"We'll just be a moment." Evan closed the door.

Jana felt relieved. She'd prevailed. Virgil had listened. She . . .

Looking at her, Virgil bared his teeth and said quietly, "Those youngsters better be safe with those humans."

"They will be."

"If they're not, I will tear out the throats of those two humans—and then I'll tear out yours."

Moments later, Evan and Kenneth left their room and followed Virgil for their meeting with the mayor.

Jana stood in the corridor, waiting for her heart to stop pounding, for her body to stop shaking. When she finally regained control, she went downstairs to find Anya Sanguinati and arrange for some meat and fruit to be sent up to the children.

Jesse looked at the Simple Life women and wondered how two of them had been able to hide their lack of tolerance from the leaders of the Lakeside Courtyard. They might be excellent housekeepers and cooks, but they would be hard neighbors. Something she needed to point out to Tolya, but that could wait. The women were already committed to going to the ranches tomorrow, and she had another concern right now. "Mr. Sanguinati? If I could have a minute?"

Tolya had sent Joshua Painter on his way but had remained in the general store. Jesse wasn't sure why he had stayed, but her left wrist had quieted to a dull ache, which should be a good sign that the crisis was over, but she needed to be sure.

"We'll just get these boxes filled." Candice grabbed a box, her list . . . and Lila.

Jesse led Tolya to the stock area of the store, where they were out of sight and hearing of the other people.

"Are you okay with them living here? The men, I mean?"

He looked puzzled. "Should I object?"

"No," she said quickly. "I . . . wasn't sure if you'd encountered same-gender mates before."

"Among the *terra indigene*, mating is about having offspring and requires male and female. That doesn't mean we don't form bonds with those of our own gender, but it is not the same as mating." He looked polite but uninterested. "Is there anything else?"

"Those men are Intuits. They wouldn't have brought those children here if they'd done anything wrong."

"Deputy Jana seems to be of the same opinion."

Jesse wondered what Deputy Jana had said, but apparently it had been enough to sway the decision to let the family stay in Bennett. "I'd better get back out there. Those women are heading to the ranches in the morning. I want to make sure they have everything they need. Being from the Northeast, they might overlook something that would be real useful."

"If you need anything, I will be at my office. Virgil is bringing the men over to discuss work and houses."

She should have been relieved. Instead, she felt there was still reason to worry.

Tolya was barely out the door when Jesse's mobile phone rang. "Jesse Walker."

"It's Rachel. I smelled mouse in the back room of the store. Can I chase it?"

Damn it, mice were the last thing she needed in her store when she had packed it with all the foodstuffs she could buy before things had gone so wrong. She didn't need Rachel, in human or Wolf form, knocking into shelves and smashing glass jars.

"Just take a look around and make sure the mice haven't gotten into any of the food," Jesse said. "I'll be home tomorrow."

She spent a couple more minutes talking with Rachel, then made sure the women heading out in the morning truly had everything they needed.

Tolya looked out the window of his office. People walked or rode bicycles on the main street. A few got on the bus to go home or go to wherever they were doing sorting that day.

Apparently Deputy Jana had been vehement in her belief that the youngsters should live with the men they saw as their parents. And Jesse Walker had recognized the men as Intuits. Would that kind of human come to a town full of *terra indigene* if the youngsters had not been orphaned as they had claimed? He didn't think so. Adults would gather; questions would be asked—*especially* about the Wolf pup since so many Wolves had been killed by the humans who had belonged to the Humans First and Last movement.

Bennett was *not* the place for humans to bring stolen *terra indigene* young. But if the men wanted those youngsters to learn about their own kind and still have that family made up of many different forms, a town like this was the place to bring them, the place to try for acceptance.

As for the blood prophet . . .

The euphoria that filled the girls when they began to speak prophecy after their skin was cut provided a veil against the visions, protecting them from the things they had seen. But when a girl was prevented from speaking—or chose not to speak in order to see the visions—there was no protection, no euphoria. There was only agony and the possibility of seeing something so terrible the girl's mind would break.

The Maddie girl was young and so small—and mute. But Meg Corbyn and Hope Wolfsong were showing the rest of the blood prophets that there were other ways to "speak" without cutting or words. Meg was exploring the use of fortune cards being converted into prophecy cards, and Hope slipped into a trance and drew her visions. Perhaps there were other ways to speak that hadn't been explored yet.

He wished he still had direct contact with the Lakeside Courtyard and Meg Corbyn. Even if he had contact, it wouldn't be fair to ask for more help after all the work they had done to run the job fair and find suitable humans to resettle the town. But he did have direct access to Jackson Wolfgard and Hope Wolfsong. Hope had already drawn one warning that concerned Bennett. Maybe, if he provided some information, she might show him some possibilities of what to do with the sweet blood girl.

Turning away from the window, Tolya placed a call to Sweetwater and left a message at the communications cabin, asking that Jackson call him as soon as possible.

CHAPTER 18

Firesday, Messis 17

Abigail pushed the edge of the curtain to one side and peered out the window at the people getting off the small bus. She wasn't being nosy. There were reasons why she needed to know who lived around her, needed to know if any of her neighbors posed a threat to her maintaining the sweet Abigail persona. Not everyone was as gullible as Barb Debany, including Barb's housemate, Deputy Jana Paniccia. Abigail had a feeling that the deputy didn't buy into *anyone's* persona—maybe even her own.

That niggling doubt about her own abilities might be enough to work with to keep Jana from looking too closely at the neighbors.

Abigail recognized Tolya Sanguinati and Virgil Wolfgard, and she'd seen the young guy and the golden-haired man walking around the town square when she'd ventured beyond this street for her cleaning job or to put in her required hours of sorting work. But the other two men and the four children were strangers. The men didn't *look* dangerous, but the most dangerous men often didn't.

When Jana pulled her official police vehicle into the driveway of the house next door, Abigail went outside to find out what was going on. It would be natural to be curious.

Barb came out of the house she was sharing with Jana, said, "Hi, Abby," then looked at Jana. "What's up?"

"Several things," Jana replied, stopping to watch the group of people stand in front of each house on the street. "Since the guys making deliveries of household goods are up to their eyeballs in requests, the sheriff told me to load up my official vehicle with goods we'd earmarked for the house in exchange for letting said vehicle live with us."

"It's a car, not a puppy." Barb studied the vehicle. "We can haul things in it?"

"Yes. You being the next thing on my hauling list as soon as we unload." Jana opened the back, pulled out a box, and handed it to Barb, who stood there with her mouth open.

"I'll take one," Abigail said, wondering what was wrong with Barb.

"Did *he* send you to put me in the Me Time cell?" Barb demanded. "What did I do *now*?"

"Shh," Jana said when Virgil turned to stare at them, proving just how sharp Wolf ears were when it came to picking up sounds. "No, this is about getting some of the pets adopted. So help me get these boxes in the house and we can be on our way."

Abigail waited until the three of them carted the last load of boxes into the house and Barb went to fetch her daypack and house keys. Then she asked, "Why are the town leader and the sheriff looking at houses with those men?"

"One of the children is . . . special . . . and Joshua Painter says she needs a house that doesn't have a stain of darkness—which is something specific that Joshua can sense but can't explain," Jana replied. "That's why they're all out there looking at houses. They looked at houses that had already been cleared out on another street, but none of those places were right."

Special like Becky Gott? Or special like drawing pictures that showed something that could happen in the future? If she hadn't seen a picture like that when she'd lived in Prairie Gold, she wouldn't have sensed that Jana's hesitation revealed more than the deputy realized. Special could be like finding the mother lode. Or being able to identify that kind of special could be information she could trade if the wrong kind of people came wandering down the street and found *her*.

"I'm ready," Barb said, joining them.

They locked the house on their way out, then paused to watch the group conferring on the front yard of one house before moving on to the next.

"Think we'll have new neighbors?" Abigail asked, trying to sound casual.

"If they choose a house on this street, they won't be the only new neighbors," Barb replied. "Some of the *terra indigene* would move into houses around here to keep watch. They're kind of intense about protecting—"

"Barb!" Jana said sharply.

For a moment, Barb looked hurt. But Jana looked alarmed at what her housemate was about to reveal, confirming that one of the children *was* the lucrative kind of special.

"Sorry," Barb said.

"It's all right," Jana said. "I'm just skittish from yesterday."

What had happened yesterday? Nothing that had made the rounds of gossip.

Jana jingled her keys and looked at Barb. "Let's get going so I can spend some time with my four-legged ride. See you later, Abby."

"See you." Abigail watched Jana and Barb drive off before retreating to her own house.

Kelley wasn't happy living with her anymore. He had a separate bedroom now and was clearing it out and cleaning it up. But he made no effort to help her with the rest of the house. Which meant he didn't know what was in the house and what wasn't—including the things they were supposed to turn in.

And since Kelley wasn't sharing a bedroom with her, he also didn't know about the pack she'd hidden in the closet—the emergency pack of essentials she would need if she had to run again.

"What I told you about Maddie was said in confidence," Jana said as she drove the few blocks to the town square. "We can't talk about her to anyone."

"But you said there were lots of people in the store when those men arrived with the children," Barb protested.

"And Mr. Sanguinati stopped the men from saying Maddie was a blood prophet. There's no reason for anyone to know by what *he* said unless they'd already met one of the girls."

Barb stared at her. "Then how did you know what Tolya was talking about?"

"Your brother told me key words the Others use when talking about the girls. Since he was the one who told me, I thought it would be okay to tell you."

She'd been shaken last night when she'd arrived home, had needed to talk to someone. She didn't tell Barb about Virgil's threat. She hadn't wanted anyone to know because she had to work past it. Gods, did she have to work past it or she'd be a wreck before she'd been on the job a week.

"Look," she said. "If Virgil or Tolya thinks Maddie is in any kind of danger from neighbors, even if it's just people acting too curious or asking too many questions, they'll take the girl away."

"You mean relocate the family?"

Jana shook her head. "The other children would be relocated, separately or together. The dads wouldn't survive."

Barb stared straight ahead. "Someone will figure it out."

Jana nodded. "But I don't want the blame for that landing on our doorstep. Okay?"

"Okay. But . . . Abby is really nice."

"Burch is her married name, right?"

"Yes."

"Who was she before she married Kelley?"

"I don't know."

"And that's the problem, isn't it?" Jana glanced at Barb. "This is a fresh start, a new beginning, call it whatever you want. But that means we don't know who people were before they arrived in Bennett."

Barb slumped in the seat. "I don't want to think like that. I don't want to talk to people and wonder what they're hiding."

"I know. I'm sorry. And you don't have to wonder. Just don't tell anyone about Maddie."

"Did you think being a police officer would be like this? I used to tease Michael about running background checks on my dates, but now I wonder if he did."

Probably, Jana thought.

"So did you think it would be like this?"

I will tear out the throats of those two humans—and then I'll tear out yours.

"No," Jana said. "I really didn't think it would be like this."

Standing at the gate of the fenced-in yard that held the dogs to be adopted, Tobias scratched and petted the dogs who came up to greet him while he waited for the almost-vet who was taking care of the animals.

"I appreciate you giving me a job. I learn fast," Edna "Ed" Tilman said.

Everything he'd sensed about this new hand indicated that she wanted to be one of the boys, but Tobias still gave her a smile that said clear enough that he was the boss and she was one of his men—and he hoped he wasn't wrong about her and would end up actually having to say he wasn't going to allow them to be anything more. His mother hadn't voiced any concerns about the girl when he'd introduced them. Ed wanted to work on a ranch as one of the hands and not as household help. She'd been real clear about that. She'd demonstrated her ability to ride a horse and lasso animals in a corral. Whether she'd really thought about what it was like to spend a day in the saddle was anyone's guess.

Then again, working with someone who wasn't an Intuit was like learning a different language, so maybe he had been hearing flirting where there was only nerves and enthusiasm. They'd all find out soon enough, and Ellen Garcia, who took care of the Prairie Gold ranch house and the accounts, would take the girl in hand—one way or another.

Funny how he understood the Wolves who were in charge of the *terra indigene* settlement near Prairie Gold better than he understood other kinds of humans. He understood Virgil Wolfgard too, and Morgan Wolfgard had told him enough about Virgil and Kane for him to appreciate why they were an asset to Tolya Sanguinati and a danger to the humans settling in Bennett.

As a sheriff's department vehicle pulled up, Tobias and Ed turned away from the enclosed yard full of barking, excited dogs. The passenger hopped out and rushed toward them.

"Tobias Walker? I'm Barb Debany. Tolya said you wanted to adopt some dogs and cats?"

"Yes, ma'am." He looked at the other woman getting out of the vehicle. Glossy brown hair pulled back in a tail. Brown eyes that held friendliness and wariness in equal measure. Trim figure. And the gun attached to her belt and the badge pinned to her shirt made her that much more interesting. Since she wasn't the sheriff . . . "Deputy . . . ?"

"Jana Paniccia."

"Mr. Walker is going to adopt some of the dogs and cats and take them to the ranches," Barb said, pulling a set of keys out of her purse. "Hush up all of you and look adorable."

Since she'd raised her voice, he assumed she was talking to the dogs and not the people. Even so, he was looking for working dogs, not adorable puffballs. Having been one of the humans who had freed the trapped dogs and set up the feeding stations, he knew most of the dogs wouldn't suit his needs or the needs of the people on the other ranches. And his mother, who had agreed to take a dog on a trial basis—the trial being that the dog could get along with Rachel Wolfgard and vice versa—wasn't interested in a puffball either. Jesse Walker was not a puffball kind of woman.

"Well, I'm going to take a look, anyway," he said. "Looking for barn cats mostly, and dogs that can earn their keep on a ranch, one way or another."

"Then let's look at the cats first." Barb led them to the single-story house next door.

As Tobias held the door open to let the women go in first, he noticed the deputy eyeing his revolver. "Sheriff Wolfgard and Tolya Sanguinati gave me special permission to wear a weapon in town."

She nodded as she entered the house ahead of him, but he wasn't sure if that was acknowledgment of information she already had or that she'd be checking with the sheriff to confirm his statement. In her place, he sure would.

The cats had the run of the living room, and despite living around animals, he wasn't sure he'd want to take over this house after the animals were relocated.

"I'm doing most of the sorting in the rooms that weren't cleared out before we turned the place into a pet hotel," Barb said. "Turns out some people are allergic enough to cats that handling something like books from a house that had cats is enough to cause a reaction. So everything that's left in this house that can't be washed has to be boxed and labeled and stored in a separate location from the rest of the goods. The birds are in a house across the street." She looked at Ed. "Would you like a bird?"

"Ed is a ranch hand. She won't be at the ranch house every day to look after a bird," Tobias said. But he turned the thought over in his mind and wondered if Ellen Garcia would enjoy the chirp and chatter. He'd mention it to her and take a look next time he was in town if she didn't want to come up to Bennett herself.

He had a good feeling about four of the cats, that they would be happy being barn cats and partially fending for themselves by hunting mice. Barb Debany found carriers for each of them. The cats weren't pleased about the confinement, but they didn't cause too much fuss after Barb gave each of them a catnip toy as a distraction.

The cats he could take or leave. At the Prairie Gold ranch, Ellen Garcia was the one who had a soft spot for the barn cats. But the dogs crowding around him when they returned to the house next door made him sad. They were good dogs that just wanted to be loved.

Or wanted a job.

Spotting two border collies, Tobias raised a hand and watched the dogs snap to attention, ready to follow his command. When he lowered his hand and started to turn toward Barb, he could feel them accusing him of dashing their hopes.

"You have any leashes handy?" he asked.

Barb nodded. "I'll get them." She returned a minute later with a handful of leashes.

Talk about hopeful.

He let out a sharp whistle, then said, "Sit!" and watched half the dogs obey the command. Taking four of the leashes, he said, "Stay!" before walking over to the border collies and clipping leashes to their collars. These two would go with Truman Skye, who had experience working with the cattle dogs on the Prairie Gold ranch.

He eyed the rest of the dogs and decided, with regret, that he couldn't see them with the Simple Life women who would be keeping house on the other three ranches. Jesse's vehemence about which Simple Life woman would be working for Truman meant he couldn't assume the other women would provide a good home for a dog. Didn't mean they weren't good people; they just weren't the right people for these dogs.

He almost gave the release command when he noticed one young female—white with rust-colored ears and saddle—who had obeyed his command to sit but wasn't focused on him. She was focused on Jana Paniccia and was struggling to obey the stay command when she clearly wanted to rush over and make friends.

Giving the release command, Tobias waded through the dogs until he reached the deputy. "You looking for a dog to ride shotgun?"

"I've been thinking about adopting one of the dogs, but I'll mostly be on horseback when I'm on duty," Jana replied, petting the dog, who had reached her first.

Tobias crouched and studied the young bitch. Not more than a few months old. Lots of energy. She would be a good fit for the deputy, and she'd be a good fit with the right horse. Question was, was Deputy Paniccia riding the right horse?

He handed Jana one of the leashes. "She'll suit you."

"You can tell that, can you?" Jana asked dryly.

"Yes, ma'am, I can. I have a feel for animals."

"Feel? You're an Intuit?"

"Yes, ma'am."

She gave him an assessing look. "What about Wolves? Do you have a feel for the snarlies?"

If she hadn't looked ashamed for saying that, he wouldn't have answered. "That's a conversation for another time and place," he said quietly. "But I can tell you that if you use a disrespectful word for someone when you think about them, sooner or later you're going to slip up and say it out loud, maybe even within the individual's hearing, and whatever trust you had built will be gone and you will never get it back."

"I know that—and I know better. Heard enough disrespectful words thrown in my direction when I was at the police academy, and I swore I wouldn't do that to someone else. But he's so *frustrating*."

He'd known her for only a few minutes, but the way she moved and the look in her eyes told him Jana Paniccia had pluck, so he didn't need to ask *whom* she found frustrating. And he didn't doubt for a moment that Virgil found his new deputy equally frustrating. Only thing was, if pushed, Virgil would do more than bruise feelings. "Well, you're thinking like a human, and he's thinking like a Wolf. And not just a Wolf— he's the *dominant* Wolf and you're part of his pack."

"So I should learn my place?"

Tobias nodded. "Sooner you do that, the better you'll get along with him." He looked over at a couple of playpens set up in a spot that had been shady but was rapidly changing to full sun. "I have to get people and critters settled today, but I'll come back tomorrow and we'll have that talk."

"All right. Thanks."

"Hold them for a minute." He gave Jana the border collies' leashes before he walked over to the playpens, which held the puppies. A few were youngsters barely weaned. But there was one . . . Still had her puppy fuzz, but old enough to have been housebroken—he hoped. He picked her up and cuddled her against his chest while she desperately tried to give him kisses.

He wasn't sure if she was a particular breed or a mongrel. Didn't matter. There was something about this one that gave him a strong feeling that she was the right one.

"Want to come with me and meet my mother?" he whispered.

Wag wag. Kiss kiss.

"Ms. Debany? I'll need a collar for this one."

Barb Debany studied the pup. "I'll get a collar and a harness. That might work better. The storage place has dog beds and crates and whatever else you'll need." She dashed inside and returned a minute later with a choice of collars and harnesses.

He got the puppy fitted out, collected the border collies, loaded up the cats, and left Barb Debany to do her routine feeding and cleanup, while Deputy Paniccia drove off with her new friend. As he and Ed drove to the building that was serving as a warehouse for household goods and was supposed to have everything the dogs would need, he wondered if his mother was going to take one look at the puppy and then pick up her rifle and shoot him.

* * *

Pulling up in front of the household goods warehouse, Jana looked at the dog curled up on the seat beside her. She needed to pick up what Rusty would need but couldn't leave the dog in the vehicle. She could go to the office and put Rusty in the Me Time cell, but she didn't want Virgil or Kane to find the dog before she got back—and she didn't want to imagine what she might find when she got back if she did leave Rusty alone in the office before she told the Wolves she had adopted the dog.

"Deputy?"

She looked at the man who had helped her load up her household goods that morning. "Could you help me?"

"Sure. What do you need?" Then he laughed as Rusty climbed into Jana's lap to sniff the stranger. "Ooooh. Barb roped you into adopting one?"

Jana put an arm around Rusty. "This one did the roping." With some help from a good-looking Intuit rancher. "I wasn't thinking about the logistics of getting her things after getting her."

"You need everything?" he asked.

"Doubled. One for home and one for work."

He raised his eyebrows. "You're bringing her to work? Will . . . *they* . . . agree to that?"

"They will." She hoped.

He studied Rusty a moment longer. "I'll be back in a few minutes."

And he was, with two crates for a medium-size dog, bowls for food and water, and a sack that held who knew what else.

"We don't keep food here," he said when he finished loading up the back of the vehicle. "I called the feed store since the people working there are collecting animal food from the houses. They'll bring some over to the sheriff's office. Not sure if you'll be expected to pay for it since it's not food for you, but you'll figure it out."

"Thanks for your help." Jana drove to the sheriff's office and parked. Then she looked at Rusty, all bright, hopeful eyes and wagging tail. "I sure hope Virgil doesn't look at you and think I brought him lunch. Stay."

Getting out and closing the door before Rusty could follow, she hurried to open the back and get the crate out.

"What's that?"

Jana jerked in surprise, then looked over her shoulder at Yuri Sanguinati. "It's a crate."

"And that?" He pointed at Rusty, who was climbing into the back.

"That's a dog."

Yuri looked at Rusty, looked at the crate, and finally looked at the sheriff's office. Grinning wide enough to show his fangs, he lifted the crate out of the vehicle and said, "You get the rest."

"I could have done that," Jana said. She could not afford to appear weak.

"I'm sure you could, but it would have been hard to open the office door if you were holding this instead of the smaller items."

Practical, not condescending. She hadn't realized she had such a big chip on her shoulder, had to stop hearing the echoes of instructors and fellow cadets telling her she wasn't strong enough to be a cop. She had been hired for this job because Simon Wolfgard had seen something in her that he thought would suit this town and the sheriff. She'd better start showing everyone she was worthy of being hired.

"Thanks. I hadn't intended to pick up a dog today. It's thrown me off stride." She hurried to open the door and point to the spot near her desk where the crate could go. By the time she dumped the bowls and sack on the floor and rushed out to fetch the dog, who was barking like crazy, she discovered the Others, in the form of a big-ass Hawk, had already found her new friend. Or found something of interest. It seemed to be ignoring the dog—which was good—as it worked out how to open the other crate.

That was not good. Some of the dogs Barb looked after were Hawk-size meals, and if Hawks or Eagles learned how to open the crates . . .

Jana opened the passenger door, picked up Rusty, who squirmed and barked to warn everyone that there was danger, danger, *danger*, and took her inside the office. Sliding the leash's loop up a leg of one of the visitors' chairs, she hurried out to her vehicle—where the Hawk was now comfortably perched on the tailgate, surveying the part of the town square that was visible from the sheriff's office.

"I have to close up the vehicle now," Jana said.

The Hawk eyed her, and she wondered if this one could shift to a human form that she would recognize as a new resident of Bennett or if this was one of the *terra indigene* who couldn't—or wouldn't—take a form so many of them considered an enemy rather than just a rival predator.

The Hawk flew over to a recently installed hitching post at the edge of the square. Several hitching posts had been added to accommodate the horses and horse-drawn conveyances. Around the square, the grassy side was now parking for horses, mules, and donkeys. The building side of the street was parking for cars. So far there weren't many horses or cars coming into the business district, but having both using the streets was a concern that should be brought to the town council.

Jana returned to the office and to Rusty, who seemed frantically glad to see her. Crouching to give pats and reassurance, Jana said, "It's all right. It's all right. Now, you need to be good, okay? And you'll need to stay in your crate when I'm working. But once you get used to being with me, you'll be able to come out more. Now, I'm just going in the back to fill your water bowl." She needed to put in her hour working with her horse, which was considered part of her workday since she had to become a sufficiently capable rider to handle her duties as a mounted deputy. And she'd better check e-mail before she slipped up on something important.

She grabbed the water bowl and dashed into the back part of the office to fill it.

Rusty barked. Bark, bark . . .

Silence.

Leaving the bowl on the counter near the kitchen sink, Jana returned to the front of the office and froze. Kane, in Wolf form, and Virgil, in human form, stared at Rusty, who was doing her best to hide under the chair.

Smart dog.

"Sheriff." Jana's heart pounded as Virgil walked past her and went into his office. Since Virgil wasn't going to talk to her, she took a step toward Kane, whose attention remained focused on the dog. "Her name is Rusty. I adopted her. I was going to talk to the sheriff about . . ."

That was as far as she got before Virgil, now a massive Wolf, came out of his office and brushed past her.

"Sheriff . . . Virgil . . ."

Virgil knocked the chair halfway across the room and was on the dog before Jana could draw another breath. Poor Rusty yelped and tried to run, but Virgil's jaws closed over the dog's neck, forcing her down before he released her neck and used a paw to push her over on her back. As soon as she exposed her belly, he stood over her, her body between his big front paws.

"Stop it," Jana said fiercely. *Oh gods, please don't kill her just because you don't like me.*

Virgil ignored her. When he finally stepped back, Rusty scrambled to roll and run, but Kane was on her before she got her feet under her. Same forced submission.

Furious but afraid to do anything that would provoke something more lethal than this bullying, Jana held back and watched—and resisted the urge to draw her weapon.

When Kane released Rusty, Virgil moved into position, keeping the dog between them. And then . . .

Rusty timidly wagged her tail. And Virgil and Kane wagged their tails. An understated wag, to be sure, but it seemed to encourage Rusty to quietly submit to being sniffed while she licked them. And then . . .

Done. Virgil returned to his office. Kane went outside. Jana lunged, grabbing Rusty's leash before the dog could dash outside and flee.

"Come here, girl. Good girl. You stay with me. Come over here." Coaxing, Jana half led, half carried Rusty to the crate and put her inside before unclipping the leash and securing the door. Dropping the leash, she stormed into Virgil's office, too mad and scared to think until she saw him adjusting himself before he zipped up the jeans.

"What?" Virgil said.

"Why did you do that? She's young and—"

"She's yours now?" he interrupted.

"Yes!"

Virgil reached for the checked shirt. Blue today. "Then it's important for her to know her place in the pack. It will keep her safe."

Jana stared at him. He sounded so unconcerned, so matter-of-fact.

Virgil returned her stare. Jana lowered her eyes and stepped to one side when he approached. He walked out of the office, buttoning his shirt, then stopped when he reached her desk and the crate nearby.

"That is like a den for her when we aren't around?" he asked.

"Yes." Scrambling to adjust her thinking, she added, "I just picked her up, so it's better for her to stay crated or on a leash until she gets to know me—to know us."

He considered that. "You should let her out to sniff around so that she recognizes the scent of her new territory."

"I will. I'll let her settle down first." *And give myself a chance to stop shaking inside.*

"When Kane comes back, you should ride the horse. Then she will still have pack nearby and know she's not alone." Virgil gave Jana one sharp look before leaving the sheriff's office.

Jana collapsed into her chair and remembered Tobias Walker's words: *You're thinking like a human, and he's thinking like a Wolf.*

Could it be that simple? This was her third day on the job, and she'd been angry about having all the desk work dumped on her, had been angry about Virgil walking her around the square like some inadequate pet while he made the rounds. Even when he'd scared her yesterday, she'd been thinking of him as a human male sending the message that she couldn't be a cop on her own, but what if she considered his actions from the point of view of her being part of the pack? Virgil was domi-nant. Even in human form, Virgil was darn scary. In Wolf form . . . She wouldn't want to see him coming after her. Kane was next, being the senior deputy, not to mention being a Wolf. That made her third in the pack. That didn't make her *less*; it was simply her place. And the typ-ing and filing and handling the e-mails? Her ability to do those things were human skills she was providing for the benefit of the pack, like Virgil's and Kane's superior sense of smell and ability to track because they were Wolves. Like their ability to communicate with other *terra indigene* even when those beings weren't in human form.

Virgil hadn't thrown her down and rolled her on her back, forcing submission the way he'd done with Rusty, but had he been sending clear, to him, signals that she needed to acknowledge his dominance and her place in the pack?

Jana went into the kitchen and returned with the bowl of water. She opened the crate door enough to let Rusty have a drink and managed to close it before the dog could escape. Then she turned on the computer and checked the e-mails.

More there than she expected. There were probably a ton of e-mails sent to the previous occupants of the sheriff's office, but she didn't know the username or password. Maybe there was someone in town now who had the computer skills to get access to those e-mail accounts or just eliminate them.

Rummaging in her desk, she found a notebook. Dating the top of the page, she wrote a summary of each e-mail, putting a big star in front of the time-sensitive ones—like the meeting of the town council that Tolya Sanguinati had called for tomorrow afternoon. She printed that one out and put it on Virgil's desk. She could show him the others if he wanted to read the full text.

The only message that gave her a moment's pause was from someone named Jackson Wolfgard, who was located in a place called Sweetwater. He asked for confirmation that this was the correct e-mail address to reach Virgil and Kane Wolfgard and also asked for confirmation of the phone number.

Jana hesitated. The name Wolfgard meant he was a *terra indigene* Wolf, but being a Wolf didn't mean he was a friend. Still, this was a public e-mail address and phone for the sheriff's office, and other communities should know how to contact them.

She replied to the request for information, signing the e-mail as Deputy Jana Paniccia, Bennett Sheriff's Department. Before pushing the SEND button, she copied the e-mail to Tolya Sanguinati. Having finished that administrative task, she sat back and considered what her role as the human deputy could be.

Jesse eyed her son, who was holding a fuzzy gray puppy against his chest, the fingers lightly scratching the pup's neck and shoulders. Damn him, but he'd always known which critter would tug at her heart if he brought it home. Didn't mean she wouldn't put up some resistance.

"When I said I'd consider adopting a dog, I didn't mean I wanted to raise a baby." She gave Tobias a stern look.

"But she needs a mom." Tobias looked at the pup, then looked at Jesse. "I already took her to the vet and had him look her over. She's weaned, and the vet gave her the shots she needs right now."

"Weaned doesn't mean housebroken."

"No, but she'll learn fast. She's got a real good brain inside that small head. And given her age . . ."

Jesse drew in a breath. "Weaned" meant older than eight weeks, but the puppy still had the baby fuzz. The pup would have been born shortly before the Elders and Elementals had torn through the continent of Thaisia, wiping out the entire human population in some towns—like Bennett. So there hadn't been anyone to teach the pup.

"Where is her mother, her littermates?" she asked, trying to resist reaching for the furball just a little bit longer.

"Don't know," Tobias replied. "Didn't see a bitch hanging around the puppy pens Barb Debany had set up. Didn't see any other pups around her age."

Giving in, Jesse held out her hands. "Let's see her."

To give him credit, Tobias didn't smile, didn't indicate in any way that he'd known this would happen. Of course he'd known. He had a feel for animals, just like she had a feel for people.

"Rachel can be an honorary big sister," Tobias said.

"Don't push it." Wolves cared about the pups in their pack, but Jesse wasn't sure how a juvenile Wolf would react to a young dog.

"Did you think to pick up what this one will need?"

"Yep." Now Tobias grinned. "Want me to put it in your car? I have to be heading out to help Truman move to the Skye Ranch and make a list of the folks who will be working for him. Then I'm heading to the Prairie Gold ranch to get my own new workers settled and introduced to Ellen and Tom Garcia."

"Have you decided on what to do with the girl? She can't bunk with the men."

"Tom and Ellen have their own cabin behind the main house, so the housekeeper's suite is available. Figured I would talk to Ellen about putting Ed there."

Jesse hesitated. She didn't have any concerns about the girl, but the distance between living in a Northeast community, no matter how small, and living within sight of the Elder Hills—and knowing what lived there—was a distance of more than miles. And the reality could easily change expectations.

"Having her work for you instead of other Simple Life folks who might resent her breaking away from traditional roles is good of you, but you should be careful that she doesn't start thinking that being given use of the housekeeper's suite is a step toward sharing the master bedroom." Being the only single woman on the ranch would garner the girl plenty of attention.

"I get the feeling that Ed is looking for the freedom to be one of the boys rather than someone's missus." Tobias raised his eyebrows. "Don't you?"

Put that way . . . Smiling, Jesse studied her son—and felt an interesting tingle. Even if Ed hadn't wanted to be one of the boys, Tobias wouldn't be looking in her direction. "Something else before you haul this one's supplies to my car?"

"What do you know about the new deputy?"

The boy was about as subtle as getting whacked with a two-by-four when he was trying to act as if his interest in the answer was casual to the point of indifferent. Tobias was never indifferent when it came to people or critters.

"She arrived on Sunday, started work on Windsday, and despite some grumbles and growling, she and Virgil haven't had a full-blown fight. Yet." Although she had the feeling that *something* had happened between them when they escorted that mixed family to the hotel.

Tobias looked concerned. "You think that's likely?"

Jesse thought for a moment. Morgan and Chase Wolfgard, the new leader and dominant enforcer of the Prairie Gold pack, had come from a pack that had been too far from human settlements to be found by the Humans First and Last movement when those men had slaughtered other Wolf packs. They left their home pack because they were needed in the *terra indigene* settlement at the southern end of the Elder Hills. But Virgil . . .

"Were you told about Virgil?" Jesse asked. She wasn't sure who had decided to make Virgil the sheriff. It hadn't been Tolya. He'd been given orders and had to deal with the result as best he could. She did know Virgil was the reason Tolya had wanted a human deputy to be hired to work in Bennett.

"I know about him. Don't think Deputy Paniccia was told." He didn't meet her eyes. "I'm coming back tomorrow to look over the horse she chose. I have a feeling it's not the right one for her."

"Why don't you help her choose a dog?" Jesse suggested dryly as the puppy tried to squirm out of her arms and sniff whatever was in reach.

Tobias grinned. "I already did."

In Wolf form, Virgil and Kane roamed some of the residential streets of their territory. Old human scents. They found the carcasses of a couple of the roaming dogs—and they found the fresh scent of some Elders on a blue post office box at an intersection that was part of the new boundary for human settlers. They both marked the box on the opposite side, acknowledging the boundary.

Easy enough for them to scent the line between where humans would be watched but not harmed as long as they themselves did nothing harmful, and that one step that would put them in the wild country, regardless of the houses on the street. But humans wouldn't be able to tell where the boundaries were.

They turned a corner and Virgil stopped when he spotted Tolya Sanguinati standing in front of a house in the middle of the block, talking with Saul Panthergard and Joshua Painter.

<What?> Kane asked.

Instead of answering, Virgil headed for the Sanguinati.

A shift in the wind direction had Saul turning toward them before the other two males noticed his approach.

<Where is the sweet blood?> Virgil asked.

Tolya gestured toward a house a few doors down on the opposite side of the street. <Barbara Ellen is looking after the children while the adults in that pack look over this house.>

<Then you found a den for them?>

<Joshua Painter says this house has no stain of darkness and will not torment the sweet blood. The adults are looking it over to make sure it has all that their pack needs in other ways.>

Had the *terra indigene* known that sweet bloods could be tormented by a place? Did Simon Wolfgard know that? Or had Broomstick Girl

simply found a comfortable den and settled in at the Lakeside Courtyard? What about the pup living with Jackson Wolfgard?

In both those cases, the sweet blood had been given a den among the
terra indigene instead of claiming a den that previously had belonged to
humans. Maybe that was the reason this search was different.

Or maybe the choice of den was more important because this pup
couldn't howl and would suffer in silence.

<I'll check the rest of the street,> Kane said.

Virgil ignored the comment. He'd seen the small bus pull up. When
the door opened and the Jacob pup leaped out ahead of the rest of the
Gott pack, he knew why Kane was heading that way. If one of them kept
watch over the Becky girl, the adult females would have time to make
food for the pack while the boy pup could run and play and the Becky
girl could explore a bit around the family den.

The adult males, Kenneth and Evan, came out of the house.

"As far as we can tell, the house looks solid," Kenneth said. "All the
appliances are in good condition. There are bunk beds in one room that
will work for the boys." He stopped and swallowed hard.

"There is a room that would work well for the girls, but we would
need to find two single beds," Evan said. "And it would be less . . . emotional . . . if we could remove all the personal belongings quickly."

"That might be possible," Tolya said. "I will let you know tomorrow.
Are you saying you will take this house?"

The men looked at each other, then nodded.

"Very well. I'll draw up the papers." Tolya looked at the small bus.
"The driver is waiting for you. You should gather your young and go
back to the hotel now."

Virgil watched the men walk down the street. <So the sweet blood is
going to live within sight of Barbara Ellen and the wolverine?>

Tolya made a sputtery sound. <The wolverine? Deputy Jana is human.>

<Are you sure? If her mother had mated with one of the Weaselgard,
she could have been the result.>

<Even if her mother had mated with one in his human form, humans
and *terra indigene* are different species. We can't mate and produce offspring.>

<I know.> Virgil huffed. <But if her mother *had* and we *could*, that would explain so much about *her*.> He could tear out Jana Paniccia's throat before she could blink, but she still filled a room with attitude: *I might be smaller, but I can take you.* If that wasn't a wolverine, what was?

And wasn't she going to howl about what he'd decided?

<The house at the corner,> he said.

<What about it?>

<The Wolves will make it their den now.>

Tolya studied him. <Why?>

Virgil studied the Sanguinati in turn. <Will the Sanguinati claim a house?>

Tolya smiled. <We will. We have already claimed two in different parts of the town. Yuri will reside in this one. I am arranging for humans who know how to inspect houses to look at the other ones the Sanguinati have claimed. They can look at yours too.>

The stink of humans in his den? <Very well.>

<Ravens will take one house on this street, Eagles another.>

<The sweet blood will be protected.>

<Yes, she will.>

CHAPTER 19

Watersday, Messis 18

Tobias set the nozzle into its slot on the pump and winced at the total cost. At this rate, he was pouring his pay into the pickup's gas tank. Sure, the gas station was running a tab so that anyone from the Prairie Gold ranch could fill up here in Bennett, but more new people coming into the town meant more vehicles would be put back on the roads—and if he wasn't careful, those people could come to resent the Prairie Gold folks for being given special treatment when it came to some rationed goods like gasoline.

"Good morning, Mr. Walker." Tolya Sanguinati approached him, having come from . . . somewhere. "I thought all the new employees had gone to their assigned ranches yesterday."

"They did. I'm not concerned about the old Black ranch, which is now the Skye Ranch. Truman's a good man, and he knows the importance of being a good neighbor." Truman had been with him the day Joe Wolfgard had told them about the Elders, the day they had *seen* a half-grown bison being carried away from the animals that had been slaughtered by the Humans First and Last movement. Had seen the bison, anyway. The human eye couldn't see the *terra indigene* in their true form, couldn't detect anything more than what could be mistaken as a shimmer of heat. "I came back this morning to help Deputy Paniccia choose a horse."

"I thought she had a horse. She is at the stable now, riding it."

"She needs the right horse." Unsettled, Tobias removed his hat, ran his fingers through his hair, then put the hat back on. "I'll make it a point from now on to fill the truck before I leave Prairie Gold when I'm coming up for personal business."

"Choosing the right horse would be important for Deputy Paniccia to fulfill her duties?" Tolya asked.

"I think so." How much did the *terra indigene* understand about human romance? Especially when a man wasn't sure if his interest would be reciprocated?

"Then I think this tank of gas should go under the column for town business." Tolya smiled and walked away, leaving Tobias to wonder if the Sanguinati, at least, understood more about humans than humans realized.

Jana rode round and round the corral and felt keenly disappointed. She was riding a horse, which was what she wanted. She would be a mounted deputy, which was what she wanted. But she felt like a little girl riding a pony in a ring while the grown-ups stood on the other side of the rails smiling and nodding indulgently.

And now there was Tobias Walker standing with the men who were in charge of the livery stable, and wasn't that just perfect? She knew she was a beginner, but she hated looking foolish. And she hated feeling disappointed when she and the bay circled round again and she realized Tobias wasn't standing there anymore.

Then Tobias walked out of the stable with a caramel-colored horse and headed for the corral at the same moment the bay bolted to the far end of the corral. Jana grabbed the saddle horn and managed to hang on instead of landing in the dirt, but it was a near thing.

"Dismount and bring him over," Tobias said as he opened the gate and led his horse into the corral.

Embarrassed and shaky, Jana dismounted and tried to lead the bay, but the horse wasn't having it.

Dropping his horse's reins, Tobias walked over to them, grabbed the reins under the bay's chin, and said firmly, "That's enough of that. If he was going to hurt you, he'd have done it by now." Tobias led the bay to the rail and tied him before returning to the other horse. Then he wagged a finger at Jana.

Jana moved slowly, trying to figure out who the *he* was that might be doing the hurting. Not seeing anyone except the Simple Life and Intuit men who had been watching her ride, she approached Tobias.

"This is Mel," Tobias said.

"Is that short for Caramel?" she asked.

Tobias grinned. He was amused, but she didn't feel like he was laughing at her.

"I can see how you might think that, with him being a buckskin. But, no, Mel isn't short for anything. Mount up and I'll adjust the stirrups for you."

Mel snuffled her, then gave her a shove that knocked her back a step.

"Mind your manners, boy," Tobias said sternly. Then to her, "He's a gelding with a stallion's ego. He expects to be petted and praised." A beat of silence before he added, "Much like the rest of us."

Was he flirting with her? Did she want to flirt back? Time to sort that out later. Right now, she had another male demanding her attention.

"Hello, Mel." Jana stroked the horse's nose before running a hand along his neck beneath the black mane. "You are handsome, aren't you?"

Mel tossed his head as if agreeing with her.

"Mount up, Deputy."

She hesitated, looking over her shoulder at the bay. "I have a horse."

"And he's a good horse," Tobias agreed. "But not the right horse. You're going to be answering calls and providing assistance in a town that's just a kiss away from the Elder Hills. You need more than a horse. You need a partner. And . . ."

The bay snorted and fought the reins tying him to the rail.

"I'll bring him in," one of the men said, ducking between the rails.

"No, just stay with him until I get Deputy Paniccia settled." Tobias looked at Jana. "That right there is a big reason why the bay isn't the right horse for you." He nodded at Mel, whose ears were pricked and whose attention was on something outside the corral.

Jana looked in that direction.

Virgil in Wolf form stared back at her.

"Mel and your coworkers have made friends," Tobias said. "He's not going to spook if one of them is running with you or approaches you when you're on horseback. And he was bred from Prairie Gold stock and has been running on land like this his whole life. He'll listen to you, but you have to listen to him too when he's telling you there's something around that could be trouble."

Jana mounted, then waited while Tobias adjusted the stirrups and handed her the reins. As soon as she gathered the reins and held them as she'd been taught, Mel walked over to the rails where Virgil waited. Horse and Wolf did their greeting snuffle-sniffs.

"Time to work," Tobias said.

Mel's head came up. Ears wagged forward and back.

"Take him in a circle at a walk," Tobias said. "And stay away from the bay for now."

She'd been told the bay was a good horse for a beginner, but riding Mel was a totally different experience. They moved together, so smooth and easy.

"Jog," Tobias called.

Before she could give Mel any signals, the horse began to jog in response to Tobias's command. This wasn't the pounding that made her wonder if she'd lose her ability to control her bladder by the time she was thirty; this was an easy cruising speed that gave her time to observe what was around her.

"Lope."

Again, Mel obeyed before she did, and she felt the reality that matched what she'd always imagined it would be like to ride a horse. She could see herself riding across the open spaces and . . .

"Walk."

Mel immediately dropped to a walk, jolting Jana out of her happy fantasy. She beamed at Tobias—and noticed Virgil standing on his hind legs, one paw on the rails for balance, watching her from the other side of the corral.

Tobias stepped away from the rails. "You two get acquainted while I deal with the bay."

She discovered that 'deal with the bay' meant adjusting the stirrups and mounting. The bay seemed fine, calm, the easygoing horse she'd ridden for the past couple of days—until Tobias aimed the horse toward the front of the corral . . . and Virgil.

"He's afraid," she said, worried that Tobias would hurt the horse.

Tobias reined in. "Yep, he is. That's no reflection on him. He's obeying instincts that would keep him safe in most situations. But it also means he's not trusting his rider to tell him it's okay to ignore those instincts, and you can't be out there on a horse that can't trust you. Which is why you're going to ride Mel." He dismounted and handed the bay to one of the livery men. Then he walked past her, opened the gate, and smiled. "You aren't going to learn enough riding in circles in a corral. Time to go out there and learn how to ride."

"But . . ."

"The town square runs the length of the business district. You can circle around that a few times and get the feel of moving through trees and on grass. Get the feel of riding past people and the *terra indigene*. I'll see what else they have in the stable and join you, if I may."

"I'd appreciate that."

"Go on, then. I'll catch up."

The moment Mel's feet touched the grass in the square, Jana felt the change in him, as if he'd been bored before and now he wasn't. She understood the feeling.

"We're still walking," she told him when she felt him gather himself for something a little more speedy. One ear swiveled back at the sound of her voice, but his attention was still on something ahead of them.

A moment later, Barb Debany and her blue-roan gelding, Rowan, cut across the square and jumped the little creek.

"They let you out of the corral," Barb said, turning Rowan to walk beside Mel.

"Tobias Walker has a different opinion about how a person should learn," Jana replied.

Barb admired Mel. "What happened to the bay?"

"Tobias had opinions about that too, and now I have a new riding partner. And it looks like Mel and Rowan are barn buddies."

Barb laughed. "Didn't think of it that way, but it sure looks like it."

Now that they were riding together, the horses seemed content to keep to an active walk.

"You're not wearing your six-gun," Barb said when they turned at the end of the square. She waved at three children playing in the little garden next to the Universal Temple. They waved back.

"I left it at the office. Figured that was better than accidentally shooting me or the horse."

"You'll have to ride and carry when you're officially on duty, right?"

"Right." She'd worry about that later. Better yet, she'd ask Tobias about riding while wearing a gun.

"You girls out for an Earthday stroll, or are you out to ride?" Tobias asked as he rode up to join them.

"Rowan and I are cooling down from our ride," Barb replied. "I was just keeping Jana company until you got here." She grinned at Jana. "See you later." Then she mouthed, *Or not.*

Feeling her face heat, Jana shortened the reins before Mel decided to follow his buddy.

"Warmed up now?" Tobias asked.

She nodded. She knew he meant the horse, but, yeah, she was feeling plenty warm right now. As the town's only female—and human—deputy, she couldn't afford to gain a reputation for being an easy ride, and she wasn't sure if Tobias had caught Barb's silent, teasing remark.

"Then let's ride."

For the next half hour, they jogged and loped and circled and changed directions. They stopped and backed up. Jana was pretty sure she wasn't more than a passenger and Mel was following Tobias's commands, but she learned how it felt to be on a horse that was moving over ground that wasn't a corral. Finally they were circling the town square at a walk, giving the horses a long rein to stretch their necks.

Tobias smiled. "Pretty good for your first time out."

"Mel did all the work."

"You have all your gear? I noticed you weren't riding with it in the corral."

Jana frowned at him in puzzlement. "Gear?"

Tobias shook his head and sighed. "Well, it's all farm folk and city folk who have come to town, so I guess it's not surprising that no one told you what you should have out here."

Jana's eyes widened as he listed the things she should be carrying with her. "I'm riding a horse, not driving a car with an empty backseat."

"You'd be surprised what you can fit into saddlebags."

"And the rope?"

Tobias eyed her. "Do you know how to use a lasso?"

"As in, rope that cow?"

"Or that bank robber—unless he's got a gun, which is likely. But you never know when you might need to throw a rope over something or someone."

"Another skill I didn't learn."

"Hard to learn a skill without a teacher."

"Are you offering to teach me?"

"I surely am. How about this afternoon? I'm in town today but need to get back to the ranch and put in some time there, especially since I've got some new hands to break in."

"I have to be at this town council meeting early this afternoon, but I'm free after that."

"Don't get in trouble with your boss on account of me."

Jana looked around. "Speaking of my boss, you had something to tell me?" After dealing with Virgil for the past couple of days, she needed all the information she could get.

Tobias looked away and said nothing until they rode past the sheriff's office and were out of earshot—of anything she could see, anyway.

"Regular wolves have an alpha pair," he said quietly. "They're the ones who mate, and the pack works together to raise those pups. Can't really afford to have more than one litter of pups to feed. But the *terra indigene* don't follow the traits and behavior of the predators whose forms they absorb, not right down the line. With the Wolfgard, the dominant pair will mate and the pack will raise those pups. But the following year, if the dominant enforcer in the pack has a mate, *they'll* be the ones who breed and the pack will help raise their pups.

"Virgil was the dominant enforcer in his pack and Kane was another enforcer. They had been out tracking something—prey or adversary, I don't know which. But they weren't with the rest of their pack when men in the Humans First and Last movement targeted the pack and killed all of them. Even the pups." Tobias said nothing for a moment. "I have the feeling that Virgil isn't proud of being able to shift to human form well enough to almost pass for human. But he was offered the job of being the dominant enforcer for this large mixed pack, and he accepted. That doesn't mean he feels any tolerance for humans."

"Do you think he had a mate?" Jana asked.

"I do. And I'm guessing some of the young who were killed were his."

Sobered by what she'd just learned, Jana rode back to the livery stable. When she realized she had just enough time to run back to the sheriff's office and take Rusty out for a piddle break before going to the council meeting, she accepted Tobias's offer to unsaddle Mel. She'd need to learn how to do that for herself, as well as take care of her horse, but she had enough to deal with right now.

"I'll swing by your office later this afternoon," Tobias said.

"See you then." Feeling lighthearted about seeing Tobias again, and vowing to try to be more understanding when she dealt with Virgil, she jogged to the office, took Rusty to the square for a few minutes, and then checked e-mails in case there was something she should report at the meeting.

Jesse walked into the meeting room with a box lined with a piddle pad in one hand and a puppy in the other. The daypack she usually carried weighed twice as much today because Tobias, damn and blast him, had talked her into this. She hadn't had to lug this much stuff around since her boy was in diapers.

She looked down for just a moment as she set the box next to a chair. She looked up to find herself sandwiched between two Wolves in human form—if you didn't count the furry, Wolf-shaped ears.

"What's that?" Virgil said, his attention fixed on the gray puppy.

The puppy, who was either very brave or not too bright, yapped at him.

To Jesse's surprise, Virgil grinned and held out a hand for the pup to sniff.

She said, "This is the new addition to my family."

Virgil gave her a sharp, assessing look, but he didn't comment about her choice of words.

Setting the puppy in the box, Jesse slipped the daypack off her shoulder and tucked it under her chair. The puppy whined and tried to climb out of the box. As she wondered about the wisdom of distracting the puppy with treats—and teaching the pup that bad behavior would be rewarded—Virgil settled the matter by sitting on the floor next to the box. He picked up the pup and said, "See? You're mom is right there." Then he cuddled the puppy against his chest and said nothing when those sharp puppy teeth gnawed his hand.

Jesse dug out one of the bone-shaped treats. "Let her gnaw on that instead of your thumb."

He took it and smiled as the pup settled in his lap with her treat.

He had been a father once, Jesse thought. The certainty of it made her heart hurt as she watched Virgil with the pup. She glanced at Kane, who had taken the seat next to Virgil and was also focused on the pup. *And he had been an uncle. Their family is gone now, casualties of war.*

Jana Paniccia came in and sat beside her. "Didn't have time to shower. Sorry."

Virgil leaned forward to see past Jesse's knees. "Why sorry? You smell like the horse who is not meat. That is good."

Fortunately neither woman had to respond to that because the Sanguinati arrived along with two young Intuit men.

"I have called this meeting because a request was made to expand the boundaries of the town to include one of the two full-size grocery stores in Bennett," Tolya said. "Fagen and Zeke will present their proposals for us to consider."

Fagen talked about how he and the people working with him would take responsibility for finding the food-processing plants that had survived the war. He explained how his group would also collect food from the houses and warehouse it to stock any small neighborhood stores, as well as the general store located on the town square.

Jesse wasn't sure the Sanguinati appreciated the charts, but Fagen had thought through what his group wanted to do.

"The collection of food and distributing it is what you've been doing since arriving in Bennett," Tolya said. "How is this different?"

"When we first came to Bennett, we came for the adventure and be-cause we believed helping you secure the town would earn humans the right to have a place in the town's future," Fagen said. "We worked for room and board and, basically, spending money. And we worked for the town council—or you, as the mayor. But not everyone works for you now. You've got doctors and lawyers and dentists, and that's a good thing. But those people will charge for their services, so those of us who are staying need to earn our own living because you need to pay the folks who are actually working for the town, like you and the sheriff and his deputies. Like the people who are needed to collect garbage and maintain the streets in summer and winter."

"We will consider what you have said," Tolya said.

Zeke's proposal was much the same as Fagen's, only Zeke and his group wanted to be the salvage business that cleared out houses. More charts explained how each house would have careful documentation so that jewelry would be taken to Kelley Burch for assessment and private papers would be packed up for the lawyers to review in an attempt to find any heirs who might have lived elsewhere and survived. Zeke's group had information about a few towns—most of those places being no more than a handful of buildings—that, most likely, had been resettled by *terra indigene*. Part of the salvage business would be to drive out to those places with a van packed with goods that the Others might find useful: human clothes, books, games, canned goods that could tide someone over if the hunting was lean.

Tolya thanked the men and asked them to wait outside the room while he and the town council discussed their proposals.

Jesse wondered how much discussion there would be and how much had already been discussed by the Sanguinati using the *terra indigene* form of communication.

As soon as the door closed, Tolya turned to her. "You feel people. What do you think about them?"

Jesse considered what she'd felt during the meeting—and realized Tolya had been watching for her tell. But her left wrist hadn't tingled or ached in warning. "Zeke and Fagen were among the first Intuit men who came to Bennett to help out. I think they have a frontier sense of adven-ture, much like the Intuits who settled Prairie Gold." She smiled. "Much

like the Intuits who still live in Prairie Gold. The people who came here
from the Lakeside job fair all have skills we wanted for the community—
not just the doctors and lawyers but the electricians and plumbers and
carpenters too. And those people, who are skilled in their trades, have
promised to hire youngsters as apprentices to learn those trades. People
coming in now have to clear their own houses of the personal effects of
those who lived there before them. It's time to stop requiring sorting of
goods to be part of every person's workday. Let Zeke and Fagen start their
own businesses to do what is needed."

Tolya nodded, an indication that he had listened to what she'd said.
Then he looked at the Wolves. "Virgil?"

"One of those stores is close to the new boundaries," Virgil said. "I
think the Elders would agree to expanding the town boundaries that
much."

"That store also has other stores nearby, like the one that has many
different kinds of things," Kane added.

"A department store?" Jana asked.

Kane shrugged. "It is a store with many things."

"The other food store is too far beyond the new boundaries," Virgil
said. "It is in the wild country now. It would not be safe for humans to go
there with new food."

"But there would still be a lot of foodstuffs on the shelves or in the
stock room," Jesse said. "Most of the fresh food will have rotted by now,
but the food in cans and jars should be good."

"The *terra indigene* who have claimed some of the houses in that part
of the town will use the food," Virgil said. "They will need it since they
will spend part of their time watching for enemies. Also, being in human
form to do human tasks means there are many days when we can't hunt
properly to bring down meat. We will need to eat meat killed by humans
or go hungry."

Jesse doubted any *terra indigene* would go hungry. Since humans
weren't allowed to carry guns within the town limits, they would be easy
prey, despite the understanding that Bennett's human residents were considered not edible—at least by the *terra indigene* residents. Whether the
Elders thought the humans were like chickens in a pen wasn't something
she wanted to know.

"Two humans arrived on yesterday's train, looking for work," Tolya said. "They offered to open the land agent's office and take responsibility for recording who lives where and which businesses are now open. They talked about mapping which houses and businesses are already taken so that newcomers can be shown the houses that are still available and not have to wander."

Everyone thought that was a good idea. Tolya nodded. "Then I will tell Craig and Dawn Werner that they have jobs and may select their own house."

After informing Zeke and Fagen that their businesses were approved and setting up a time for them to meet with him and take care of the paperwork, Tolya adjourned the meeting.

Virgil stood, still holding the puppy.

Jesse eyed the pup. "She needs to go outside and do her business."

The Wolf stared at the box. "She's going to live in that?"

The growl in his voice made her shiver, but she answered briskly. "The box was small enough to bring in for this meeting. She has a puppy playpen that I'll set up in my own store. She has a bed for when she's a bit older. She has a crate to stay in when she needs quiet time." When Virgil said nothing, she added, "Better get her outside before she pees on you."

Virgil headed for the door, leaving Jesse to grab the box and her daypack. Then he stopped. "What's her name?"

"She doesn't have one yet."

The stare he gave her wasn't friendly. "Why not?"

"Because I want Rachel Wolfgard to help me choose a name. Since the pup will be spending as much time with Rachel as she spends with me, I would like my friend's input on a name."

She wouldn't say he softened toward her, but she had a feeling that she'd given Virgil a reason not to think ill of all humans.

Jana washed her hands, then splashed cold water on her face. Virgil hadn't said anything about the Wolfgard taking over the house at the corner of her street. She wouldn't have known if she hadn't run into John Wolfgard outside the bookstore and learned about the move. John was pleased to be able to observe humans going about their usual tasks. There had been a human pack in Lakeside and interacting with them had been educational.

She wasn't sure she wanted to be the equivalent of the educational channel on TV, but she could guess why some of the strongest predators in Bennett were moving into houses on that street.

The blood prophet.

She didn't know enough about the *cassandra sangue*, and she needed to learn—fast—because she was the law as well as a neighbor. She should know what to watch for that might indicate signs of trouble.

As she debated whether to approach Tolya Sanguinati or Jesse Walker to find out what information they might have—and assess their willingness to be forthcoming with her—Jana walked into the front part of the office and noticed the way Virgil and Kane were staring at Rusty, who should have been in her crate and wasn't.

Virgil smiled—actually *smiled*—at her before focusing on Rusty again. "She eviscerated the bunny. Good girl!"

Rusty wagged her tail, looking thrilled to receive her pack leader's praise.

Jana stared at what was left of the toy she'd given the dog that morning. "No, *not* good girl. Bad girl!"

Rusty stopped wagging her tail, dropped the bunny's head, and whined.

Virgil swung around to face Jana and growled, "Why bad girl?"

Dominant Wolf or not, she could *not* allow him to intimidate her, especially when they were in conflict about something that was none of his business. She took a step forward so they were almost toe-to-toe and looked up at him. "She's not supposed to rip up her toys."

"Then why did you give her a toy that looks like prey?" he demanded.

"I didn't think she'd know what a bunny looked like!"

Stupid human. He didn't say it. He didn't have to.

"If she swallows some of that stuffing, it could make her sick," Jana said.

He bared his teeth and looked a lot less human.

"Some toys are meant to be chewed, but not the stuffie toys." She tried to sound reasonable. She really did. But even she heard the growl in her voice and wondered how close she was to challenging his dominance and being bitten.

He made a sound somewhere between a grunt and a growl and walked out of the office, followed by Kane.

Rusty crawled to Jana and rolled over, exposing her belly.

Sighing, Jana crouched and rubbed the dog's belly. "It wasn't your fault. You're still a puppy and everything is new. I just hope every part of your training isn't going to include a confrontation with *them*."

She put Rusty in the crate and swept up the remains of the bunny. She dumped the bits into the wastebasket, then considered the puppy and dumped the wastebasket into the garbage can out back. Afterward, she tried to settle down and get some work done so that she could have her roping lesson with Tobias.

The phone rang, making her jump. "Sheriff's Office, Deputy Paniccia speaking."

"You sound so official," Barb said.

"I *am* on duty."

"What are you doing after work?"

Jana suppressed a sigh. "That depends. I made plans but I could break them."

"Would those plans include a certain rancher?"

"He offered to teach me to use a lasso."

"Is that what we're calling it here?"

"Barb!" She could hear the sparkle in her friend's voice.

"Okay, I'll stop teasing. But he is good-looking, and he is giving you riding lessons—which is not another way of saying you know what—and . . . Hey, he's single, isn't he?"

"As far as I know." And in this town, she doubted anyone could keep their marital status a secret.

"Well then, enjoy a little lassoing and smooching." A beat of silence. "And if you write any letters to anyone in Lakeside, *do not* say I said that or Michael will start wondering what *I'm* up to—which is nothing that I couldn't tell my mom about—and find a way to be on the next train out here."

Jana laughed. "I won't mention it." She hung up and went back to work.

Unsure of Virgil's and Kane's moods when they returned an hour later, Jana moved to the center of the room so that she wouldn't be trapped behind the desk—just in case Virgil decided to do more than growl at her.

Kane remained in the doorway. Virgil stepped within arm's reach, held out a toy, and growled, "Acceptable?"

Jana smiled as childhood memories flooded her. "It's Cowboy Bob."

As a child, she had loved the *Cowboy Bob* TV show, where Bob, a cloth doll, could change into a real cowboy who helped the children living in a frontier town. But he became real only when the adults weren't around to see him.

This Cowboy Bob, complete with his hat, boots, and six-gun, must have been printed on the material—front and back—then sewn together and stuffed. She hadn't known such a thing existed and wondered if a TV station in this part of Thaisia still aired the old shows.

When she reached for the doll, Virgil pulled his hand back. "Acceptable? It doesn't look like prey." He paused before adding, "At least to her."

Now, that was just being mean. "Yes, it's acceptable."

Before she had time to thank him, before she had time to react, Virgil grabbed the back of her neck and vigorously rubbed the doll over her chest, then her face, and finally her hair before he let her go.

"By all the gods!" Her heart pounding, Jana stumbled away from him and watched as he held up the doll and *sniffed it.*

"We already rolled on it. So did John. That left you."

There were plenty of things she wanted to say. Plleeeennnnty. She just couldn't form the words.

Would she have to arrest herself if she whacked him over the head with a stapler? That assumed she could get close enough before Kane intervened.

Virgil crouched, held out Cowboy Bob, and waited for Rusty to creep out of the crate and approach him.

"Pack," Virgil said firmly.

Rusty sniffed Cowboy Bob. Her tail began to wag.

Virgil set the doll on the floor, belly side up. "Pack."

The tail wagging became more vigorous. Then Rusty snatched Cowboy Bob and darted into her crate. With her new pack mate nestled between her paws, she settled down for a nap, leaving the adults to sort things out by themselves.

Virgil straightened and turned to stare at Jana.

She huffed and she puffed and finally forced out the words: "Thank you. That was kind of you to find her another toy."

He continued to stare. "We're going out to patrol. Tobias Walker says he's going to teach you to rope things because it is a skill you will need. We will be back before it's time for you to leave."

"Okay."

As he walked out the door, Virgil grumbled something about wolverines. Jana didn't catch most of it, and she figured it was better for both of them if she didn't ask him to repeat it.

When she didn't get an answer the first time, Barb knocked a little harder on Abigail Burch's screen door. Abby could be in the bathroom; it always seemed like someone who wasn't expected knocked on the door just when you needed to bring a book or crossword puzzle into the bathroom.

She'd turned away from the door and picked up her boxes when she heard footsteps. She offered Abby a big smile that dimmed as she looked at the other woman.

"I guess this is a bad time. Sorry to have bothered you."

"It's all right," Abby said. "Personal stuff."

"Want to do something for a neighbor?" Barb felt bad about asking someone who already looked worn-out, but she was asking everyone who already lived on the street. Even John Wolfgard was coming over to help, and the Wolves hadn't done anything about moving into their own place except pee on the house.

Abby stepped outside. "You need help?"

"The new neighbors do. Because of the kids, their house needs to be cleared out of everything but the furniture."

Abby nodded. "I've got a job now as a cleaner. I told them I prefer doing office buildings to houses, but we're all coming over to give that house a good scrubbing because of the girl."

Because of the girl. Normally, Barb would have responded to the curiosity and the question under that statement by telling her friend about the girl. But Jana was sincerely spooked about people finding out about Maddie, and it did seem odd to single out one of the kids when they'd barely been seen, so Barb said, "I heard someone was going to do the cleaning, but the house needed to be cleared first. That's why I'm asking the people on the street to go over and help. The faster it's cleared out, the faster Kenneth and Evan and the kids can move in."

When Abby didn't respond, Barb wondered if the other woman had some objection to the new neighbors.

Abby said, "All right. I'll go over with you and help for a while."

"That's great." But it didn't feel great.

Abby hesitated, then shrugged. "I guess I don't have to lock it."

"Do you want to leave a note for Kelley?"

"What for?"

Abby sounded so sad, Barb didn't know what to say. She just headed for the house across the street and a few doors up from her own home.

"Don't they want any of this stuff?" Abby asked when they entered the house and looked around.

"They might, especially some of the books and food and linens. For now, Zeke and Fagen are bringing two of the vans they've been given for their businesses and will drive all the goods over to the community center. Evan and Kenneth will look over everything and bring back the things that will be useful for their family." Barb took a scrunchie out of her jeans pocket and pulled her hair back in a short ponytail. "The guys can pack up the living room and family room when they get here. Hannah and Sarah Gott said they would take care of the kitchen. John can pack up the books since he's in charge of the bookstore. You and I should pack up the bedrooms and bathroom. That's where the really personal stuff will be."

"I'll start in the bathroom." Abby took one of the smaller boxes.

"Let's see if there's a shoebox in one of the bedrooms that you can use for any prescriptions we find. Those need to be boxed separately from everything else."

They went into the master bedroom. Easy enough to find a shoebox. The woman who had lived there must have bought a couple of pairs of shoes just before . . . things went bad. Barb removed one pair of shoes and turned to hand the box to Abby—and wondered why Abby looked like the top of the dresser was filled with venomous snakes instead of a scatter of pendants and bracelets.

"You okay?" Barb asked.

"Yeah." Abby grabbed the shoebox. "Fine." She bolted out of the room.

Barb found suitcases tucked under the bed. As she filled them with the nicer clothes in the closet, she wondered why a woman who felt such revulsion for jewelry would marry a jeweler.

A bigail stared at the items in the medicine cabinet. What were they supposed to do with an open bottle of aspirin or cough syrup? If people threw the things out, would they regret the waste a year from now if the companies that made those things didn't exist anymore? But who wanted to use aspirin or cough syrup from a stranger's house?

She reached for a pill bottle. What about prescriptions? The mayor and sheriff had approved this house for the new family, but had whoever vetted it known that the woman who had lived in this house had used pills in order to sleep? She hadn't found anything besides over-the-counter drugs in her house, but that didn't mean sleeping pills were uncommon. Prairie Gold had been just as close to the Elder Hills as Bennett, and everyone had a sleepless night on occasion, but the people in Prairie Gold hadn't felt—and still didn't feel—threatened by the Others. Maybe the people here had always felt threatened. Maybe that had made it easier for them to side with the HFL.

She opened the bottle of sleeping pills. A quick search in the cabinet that held personal kinds of supplies netted a bag of cotton balls. Stuffing a cotton ball into the pill bottle, she closed it and slipped it into the pocket of her dress, then shimmied a little to make sure nothing rattled.

Hurrying now, she cleaned out the medicine chest and cabinet. She filled one of the larger boxes with towels that looked almost new and just needed a wash.

By the time she returned to the master bedroom, Barb had the bed stripped down, had the suitcases standing near the door, and had filled two boxes with clothes from the dresser. As she stepped into the room,

Barb opened one of the top drawers, removed a large jewelry box, and set it on top of the dresser.

"There are two jewelry boxes here," Barb said. "Maybe one was for costume jewelry and one for good?" She opened the box on the dresser. "Oh, this is so pretty. Maybe I could buy it." She held up a necklace made of turquoise beads on a gold chain.

Abigail could feel the dissonance between Barb and the stones from where she stood, and anything that brought even a little darkness into Barb's life would also bring it too close to hers. "Put it back. Don't touch it."

Barb looked puzzled and a little hurt. "I don't think it's an expensive piece. And it would suit me."

No, it wouldn't.

"I'm not going to pocket it," Barb said. "I'll just put a note in the jewelry box to say I'm interested and ask Kelley what it's worth." She moved her other hand to cup the turquoise beads.

"No!" Abigail screamed. "Don't touch it. The stones are soured!"

Startled, Barb dropped the necklace.

Abigail started to cry. "I'm sorry. I'm sorry. But you're so . . . bright . . . and happy, and those stones have been soured by someone who was neither of those things."

"But . . . this house is supposed to be okay for . . . the kids. Joshua told everyone it didn't have a stain of darkness."

"Maybe the place doesn't. Maybe nothing happened here that he would recognize as a stain."

"Why do you?"

Abigail pointed at the jewelry box and made her hand shake. "The stones. And these." She took the pill bottle out of her pocket.

Barb looked at the bottle. "Were you going to take that bottle without telling anyone?"

"Yes."

Barb wasn't an Intuit, but she had an older brother who was a cop. "Is this connection you have with stones the reason why there's friction between you and Kelley?"

"He doesn't know. No one knows."

"Don't you think it's time you told someone about what you can sense?"

Abigail shook her head. "If people know, something might be said and the wrong person will overhear it—and then I'll end up dead. I've been running since I was seventeen, but there aren't that many places to run anymore, even if I could get there."

"You've been hiding since you were seventeen?"

"Yes."

Barb sat on the bed. "Abby, you have to tell someone. The Others aren't going to care if you can sense whatever you sense in jewelry, but they'll care a lot if they think you're keeping a secret that ends up causing trouble here."

Abigail forced herself to move, to sit beside Barb. "I can't. Barb, you don't know them. You don't know what it's like to be controlled by them." She closed her hands around Barb's in a bruising grip. "I can't support myself in Prairie Gold. If the Sanguinati decide I can't stay in Bennett, where will I go?"

"Tolya will listen," Barb said. "And if you can't tell him directly, tell me, and I'll tell him."

Ally and advocate. Yes, that would work nicely. She would become another secret. Like the girl.

Abigail released Barb's hands and said, "Have you ever heard of the Blackstone Clan?"

CHAPTER 20

Earthday, Messis 19

Sitting across from the three women, Tolya studied the way Abigail Burch clung to Barbara Ellen—and the way Deputy Jana rested one hand on Abigail's shoulder.

Was that hand on Abigail's shoulder a gesture of unspoken support or was it something else?

Barbara Ellen had called him last night, saying there was something important she had to tell him, something that might have an impact on the whole town. That was the reason he had called the town council to meet this morning and hear what Barbara Ellen had to say, despite Earthday being everyone's rest day.

Now he wished he'd asked Jesse Walker to drive up from Prairie Gold to listen to whatever would be said. She understood human females, and what he was seeing in the three females sitting across from him made him decide that, Earthday or not, he would call Jesse to relay whatever was revealed here.

<Why are those two huddled together like that?> Virgil asked, taking a seat next to Tolya.

<Fear?> Tolya replied dryly. Virgil had also recognized that slight

distance Jana had put between herself and the other females and hadn't included her in the huddle.

<I haven't snarled at any of them today. Not even the wolverine. Haven't even needed the Me Time cell lately.> Virgil sounded disappointed.

Tolya continued to study the women as rest of the Sanguinati arrived and filled the chairs. <If they were prey, who would you go for?>

<Barbara Ellen and Abigail,> Virgil replied without hesitation. Then he did hesitate. <The wolverine looks like she's with them, but she's not. At least, not all the way. She's caught the scent of something that makes her wary.>

Not how he would have described it, but it matched his thinking. Jana must already know what Barbara Ellen wanted to tell them—and she was keeping watch instead of standing with her friend. <Do you remember the warning Jackson sent us? The picture with the people made of black stones?>

<What about it?>

<The unknown female with Barbara Ellen . . . >

<Was the wolverine.> Virgil said, finishing the thought. <The Hope pup drew her before any of us knew what she looked like.>

Even in the picture, Deputy Jana had been keeping watch.

Tolya looked around and realized one of them was still missing. <Where is Kane?>

<The Becky girl found a hairbrush and wanted to make him pretty.>

Tolya didn't smile. Did. Not. Smile. He did, however, find it fascinating that the Wolves displayed such a high tolerance for certain humans. He couldn't imagine Virgil or Kane allowing any other child to brush them to make them pretty. Maybe it was Becky Gott's simplicity and innocence. Maybe Wolfgard young—at least the ones who were able to shift to human form—did the same kinds of things as a way to learn. He'd probably never know, but he did understand that every human Virgil tolerated made him a more dangerous threat to the rest of the humans because he was taking them into his pack—and having lost one pack, he would kill anything that threatened this new one.

Tolya said, "Shall we begin?" When they all nodded—all except the three human women—he focused on Barbara Ellen. "There is something you need to tell us?"

Barbara Ellen looked around the room, just as he had a moment ago. But her skin was so pale now, the freckles were the only color left in her face.

"I didn't expect . . . I thought . . ." She took a deep breath and blew it out. "Can I tell it as a story?"

"This is a teaching story?" Virgil asked, leaning forward and bracing his forearms on his thighs.

"A family story to impart information rather than entertain," Jana replied.

All the *terra indigene* nodded. Tolya wondered if the females understood how closely their words would be heeded. Entertainment, if not appealing to an individual, could be ignored. A teaching story never was.

Barbara Ellen glanced at Abigail. So. This story was not about Barbara Ellen or her family. She was the designated teller—but had Jana helped shape the information into a teaching story to make sure he and Virgil heard what they needed to hear?

"Once upon a time," Barbara Ellen began, "there was a young Intuit girl who came from a family of gamblers and swindlers. Being Intuits, the gamblers used their abilities to sense things that were tied into their skill with cards and other games of chance. They knew when to bet and when to fold—and sometimes they cheated by folding when they could have won a hand so that the people playing with them wouldn't start to wonder about why they won so much. And the swindlers always sensed who would be most vulnerable to whatever con they were playing.

"Sometimes they worked different swindles in the same town or split up and worked in a couple of towns close to each other. Sometimes the whole family would work one con. But they always stayed in touch and they always left the area around the same time because moving around was safer—and because there was less chance that one of the youngsters might say something that made a mark realize he was dealing with Intuits.

"See, their being Intuits was the big family secret, the thing you could never ever tell anyone else." Barbara Ellen looked around the room. "You could never tell. And if you were a part of the family, you could never leave."

"And if you did leave?" Tolya asked softly.

"Death," Abigail whispered, her blue eyes blind and staring. "If you're out of the life, there's always the chance you'll snitch on the rest of them, so . . . death."

Barbara Ellen resumed the story. "The girl's Intuit gift was unusual. Some people believe that gemstones of all kinds have healing or magical properties and can help the person who wears them. But the girl knew exactly which stone would resonate with a particular person. Even if a hundred stones were on a table, she could tell which one truly suited a person and would bring good things, positive things, into that person's life—or help keep bad things away. But just as some stones would be good for a person, other stones would open a person up to bad things. Sometimes little things, like spilling coffee on your shirt just before an important meeting or missing out on having lunch with a friend because your car had a flat tire. Little things, day after day. And not so little things. Like sitting down at a poker table and gambling away your family's life savings.

"The girl and her uncle had a particular part to play in the rest of the family's endeavors. They would rent a booth at a fair or an open market. The uncle would repair jewelry and clean jewelry while the girl did the patter about choosing a stone for luck or love or good fortune. Some of them were tumbled stones you would keep in a bowl while others had a hole through them so they could be strung on a cord or a gold or silver chain—which the uncle would sell to the mark. And because the girl was young and pretty, people never suspected they were being cheated in some way.

"The thing was, if the uncle had a feeling the mark had money or something else of use to the family, he would signal the girl to select a dissonant stone—something that would sour the person's life in some way and make them vulnerable. And the girl did it because she was young and they were her family and she depended on them for her survival. So someone would carry his 'lucky' stone into the saloon where the girl's father was playing poker—and end up owing so much to *all* the players at the table that he would be ruined financially. Or a woman would wear a necklace that was supposed to bring her good fortune and end up being dragged into an alley where she'd be roughed up—and sometimes worse—before having her purse stolen.

"The girl didn't understand these things when she was young, but when she reached her teens and realized what happened to the people who were given bad stones . . ."

"She ran away," Abigail whispered. "She kept running and hiding, choosing places too small to be of interest to the family, or hiding in larger cities, doing whatever work she could to get by. She was in one of those cities when she met a kind man who fell in love with her. She married him but she was too afraid to tell him the truth about her abilities or her past, and when he found out, he . . . didn't love her anymore."

Tolya noticed Barbara Ellen's face settling into a tiny frown—noticed Deputy Jana's sharp look. <They've heard a lie,> he said to the rest of the *terra indigene*. <Something isn't the same as the story Abigail told them before.>

<Do we challenge?> Yuri asked.

<No,> Virgil replied. <We don't challenge—yet—and we don't trust.>

<Agreed,> Tolya said.

A tear ran down Abigail's face. "They'll come here. On the train. Her father likes to travel by train. Sooner or later, they'll come. To gamble, to plunder. To kill. They'll come." She was still telling a story instead of admitting she was talking about herself.

"What are these humans called?" Tolya asked.

"Blackstone. They're the Blackstone Clan."

Abigail and Barbara Ellen leaned against each other, exhausted. And Jana?

<Are you going to talk to Deputy Jana about the picture the Hope pup drew?> he asked Virgil.

<Not yet,> Virgil replied.

"Thank you for this story," Tolya said, addressing the humans. "You have given us many important things to consider." *More than you realize.* "I hope you can put this aside now and enjoy the rest of your day off."

"We're all helping Kenneth and Evan at their house," Jana said with a strained smile. "Today's plan is to haul the rest of the personal belongings out of the house so the cleaners can come in later this morning and scrub it from top to bottom. Then we'll give the children's bedrooms a fresh coat of paint."

Tolya thought that sounded like an appalling way to spend a day off, but he smiled since he was pretty sure that was the correct thing to do. "Then we won't keep you any longer."

The *terra indigene* waited until the humans left the conference room. Then they all looked at each other before Tolya turned to Virgil. "Black stones. Blackstones."

Virgil nodded. "Looks like the Hope pup was right about that too."

"Walker's General Store, Jesse speaking."

"Jesse Walker, this is—"

Recognizing Tolya's voice, Jesse focused on the new member of her family and said firmly, "Down, Cutie."

A beat of silence. "I beg your pardon?"

His tone of voice, somewhere between bewildered and insulted, made her laugh. "I was talking to the puppy. She's in her pen"—Jesse took the couple of steps needed to reach the pen and quiet the puppy, who had been trying to climb out to be closer to her—"and has to stay there." To make sure the pup did, she crouched beside the pen and began petting.

Another beat of silence. "You named her Cutie?"

"Are you going to tell Virgil?"

"No. Absolutely not." Now he sounded horrified.

"Her official name is Cory Walker, but Rachel insists on calling her Cutie-pup or Cutie for short."

"Rachel Wolfgard named the puppy?"

"She did."

Tolya sighed, a long exhalation.

Jesse's humor faded when she realized she'd stopped petting the puppy and now had her right hand wrapped around her aching left wrist. "You didn't call to ask about the puppy."

"No, I called to ask if you had heard of the Blackstone Clan. They're a family of Intuit gamblers and swindlers."

A chill went through Jesse. "I've never heard of them. Why have you?"

"Abigail Burch is from that family and says she has been hiding from them for many years now. She believes they'll kill her if they find her."

Jesse's hand tightened around the wrist that now throbbed as a confirmation of Tolya's words, and remembered the drawing Hope Wolfsong had made that showed Abigail dead. "They will." She thought about Abigail, who had made soaps and candles and worn old-fashioned dresses and read tarot cards—and who had hidden her real self so well even Jesse hadn't sensed the truth about her.

"Apparently she can sense if a particular stone will bring a person good luck or bad," Tolya said. "This is an unusual skill?"

"Yes." Being able to bring about a run of bad luck would certainly benefit gamblers and swindlers.

Cutie started yapping, craving attention. Or needing something else. "Tolya? I'll call you back." Jesse hung up, grabbed Cutie and a leash, and rushed through the back of the store and out the door. She walked the pup for a few minutes, letting Cutie become familiar with the scents and land behind the store.

An excuse, to give herself time to think before she called Tolya.

Had the soaps and candles and long dresses and tarot cards been Abigail's attempt to reinvent herself and get away from a corrupt life, or had it all been a disguise? Oh, Jesse was sure the girl had had reason to hide, but she also had a feeling that everyone in Prairie Gold had been played—and now she wondered if Abigail had moved to Bennett to try to patch things up with Kelley or to get away from her, an Intuit who sensed people and would no longer accept the disguise at face value? Was giving Tolya this information about the Blackstone Clan just a piece of a game?

She didn't want to be responsible for the girl being driven out of town, especially if Abigail really was trying to make a fresh start. But if Abigail had a different agenda, what sort of damage could she do in a mixed community where she would find marks for a different kind of con?

Or had she already found some?

In small Intuit communities—and most of their communities were small, given that they were tucked away in the wild country—there was almost no crime beyond occasional mischief and the rare times when an individual snapped without warning and did grievous harm to someone.

That didn't mean all Intuits were good people. It didn't mean their kind of human didn't spawn liars and thieves. It just meant that kind of person didn't prosper in an Intuit community. *Couldn't* prosper. But in other communities where you could hide what you were and use your extra sense to do unlawful deeds?

There had been Intuits who had done such things. Maybe the most successful outlaws who had lived a century ago had been Intuits who sensed what to rob and when—and sensed when it was time to retire and become something else. Maybe they got married and raised children and quietly taught their sons and daughters skills that were outside of polite society. And maybe there were some of those progeny even now who knew when to move on and let the marks recover before coming back around, like some kind of outlaw migration.

A family of gamblers and thieves. A clan, Tolya called it. No, she'd never heard of the Blackstones, but she had a very bad feeling about what would happen in Bennett when the next member of that clan showed up.

Virgil helped haul boxes into the two vans while he tried to decide if he could justifiably snarl at Deputy Jana for not telling him about the Blackstone humans yesterday when she'd first found out about them. Except *he'd* known about humans made of black stones days before Jana arrived in Bennett and hadn't shown her the picture the Hope pup had drawn.

Was he just as wrong for not telling? More wrong? No. *Not* more wrong.

He snarled and felt his canines lengthen to Wolf size—and watched one of the salvage humans stumble away from the van, dropping a box as the man fled back into the house.

Moments later, Jana rushed out of the house. Of course the wolverine would come rushing out to puff up and snarl.

"What happened?" she demanded. "Larry said something about teeth and is pretty freaked-out."

Virgil bared his teeth.

Jana almost took a step back, then took a step forward, kicking the box, which, from the sound of it, had been full of breakables that were now broken.

"Oh," she said. "Well, why did you snarl at Larry?"

"I wasn't snarling at Larry; I was snarling about *you*."

"What did I do?"

That tone was a challenge to his dominance. It really was. If he was certain she was the one who was more wrong, he'd bite her—but he'd use his mostly human teeth. Those wouldn't hurt her as much, but enough.

And if she bit him in retaliation?

He shoved his box deeper into the van, then swung around her to fetch another one that wasn't full of broken things. As he passed her, he growled, "You're confusing the puppy."

Jana threw her hands in the air. Why? Who knew? It was one of those weird things humans did.

"How?" she yelped. "Why? She's not even here!"

As he walked into the living room, Virgil heard a box full of broken things being thrown into the van—and he smiled.

Jana stood under a cool shower, washing away dirt and sweat. They'd done a lot of good, hard work today, and tomorrow Evan and Kenneth's family would move out of the hotel and into their new house—where it was less likely that Maddie would be seen by someone who would realize what she was and see nothing but profit.

The day had wrung her out. Not just the physical work, and not just the niggle of doubt about some of the details in Abigail Burch's story, but the gnawing sense of guilt that maybe she *was* confusing the puppy. She needed to have a firm idea of what she wanted to accomplish with—and for—Rusty and then find out how to do that. And once she figured *that* out, she had to convince the big bad Wolves to follow *her* rules when it came to *her* dog, or poor Rusty would get caught in the middle of mom-and-dad squabbles about how to raise the kid.

Gods. Perish the thought of Virgil in that role. Except . . . he was the sheriff and that made him the dominant enforcer in the town and that made him the dominant Wolf in the town. Or maybe being the dominant enforcer was the reason he'd been given the job of sheriff. Whatever. The point was that she and Virgil had to agree on how to oversee Rusty's education.

She was so not looking forward to that discussion. But she didn't have to think about it for the rest of the day. She would take Rusty for a walk and then some playtime in the backyard. But right now, all she wanted was some food and a glass of beer. Or a large whiskey. Or . . .

Even under the water, she heard the howls coming from her neighbors down the street.

. . . a sledgehammer.

She turned off the water, dried off as quickly as she could, and threw on some clothes when she heard Rusty howling in the living room—and heard Buddy the parakeet making a loud scoldy noise that was either the parakeet version of a howl or an objection to the sound Rusty was making.

"Hey, girl," Jana said as she moved toward the dog.

Rusty looked at Jana, wagged her tail, and howled again—and was answered by Virgil, Kane, and John.

Jana grabbed the leash from the basket near Rusty's crate and snapped it on the dog's collar—just in case Rusty tried to go through the screen door to join the Wolves.

"We are here," Barb said, walking out of the kitchen.

Jana studied her housemate. "And . . . ?"

"I think that's the message. We are here. The Wolves in the Lakeside Courtyard would howl at night and my brother said that was the message. Or one of the reasons they howled."

"Who were they telling?" She didn't think the humans who lived in Lakeside were that thrilled to know the Others were close enough to be heard.

A howl. A sound so deep Jana felt it vibrate in her bones and freeze her blood. A huge sound.

A second howl. A third. So close the windows rattled.

"Hold her," Jana said.

Barb rushed forward to grab the leash. "Don't go out there. Humans shouldn't go out there."

"I'm a cop." She wanted to run into her bedroom and grab her weapon, but she wasn't dressed like a cop, wasn't going about official business—and she didn't think that whatever was outside would notice if she pinned a badge to her T-shirt. It would notice the gun—and kill her for carrying a human weapon.

All right, then. She had faced down a few bullies at the academy with nothing but attitude; she could do it here too.

After checking that Barb had a tight grip on Rusty, Jana slipped outside and walked into the street just as the Wolfgard answered those deep, terrifying howls—and were answered in turn.

How close were those things? *What* were they? Elders, sure. But what did that mean? They were howling, so . . . gigantic Wolves? Or something that howled but was even older and more primal than the Wolfgard?

She didn't know—and understood on a gut level that she *couldn't* know and survive. She also understood something else. The humans living in Bennett needed some way to know the boundaries, needed to know where the lines were now drawn that separated streets that were within the jurisdiction of the police and town government from the streets that were in the wild country and were under the jurisdiction of *them.*

"Virgil?" Jana called softly, hoping her voice wouldn't carry much beyond the Wolves.

He turned to face her. Kane and John continued to face the direction of the Elder Hills.

"We need to talk about some things tomorrow," Jana said.

He made a sound she took to be agreement.

She nodded. "Okay, then." She looked toward the Elder Hills and saw nothing—and wondered if there was an Elder in its true form standing a few yards beyond the boundary, watching her. "Okay."

Forgoing the walk for the dog's sake—an excuse Barb didn't question—Jana and Rusty played in the backyard while Barb put together a simple meal of sandwiches and salad.

Late that evening, as she wrote a short note to Tobias, asking for book recommendations on dog training, she thought about the howling.

We are here. According to Barb, the Wolves meant it as reassurance that they were keeping watch. But the answering howls? We. Are. Here. Should the humans hear that as a reminder or a threat?

The door to the private railroad car opened a finger's length—enough for the barrel of a gun to be aimed at anyone sitting at the card table. But no gun appeared or was fired. Instead, Judd McCall said, "Parlan?"

"Come in." Parlan placed the derringer on the table and resumed shuffling a deck of cards. He waited while Judd scanned the public side of the room, then fixed on the door that provided entry into what was, most of the time, his private space.

"Any company waiting for you?" Judd asked.

"No." When the mood struck, he'd pick up a woman and use her well for a day or so, sometimes even letting her travel with him for a while if she had some interesting—and uninhibited—skills. Plenty of the saloon whores had indicated interest in having him for a night instead of some rough-and-tumble man, but he hadn't reciprocated the interest lately.

The northern half of the Midwest Region was even more barren than he'd realized in terms of large towns and people who still had money. The southern half still had a few human-controlled cities along the gulf—places where the clan had previously set up shop for a few weeks before moving on—but he hadn't paid enough attention and hadn't realized the Midwest Region had been split and they would need another set of travel passes to reach the cities along the gulf.

No, that wasn't true. He had been paying enough attention ever since that damn war, but people were still discovering the repercussions of the HFL movement trying to wrest control of the land from the Others. And the clan finding themselves in the wrong half of the Midwest Region was one of those repercussions.

He dealt four cards, faceup.

Judd raised an eyebrow. "Blackjack?"

"To pass the time."

Everyone else in the clan liked to gamble, but some weren't allowed to gamble outside the clan because they couldn't always be trusted not to put something on the table that they shouldn't. But Judd didn't gamble. Not with cards or dice. And Judd wasn't what you would call a rough-

and-tumble man. He was too damn dangerous for that because Judd
McCall liked to gamble with guns and knives. He liked to gamble on
how long it might take a man to die from a particular wound.

"Game broke up early?" Judd tapped the table to indicate he wanted
another card. "Busted."

They set those cards aside and Parlan dealt another hand. "The ones
who joined the game because it's Earthday and they were bored and
looking for something to do until the train could leave in the morning
didn't have enough cash to see them past a couple of hours of play. And
the ones who hoped I'd take markers because they never figured to lay
eyes on me again . . . I persuaded them to move along." He sighed. "Barely
making enough to meet expenses since those HFL idiots lost the war."

"Sometimes you're the one who floats us . . ." Judd pulled a handkerchief tied up as a bundle out of his coat pocket. "And sometimes another
branch of the clan makes the profit." He untied the bundle.

Parlan set the cards aside and picked up a diamond and emerald
necklace. A modest piece. Probably a gift for an important anniversary—
or the kind of gift a married man might give his mistress to keep her
sweet and believing that he really was going to leave his wife. "Where did
you find this?"

"Charlie Webb and Sweeney Cooke reported in. They found another
of those hole-in-the-wall towns. They were thinking it might work as a
base of operations for some in-and-out jobs, but Charlie noticed that two
of the houses were occupied and figured they shouldn't be touched since
he wasn't sure who, or what, occupied those places. They entered one of
the other houses and helped themselves to whatever easily fit in the car.
Some cash and jewelry that couldn't belong to anyone living in that town.
A couple of handguns and a rifle, along with ammunition. Clothes and
cans of food. Sweeney wanted to do a bit of crazy and smash windows,
make a mess, but Charlie calmed him down. Said if they left quiet, they
could slip back into town and clean out another house."

"Good thinking on Charlie's part." Parlan dealt cards, not even asking if Judd wanted to hit or stay. "Is Sweeney becoming a problem?"

"Might be. But not yet. I'll deal with him when the time comes."

Parlan nodded. "Did Lawry have a look at those?" His brother,
Lawry, was their jewelry expert—and their jewel fixer. Lawry always

knew which stones could be popped out of a setting and replaced with paste with the mark none the wiser, and could make the switch in the time it took to fix a broken clasp.

"Not yet. He and Dalton went off in a different direction. Heard some rumors about abandoned ranches." Judd gave Parlan a sharp smile. "Rustling isn't much fun when there's no one around to notice the stock is missing."

"Not practical either unless we already have a market for the animals. Besides, that's not really our line of work." Parlan tossed the deck on the table and sat back. "I've squeezed dry everyone I can squeeze on this train, and I don't have the feeling that any fresh marks will be boarding tomorrow. I'll make arrangements to have my car hitched to the east-bound train with an eye to changing to a southbound line before I reach the Midwest Region's border."

"You're thinking the people coming out here to live might have some cash?"

"No, I'm thinking it's time to take off the gambler duds, put on my suit, and charm some of the businessmen's wives by gallantly offering to make up a foursome for bridge. Some of those women have been travel-ing with their husbands on business for weeks now to escape whatever was happening in their hometowns and are desperate for fresh company. They'll be a likely source of information about towns that have become nothing more than stops for the train and which ones might have poten-tial for us." Parlan walked over to a cabinet and opened the drawer that held maps. Taking out the map for the Midwest Region, he returned to the table and opened it.

Judd came around the table to stand beside him. "Not a lot of choices."

"Not a lot," Parlan agreed. Some he already knew weren't more than the station with a few houses and a couple of stores for the railroad em-ployees. And some didn't have even the employees anymore, despite the hazard pay that went with manning such a place. "Here." He pointed to a town that had been of modest size before the war and might still be. Not every human place had been decimated, and there was something about that town . . . "We'll meet up here."

"Why?"

"It has an east-west connection right across this half of the Midwest.

A northern line begins there as well and looks like it runs all the way to the east-west line we're on now, near the High North border. That kind of loop could be useful to us. And it has roads that will give us even more access to any towns around the area." Parlan ran his finger along the westbound track to the town located at the northern end of the Elder Hills. "I have a feeling this is where our luck will change." He tapped the town's name.

Bennett.

CHAPTER 21

Moonsday, Messis 20

Jana stared at the ceiling, then looked at the clock on her bedside table. Stared at the ceiling. Looked at the clock.

Too early to get up. Humans weren't being held to a dark-to-dawn curfew within the boundaries of the town, although no one was guaranteeing their safety if they went out when it was dark. As a deputy, she didn't have to heed *any* curfew when she was on duty. But those howls she'd heard yesterday had come from beings that were way too close to her house, and she had no desire to cross paths with one of *them* just because she couldn't sleep.

"If you're not going to sleep, do something useful." Patting the bedside table until she found the scrunchie she'd left there, she pulled her hair back into a tail, shoved her feet into the sandals she was using in lieu of slippers, and headed for the office/workroom she and Barb were still setting up. But a whine from the living room had her changing direction.

"Hey, girl," Jana said softly. "Quiet, now. We don't want to wake up Barb."

Rusty whined again.

Would she rather let the dog pee on the pad in the crate and then have to wash it or accompany Rusty outside—in the dark—and let the pup do her business in the backyard?

It's our darn yard, she thought as she opened the crate and reached for the leash.

Nope. No leash. Rusty rushed past her to the back door.

Jana followed, flipped on the kitchen light over the sink and the back door light that lit part of the yard. She unlocked the back door and pushed the screen door open. Rusty bolted outside and squatted just beyond the steps, which meant the dog hadn't yet learned what part of the yard was meant to be her lavatory or she just couldn't hold it anymore.

Snagging the big flashlight they were leaving on the kitchen counter, Jana went outside. The light at the back door didn't reach the farthest end of the yard, and she didn't want to step on something that might object when she took the dog back there in case Rusty needed to do more than piddle.

The pup found something of interest back there, and whatever it was it didn't slither or crawl away from the flashlight beam. Then Rusty looked toward the house and wagged her tail.

Something in the dark, moving toward them. Must have climbed over the fence. Or jumped over the fence.

Gods, was this one of the fighting dogs she'd been told to watch for because they were a danger to the children in town as well as to pets?

She reached for the gun she wasn't carrying as she aimed the flashlight beam toward a big shape that was just a little darker now than the yard—and got an annoyed growl in response as she shined the light right into Virgil's eyes.

She jerked her wrist to shine the light down. "Sorry. Didn't know it was you." Now she felt foolish for thinking the dogs would come to a settled street that had Wolves living in the house at the corner. But better to think about the dogs than to think about the fact that she was wearing nothing but her tank top and boxer pajamas since she hadn't expected to be seen by anyone except, maybe, her housemate.

Virgil gave Rusty a quick sniff and lick, which must have been enough reassurance, because the pup went back to exploring the yard. Then he stood on his hind legs and shifted.

Jana looked away but not before she'd seen more of her boss than she wanted to see. Did he think her clothes were some kind of invitation? Or . . .

"What?" Virgil sounded like his usual gruff self.

Act like you're both in uniform. Act like you're not in your pj's and he's not naked. "I wasn't expecting to see anyone. You startled me."

"You said you wanted to talk. You were outside with Rusty and awake." He cocked his head and studied her with those amber Wolf eyes. "Maybe awake."

Oh, she was plenty awake now. Plleeeennnnty.

"You wanted to talk," Virgil repeated.

Yes, she did. But not in her backyard in the dark when she was and he was . . . Gods.

"Why are you up so early?" she asked, changing the subject because she couldn't remember what she'd wanted to talk to him about. Not looking at him but knowing what she'd see if she did look was darn distracting.

Virgil focused on her house. "Some humans who settled a few streets from here took cats to be part of their packs."

"Adopting the animals left behind is good." She knew Barb was planning to approach Evan and Kenneth about giving one of the available parakeets to Maddie since the girl had been so taken with Buddy the day Barb had looked after the children.

"The bad dogs found the cat who went outside. Cats are fast, but it wasn't fast enough. Not against that pack."

"Oh gods." She'd have to tell Barb.

Virgil growled. Rusty immediately stopped exploring and returned to Jana, pressing against her leg.

"Barbara Ellen wants to believe they are not bad dogs," he said, the growl still under the words. "But they are. They don't hunt to eat. They hunt to kill because they like to kill. Do you see the difference?"

"Yes."

"Big dogs. Big pack. They can take down bigger prey—or prey with weapons."

Suddenly Jana understood what Virgil was doing in her backyard. The pack was out there, close enough to be a possible threat. And she and

Rusty, who were now members of *his* pack, were outside in the dark. Vulnerable.

"Rusty is young," he said, "and your teeth would do no good in a fight."

If she and Rusty were vulnerable, what would happen if the dogs attacked someone like Maddie? "We have to find them and kill them."

"Yes."

That simple. Driving the dogs away hadn't been enough. They were dangerous adversaries who had returned to his territory and now had to be eliminated.

"I'll head over to the office as soon as I can." As he turned away, she said, "Virgil? Are you okay with me bringing Rusty to the station?"

The sky had lightened enough that she could see his bafflement. "When we hunt, she needs to be in the den where it is safe. When we are not hunting, she should be with her pack. How else will she learn?"

That, too, was simple for him.

Jana petted her dog. "Come on, girl. Time for breakfast. Breakfast?"

Virgil snorted a laugh. "Do you expect her to know all these words?"

"Not all of them," she said defensively. "But she's smart enough to learn words."

"Food. It is one word that means the same thing whether it's morning or night. That one she will learn quickly."

He walked with them. Walked into the light from the back door just as Barb opened the screen door.

Jana recognized shock—and was certain her friend was blushing when Barb squeaked out, "Morning, Sheriff."

"Barbara Ellen." He paused a moment, as if trying to figure out why she was acting . . . odd. Then he shifted to his Wolf form, jumped the fence, and disappeared.

"Coffee's ready." Barb filled two mugs as soon as Jana came inside.

Jana busied herself with giving Rusty a scoop of kibble and didn't look at her housemate.

"Okay," Barb said. "I'm not an expert or anything, but Sheriff Wolfgard . . . He's pretty . . . manly. Don't you think?"

"I guess." Really didn't want to think about it. Really didn't.

"Do you wonder . . ." Barb set her mug on the counter. "I mean,

the Others can shift, right? So . . . do you think they can . . . adjust . . .
parts?"

Jana spit a mouthful of coffee on the counter. "Gods, Barb!"

"Haven't you ever wondered?"

"Not until now!"

"Oh. Well, I've wondered, and it's not like you can ask any of them."

Jana mopped up the coffee with a dishrag. She rinsed it out and hung
it to dry before grabbing what was left of her coffee. "I have to head in
early."

"Can I catch a ride? I wanted to sort some books before I take care of
the animals." She paused before adding, "Joshua is meeting me. He sent
a message that he has news."

"Sure. I just need a quick shower since I cleaned up last night."

Grabbing her robe from the back of her bedroom door, she spotted
the note she'd written to Tobias last night. Had to mail that this morning.

It had been a long while since she'd met anyone as nice as Tobias who
also made her hormones flutter, and he filled out his jeans quite well,
thank you very much. But she hadn't *seen* him, so it wasn't her fault that,
while she took a cool shower that bordered on cold, she kept picturing
Tobias's head on top of Virgil Wolfgard's body.

Virgil continued his inspection of the front of the wolverine's house—
the inspection that had been interrupted when he'd heard her and
Rusty outside in the yard. In the dark. The bad dogs *should* be denned
somewhere since some of the Elders who lived in the hills were nocturnal
hunters and very good at taking prey that had bedded down for the night.
Like bison and deer . . . and humans.

No scent of dog except for Rusty. That was good. Choosing the large
rock near the front step—a rock, he'd been told, that was decorative, although he couldn't see the difference between it and all the other rocks
outside the town—he lifted a leg and marked it to warn off the bad dogs
and to inform the Elders who prowled these streets that the Wolves paid
particular attention to the beings in this house.

Kane joined him a minute later.

<No scent of the bad dogs near the Becky girl's house or the den with the mixed pack,> Kane said. <I marked those places.>

<I marked this one,> Virgil replied.

From the back of the house, Virgil heard the wolverine make a sound that was close to a yelp. Words, yes, but . . . yelp.

They listened, but there were no other sounds of possible distress. What they did hear was water. Someone in the shower.

<I'll help John prepare food for us,> Kane said.

<Yes. I'll be there soon.>

Kane trotted up the street, a dark, silent shape. Virgil stayed and listened to the water.

The bad dogs had retreated from the Wolfgard territory, but now they were returning. There had been more than two dozen dogs in the pack, but Virgil doubted there were that many left. The dogs might have stayed around houses outside the new town boundaries forever, hunting prey or scavenging what food they could find in the houses that had the little animal doors without fighting the Wolfgard. But they had drawn the attention of the Elders, and now the dogs were being hunted instead of being the hunters. Now they were being driven back into Wolfgard territory, squeezed between two kinds of *terra indigene*. They would try to take the Wolfgard territory. It was the only place they could go, but it would make no difference. One way or another, the bad dogs had to die so that the Elders would tolerate the dogs that were useful . . . or not a threat to anyone. Like Rusty.

The bad dogs had to die before they killed more than cats. There were young among the humans living in Bennett—and if the adults weren't vigilant, the young were always the easiest prey.

The water stopped. How long did it take a human female to groom herself after washing? More to the point, how long did it take the wolverine?

Figuring the answer was *not long*, Virgil ran back to the Wolfgard house. When he reached the front door, he almost shifted to human form to let himself in, but there were lights going on in some of the houses. Not in the houses closest to the one the Wolfgard now claimed, but some humans were awake and might open a door or look out a window and see his human form. Which shouldn't matter since he was a Wolf regardless of form, but Barbara Ellen getting squeaky reminded him that looking human meant wearing human clothes because *naked* meant something to humans, who got strange about something that meant nothing except that humans couldn't adequately communicate with *terra indigene* who weren't in human form, so sometimes shifting to that form was required even if clothes weren't available.

The wolverine hadn't squeaked about him shifting in order to talk to her. He approved. She had enough inadequacies, being human and all, but she was showing that she had potential to be a good working member of the enforcer pack. And she had enough bristly, puffed-up attitude most of the time that he wasn't giving up on the idea that one of her ancestors had been a Wolverine, despite the possibility being impossible.

Or . . . She said she'd been raised by foster parents. Maybe *they* had been Wolverines and she'd learned the attitude from them.

Entertained by that thought, Virgil trotted around the house before shifting to human form and opening the back door. John and Kane were in the kitchen, pulling things out of the fridge and cupboards to make before-work food.

"Kane, I'm going to pack one of those carryalls with clothes for both of us," Virgil said. "John, when I've packed what we need, you run down to the wolverine's house and put the carryall and our shoes in her vehicle. She will be going to work early."

"I'll ride with her," John said. "I want to start work early today too. Joshua Painter is going to work in the bookstore with me. He likes books and needs to learn a trade if he's going to live around humans."

"Barbara Ellen likes books," Kane said casually as he cut up a rare-cooked beef roast into slabs of meat for the three of them. "She spends more time helping to sort books than she needs to."

"Is Barbara Ellen receptive to mating?" John asked as he opened two cans of peach slices. The Wolfgard ate meat, but in human form, other foods were . . . tasty . . . and eating sweet fruit with the meat was surprisingly pleasant.

"Don't know," Kane replied. "But Joshua isn't. At least, not yet."

Not interested in discussing human mating rituals, Virgil walked out of the kitchen, pulled a small carryall out from under his bed, and filled it with two sets of clothes for him and two for Kane. He found another carryall that was big enough to hold the boots Kane wore when he was in human form and the shoes Virgil preferred. The boots were more like what the human males wore on ranches, but Virgil, being in human form most of the time when he was on duty, had decided he wanted a shoe that was comfortable to walk in and easy to remove if he had to shift to Wolf form quickly.

He didn't want to think about Barbara Ellen being receptive to mating—or the sex thing, which, from what he could figure out, wasn't the same as mating. He was sure the wolverine would tell him it wasn't any of his business, that humans were free to do the sex thing with anyone they pleased. But it *was* his business because Barbara Ellen had ties to Lakeside, and he and Tolya wanted to remain friends with the *terra indigene* who lived in Lakeside.

Virgil closed the carryall but didn't pick it up because another thought occurred to him.

What about the wolverine? How close were *her* ties to the Lakeside Courtyard and the police pack that was connected to the Courtyard? And how receptive was *she* to a human male's mating overtures?

Tobias drove through the early morning light, wondering if he was acting like a fool. He was the foreman of Prairie Gold's ranch, and he had work to do and responsibilities to meet. But, damn it, there was that spark he felt whenever he was around Jana, and he thought she felt some interest in him too—and not just as someone who could teach her to rope and ride. But even if she wasn't interested in getting better acquainted on a personal level, even if the spark he felt fizzled, he wanted her to ride well and develop a partnership with Mel. Sure, she was supposed to be patrolling streets that were part of the town or had been part of the town, but anything could happen once you were in the wild country. And people being people, anything could happen within the town.

He wasn't a stranger to women. He liked their company and had accepted invitations over the years to participate in mutual pleasure. But some had never gotten past a kiss because, even though his mother was the one who could sense other people, he'd had the feeling some of those women had wanted him because they wanted to be a foreman's wife in order to rule the house and the ranch's bank account.

And there hadn't been this kind of spark, even with the women whose company he'd enjoyed in all manner of ways. An attraction, sure, but not the kind of spark that was pulling him back to Bennett when he should be putting in time on the ranch.

"She's not an Intuit."

"I know that, Mom. I know she's not one of us, I know she's got a job in Bennett, and I work at the ranch, and there's a fair piece of driving between those two places."

"Nothing wrong with a phone call between visits. Or a letter."

"A letter? I'd probably be the one driving our post up to the Bennett office."

"A letter is something that can be enjoyed between friends, but it's also an old-fashioned kind of courtship. A woman can revisit a letter when the man isn't around. Gives her a reason to think about him. Speaking of letters, since you're making the trip anyway, take the sack of mail Phil has ready and bring back the mail for the town as well as the ranch. And check with John Wolfgard to see if he has any of the books I asked about."

He'd called Truman Skye after leaving his mother's house that morning and offered to pick up any mail for the Skye Ranch since it would be on his way back home. Truman sounded grateful to eliminate one chore from his list and asked if Tobias could bring back a few things from the general store, if the items were available.

He couldn't complain if his social call had turned into a delivery run. It justified the use of the gasoline.

"Joshua is going to work for you at the bookstore?" Barb twisted around to look at John, who was in the cargo area with Rusty, the carryalls, and the carry sack of food he'd had with him when he'd informed Jana that she was giving him a ride to the town square.

"He likes books," John replied. "That's why he spends extra time sorting the books that come in from the houses."

"Is that our story?" Jana asked dryly, looking into the rearview mirror.

John hesitated, then gave her a delighted smile. "Yes. That is our story."

"Okeydokey." Jana didn't glance at her housemate. Did. Not. After that crack about whether Virgil had adjustable parts, Barb deserved a little teasing.

"Well, he does like books," Barb said defensively.

Jana smiled. "Then it's a good fit. Joshua does work he likes and gets to interact with people who are, for the most part, coming in for something that will please them."

Barb looked out the window and said, "We're just friends. I have *lots* of friends. Besides, Joshua is too young for me."

Definitely too young and too . . . undomesticated . . . to cope with some human behaviors. But being a true wild boy, Joshua is the only friend you're hoping no one mentions to your brother.

Jana looked in the rearview mirror again. John met her eyes and nodded. If Michael Debany found out about Barb's friendship with Joshua Painter, the news wouldn't come from either of them.

Tolya turned on his computer. He'd never had a reason to be grateful for the Earthday rule of most businesses being closed—including government offices—but as Bennett was swiftly being transformed back into an inhabited town, he appreciated having one day when he could ignore the human residents and their helpful ideas and the requests to reopen more of the businesses. Reopening businesses was a good thing, certainly, but all those humans made his job more demanding. At least handling the paperwork and keeping track of who was living where and running which business was no longer his problem now that he had hired the two humans to be land agents.

His mobile phone rang. He glanced at the clock as the phone rang again. Too early to be a personal call. Too early to be anything but trouble.

"Tolya Sanguinati."

"It's Stewart Dixon. Do you remember me?"

"Of course." A rancher who lived north of the Elder Hills, Stewart Dixon had been helpful when the Prairie Gold Wolves had shipped eleven bison to Lakeside. "What? Please repeat your words." The signal faded and came back.

"A stranger came to the house. Tried to force himself on my daughter. Ranch hand came in and interrupted. My man's been stabbed. I've got him in the truck and I'm heading to Bennett. Please gods, tell me you have a doctor there."

"We do. Come to the government building when you reach the town. I will escort you to the doctor from there."

"Got my wife and daughter with me," Dixon said. "My sons and some of the hands are watching the house and the horses."

Tolya disconnected the call, then used the desk phone to call one of the doctors who had been hired through the Lakeside job fair. The doctor's wife was a nurse and midwife and worked with her husband, so he didn't have to call anyone else. But after a moment's thought, he called the other doctor as well as the vet, who also had been hired through the job fair. Tolya wasn't sure the second doctor would be required or that the vet would be useful to a human who had been stabbed, but he wanted all of the town's bodywalkers awake and ready.

Next he considered the females coming in with Dixon. He wasn't sure if the daughter was injured, but he was certain that, with Dixon needing to be present to help the injured man, the females would be on their own and vulnerable.

He called the Bird Cage Saloon. "Scythe?"

"Yes." Her voice sounded rough, as if she wasn't fully in her human form yet.

"It's Tolya. I need you to provide hospitality to some human females who will be arriving soon."

"Why bring them to the saloon instead of the hotel?" Curiosity, not challenge.

"Because you're at the saloon." And no one would harm those women with a Harvester standing guard.

"I'll be ready," Scythe said.

With nothing else to do until Dixon arrived, Tolya checked his e-mail—and felt his body tighten as he opened the message from Jackson Wolfgard and downloaded the picture that was attached.

He printed out two copies of the picture—one to keep and one for the sheriff's office. Then he forwarded the picture, along with Jackson's message, to Jesse Walker.

If Stewart Dixon hadn't called, the picture would be no more than a curiosity this morning—a young woman with pale red hair looking in a mirror, but instead of her own reflection, the mirror showed a young, dark-haired man. The woman was starting to turn away, as if wanting nothing to do with the man.

Tolya recognized the woman—and he suspected Abigail Burch would be able to tell him the name of the man.

Scythe's hand rested on the phone. She was a hunter, a predator, a Harvester. Such an odd feeling to be asked to protect anything, let alone humans.

What was needed? What should she offer? And who should she have with her who would better understand what these females required?

She called Garnet Ravengard, who would keep watch from one of the trees in the town square and give warning if an enemy approached. Then she called Candice Caravelli and Lila Gold, waking both. When she told them to come to the saloon and why, Lila had questions about the females who needed protection. Candice did not, which made Scythe think that Candice knew more about needing help than Lila did. Her last call was to Yuri Sanguinati. The Intuit males who worked in the saloon were good workers, but she thought another predator would be more useful right now.

She combed out her hair, still wet from the shower, then dressed in jeans and a T-shirt—a simple outfit that matched the kind of clothes Candice and Lila wore before they reported to work. Casual attire. Something a business owner might wear before the business opened for the day and she dressed in the costume that was part of the ambiance of the Bird Cage Saloon.

She gave Yellow Bird fresh food and water and changed the papers in the cage as Barbara Ellen had shown her how to do.

"I will return later and listen to your singing." She didn't know if it made a difference to the bird, but it seemed sad for the bird to sing and not have anyone listen.

As a last check, she stood in front of the full-length mirror. The clothes were appropriate and would not alert the threat, whatever it may be, that she was more than the other females in the saloon. And the hair—mostly gold with streaks of blue and red—now had the waves that Lila Gold always complimented without understanding their significance.

A door opened downstairs—and Scythe's hair began to coil. A sharp whistle made her hesitate at the door of her suite.

<Scythe?> Yuri called.

<I'll be down in a moment. The girls will be here soon.>

Yuri laughed. <Human females at this hour of the morning? I'd better make coffee.>

Yes, Scythe thought. If the enemy came to her door, he would expect no trouble—right up to the moment when her hair turned black and simply looking at her would have his organs turning to sludge.

Jana opened the door of the sheriff's office and dropped her daypack on her desk.

"I'll put the food in the fridge for Virgil and Kane. Where do you want these?" John asked, lifting the carryalls as he walked past her.

"Put the clothes in Virgil's office." She almost told him to put the clothes in the Me Time cell, but that would be like pulling Virgil's tail—not something she wanted to do when they were almost getting along.

As soon as John left, Jana dropped Rusty's leash and turned on the computer. "I'll take a quick look at e-mail and make sure nothing urgent came in last night; then we'll drop off this letter at the post office and take a quick walk around the square. Okay?"

E-mail from Tolya, asking Virgil to meet with him as soon as the Wolf was on duty. Another e-mail from Tolya, specifically to her, telling her to report to him immediately to deal with a situation that had occurred on a ranch north of Bennett.

Did they have jurisdiction there? She hadn't been in town a full week yet and had been so focused on getting settled and learning the town's boundaries and its citizens that she hadn't thought about who else the Bennett Sheriff's Department was expected to protect. She'd study a map of the Midwest and find out where the towns had been before the war—

and make a note of which ones still existed. That would give her some idea of where the next human law enforcement might be.

Jana closed the e-mail program and headed for the door, snagging the letter to Tobias from the front pocket of her daypack as she passed her desk. "Okay. Let's go to the post office and then see Mr. Sanguin . . ."

Rusty huddled in her crate. Now that Jana thought about it, the pup had seemed overly eager to get inside the office this morning.

Crouching, Jana held out her hand. "Rusty? Come on, girl. It's okay. Come on out. Quick walk."

Rusty came to her but balked at the office door. Should she let the dog stay or insist on being obeyed?

"Come on, girl." She really needed a dog-training book. Or a book on human-dog relationships. Virgil could interpret dog, but she didn't want to ask him about Rusty's behavior since it would prove she knew less than he did and that would give him more reason to ignore what she thought about Rusty's education.

The dog came with her but didn't do her usual pulling on the leash to explore as much as possible. Instead, the only pulling was attempted dashes back to the sheriff's office. And when the pup wasn't trying to go back to the office, she was pressed so close to Jana's leg that Jana had to watch each step to avoid stepping on Rusty's feet.

As they came out on the other side of the square, Jana spotted Isobel Sanguinati outside the post office.

"Morning!" Jana called.

Isobel turned—and Jana jerked back a step. The Sanguinati who were in charge of Bennett had originally lived in Toland, an East Coast city that had been one of the largest human-controlled cities on the whole continent. They always sounded so educated and looked so sleek in their black clothes, it was easy to forget they weren't some high-society family who had made their fortune in banking and investments; they were predators. They were a form of *terra indigene*.

Looking at Isobel now, Jana knew she wouldn't forget it again.

Isobel smiled, carefully not showing even a hint of fang. "Your dog is nervous."

"Yes. We usually take a walk in the morning, but I think I should put her in her crate for a while."

"It would be harder for an enemy to reach her if she was in a larger cell." Isobel held out a hand. "You have mail? I will take it."

"Thanks." Jana hesitated a moment before stepping forward and giving Isobel the letter. "Why do you think Rusty needs a larger cell? What's going on?"

"Perhaps nothing. Perhaps a fight." Isobel walked into the post office.

Oh gods. Who's fighting? Forcing herself to steady her breathing, Jana looked around. An Eagle perched on one of the new hitching posts, watching her. Hawks soared overhead. Ravens or Crows flew from one tree in the square to the next, but they were silent. Whatever communication was being shared, it wasn't vocalized.

A little ways down the street, Jana noticed Becky Gott taking her morning constitutional. Hannah and Sarah Gott had taken over two of the alleyway stores for their used-clothing business, and Becky had the job of sorting buttons taken from clothes her aunts deemed fit to be rags or quilting squares, filling glass containers with different colors. But every morning Becky took a walk around the square, waving at people as they opened their stores. Eventually her brother, Jacob, would fetch her and guide her back to the Gotts' store.

Today, with Rusty whining and Isobel Sanguinati's comment about a fight still circling in her head, seeing Becky on her own gave Jana a chill.

"Deputy? Morning, Jana!"

Jana worked up a smile as Craig and Dawn Werner, the new land agents, hurried toward her. In their mid-twenties and married just before the war that swept over the continent earlier that summer, they had had the misfortune of losing their jobs a couple of days before the wedding. With some cash from friends and family, they had packed their belongings into two large backpacks and headed out to see some of Thaisia. Then the Elders closed the borders between the regions, making travel difficult if a person didn't have a work permit. Caught on the wrong side of the border and unable to return to the West Coast town where they had grown up, they had scrambled for food and shelter and safety until they managed to convince someone that they were heading for jobs in Bennett and bought tickets on a bus that covered travel between towns not serviced by the trains.

"Morning. Who is this?" Jana asked, looking at the black-and-white puppy.

"We just got him yesterday and haven't settled on a name," Dawn said. "We're not even sure what breed he is, but we're hoping he doesn't get too big."

Studying the puppy, Jana thought Dawn should hope a lot harder.

When both puppies started whimpering, Jana figured she'd delayed long enough. "I have to—"

"We have a business proposal for reopening the movie theater," Dawn said hurriedly, holding out a sheaf of papers. "Small scale to start since we're running the land agent office. Just weekends. I would take care of tickets and the books."

"I worked part-time in the projection booth of theaters in our home town and could take care of showing the movies," Craig said.

"Could you . . . ?" Dawn glanced toward the government building, then quickly looked away when Tolya Sanguinati stepped up to the open window and looked down at them.

"Yeah, okay." Aware that she should be heading up to the mayor's office to talk to Tolya, Jana looked at Becky, who seemed to be studying something in the grass. She hoped it wasn't poop. "Drop the proposal off at the sheriff's office this afternoon and I'll take a look at it. Right now, I need a favor. That's Becky Gott."

"Okay," Craig said.

"I'd like you . . ."

Horses. Screaming.

The Eagle launched itself skyward. The Ravens were suddenly in motion.

A fight, Isobel had said. Looked like it had arrived. But who were they fighting?

Jana gave Craig a shove. "Grab Becky and get inside."

"Where . . . ?" Dawn began, scooping up her own puppy.

"Anywhere! Just get inside. Now!" Certain that Rusty would run away from strangers if she gave her to Dawn, Jana unclipped the leash from the pup's collar and dropped it. Better to let the dog run and hide than have the leash tangle in something and leave Rusty vulnerable to whatever had frightened the horses.

Drawing her weapon out of the holster, she strode across the square, trusting Craig and Dawn to look after Becky. If she could reach the office, she'd take a moment to shut Rusty inside.

She was almost across the square when she heard gunshots coming from the direction of the livery stable.

As she looked in that direction, a woman on the other side of the square screamed—Dawn or Becky. Rusty stopped suddenly and barked, a frightened, frantic sound.

Pivoting, Jana cocked the hammer and raised her gun.

Two dogs racing toward her from the direction of the stables. The one in the lead was a big brute. Nowhere near as big as the Wolves, but the biggest dog she'd ever seen.

In the second before she pulled the trigger, she wished she'd asked about a firing range where officers must have practiced, wished she'd tested the revolver. Wished . . .

Sound exploded around her. Even as the gunshot filled her ears and head, she heard the sound of fighting off to her right and saw both dogs still coming toward her—not running from the livery stable, running at *her*.

No time. No time.

She shot the first dog in the chest and put two bullets into the second dog just before it launched itself at her. A savage cry had her spinning around in time to shoot the dog that had been charging her from behind. She had one round left, and the fourth dog . . .

She jerked the revolver skyward to avoid shooting Joshua Painter as the dog grabbed the boy's left arm, exposing its own belly. Joshua's right hand lashed out, and the claws on the specially made leather glove ripped the dog's belly open.

Jana took a step toward the fight still taking place on the other side of the square. One dog ran toward her, trying to flee from the Wolves' attack. Before she could take aim, smoke raced above the ground and overtook the dog. Hands formed, grabbed the dog, and snapped its neck. When the dog dropped, the smoke shifted into Tolya Sanguinati.

Silence, followed by a savage, furious snarl.

And then a lone Wolf howled.

Jana looked back. The dogs she'd shot were dead or dying. Either way, they were no longer a threat. Neither was the dog Joshua had gutted. But the boy . . .

"Joshua?" She kept her gun lowered but ready as she studied the savage expression in those gray-ringed green eyes. "You okay?"

He rose from his crouched position over the dog. His eyes took in her badge, her gun, and . . .

She knew Rusty had returned before she felt the pup press against her leg. She crouched, her eyes never leaving Joshua's face, and rested one hand on the pup. She didn't know where Rusty had gone, if the pup had stayed near her or had run and now returned. She'd been focused on keeping them alive.

"It's okay, girl. It's okay. You okay?" She risked a quick glance at the pup. No blood. A quick feel revealed no injuries that she could detect.

"She belongs to you?"

She stopped the instinctive move of raising the gun. In that moment of distraction, Joshua had closed the distance between them without making a sound.

He might be human, but he'd been raised by the Panthergard and was, in his own way, just as much a predator as the *terra indigene*. That was something she couldn't afford to forget.

"Yes, she's mine," Jana replied.

He nodded. "She stayed close. Would have died if you hadn't been a good predator, but she stayed close." He met Jana's eyes. "Loves you."

She swallowed hard. Did his being an Intuit make his certainty more powerful? "Your arm?"

He held up the left arm and gave her a feral smile that made her shiver. From wrist to elbow he wore a quilted sleeve over his shirt. Thick, puffy thing—slimmer than the suits officers wore when training dogs for police work, but it had done the trick.

"Might have bruises," Joshua said as he considered the arm. Then he shrugged.

A Wolf howled again.

Jana sprang to her feet. Only one Wolf howling—and many *terra indigene* flying toward the spot where the Wolfgard had fought the dogs.

"Jana!" Barb ran toward her from the direction of the diner, then skidded to a stop when she saw the dogs. "Oh." Her eyes filled with tears. "Oh."

"They were enemies," Joshua said, his voice hard.

"I know, I know." Barb wiped the tears off her face, then paled as she stared at the bloody, clawed glove on Joshua's hand and understood what it meant.

Looking at Barb's face, Jana understood the dogs weren't the only thing that had died on the square that morning. She wouldn't be surprised if the stack of romances about the wild man tamed by love were quietly returned to the book-sorting room.

"Barb," Jana said softly.

Barb sniffed. "Is Rusty okay?"

"Yeah. Can you take her to the office for me? I need to check on Virgil and Kane."

"Sure." Hooking a couple of fingers under Rusty's collar, Barb led the pup to the sheriff's office. Joshua watched her go but didn't follow.

Jana holstered her gun and ran to the other side of the square.

With a furious snarl, Virgil tore out the throat of the last enemy. Then he howled.

We are here. A message to the other *terra indigene* who had joined the fight as well as a message to the Elders. *We are here.*

<Kane?> The Wolves had needed to meet the enemy pack, so he'd ignored the gunshots coming from the building where the horses lived. And he'd heard another gun being fired in the square. He needed to find the rest of the fighters, but first . . . <Kane!>

<Hurt.>

Virgil leaped over the bodies of the dead dogs to reach his brother, who struggled to stand on three legs. Kane's left hip was ripped and bloody—was still bleeding.

Standing next to Kane so his brother could lean against him, Virgil howled again—this time, a cry for help. In the wild country, the Wolfgard would have licked the wound to clean it, would have found the safest place for a packmate to rest—and if their pack didn't have a bodywalker who had learned how to set bones and close up wounds, they would have hunted for their wounded, starving themselves if game was scarce.

But here the Wolfgard were too few, and the dogs had been many, despite the Wolves receiving help from the Sanguinati.

"Virgil? Kane?"

Virgil watched Jana as she ran toward them, as Tolya Sanguinati headed toward them.

They were few, but that didn't mean they didn't have a pack.

Movement coming from the side. Virgil turned his head and snarled.

Tobias Walker, his gun still in his hand, stopped moving. Raising one hand, he carefully holstered his weapon.

"Anyone hurt?" Tobias asked.

"Kane," Jana said. "Gods, he's bleeding."

Her voice sounded . . . strange. High. Not like the wolverine who challenged him all the time.

"I called the vet for another reason," Tolya said. "He'll be at his clinic now."

"My truck is at the livery stable," Tobias said. "I'll throw a couple of blankets in the bed for padding. We'll get him there."

"I have the official vehicle," Jana said.

"Let Tobias Walker drive," Tolya said.

Something in the Sanguinati's voice warned that there would be no discussion—and that made Virgil look closer at the wolverine. No blood on her. He hadn't noticed her having trouble moving. But Tolya recognized there was something not right about her. He couldn't put a word to what he sensed, but he agreed.

Tobias ran to fetch the truck.

<Virgil.> Even using the *terra indigene* form of communication, Kane sounded weak. <You have to stay and help Tolya. Your job as the dominant enforcer.>

He knew that. He didn't like it, not with Kane so hurt, but he knew it. <Do you trust Tobias Walker enough to be with him when you're hurt?>

<Tell Deputy Jana to come with us.>

Yes. She wasn't a Wolf, but she was a member of their pack.

Tolya met his eyes, then looked at Jana. "Virgil needs to help me deal with this. You should go with Kane and Tobias."

Jana nodded. "What about the other thing you wanted me to do?"

"Stewart Dixon isn't here yet. Scythe will look after the females until you return and are ready to talk to them."

Crowgard cawed a warning moments before Tobias appeared with the truck. The Intuit drove carefully, turning the truck around so that the back was close to the Wolves. Tobias hopped out and opened the tailgate.

Tolya stepped forward. "I'll lift Kane into the truck." The Sanguinati smiled, showing a hint of fang. "He's heavy."

Tobias eyed Kane and nodded.

It was easy to forget the Sanguinati were strong. As smoke, they did not look strong, even if they could outrun Wolves in that form. But Tolya lifted Kane and set him on the tailgate before shifting to a form between human and smoke and flowing into the bed of the pickup to help Kane take a few staggering steps to the blankets Tobias had piled up as a nest.

Jana did a twisty hop that ended with her sitting on the tailgate. She scooted over to Kane, one hand resting on his shoulder as he lowered his head to her thigh and sighed.

Tobias looked at Virgil. "We'll look after him."

He had to trust. But he waited until Tolya was the only one close enough to hear him before he let out a quiet, distressed whine.

CHAPTER 22

Moonsday, Messis 20

"You should clean those wounds," Tolya said quietly. "I don't think Deputy Jana noticed because your wounds aren't as serious as Kane's, but you should take care of them before she shakes off her distress over the fight and sees you again." A pause. "Do you need help?"

Virgil stood absolutely still. There had been no Sanguinati where he'd lived before. With the exception of John Wolfgard, none of the shifters now living in Bennett had had any experience with that form of *terra indigene*. But Simon Wolfgard worked with one of the Sanguinati, even ran a bookstore with him.

<I don't need help.> He had no reason *not* to trust Tolya, but being around other strong predators when he was hurt made him uneasy.

Tolya nodded as if he understood the reason behind the words and would have given the same answer. "We have humans coming in from a ranch and another problem that needs to be addressed. If you can shift to your human form without doing harm to yourself, I would appreciate it."

<I'll be back.>

"I'll arrange to have the carcasses picked up. They're meat?"

<Yes.> He considered the humans whose lives brushed against his.

<Take them beyond all the houses. Animals and *terra indigene* will welcome the meat.>

"Best if Barbara Ellen and Deputy Jana don't have to look at that particular truth today."

The wolverine had sounded squeaky, but she would shake that off, and once she did, he didn't need her snarling at him today.

Leaving Tolya, Virgil trotted across the square. He stopped to sniff the ground and the dogs he found within sight of the sheriff's office. One was gutted; three were shot. The largest of the dogs had a hole in its chest and a bloody straight line along its shoulder that looked too shallow to have done more than annoy the dog. But the three dogs told him why the wolverine had sounded squeaky. She'd been in her own fight and had stood her ground.

He crossed the street to the sheriff's office, then shifted his front paws enough to open the door. He stepped inside and stopped.

Kneeling in front of Rusty's crate, Barbara Ellen twisted around to look at him.

"Oh, Virgil."

She didn't say anything else, so he went into the bathroom and, once again, shifted his front paws enough to turn on the water in the shower cubicle. Then he stood there in his Wolf form, letting water wash away the enemies' blood and wash out his wounds. The wounds hurt, but none of them were crippling and most weren't that deep.

He was big enough and strong enough—and skilled enough—to bring down a half-grown bison by himself, tearing at its legs until it collapsed. Even so, he and Kane had been outnumbered by dogs that also knew how to fight. They would have lost this fight on their own. He knew it. So did Tolya. But the Sanguinati *had* entered the fight. So had the Eagles and Hawks.

So had the wolverine.

Once he was clean as a Wolf, he shifted to his human form and washed that too. The wounds looked worse on a human body. Why was that? But looking at his arms reminded him that he hadn't heard from the other member of the Wolfgard pack. <John?>

<I'm all right. Didn't have time to shift all the way before one of the dogs attacked me. I crippled it, and Yuri Sanguinati killed it. I think my

being in the between form scared some of the humans who were watching the fight. What about you and Kane?>

<I'm all right. Kane is hurt. The wolverine and Tobias Walker are taking him to the vet.>

<What do you want me to do?>

<Help Tolya with the carcasses until I get there.>

Shutting off the water, Virgil patted himself dry. Finding a healing ointment in the medicine chest, he dabbed some on the wounds he could reach. There were tears in the flesh on his back that might benefit from the human medicine, but he couldn't reach those. He considered asking Barbara Ellen to help, then decided against it and put the ointment back in the medicine chest.

Once he was dressed in his usual jeans and shirt, he stepped into the front part of the office. Barbara Ellen had left a pink message on the floor in front of Rusty's crate, saying she had to feed the other animals.

Virgil knelt as he opened the crate, then sat back on his heels. Rusty came to him and licked his face, so glad to see him. But he knew she was looking for someone else too.

"Your mom has to help Kane right now." He buried his hands in the puppy's fur. "I guess this was her first real fight, and maybe she was afraid. But she stood for you, kept you safe."

His mate would have fought to protect their pups, along with the rest of their pack. Hadn't made a difference in the end. Too many of the enemy with weapons that could bring down bison. There had been only Wolfgard there in that remote spot that should have been safe since they'd had limited contact with humans.

Not safe enough.

"In you go, pup." After coaxing Rusty into her crate, Virgil hesitated before opening the bottom drawer of the wolverine's desk, taking out the plastic tub, and removing one of the chewing treats. It was shaped like a bone—but not like any bone *he'd* ever seen—and was supposed to be tasty. He'd eaten one when the wolverine wasn't around and decided that if dogs thought those things were tasty, there was something wrong with dogs.

But the pup wagged her tail and made happy sounds when he opened the door wide enough to give her the treat.

"Don't tell your mom."

Putting the tub back in the drawer and making sure the crate door was secured, Virgil left the office so that the citizens of Bennett could see what would tear out the throat of any threat, whether that threat was a dog or a human.

Tolya watched John Wolfgard and Yuri Sanguinati toss the carcasses into the back of a pickup. Then he scanned the street. Most of the humans had been inside their shops or hadn't reported to work yet. That was good. The fewer humans who saw proof of what the *terra indigene* could do, the less fear would scent the air and excite the predators among them. And since half of Bennett's residents were predators, it was better if the other half didn't turn themselves into scent lures.

Scythe crossed the street, not even glancing at the dead dogs. Their life force was already spent, so they held no interest for her.

"Should I have fought?" she asked. "I was close enough, but I thought the Wolves would see and . . ."

"And die," Tolya finished for her. "You were right to stay out of it."

"What about the females who need protection?"

"They'll be here soon."

As Scythe headed back to the Bird Cage Saloon, Candice Caravelli and Lila Gold piled out of a taxi and hurried to follow Scythe.

As soon as those two females left the taxi, Dawn Werner ran out of the saloon and waved her arms at the driver, followed by her limping mate, who had a scarf wrapped around the calf of one leg.

"Dog bite?" Virgil asked, coming up beside Tolya.

"Looks that way. I had called the doctor about another matter. He will be in his office soon, if he's not there already." Wondering what had happened to the puppy the woman had been holding, Tolya watched the two humans get in the taxi, which sped toward the medical building on the other side of the square. "There are things we need to discuss, but they can wait until Stewart Dixon arrives."

"What is there to discuss?"

"The face of a potential enemy."

*   *   *

The vet and Tobias used one of the blankets to carry Kane into a treatment room. Jana watched, not sure what she was supposed to do.

"Should we step out?" she asked, pointing to herself and Tobias.

"No," the vet said too quickly.

Well, she couldn't fault the man for wanting familiar humans in the room with Kane. Patching up one of the Wolfgard after a fight wouldn't be a usual part of the vet's training.

"I'd like to use anesthesia . . . ," the vet began.

Kane swung around, snapping and snarling, and would have fallen off the table if Jana and Tobias hadn't grabbed the Wolf.

"That's not an option," she said, hoping she sounded official.

"But I need to shave the fur around the wounds and . . ."

Kane's snarls became more threat than warning, and the vet stepped back from the table.

Jana felt sorry for the man. He couldn't use a muzzle or any other kind of restraint to keep himself and his patient safe. But working on Kane, who was already hurt and upset, with no kind of restraint? She wouldn't do it.

Of course, she was the one holding on to both of Kane's front legs, which put her hands and forearms in easy reach of those big sharp teeth.

She was an idiot.

"Vet's right about shaving the area around the wounds," Tobias said. "Doctors shave the hair around a wound on humans too. That sucks, but sometimes it needs to be done."

"Stitching the wounds will hurt." The vet was still standing back from the table.

"What about a local anesthetic? The objection is about feeling vulnerable, right?" Tobias's first question was for the vet. The second was directed at Kane, who replied with a grunt and growl. "A local would numb the area around the wounds that need to be stitched and make it easier for everyone, but Kane would still know what's going on around him." Now he looked at Jana.

Since Kane couldn't speak for himself without shifting—and that didn't seem like a good idea right now—she, being his fellow deputy, was apparently his medical proxy.

"Local anesthetic." She looked at Kane. Was she imagining the fear in his eyes? Remembering why Kane and Virgil were the only survivors of their original pack, she added, "I'll stay here and keep watch."

That must have been the right thing to say, because Kane lowered his head and sighed.

"You might feel a prick," the vet said as he approached the table with a syringe.

Kane either didn't feel it or was hurting too much to care. But the sound of the clippers had the Wolf rearing up and showing his teeth.

"It's all right," Tobias said, laying a hand on Kane's shoulder. "The fur will grow back. Right, doc?"

Maybe it was the sound, or maybe it was the feel of something on his skin so close to the wound, but Kane wasn't having it until Jana snapped, "Stop being such a baby about this. The vet is going to shave off the fur and stitch you up and that's that."

All three males stared at her.

She stared back and showed her teeth. "What? Is this Testosterone United?"

"When dealing with feisty women, we males have to stick together," Tobias said. "It's kind of the T.U. code."

She might have said something unforgivable if she hadn't seen the satisfied *so there* look on Kane's face.

She gave them all a "Danger! Angry woman" face. Kane closed his eyes and pretended to ignore her. Tobias winked at her and said nothing. The vet worked.

After a few minutes, Tobias said, "If you don't need me right now, I'll step out and make a couple of calls, find out how everyone else is doing."

Jana nodded. After Tobias left the room, she said, "Kane has some cuts on his face."

The vet handed her a bowl filled with liquid and a clean cloth. "Wash them with this."

As the vet went back to stitching up the worst of Kane's wounds, Jana carefully washed the cuts on the Wolf's face and the gash in one ear.

"When you train to be a cop, you know you might have to shoot someone in the line of duty, but I've never fired a weapon at another living thing until today. Gods, I'd never fired a weapon anywhere but at the firing range." Her breath hitched. "I've never killed anything before. I've never gone hunting or anything like that. I know it was the dogs or us, but . . ."

She didn't realize she was crying until Kane raised his head and licked her face.

"I should put a dressing on this, but I doubt he would tolerate it," the vet said.

"He'll want to keep it clean his own way." Jana leaned forward until she and the Wolf were nose to nose. "But he promises not to pull out the stitches. Right?"

"*Grrf.*"

She took that as agreement.

Tobias slipped back into the room. "One man was bitten and is being treated by a human doctor. Nobody else had any serious injuries from that attack."

"Was there another attack?" Jana asked, alarmed that the dogs might have injured someone else in the town before reaching the square.

"Man was brought in from Stewart Dixon's ranch. He's at the doc's office now. Once we're done here, we're supposed to bring Kane back to the sheriff's office, and you're supposed to join Tolya to take someone's statement."

She nodded.

"Is that where Mr. Wolfgard will be? The sheriff's office?" the vet asked.

"During regular office hours," Jana replied. "I expect his brother will want him to be at home in the evenings."

"Then I'll stop by the office tomorrow to check on my patient."

Allowing Tobias to lift him off the table, Kane limped out of the vet's office on three legs. Jana rolled her eyes when Tobias gave her a look that made her swallow any remarks about male stubbornness. And she swallowed any comments when Kane stood on one hind leg and planted his front legs on the tailgate since he didn't snarl about Tobias lifting his back end and then helping him get settled in the pickup bed.

Since Kane didn't need her with him, she sat in the front with Tobias on the drive back to the town square.

"Testosterone United, huh?" she said after a minute.

He grinned. "It worked, didn't it?" The grin faded. "After Tolya told

me about the attack at the Dixon ranch, I called my mother, as well as
Ellen Garcia at the Prairie Gold ranch, and the resettled ranches between
here and Prairie Gold. Wanted to let them know we had a gang of marauders in the area."

"Wouldn't they have to come through Bennett to reach the places
south of the town?" Jana asked.

"They could take a roundabout route and come up from the south,
but, yes, if they hit a ranch north of us, it's a good bet they'll be coming
to town or hiding out somewhere nearby. There are a few places around
here that are nothing more than way stations with a combination gas station and general store, and a couple of houses, if that."

Gang of marauders. How often did Tobias drive around alone?

"Are you staying in town today?"

"Wasn't planning to stay the whole day, but looks like I will be now.
I'll see about getting a room at the hotel for the night." He glanced at her.
"You've got work to do, but maybe we can take a ride later? That buck-
skin will get up to some mischief if he doesn't get enough work."

"I'd like to get out for awhile."

He smiled and said, "Good."

Tobias had a really nice smile.

B arb knelt in front of the large crate that held a litter of puppies and
listened to the dogs in the fenced yard, barking and barking. The
puppies needed to be socialized with people and other dogs. They needed
care and training and love. They needed more than she could give them
on her own.

People helped her when they could, but not everyone was interested
in the animals—and even fewer people wanted to deal with so much
poop. But time was running out. The Others didn't understand the human desire to have a pet, a companion, something not-them that would
share their living space.

Well, they might understand about sharing their living space with
something that was not them. After all, they had allowed humans to
settle on this continent when travelers first arrived from other parts of
Thaisia centuries ago. But understanding didn't mean they wouldn't put

down anything they viewed as a threat. They'd done it with the people who were part of the Humans First and Last movement—and they had done it today with the dogs.

"Are you angry with me?"

Trying to stand up and twist around at the same time, Barb fell on her butt and yelped. Which set off the puppies.

Joshua stepped closer and crouched in front of her. He held his hand out—not to her, but to the puppies in the crate—and let them sniff him.

"Why would I be angry with you?" Barb wrapped her arms around her knees, ashamed that she didn't feel comfortable being around him right now. She looked at his hand and only saw the blood on that clawed glove he sometimes wore—and saw the gutted dog. No, she couldn't be angry with him any more than she could be angry with Jana for killing the dogs, but today she realized that, despite his human biology, Joshua Painter was more Other than human—and maybe he always would be.

"I killed one of the dogs."

Misery swelled inside her. "I felt so optimistic when I got off the train a few weeks ago. I was going to work with animals and have a horse and it would be a big adventure."

"You're doing all those things."

Yes, she was. But today had scraped off some of the shine, revealing a harsher reality than she'd imagined. She looked at the puppies. "Help me take them outside. They all need piddle time."

They took the puppies out front to a strip of dried, yellow grass instead of taking them into the backyard with the mature dogs.

"A lot of small towns in the Northeast had a larger population than Bennett, but there's maybe a few hundred citizens here now—and that's figuring in humans and the *terra indigene*. No one's thinking of adding a pet to their household when most people are still trying to figure out where they're going to live, and even when they do select a house, they have to clear out the personal effects and get themselves settled while working at whatever business is their livelihood."

She watched Joshua with the puppies as they returned the pups to their crate. The older dogs reacted to Joshua the same way they reacted to Saul Panthergard, regardless of his form; they smelled a predator. But the puppies seemed to think Joshua smelled interesting.

"The *terra indigene* will not want pets," Joshua said thoughtfully as he petted the puppies. "And the humans are too busy to think about pets."

"That's true right now. I'm just afraid that by the time they start thinking it would be nice to have a dog or cat or bird . . ." She was supposed to meet with the vet today to review her training and skills. If she was going to continue her education on an apprenticeship basis, she had to reduce the number of animals in her care by finding homes for them before the Others made a different choice.

She studied Joshua. She was about to ask him if he'd like a puppy, but she remembered that bloody glove and couldn't do it. Not today.

Joshua stood. "I'll help you for an hour. Then I have to go to work."

"Shouldn't you already be at work?" she asked.

"Yes, but John will understand."

She almost told him a human boss would be less understanding, but she wanted the help, especially today. "Thanks." When she next saw Tobias Walker she'd ask for any suggestions about finding homes beyond Bennett for the orphaned pets.

Virgil lifted Kane off the tailgate and lowered him to the ground, letting his brother limp into the sheriff's office on his own.

"He's hurting," Tobias Walker said quietly. "How about you?"

"Nothing that won't heal." Virgil watched the wolverine follow Kane into the office. "What about her?"

"She helped Kane get through the vet stitching him up."

"She killed. That was not natural for her."

"She did, and you're right; it wasn't natural. Her emotions might be . . . big . . . for a few days while she comes to terms with what happened this morning."

Virgil studied the human male. What did that mean, her emotions might be big? Weren't they always big?

"I'm going to stay in town today," Tobias said. "I'll see about getting a room at the hotel and taking care of some of the chores for Prairie Gold, but I'll be around if you need help of any kind."

Virgil nodded and walked into the office. John had done some scrounging in the warehouse that held possessions from the cleared-out houses. He hadn't found something he called a Wolf bed, but he had found a folding cot. After moving Kane's desk to one side, there had been enough room to put the mattress on the floor. John had added a couple of blankets as a mattress cover and thought it would do as a comfortable place for Kane to sleep when he was in the office.

Kane obviously thought it would do since he gave the mattress and blankets a quick sniff before lowering himself onto them with a groan.

The wolverine wasn't paying attention to Kane. *She* was staring at Rusty—or the remains of something in Rusty's crate. Then she narrowed her eyes at Virgil. "Who gave Rusty one of the treats?"

"Cowboy Bob," he replied blandly.

She looked at the toy leaning against the side of her desk, then turned back to Virgil, baring her teeth. "Cowboy Bob? Really? Is that what we're doing now? *Blaming the stuffie?*"

She looked bigger than she had a minute ago, but he met her eyes and said, "Yeah."

The sound she made reminded him of a whistling teakettle on the boil.

She brushed past him, giving him an elbow in the ribs before she grabbed one of the bowls near Kane, who flinched and then whined when he realized his injured leg wouldn't allow him to get out of the way. When the wolverine headed for the back rooms and started banging around in the kitchen doing who knew what, Virgil blew out a breath.

He was starting to understand what Tobias Walker meant by her emotions being big. Fortunately for the Wolves, there was a reason to shove her out the door and let someone else deal with her for a while.

She returned to the front room and put the bowl of water where Kane could reach it easily.

"Tolya Sanguinati needs you to talk to the females from the Dixon ranch," Virgil said. "He's waiting for you at the saloon."

"Why there?" She didn't sound quite on the boil anymore but still close enough.

"Scythe is protecting them while Stewart Dixon is protecting the wounded male, who is at the human bodywalker's office."

The wolverine nodded. Virgil stepped aside to let her pass. But she stopped when she was abreast of him and stared at the door.

"You tell Cowboy Bob that if he gives Rusty another unauthorized treat today, I will pull all the stuffing out of his arms." She walked out of the office.

<Virgil?> Kane whined.

He didn't answer, but he heard Kane sigh—and felt the same relief—when he turned the lock on the door.

<Tolya?> Virgil called. <The wolverine is on her way over to see you. She has big emotions.>

Tolya frowned. <What does that mean?>

<Be careful.>

That sounded ominous. But no matter what Virgil would like to believe, Deputy Jana was just a human female.

With a gun.

Seeing her walk into the saloon, Tolya realized he'd been too busy to have much contact with all the new arrivals, including their female deputy, and had been assuming she was some combination of Barbara Ellen bounce and Jesse Walker grit—they being the two human females he'd had sufficient contact with to gain some understanding of that gender in the human species. Now he had a better appreciation of why Virgil referred to Jana as a wolverine.

"Mr. Sanguinati," Jana said. "You wanted to see me?"

"There was an attack on a ranch early this morning."

"I saw your e-mails. Ranches north of the town are part of our jurisdiction?"

"There is a Wolfgard pack who keeps watch in that area, but I don't think there are any human police, if that's what you're asking."

Jana nodded before looking at the four women sitting at the table farthest from the door. "If the daughter was attacked, I'll need to ask some personal questions. They may want to do that somewhere more private."

"They have use of the female dressing rooms upstairs, or we can use Scythe's office," Tolya said.

"You're sitting in?"

"Yes. I, too, have some questions."

"Does Scythe have a pad of paper and a pen? I left the office without them."

Tolya silently made the request. Scythe walked out of her office a moment later and held out the items.

"Thanks." Jana walked over to the table. A moment later, Candice Caravelli and Lila Gold said their good-byes and walked up to the bar.

"There's been no trouble here," Scythe said. <Yuri is here.>

"Good." The word acknowledged both messages. Tolya looked at Candice and Lila. "Anything I should know?"

"Melanie is really scared," Lila said.

Tolya wasn't sure if Candice Caravelli's silence meant she had nothing to say or nothing she wanted to say to him and Scythe. He would consider that later.

He joined Jana and introduced her to Melanie and Judith Dixon.

"What happened this morning?" Jana asked.

"Ranch work starts early, as soon as we can," Melanie began. "Mom was out collecting eggs from our chickens, and Dad was in the stable taking care of the stallion while my brothers and the hands were tending the other horses and putting them out in the paddocks. The house's front and back doors were open to let in the cooler air. We lock up at night, but it's always been safe to leave the doors open during the day when someone's around."

"That makes sense," Jana said.

Tolya listened and struggled to comprehend the undercurrents. He'd had more interaction with humans in the past few weeks than he'd had in the whole of his life, and he wasn't always sure if he was reading humans correctly. It sounded like Jana was confirming that the females had done nothing wrong by leaving the doors open. Why would that have been wrong?

"I was setting out food to make for breakfast when I heard a couple of cars drive up." Melanie frowned. "Didn't see any headlights, but I didn't think about that. Could have been the hands coming in from the cabins."

"Cabins?" Tolya asked.

"We have two cabins on the land we . . ." Judith stopped. "On the land we lease for grazing. Men will stay there for a couple of days at a time to check on the cattle, as well as ride out and make note of the available grass and water. Sometimes, if we get a fast-moving storm or a heavy snowfall, it's a place to shelter. My husband told the Wolfgard that the *terra indigene* are welcome to use the cabins too. We keep them supplied with cans of food and jugs of fresh water, as well as seasoned wood for the stove."

Tolya nodded. He knew the Wolfgard had no quarrel with Stewart Dixon and his family. He also knew the Wolves and Dixon had hunted together to bring down meat for both their families.

"I heard the back door open," Melanie continued. "I started to turn away from the counter, figuring it was one of my brothers coming in for coffee. But it was a stranger. He shoved me up against the counter, shoved me hard, and put a knife against my face. He said he could tell I needed a good humping, and if I stayed quiet no one would get hurt. He . . ." Her hand shook as she picked up a glass of water that was on the table and took a sip. "He grabbed my breast, then started pulling at my jeans. But he wasn't getting them open fast enough, because the next thing, he pushed me down on my knees and started to pull down his zipper. That's when another man came into the kitchen, just for a moment. He said, 'By all the dark gods, we don't have time for that. Someone sounded an alarm.' He ran off, and I heard the screen door in the front of the house squeak and thought Dad was going to be mad because he asked my brothers to oil the hinges last week."

"Who sounded the alarm?" Jana asked.

"The Owlgard," Judith said. "A pair of them moved into the hay barn after the troubles. Stewart installed an Owl door for them and built a kind of platform under it so that, once the chicks hatched, the adults could be outside if they wanted and still be close to the nest." Taking the glass from her daughter, she sipped some water before handing back the glass. "Anyway, all of a sudden one of the adults was swooping around the chicken coop, which they've never done before, and I guess one of them went to the stables and shifted to tell the men there were strangers in the house. Stewart and the boys came running, but Manuel had been heading for the house anyway because he heard a car driving away fast and felt uneasy enough that he wanted to check on Melanie."

"Manuel rushed in, shouting when he saw the man and realized . . ." Melanie gagged a little before regaining control. "The man rammed the knife into Manuel before running out the door. I heard Dad shouting and he shot at the car, but the men got away."

"The car has a broken taillight now and a broken window," Judith said. "We saw the glass when we were getting Manuel to the truck to bring him here." She thought for a moment. "Stewart said the getaway car swerved, and he thinks he might have hit the driver."

"You've never seen the man before?" Jana asked. "Could he be someone who works at another ranch, or someone who used to stop in Bennett and might be doing that again?"

Mother and daughter shook their heads.

Tolya opened the slim leather case he'd brought with him, took out a picture, and set it on the table. "Was this the man who attacked you?"

Melanie stared at the picture. "No. This is the other man, the one who warned him to get out."

Abigail swept and polished and vacuumed. She dusted the blinds and mopped the hallways and cleaned the restrooms in the office building that held a variety of small businesses. She didn't mind cleaning the offices. At least there weren't any surprises. The two attorneys who had come to Bennett didn't keep bowls of tumbled stones on their desks. And the desks intended for their personal assistants didn't have anything like that either.

Each office was made up of two rooms, and as houses were cleared, the attorneys' rooms were piling up with boxes that contained documents that might help locate living heirs.

She considered approaching the men and asking if they needed help sorting the mail that was still coming in for Bennett's previous residents. If someone sorted the personal mail from all the rest, that would be helpful, wouldn't it?

And seeing the personal mail would help her figure out which cities still had survivors and might be a place where she could disappear if she needed to disappear again.

Out of the corner of her eye, Abigail saw a shape where a shape shouldn't be. She stumbled back a step, almost getting her feet tangled in the vacuum cleaner's cord.

"Gods above and below, you scared me," she said.

Virgil Wolfgard stared at her. "Tolya wants to see you."

"Why?"

Virgil said nothing.

"I have work to do. We're all behind today, and I have more offices to clean." Her heart beat so hard, she wondered if he could hear it.

"They'll wait. Tolya won't."

"I have to tell my boss. I can't leave work without telling my boss. She's just down the hall."

Virgil bared his teeth, revealing fangs that weren't meant for a human mouth.

Abigail felt a desperate need to pee and wondered what he'd do if she wet herself. Probably wouldn't matter to him. He'd drag her out of the building and up the street to wherever Tolya waited.

"Let's go." Virgil stepped back from the doorway.

She bolted past him, then stopped. "I have to lock up. I have to . . ."

He grabbed her arm and pulled her down the hallway, down the stairs, and out of the building.

"Why are you angry with me?" she wailed. "I didn't do anything!"

People—humans—came out of shops and some looked like they might help. Until they saw Virgil, saw the red flickers in the amber eyes—a sign of anger in the Wolfgard. Then they slunk into their shops.

She should have known she wouldn't get any help from these gutless wonders. Not even Kelley, who came to the door of the jewelry store but didn't even ask what was going on.

When they reached the Bird Cage Saloon and Abigail saw Jana, she hoped she had at least one ally. But she wished it had been Barb Debany in the saloon instead of Jana. Barb was a sure thing. Jana was still a question mark.

"I have to pee," she said. "I really have to pee."

Virgil released her arm and looked at Jana. "Go with her."

Abigail hustled to keep up with Jana as they headed to the toilets, which were located past the pool table, which she thought was fine for the men, but would the women feel easy about using the facilities when the pool table was in use? In her experience, only rough men—the kind women were smart to avoid—drank and played pool in saloons.

She wasn't assigned to clean the saloon, so the facilities were an unwelcome surprise. Not individual stalls. It was just a single room with a toilet and sink. She hurried inside and started to close the door, but Jana put her shoulder against it and had a hand on the doorknob.

"I won't come in with you, but the door has to stay open a little ways," Jana said.

"What? Why?"

"Abby, if you really have to pee, do it." There was a hurtful sharpness in Jana's voice.

"I guess being a friend doesn't count for much here."

Jana didn't respond to the verbal jab, confirming that the deputy wasn't as gullible as her housemate.

She did what she had to because she really had to. When she tugged on the door to exit, Jana released her hold on the doorknob but looked ready to ram the door if Abigail tried to lock herself in.

"Why is everyone being so mean?"

"No one is being mean," Jana replied. "Just cooperate, okay? We believe you can answer some questions about an attack on a ranch early this morning."

"An attack? But I was *home* until I reported to work. Ask Kelley. He'll tell you." He might not have come to her rescue just now, but he wouldn't lie to get her in trouble. Not with the Sanguinati or the Wolves.

"No one thinks you were there, just that you have some answers."

Jana escorted her to the table farthest from the saloon's entrance, where Tolya waited. Abigail sat in the chair opposite the Sanguinati while Jana took the seat beside her. Virgil stood behind her, and every breath he took felt like a threat.

She'd been this scared at other times in her life, but she'd always managed to keep her nerve enough to get out of trouble. She'd keep her nerve this time too.

A sheet of paper lay in the center of the table. Tolya turned it over and pushed it toward her, saying nothing.

He didn't have to say anything. She'd seen a drawing like this before when Jesse Walker had been asking about fortune-telling cards and she'd shown Jesse and Shelley Bookman her decks of tarot cards.

"The blood prophet drew this, didn't she?" Abigail said, her voice barely loud enough to be heard by sharp ears.

"Yes," Tolya replied.

Bitch. No denying that she was the woman in the drawing.

Tolya leaned forward and tapped the other figure. "Who is he, Abigail?"

Do you know what we do to traitors, to anyone who talks about the clan?

She remembered the man her father and uncle had brought in to do a job with them. She remembered what had happened to him after the job because he'd drunk too much and talked too much, telling secrets to the whore he'd bounced on that night.

She remembered her father's hands on her shoulders, holding her in the chair, while Judd McCall—the one some of her father's associates called the Knife, the one she had feared even more than her father—unwrapped a stained handkerchief and showed her the traitor's tongue.

"A man who was with him attacked a young woman and stabbed a ranch hand who came to her aid," Jana said. "You can't protect him, Abby."

Do you know what we do to anyone who talks?

"They'll kill me if I tell," she whispered.

"Based on this picture, we can guess who he is, but we need a name," Jana persisted. "We need his name, Abby."

She could claim she didn't know, couldn't be sure. He'd been nineteen the last time she'd seen him and still had a bit of a baby face. That softness was gone now—at least in the picture.

"You can tell us, or you can be on the next train out of Bennett," Tolya said.

"To where?"

They didn't answer.

Abigail shuddered. She'd already told them some things about her family, but naming individuals, *identifying* individuals . . .

The Knife, the man she feared more than her father, had rubbed that severed tongue over her lips, pressed it against her mouth—then stepped away as she vomited on herself, her father's hands not allowing her to lean forward and puke on the floor.

"Dalton," she finally said. "That's my brother, Dalton Blackstone."

Businesses were blooming like flowers after a good rain. Tobias put the large pizza and sandwiches on the passenger seat of his pickup, then looked around the town square.

Was the town blooming too fast? A month ago there had been fewer than a hundred people, mostly young men looking for adventure and opportunities. They had ignored any squeamishness they had felt about coming to a place like Bennett and had focused on the chance to learn a trade or run their own businesses. Bennett was an empty place that could be filled, and it seemed like there were new people arriving by car or train every day—and humans were quickly outnumbering the *terra indigene* who were, in a very real sense, the only protection these newcomers had against what lived beyond the town's lights.

Just that afternoon, he and Jana had taken the horses out and ridden past the newly defined boundaries of the town so that she could look around when she wasn't alone. And he'd wanted to go out a few blocks beyond the new boundaries to look for any signs that some of that dog pack might have survived. They'd found no sign of dogs. Instead they'd come across two cars full of people who were snooping around some houses, looking for a way inside. The strangers had become wary when they noticed the badge pinned to Jana's shirt.

She'd been polite about explaining that, despite the civilized trappings, they were standing in the wild country. The strangers hadn't liked being asked about where they were from and why they were on the outskirts of Bennett instead of coming into town.

They weren't outlaws or serious looters. For one thing, even the girls—and they were barely old enough that he would call them women—had been half drunk, which meant they'd carried the booze with them or had broken into a house or two already and hauled away some ill-gotten gains. But seeing the way one of the men kept a hand behind his back, Tobias had been sure the man had a gun tucked under his shirt. That didn't make the man an outlaw, but it did make him a fool's kind of dangerous.

That was the moment when Mel had begun snorting and dancing and trying to move out despite Jana's hold on the reins. Having raised and trained the buckskin, Tobias knew the warning signs and knew there was nothing Jana could do, so he had urged his horse forward, leading them to the nearest side street and away from the other people.

Moments after they were out of sight, there were yells and screams. Twisting around, he and Jana had watched a mangled garbage can sail over the roof the house where the strangers had been poking around and smash into one of the cars.

The snarl that followed had both horses bolting as car doors slammed and engines revved. He hadn't heard the cars peel out and drive away. Jana had looked sickly pale, and he'd figured that she was also imagining the worst-case scenario.

He hadn't told her there was no point going back. She'd already known that. They were in the wild country, out of her jurisdiction. On any other day she might have turned around anyway to see if she could help. But not today.

Once she'd brought Mel back under control, she'd said, "That's how he responds to Elders?"

And Tobias had replied, "To Elders and rattlesnakes. If he's uneasy, it's good to pay attention."

They had finished their ride without further incident, but she had returned to the sheriff's office determined to have street maps printed with the new and official boundaries. He'd spent the rest of the day buying supplies and making arrangements to pick up any perishable items first thing in the morning.

Too many things had happened that day that would chase him in his sleep, so he'd been glad to receive the invitation to a movie night at Virgil's house. Barb had Wolf Team movies, which were something none of them except Barb and John Wolfgard had seen.

As he parked in the driveway of the Wolfgard house and collected the food, Tobias felt the weight of something on his skin—a sensation of being watched. He felt that weight lift when Virgil stepped out of the house and said, "Need a hand?"

"No, I've got it. Wasn't sure what everyone might like, so I brought a few things."

"Barbara Ellen brought a roast for Kane." Virgil frowned. "The wolverine says the puppy has to stay at their house."

Tobias stopped short and stared at the Wolf. "The wolverine? You mean Jana?"

A growl was the only answer.

"The pup had a pretty traumatic day. She could use some quiet time in a familiar place. And she'll have the bird for company."

Now a grunt was the reply as Virgil opened the door for Tobias.

Since he didn't think Virgil and Kane knew much, if anything, about televisions or electronics of any kind, Tobias figured the big TV and disc player, along with a stereo system that produced a pang of envy, had been in the house with the rest of the furniture.

Food and plates were set out on the dining room table. After everyone made their selection, Tobias, Barb, Jana, and John took their places on the sofa and chairs. Virgil sat on the floor near Kane, casually tearing the crust off his piece of pizza and giving it to his brother before concentrating on filling his own belly.

Barb figured out how to work that model disc player, and they settled down to watch one of the movies about the Wolf Team, which Barb explained were movies produced by the *terra indigene* and were based on books about the same characters.

A pack of juvenile Wolves who investigated when the *terra indigene* thought humans were doing something sneaky or were otherwise up to no good, or came to the rescue when someone—or something—needed rescuing.

"Oh, *forelock*!" Barb clapped one hand over her eyes and then spread her fingers to see part of the screen. "I've seen this movie before but I forgot when this part came up."

Jana sucked in a breath but didn't look away. Virgil and Kane cocked their heads and watched with focused interest.

This should be required viewing for everyone who wants to live in Ben-

nett, Tobias thought. *Maybe humans would be more careful if they knew this is what the Others thought of us.* He considered Virgil's reaction to the story and the characters. *It's certainly the way Bennett's sheriff views humans. Most humans.*

He wondered if Jana knew Virgil called her the wolverine. It sure wasn't a compliment, but he thought Virgil said the word with a kind of wary respect for another predator.

There were places in the movie when he laughed even though he wasn't sure the humor was intentional. And there were places where he cringed, thinking about his mother dealing with Morgan and Chase Wolfgard. By the time the credits were rolling, and he noticed how many names ended in "gard," he'd decided he needed a copy of at least one of the Wolf Team movies as well as the books, which he was sure had never been sold in the Bennett bookstore. Fortunately, John Wolfgard had brought two full sets of the Wolf Team books to sell, along with thrillers by someone named Alan Wolfgard. After telling John he would stop by the bookstore before heading home in the morning, Tobias thanked his hosts and prepared to call it a night.

"You're going to the hotel?" Virgil asked.

"Yep. They're almost full up with people waiting to choose a house, but Anya Sanguinati has decided to hold some rooms for overnight guests."

"I'll go with you. It is dark. Humans should be going home."

And the Elders will be moving through the town, watching.

It wasn't said, but Tobias understood the protection Virgil's presence offered—and he appreciated it.

"Thanks. I'll walk Barb and Jana to their house and be back."

"Oh, you don't . . ." Barb glanced at Jana and pressed her lips together.

As they walked outside, Tobias said, "Hold up a minute." He went to his pickup and retrieved the book he'd tucked into the storage compartment behind his seat. "I picked this up for you."

Jana took the book and tilted it to read the title in the light spilling out of the house. "A book about training puppies?"

"I thought it would come in handy."

She laughed. "This explains why John got so flustered when I asked him if there was a book like this in the store. You'd already bought it."

They started down the sidewalk, Barb a few paces ahead of them.

"Thanks for all your help today, with Kane . . . and everything."

"I'm glad I was here to help. Keep working with Mel, and remember to pay attention to what he's telling you." He smiled at her. "I got your letter."

"How could you? I just mailed it this morning, and you haven't been home yet."

He laughed. "When I went to the post office to pick up the mail for my ranch, the Skye Ranch, and Prairie Gold, Isobel Sanguinati handed it to me. Special delivery."

"I have a weakness for stationery."

Tobias stepped closer. "Then I'll look forward to receiving more letters." And damn if his mother hadn't been right about the anticipation of receiving a letter being its own kind of pleasure.

He kissed her. A soft kiss. A warm kiss that both asked a question and gave an answer.

"Am I the only one feeling this spark?" he whispered.

"No, but . . ."

He pressed a finger lightly against her lips. "No need to be going into the 'buts.' Courting has to be a little different out here. Besides, you're going to write me letters when I can't come up to town."

"Are you going to write to me too?"

"I just might." He smiled—and heard a Wolfish *huff* right behind him. "Guess I'd better go."

He watched Jana go into her house and close the door. Then he turned to look at Virgil. Big damn mother of a Wolf and not someone he wanted to cross.

"You have any objections to me courting her?" he asked.

Virgil trotted up the street and leaped into the bed of the pickup—and Tobias had a feeling the Wolf was laughing at him for taking on the wolverine.

Parlan Blackstone stared at Dalton and Lawry. "You went to an occupied ranch when there are so many abandoned places in this region? By all the dark gods, what were you thinking? *Were* you thinking?"

"Charlie Webb and Sweeney Cooke had scouted the place." Lawry glanced at Judd McCall instead of Parlan as he stumbled to explain. "They claimed there was no one in the house just before first light, that the owners and ranch hands were all out doing chores before breakfast and we'd have a clean run of the house. And they said the doors were left open. The way stations we'd checked had already been cleaned out of anything useful, and what passed for towns were too small for us to try to sell off anything we'd acquired."

"Should have been simple, Pa," Dalton said.

Judd McCall smiled at Dalton and Lawry. "Should have been."

"Should have been." Lawry sounded angry and bitter.

Good. If Lawry tried to shrug it off, he might "accidentally" fall on Judd's knife, and that could attract attention to the whole clan. This fiasco had already attracted enough attention.

"*Would* have been if a girl hadn't been in the kitchen and if Sweeney was capable of keeping his cock behind his zipper," Lawry continued. "Gods, I swear, Parlan, that man isn't right in the head whenever he sees a female. He was supposed to grab a couple of sacks of food and get out. Instead . . ."

Lawry stopped talking.

"Did the girl see anyone besides Sweeney?" Parlan asked. He listened to the clock tick, tick, tick.

"She saw me," Dalton finally said. "But only for a second. I'm not sure she saw much. She was on her knees and Sweeney was in front of her and I was in the doorway for just a second to tell Sweeney we had to get out. Then I went out the front door and me and Uncle Lawry drove away."

"Dalton told me no names were used," Lawry said. "Even if the girl got a glimpse of him, she doesn't know who he is."

"You act like we don't sense things, get feelings about when a deck is stacked against us and we need to walk away," Parlan said.

"Dalton did his part," Lawry said heatedly. "He came away with some nice bits of jewelry and a stack of cash in a cashbox that was right out in the open. Something warned them, something Sweeney and Charlie missed."

Parlan stared at his son. "Did you handle those nice bits of jewelry?"

Dalton returned his father's stare, but he paled. "That was just a con, the distraction to give Uncle Lawry time to work."

No, it wasn't. Maybe Dalton resented his sister having that odd bit of talent when he didn't and that's why the boy had always dismissed it as nonsense. How could a gemstone bring good fortune or leave someone open to misfortune? Except it wasn't the stone itself. Never the stone itself. It was a particular stone matched with a particular person that seemed to do the impossible.

So the question was, did the ranch have a warning system that Sweeney and Charlie missed when they cased the place, or had their luck turned the moment Dalton grabbed some jewelry that had stones that created opportunities for misfortune?

Better for the family if everyone believed the trouble was because of Sweeney Cooke and Charlie Webb.

"We need to be able to settle for a few days in each place before we pick up and move on," Parlan said. "We need that more now than we ever have before. Journeys from East Coast to West Coast aren't possible anymore. We can't even get out of this damn region. So we can't put the clan at risk because Sweeney Cooke thinks with his dick."

"Where are Sweeney and Charlie?" Judd asked.

Dalton shrugged. "Charlie had pulled up near the back door of the house, so Sweeney should have gone out that way."

"I heard gunshots when we were driving away," Lawry said. "Tire could have been blown out—or one of them could have been shot."

"If one of them was shot and they managed to get away, they'll have to hide or find a town that still has a doctor," Judd said. "Either way, I think Dalton and Lawry need to lay low for a couple of days while I see what I can find out."

"You good with that, Lawry?" Parlan asked.

Lawry nodded. "Nobody saw me, and I doubt they can identify Dalton, so finding a place to squat to avoid running into Charlie and Sweeney and have someone connect us to them is the best we can do right now."

"You have mobile phones that work?"

"Yeah. Mostly. You lose the signal a lot when you get away from the towns, such as they are."

"Try to find a place where you can check in daily."

Parlan waited until Lawry and Dalton left his private car. Then he looked at Judd.

"We're not the only ones trapped inside borders," Judd said. "Been hearing about plenty of the boys who are finding it hard to adjust since that damn war."

The boys. Judd's code name for men who preferred to make a living on the wrong side of the law. Outlaws. Bank robbers and cattle rustlers. Gamblers and thieves. Killers.

"Used to be a man would settle in a town," Parlan said. "He'd buy a house, have a wife and children, go to the Universal Temple on Earthday same as the rest of his neighbors. He didn't dirty his own nest. He never did anything in that town that gave his neighbors a reason to think he was anything less than respectable. And what he did outside that town . . . That was nobody's business but his."

"You're thinking it's time to play the respectable con again?" Judd asked.

Parlan nodded. "Open a business, settle down. It will take a few years for the human towns to recover."

"If they recover."

Parlan nodded again. That was the hard truth. The towns he'd seen so far in this region were bleak prospects for a man like himself. Yes, it was time to find a place where the clan could settle down for a few years. More to the point, he was heading for the only place where they should be able to slip in with the rest of the newcomers.

"If we settle down to play the respectable con, Cooke and Webb are going to be a problem," he said.

"They're already a problem," Judd replied.

"Can you take care of it?"

Judd smiled. "It'll be a pleasure."

CHAPTER 23

Sunday, Messis 21

After an early breakfast at the hotel, Jana and Tobias crossed the street and strolled across the square. Alone, she would have taken the long way around by walking on the streets, not wanting to see the bloodstained grass or have her breath catch as she passed the spot where she'd shot the dogs. But Tobias had to get back to the Prairie Gold ranch and wasn't sure when he'd be able to return to Bennett. He had a responsibility not just to the ranch but to the whole Intuit community, since the ranch was the main source of meat for Prairie Gold.

"Ah . . . ," Tobias said.

Jana stared at the three Wolves—*and her puppy*—tearing into . . . "I left her in her crate. What's she doing out here? And what is *that?*"

"Pronghorn antelope," Tobias replied.

"She can't eat that. Rusty can't eat that."

"Actually . . ."

Virgil, Kane, and John stopped tearing off chunks of meat and looked at her like she was nuts. Rusty, hearing her voice, grabbed the severed lower half of a hind leg and carried it to where Jana stood, wagging her tail as she dropped the present on Jana's boot.

Tobias sounded like he had something stuck in his throat, but he said in a low voice, "Praise her."

She didn't want to praise the puppy. She didn't want to find other kinds of presents—and some that might not be altogether dead—being dropped on her foot because she had reinforced this behavior. But a pack shared the meat, and since she wasn't going to go down on her hands and knees and put her face in the antelope, growling at Virgil in order to claim her share, she praised Rusty and gave Virgil a look that should have singed fur.

Crouching, she wrapped a hand around the leg just above the hoof—and wished she'd eaten oatmeal instead of steak and eggs that morning, since oatmeal wouldn't have scampered around the Elder Hills before becoming someone's meal.

"Since she's not used to it, it's probably best not to give the pup too much fresh meat at one time," Tobias said in a conversational tone, looking at the Wolves. "And if you're planning to do more than sleep for a few hours, you all might not want to pack in too much meat either. Of course, you'd know better than me how your human form reacts to a full Wolf belly."

John and Virgil stopped eating. Kane, having successfully yanked off part of the meaty rib cage, hobbled a few feet away and settled down with his prize.

After giving the pronghorn a wistful look, Virgil trotted toward the sheriff's office while John headed in the opposite direction toward the bookstore.

"With me, Rusty," Jana said, waving the pronghorn leg when the pup started to follow Virgil. "With me." She indulged Rusty in a vigorous game of tug, which ended when Rusty pulled some hide off the leg and Jana, no longer having the resistance, landed on her butt.

"Need a hand, Deputy?" Tobias held out his hand.

"Don't you laugh."

"Not laughing. No, ma'am."

Uh-huh.

She accepted the hand up, and the three of them walked to the sheriff's office.

"Could Virgil have killed that animal?" Jana asked.

"Probably. He's big enough and has the speed. But I doubt he'd have dragged it all the way back to the town square. If he'd been hunting last night in the hills—which would be unusual since regular wolves don't tend to hunt at night, and from what I know of them, the Wolfgard don't either—Virgil would have brought it to their house if he'd moved it from the kill sight." Tobias stopped on the sidewalk in front of the sheriff's office. "I don't think the Wolfgard killed that pronghorn. Neither did the Panther who lives in town. None of them have had time to be out hunting for fresh meat. They've been making do with the supplies of fresh or frozen meat from all the houses, same as the humans here."

"Who would kill something and then leave it for . . ." Jana stopped when she noticed all the birds heading for the carcass. Eagles, Hawks, Ravens, Crows. Even some of the Owls. Fresh meat. The kind of meat the *terra indigene* were used to hunting and eating.

Saul Panthergard, in his Cougar form, trotted up to the kill. Kane snarled, but Jana thought that it was for form's sake. The birds fluttered and resettled, leaving Saul as the sole possessor of the hindquarters.

"Elders," Jana whispered.

Tobias nodded. "That would be my guess. Kane's hurt and Virgil's keeping watch to make sure all the pesky humans behave. Someone needs to supply meat for the pack."

And putting the carcass in the square allowed all the Others to have a piece since none of them had more right to the meat than the rest.

Jana waved the pronghorn leg, which Rusty took as an invitation to play. Holding it higher than the pup could jump, she said, "What am I supposed to do with this?"

"I'm guessing you don't want to put it in the office refrigerator."

"You guess right. For one thing, it's an under-the-counter fridge—too small to hold *this*. For another thing . . ." Jana looked at the leg. "It still has fur and skin . . . and a hoof."

"I'll see if I can locate an ice chest and some ice. Or I can take it with me and return it to the rest of the kill if that's what you want."

"That would be better."

Tobias tipped his hat back. "We feed the ranch dogs fresh meat all the time. It won't hurt Rusty. In fact, it will be good for her—and it will be easier on you to feed her meat as one of her meals than fighting with

Virgil every time there's fresh meat. She's pack, darlin', and she's furry. He might be able to wrap his mind around you not wanting to gnaw on meat that's still on the hoof, but not providing food for a pup?" He shook his head. "One way or another, the Wolves will feed her. The only way for you to keep control of what she eats is if she gets most of her meals from you."

She handed him the pronghorn leg. "I have to get to work."

"Me too." He smiled. "Too much of an audience for a good-bye kiss?"

Jana looked across the street. Everything with fur or feathers looked back at her. Watching her and Tobias. If she kissed Tobias in full view of everyone, Saul might keep it to himself, not seeing anything of interest. Kane might keep it to himself. Same with the Hawks and Eagles and Owls. But the Crows and Ravens? *Everyone* would know about a kiss before the breakfast dishes were cleared. And that was assuming the "news" didn't travel outside Bennett.

"Definitely too much audience," she replied.

The smile he gave her had enough heat to produce a nice little flutter. She wasn't sure what to do about the flutter, but it gave her a boost of confidence before she walked into the office and had to deal with a growly boss.

Tolya Sanguinati studied the two maps. One was a large map of the Midwest Region as it had been a few months ago. Even before the Elders and Elementals had raged across the continent, the human-controlled towns had been sparse in this region. There were way stations indicated on the map—Carter's Way, Silver Way, Shooting Star Way. Those places were little more than a stop for the freight and passenger trains and had a few dozen people living there at best. Other places were small Intuit or human communities that had a major roadway running through them.

And some of the more isolated places were ghost towns now, re-claimed by the *terra indigene*.

Many of those places—maybe *all* of those places—depended on Ben-nett's survival in one way or another.

Tolya shook his head. Those other places weren't his problem. Even if he had the outlandish idea that he should take some responsibility for them, he couldn't do it, because he had enough problems right here.

Putting the regional map aside, he considered the map of the town and the red lines he'd drawn last night after Air arrived at his house and told him the Elders wanted to see him.

What had stood before him . . . Not their true form. Not even the animal forms he suspected had been taken by their ancestors a very long time ago. No, these Elders had walked on two legs, but they hadn't been human in any other way. They were some of the nightmares that had wiped out the humans who had previously lived in Bennett. And they had summoned him to the edge of the Elder Hills to deliver a message: Enough.

In his smoke form, he had followed them through the streets of the town. Their claws scarred utility poles and post office boxes. By his reckoning, they were marking boundaries two streets beyond what he and Virgil had currently indicated as the town lines. He didn't know if they understood the purpose of some of the buildings that were now restored to the official part of the town, including Bennett's small hospital and a shopping center, but by the time the sun began to rise and people began to stir to prepare for the workday, he knew where the lines had literally been drawn.

Because the two official salvage companies had wisely offered jobs to any *terra indigene* who had expressed interest, they would be allowed to forage beyond the town line during the day. But those houses were now potential dens for the Others. Humans who tried to squat in any of those places would become meat.

One of the Elders left an animal in the town square to feed the *terra indigene* who were working with the humans. Today it was four-legged prey. Tolya had no doubt that, should humans become careless, the prey left in the square the next time might be someone the humans recognized.

That was one of the problems now. The *terra indigene* had been the dominant predators since the world had been new, adapting and learning the forms of the hunters around them as they changed with the world, but the Sanguinati were the only branch that had adapted to be urban predators who hunted humans as their preferred prey. That worked in

the larger human-controlled towns that had a Courtyard. Or it had before the Elders had made being out after dark a form of suicide. The
Sanguinati had hunted in the dark—smoke hiding in the shadows of an
alleyway, taking nothing but blood from an unwary passerby; a shadowy
lover in a dimly lit bar, exchanging an evening of romance—and sometimes even sex—for a fresh liquid meal.

Yuri, Anya, and Nicolai were in positions that made it possible for
them to lightly feed on several individuals during the course of the day.
Even Stazia at the bank and Isobel at the post office had opportunities to
touch humans and draw a little blood through the skin. At least until
humans became wary or even afraid of being touched.

As the leader of the town, he did not have those opportunities. He was
Sanguinati, and all of Bennett's citizens were aware of that. He would
need to make some kind of . . . arrangement . . . with some of the humans
in order to minimize their fear of his kind because this morning he
looked at a simple truth: the *terra indigene* living in Bennett were seriously outnumbered.

Most forms of *terra indigene* had a connection with the land and had
no desire to become contaminated by too much human. The ones who
were now residing in Bennett were here out of a sense of duty to the rest,
in much the same way as the shifters who lived in Courtyards and kept
watch over the humans had provided a conduit for the human goods that
were wanted by *terra indigene* who never could look human enough to
approach even a trading post—and there were many, many more who
had no desire to try to take that form.

<Tolya?> Yuri called. <We're all here.>

Taking the maps, Tolya went to the conference room to meet the
town council, as well as Virgil and Jana.

He laid the regional map on the table.

Jana leaned over the table, studied the map . . . and winced. "These
are the existing towns?"

"They were," Tolya replied. "I have not tried to ascertain if they still
exist—or if they do, in what form. Perhaps that is something you could
do as an officer of human law."

"Some of the way stations are empty," Nicolai said. "The humans
working on the trains are concerned about that because there is no one to

accept mailbags and supplies. The railroads would be willing to transfer trained workers to those places but only if the *terra indigene* would be willing to ensure their safety."

"From us?" Virgil asked.

"My impression was they were more concerned about other humans," Nicolai replied. "Some of the Owlgard have settled around our train station and keep watch at night. They also take turns listening to messages left on the answering machine in case there is an emergency."

"There was an emergency," Tolya guessed.

Nicolai nodded. "Of sorts. A human . . . held up? . . . the Carter's Way station yesterday, just before full dark. The male took money from the booth where they sell tickets, as well as a bag of food, water, and medicines that they sell in the little shop. The male had a gun; the workers at the station did not. They gave him what he wanted, but he still fired the gun and wounded one of them before he left."

"Where is that way station?" Virgil asked.

Jana found it on the map and put her finger on the name.

"Carter's Way is a stop on a north-south railroad line," Nicolai said. "If that male is one of the ones who attacked the ranch, then he's moving south."

Virgil bared his teeth. "Toward us."

"We'll deal with it," Tolya said. "Right now, we have something more urgent to deal with before the next train arrives in Bennett."

Nicolai looked at the clock on the wall. "Then there's not much time."

Tolya laid the town map on the table and moved a finger over the red lines he'd drawn. "These are the final boundaries for the town. There will be no further expansion. I will make a copy of this map for the land agents so they know where humans can live and can make a list of what stores and businesses are available for new residents looking for work."

Virgil watched Tolya. "The Elders decided?"

"Yes," Tolya said. "I was summoned last night. These are the boundaries. Room enough for the humans who are needed for the work that will allow the town to live, but no more. Anyone who wants to settle here either has the credentials to do a specific job or must be willing to apprentice in a particular kind of work and is an acceptable worker to the human who is dominant in that profession." He looked at Jana. "You will assist the Werners to determine how many residents could be supported by each business or occupation so that we know how many more people we can accept as new residents. You need to figure this out, fast, since people continue to arrive and most don't have any work papers."

She looked stunned—and then he saw the look in her eyes that was the reason Virgil referred to her as a wolverine. He appreciated the attitude needed for a small predator to challenge a larger one.

Just because he appreciated it didn't mean he liked that attitude aimed at *him*.

"Fast?" Jana growled. "*Fast?* I arrived a week ago with the rest of the people from Lakeside. We've barely had time to find homes and figure out where we're working. How much faster can we do this?"

"You were selected and approved by trusted *terra indigene* before you arrived in Bennett," Tolya said. "The ones who have been swarming into town the past few days were not." Did she not understand the difference—and the danger?

"You object to people like Kenneth and Evan?"

Virgil growled at her. Tolya pulled back his lips for just a moment, showing Jana his fangs in warning.

"They have a purpose, and that is the point," Tolya snapped. "Every human who wants to live here has to fill a position. And when those positions are filled, no more humans will be allowed to settle here. When the houses within the boundaries are filled—and not packed in like families of mice—there can be no more settlers. Humans will look at the houses beyond the boundaries and complain that there is room for them, but there is no room. The houses on the other side of the boundaries can be claimed by the *terra indigene* or not claimed at all, but they *cannot be claimed by humans.*"

"The humans already outnumber those of us they can see," Virgil said. "If they start causing trouble, the Elders will thin the human herds more vigorously than the last time."

Jana shuddered. With effort, she straightened her shoulders, but she looked pale. "What if the Werners and I find some occupations that might be better suited for *terra indigene?*"

They all looked at her in surprise.

Tolya said, "By all means, indicate those, and we'll do our best to find *terra indigene* to fill those positions."

She nodded. "The picture of the man Melanie Dixon saw at her house yesterday. I think it should be cropped to remove Abigail Burch and then sent to all the train and way stations we can contact."

"You can do this cropping?" he asked.

"Yes."

"Then alter the picture and e-mail it to Nicolai. As station master, he will send it on to as many stations and way stations as he can."

"Anything else?"

"Not today."

Jana bolted from the room.

Virgil huffed out a breath. "Yesterday's fight was her first kill."

"Ah." All the Sanguinati breathed out the sound. First kill wouldn't have distressed any of them—being able to feed on one's own was a sign of maturity—but they indicated sympathy because they appreciated Jana's ability to articulate a human perception of what was needed without displaying aggression.

Except with Virgil. And now, perhaps with him.

Tolya rolled up the maps and returned to his office. He had hoped the Elders would have given them all more time for the town and the people to find their balance. Maybe they would have been content to observe if the Dixon ranch hadn't been attacked, reminding Namid's teeth and claws that humans were, for the most part, enemies who were not only prey but preyed on their own kind.

More humans were arriving every day, looking for opportunities—or looking to steal things from the empty houses. Every human who hadn't already been approved by the *terra indigene* represented potential danger. The Sanguinati knew that. So did Virgil. He hoped Jana understood that as well.

For now, he would do what he could. And the first thing he would do was send Jesse Walker the picture Hope Wolfsong had made so that the residents of Prairie Gold would recognize an enemy if he came among them.

* * *

"Walker's General Store, Jesse speaking."

"Jesse Walker, this is Tolya Sanguinati."

She heard the puppy yapping. Cory was in an enclosed pen and *should* be safe, but . . . "Is there something I can do for you, Tolya?"

"I have sent you an e-mail with the picture of a potential enemy. Your people need to be wary of this man and any humans who are with him."

"He's dangerous?"

"He stole from a ranch, but a human with him tried to forcibly mate with the rancher's daughter."

Feeling her body tighten in response to what Tolya was saying, Jesse looked at the rifle she kept near her desk when she was working in her office area.

Yap yap *yap. I am brave. I am brave. Mom!*

"Tolya, I have to go. I'll check my e-mail in a few minutes." She almost hung up, then thought of one last thing. "Did you tell Tobias?"

"Virgil will tell him."

"I'll call after I look at the picture." Jesse hung up. She almost grabbed the rifle on her way to the back door but instead snatched the broom that was leaning near the door because she had a feeling that the broom would be enough to drive off whatever was upsetting Cory-Cutie. She pulled up short two steps out the door and shook her head—and wondered again if the pup was too brave or not too bright.

The biggest of the two male Wolves watched the pup, wearing what Jesse would call a grin on his face as his tail gently wagged. The other Wolf was trying to undo the fasteners that held a mesh covering over the pen she'd put the puppy in a few minutes ago.

"You boys want something?" They didn't come to town often, but she recognized Morgan and Chase Wolfgard.

Chase ignored her and continued working on the fasteners. Morgan shifted to human form and turned to face her.

"Why is the puppy in a cage?" he demanded, baring his teeth in a snarl.

"I wanted her to have a little time outside on her own, and I didn't want her to get snatched by a hawk or eagle," Jesse replied. Anticipating the next snarled objection, she pointed skyward. "The Hawkgard and Eaglegard are not the only ones riding the thermals looking for a meal.

They won't harm the puppy, but a regular bird of prey might go after Cory."

"Cutie," Morgan corrected. "Rachel said the pup's name is Cutie."

"Cutie will work for a puppy, but would you want to be called Cutie once you reached adulthood?"

He considered her question and finally said, "Cory is better."

Fortunately, the words were similar in sound, and she hoped the pup wouldn't become confused by having two names.

Jesse walked over to the pen, flipped a couple of fasteners, and folded back the mesh cover. Handing the broom to Morgan, who finally seemed to notice it, she lifted Cory out of the pen, gave her a quick cuddle, and set her on the ground.

"Why did you bring a broom outside?" Morgan asked. "Brooms are for sweeping. There is nothing to sweep outside."

"Brooms are also good for smacking anyone who upsets the puppy." Jesse wrapped a hand around the broom handle. Morgan didn't let go. That either meant she had to win it back or he didn't trust her not to smack him for making the puppy yap. She released the broom, hoping she conveyed that she was bestowing a favor by letting him keep it. "I have to go to the library and retrieve an urgent e-mail from Tolya Sanguinati. If you could watch Cory for a few minutes? Her piddle spot is over there." She pointed to the area she'd decided would be the canine toilet.

"We know."

Of course they did. They'd probably recognized the puppy's scent there and marked that spot themselves.

Morgan gave Jesse the broom and shifted back to Wolf form, and the three furries began to explore.

Jesse returned the broom to its spot near the back door before she hurried to the town library, where she could access her e-mail. She gave Shelley Bookman the hand signal that meant "talk to you later" and went to the bank of computers.

Not much information in the e-mail itself. The man's name was Dalton Blackstone and he should be considered an enemy. Coming from Tolya, the message was abrupt and lacking in the courtesy she was used to receiving from him.

She browsed the nearest shelf of books while she waited for the computer to download the picture. Finally . . .

A handsome young man. She could see the familial similarities between his face and Abigail Burch's. But by the time she had printed several copies of the picture, she could feel the threat this young man represented.

She stopped at the checkout desk on her way out of the library, ignoring Shelley's greeting. "Town meeting, seven o'clock this evening. Spread the word."

"What . . . ?"

She rushed out the door, giving Shelley no time for questions. She wasn't worried about the puppy—much—but the need to talk to Morgan and Chase outweighed the need to inform her own people.

It had taken time to download a picture, but she hadn't thought she'd been gone *that* long. Even so, she found Cory and the two Wolves sprawled inside the store's back room, where the floor was cooler than the ground and the room provided shade. The Wolves looked up when she entered. The puppy was down for the count, having played hard enough that she needed a nap.

Jesse crouched in front of them and held up the picture. "This man is called Dalton Blackstone. He travels with at least one other human who hurts people."

Morgan shifted to human form and lay on his belly, propped up on his forearms. "You want us to protect your pack?"

He sounded reluctant, and she understood why. Except for the nanny, Rachel, and the litter of pups, the rest of the Prairie Gold pack had been slaughtered by the Humans First and Last movement. Morgan and Chase were the only ones strong enough to protect the surviving Wolfgard.

"No, I want you to protect your pack and your settlement," Jesse said. "These humans may be smart enough to stay away from *terra indigene* settlements, but they may gamble that you won't know them and will give them supplies or let them stay among you, knowing no other humans would hunt them in your territory."

"They are dangerous?"

"Yes." She said the word, knowing it was a death sentence. As far as the Others were concerned, a dangerous human was a dead human waiting for the fangs and claws that would kill him.

"Rachel," Morgan said. "The pack's nanny is too old to mate and bear young. Rachel is the pack's dominant female now."

Rachel was the only female currently approaching adulthood, and she would accept Morgan or Chase as her mate when she was ready to have pups of her own. "She should be safe here, but if you want her to stay with the pack until these men are found, I will understand."

"We will consider your words."

"I'll put one of these pictures in a tube that will be easy to carry. You should take it back to your settlement so that all the *terra indigene* can see the human's face."

"We will wait for the tube. Then it is time to go."

She found a mailing tube, rolled the picture, and stuffed brown paper into both ends to seal up the tube. Morgan and Chase trotted out the door and headed for the settlement in the hills. Jesse tucked Cory in her crate near the desk and tried to focus on paperwork, but more often than not, every time she needed to write something down, she had to force her right hand to release her left wrist.

T obias was a few miles out of Bennett when he spotted the horse and rider in the middle of the road.

No reaction from the rider, who had to see the pickup. No attempt to move aside.

Slowing down, Tobias scanned the land to his left and right but didn't see anyone trying to approach the pickup. Deciding it wasn't an attempted holdup, he flashed his lights, not wanting to startle the horse by blowing the horn.

Still no reaction. Then a fire tornado swirled in the middle of the road. As soon as Tobias hit the brakes and stopped the truck, the tornado changed back to a horse and rider.

"What the . . . ?" The Elementals had no reason to be coming after him. At least, no reason *he* knew about.

That was when he looked in the rearview mirror and saw the Wolf running toward him. Coming fast.

Had to be Virgil.

Tobias waited until Virgil was a few yards away before rolling down the window. Reaching the truck, the Wolf stood on his hind legs, thrust his head into the opening, and dropped a mailing tube into Tobias's lap before shifting to human.

"Tolya says you need that picture," Virgil said. "All the humans at your ranch need to see that picture. There is also a copy for the Skye Ranch, and Tolya says you should talk to the other ranches so that they will look at the e-mail he is sending to them and see the picture."

Tobias opened the mailing tube and pulled out the copies of a drawing that had been cropped from a larger picture. "I don't recognize him."

"He and other humans attacked Stewart Dixon's ranch yesterday."

"I'd heard about that." Jana had told him about it over breakfast.

"I'll make sure my people know to be on the lookout." And he'd stress to Ellen Garcia that she shouldn't open the door to strangers. It wasn't their way not to be neighborly; there were *terra indigene* who showed up at the ranch house these days, looking for a drink of water or just wanting to rest in the shade of the ranch house's big porch. Ellen always took a minute to talk to them, even if they weren't in a form that could reply.

He'd talk to Ellen and "Ed" Tilman and emphasize the need for caution. And he'd talk to the folks living at the Prairie Gold farms as well. And he'd talk to Jana tonight and see if she knew anything more.

"Do you have one of those guns that shoots colored bullets?" Virgil asked.

For a moment, Tobias couldn't think of what the Wolf meant. "You mean a flare gun? Yes. I keep one in the truck."

Virgil looked at the horse and rider, then focused on Tobias. "Fire says if you shoot a colored bullet into the air, the *terra indigene* will know there is danger and will come to help."

Gods above and below. "Appreciate that." And he hoped he would never be in a position to send up a flare because he didn't want to consider which *terra indigene* would come to help.

When Virgil continued to lean in and stare at him, Tobias said, "Something else?"

"Rusty can't have meat?"

"Sure she can, but she's been fed puppy kibble up to now and you don't want to change her diet too fast."

"Kibble instead of meat? Have you tasted kibble?" Virgil bared his teeth, and Tobias had the unpleasant experience of seeing human canines change into Wolf fangs when those fangs were inches away from his face.

"Can't say I have." Obviously Virgil had—and hadn't liked it.

He had to be careful not to agree with Virgil too much, or the Wolf, already dominant, would run roughshod over Jana. Or try, anyway.

"The pup is adjusting to a new home and a new pack. Better for her to have familiar food for a while. Better for Jana to be able to give Rusty something she can provide."

Virgil's ears shifted to Wolf, as if to better hear the words. Since he hadn't backed away at all, Tobias found it . . . unsettling.

"Rusty is Jana's first dog, her first puppy," Tobias said. "She needs to learn, same as the pup, and the learning will go down easier if the teaching is . . . soft. You understand what I'm saying?"

After several very long moments, Virgil nodded. "It is good the Wolf-gard can help her learn with the dog puppy. That way Jana will know what to do when the two of you mate and have pups of your own."

"That's a thought." Oh gods. This felt like the Wolf version of a shotgun wedding. Or at the very least, an older brother wanting to know a man's intentions toward a sister. "I'd better be going. I have to deliver mail and supplies to the Skye Ranch on my way home."

Virgil stepped away from the pickup, shifted back to Wolf form, and headed for Bennett at an easy trot.

The horse and rider had disappeared, but Tobias still drove past the spot slowly before he put his foot on the gas and made up time driving to the Skye Ranch.

He'd met Jana a handful of days ago. They'd shared a couple of rides, a couple of kisses, and a movie night with friends. Sure, he was attracted to her, and a day ago, he wouldn't have turned down an invitation to become better acquainted in the physical sense. But wanting to know someone wasn't the same as being ready to marry. If Virgil thought that one thing automatically led to the other, Tobias was going to have to think hard about what he was willing to offer Deputy Paniccia.

Then again, there was that spark between them, and he liked thinking about that just fine.

CHAPTER 24

Windsday, Messis 22

Before heading for work, Jana took Rusty for another emergency run to the potty spot. She'd surely like to give Virgil a whack on the head for letting the puppy gorge on food she wasn't used to eating. But if Rusty dribbled poop on the office floor because she couldn't hold it long enough to reach grass, well, Virgil might get the message.

"Unsupervised kid in a candy store," she muttered. "It all goes in just fine, but coming out?" She glanced at the pup curled on the passenger-side floor. "Light meals for you, kiddo. That's what your auntie Barb recommended this morning."

When she reached the office, she called Move 'Em Out Bookstore and asked John Wolfgard to find her a stack of old newspapers as a preventative measure. Then she went next door to the land agents' office and arranged to escort Dawn Werner to the newly restored shopping center in order to make a list of the stores that were potential employment opportunities.

Dawn should have been safe to go on her own within the town's boundaries, but the men who had attacked the people at the ranch were still out there, somewhere. Besides, most of the *terra indigene* didn't know Dawn, and anyone watching her check out the stores might think she was doing something sneaky like those people who were looking at the empty houses the other day. But all the Others knew that Virgil's human deputy wore a shiny on her shirt that could be seen from the air, so Jana's presence would make it clear that Dawn was a resident of Bennett on official business and not a snack.

She just hoped the Elders knew what the badge meant.

W hen Zeke made a "come here" motion, Abigail reluctantly crossed the street. Thank the gods there was an official salvage business now and nobody else had to help sort through the possessions in the houses—unless that help was a kindness to a neighbor.

Since the salvage van was parked in the driveway of a house where people were hustling in and out, she didn't think Zeke was waving to her just to be friendly.

"Good morning," she said.

"Morning, Abby. You and Kelley heading out to work?"

"Yes. We were just leaving." Since Kelley now viewed the sweet Abigail persona with suspicion, she kept hoping he'd leave altogether so that she could play the brave abandoned wife and garner sympathy from her new neighbors.

"Ask him to wait a few minutes, okay? A few of us camped out in these houses last night in order to work past dark. We have all the jewelry sorted in three of the houses—at least we've got what looks like costume jewelry sorted from the nicer things. We need Kelley to assess the good pieces and assign values for all of it so that the costume jewelry can be sold."

"All right, I'll tell him." She took a step back, as if even the mention of jewelry was a source of pain.

Zeke didn't comment, but she had a feeling that he thought he knew the reason for her reacting that way.

The reason walked out of the house carrying a banker's box.

"I think a lot of the paper in this box can be shredded," Dina said. "If the attorney assigned to handle this street keeps the last couple of statements, that should be enough to confirm what was in the account."

Zeke gave Abigail a sharp look. "Something wrong?"

Everything. The dissonance surrounding this woman was so strong, she would draw negative things to everyone on this street. And Abigail's carefully tended protection stones would be completely overwhelmed by that dissonance, leaving her vulnerable to something more than a broken marriage.

"The pendant." It was a slice of rose quartz in a gold frame that gave it the look of an old oval mirror. At the top was a spill of leaves and vines that held chips of turquoise. It was exquisite workmanship, but the stones created a strong dissonance with Dina's personality.

Dina deposited the box in the van before turning to confront Abigail. "What's your problem? I didn't lift it from one of the houses. It was on display in the jewelry store, as part of the store's original inventory. I saw it, liked it, and bought it. So what?"

Dina was smart and had a sharp-edged sense of humor—and she and Abigail had disliked each other on sight. Just not compatible. Would never be friends. And now Kelley's not-so-subtle attraction to the woman was an actual reason to dislike Dina—if sweet Abigail hadn't been so hurt by the "gold girl" on Zeke's team leading her husband astray.

Abigail would have been amused that Kelley was planning to leave her because she had "played him," but he couldn't see that Dina was doing the same thing. If she didn't say anything, he'd get what he deserved when he moved in with the bitch, but if she didn't say anything, whatever trouble came would touch all of them.

Which meant revealing her little secret to more people.

"What about the pendant?" Zeke asked, sounding impatient.

"It's not in harmony with Dina," Abigail replied. "It's a beautiful piece, but it doesn't fit who she is, and instead of bringing her good fortune, it will attract a darkness to her that will cause pain and sorrow."

Dina gave her a cold, hostile look. "Bullshit. The only thing wrong with this necklace is that Kelley put it aside for me and not you." She walked back into the house.

Zeke fixed his eyes on the van. "Dina was out of line, saying that to you."

"You mean saying without saying that she and Kelley are having sex?" Abigail said.

Zeke winced.

"Zeke, talk to her. This has nothing to do with Kelley. I promise it doesn't. But I have a feeling that every time Dina wears that necklace, something dangerous will get a little closer until it catches up to her."

"Look at where we are, Abby," Zeke said. "We run the risk of something dangerous catching up to us every single day."

She'd tried to warn him, and he didn't believe her. Wasn't that perfect? When trouble came, no one could say she hadn't tried to warn someone.

Zeke raised a hand in greeting. Abigail turned and hurried across the street, passing Kelley. "I'll wait in the car."

She watched Zeke and Kelley go into the house. She watched Kelley and Dina come out—and saw Zeke take the box Dina held, stopping her from walking over to help Kelley pack the boxes into the car. It was Zeke's discomfort more than anything else that told her the sweet Abigail persona was still working with everyone but Kelley.

Parlan answered his mobile phone, pleased the erratic service hadn't affected this little town. He hadn't heard from anyone all day, and when the clan was scattered as it was now, communication became essential. "Hello?"

"Dalton's likeness is on a poster in every post office and train station," Judd McCall said in a low voice full of fury. "Wanted for questioning in the robbery of a ranch house and the assault of two people."

Parlan stopped breathing for a moment as his own fury washed over him. "Dalton said the girl got a glimpse of him but couldn't know who . . ."

"The drawing might as well be a photograph, and the poster *has his name*. I don't know who did the drawing, but putting a name to the face didn't come from the girl at the ranch."

A face without a name meant very little. Appearances could be changed. But having a name on that poster just when he was putting together a deal to play the respectable family con put the whole clan at risk.

"Do you think one of our past business associates saw the drawing and provided the name?" Parlan asked.

"No. Even the crazy ones aren't that crazy. And the boy knows better than to tell a whore his real name."

"Whore," Parlan said softly. The word reminded him of another possibility. But he didn't need to say it. Judd would have come to the same conclusion. "Dalton will have to lay low. Lawry too for the time being. Have you heard from Cooke and Webb?"

"No, but I did hear about a way station being robbed and one of the workers being shot. So I can guess where those two were a day ago. What about you?"

"I'm staying at a hotel tonight, but I'll be on the train again in the morning. I have a line on a business proposition. If my backers seal the deal, we'll have a base of operation and the clan can assemble again."

"What kind of business proposition?"

"Running a saloon that has a professional gambler in residence."

"How much are you going to have to lose to make this happen?" Judd asked.

"Oh, I'm not going to lose. I'm going to make this happen by winning very big—and then forgiving the debts in lieu of the marks being the frontmen when it comes to dealing with government officials and the law. That will keep my name off the deed—at least initially." Once he'd established himself as a respectable businessman, he'd ease the frontmen out of the business, one way or another.

Judd laughed. "I'll keep heading south, picking up what I can."

"Keep a sharp lookout."

"Always do. Where should I look for you?"

"In Bennett," Parlan said. "I've been told by my fellow passengers that there are a multitude of opportunities there for men with ambition."

"A working town probably has working law officers," Judd said.

"Officers who don't see the value of cooperation can be replaced. I'll get a feel for the town and find out whose strings can be pulled and whose strings need to be cut."

"See you there."

Parlan ended the call and stared out his hotel window.

Abigail had escaped his control and eluded him for more than three years. It would serve her right if betraying her brother to the authorities, whatever they might be, would be the very act that would cause her to stumble back into Judd's waiting hands.

CHAPTER 25

Thaisday, Messis 23

Responding to the frantic knocking on the front door and Rusty's equally frantic barking, Jana dropped her toast and rushed through the house. Anyone knocking on her door at that hour of the morning and in that way wasn't outside to tell her something good.

She grabbed Rusty's collar with one hand as she turned the locks and opened the door with the other.

"You have to come," Kenneth said. The burly schoolteacher looked ready to faint. "Maddie cut herself and we don't know what to do. She's . . . We don't know."

"Is Evan home?" she asked, then snapped, "Quiet, Rusty."

"He's dealing with the other children," Kenneth replied. "They . . ."

They want to lick the blood. Michael Debany had hurriedly told her a few things about dealing with blood prophets if she should cross paths with one, and one of those things was that the Others *should not* consume *cassandra sangue* blood because it produced a reaction in the *terra indigene.*

"Go home and help Evan," she said. "Do not let the other children lick Maddie's wound or any of the blood."

"Wounds." Kenneth sounded devastated. "More than one."

Gods. "I'll be over in a minute. You go now."

Yelling for Barb, Jana dragged a now-whimpering Rusty back to her crate and stuffed the puppy inside. Not a kind thing to do, but she could feel the seconds ticking and knew something was very wrong if a girl as young as Maddie had suddenly made multiple cuts.

"What's the matter?" Barb asked. "Why are you being mean to the puppy?"

"Maddie cut herself."

Barb gasped.

"Grab a pen and paper. You have to help me."

"Me? Why me? Where are Evan and Kenneth?"

"They have to keep the other kids away from Maddie. *Come on, Barb.*"

Jana ran out the door, trusting that Barb would follow. She stopped outside Maddie's house, cupped her hands around her mouth, and yelled, "Virgil!" Then she yanked open the screen door and stepped inside.

Maddie knelt in the middle of the living room, smacking her bloody hands on a sheet of drawing paper and making a strangled sound as if she wanted to scream but couldn't even get that much out. Kenneth held on to Zane, and Evan had a tight hold on Mace, who kept snarling and saying, "Let me lick it. I wanna lick it."

No sign of Charlee, but Jana didn't ask about her. If the young Hawk wasn't in the room, she wasn't an immediate problem.

Jana dropped to her knees in front of Maddie at the same moment the screen door opened. As Barb dropped down beside her, looking white with dread but holding a pen and pad of paper, Jana closed her hands over Maddie's wrists. "Speak, prophet, and we will listen."

Maddie suddenly stilled and stared at her with terrifyingly empty eyes that turned dreamy as the girl began to speak. "Puddle, puddle, red red red. Grandma hair walk her dog. Big water. Bumpy dark." The girl sighed and slumped forward.

Jana lowered Maddie to the floor, then looked at the two men and the boys. "You boys go to your room and stay there, or I'll arrest you."

"You can't—" Mace's protest was silenced by the savage snarl that came from the other side of the screen door.

Virgil bared his teeth as he focused on the boys. But Jana saw him quivering and took a moment to admire the strength of will that kept him on that side of the door instead of tearing through it to reach the girl with the bloody hands.

"Boys," Evan said firmly. "Go with Dad Kenneth."

Zane and Mace allowed Kenneth to herd them to their bedroom, but Mace, the young Wolf, kept looking back as if to be sure Virgil was still there to reinforce the order.

"Get some water and a cloth to clean up her hands," Jana told Evan. "We'll take the papers that have blood on them."

"And do what with them?" Barb whispered.

"Burn them." As far as she could tell, the drawing paper didn't hold anything that would help them—not a picture or any other kind of clue. "Evan, do you know what Maddie was looking at just before this happened?"

Evan shook his head as he began cleaning Maddie's hands. "We were making breakfast. The children were out here. We didn't know there was anything wrong until Charlee ran into the kitchen and told us that Maddie had cut herself. I don't know what she used, what was in the room that could . . ." He glanced around the room. "That issue of *Nature!* wasn't on the floor before, and I don't know where that picture book came from."

"I'll take them with me and see if I can figure out what she was trying to tell us." Jana rose and gathered up the magazine and picture book.

"Should we take her to the doctor?" Evan asked. "The cuts aren't deep, but there are several of them on each hand."

Jana hesitated. She wasn't an expert. Who was when it came to the *cassandra sangue?* But she was the human part of the law here. "I'll ask one of the doctors to make a house call. I think the fewer people who see Maddie today, the better." She hesitated. "You need to discover what she used to make the cuts before the other children find it. Or ask Kane to sniff around the room and find it." Virgil was right here and could do the sniffing, but she needed the sheriff and that had to be a priority.

Evan nodded, but she wasn't sure he'd heard her or understood what she'd said.

She left the house, almost smacking Virgil with the screen door in her haste to get home and finish dressing for work. She crossed the street with the Wolf trotting at her side. "You need to contact Tolya, tell him we need to meet. It's urgent. Kane should go over to Maddie's house and see if he can find what she used to cut herself. If it has any blood on it, it has to be kept away from the other children." She thought for a moment, then added, "John should come to the meeting, since he used to live in Lakeside." He was the one individual she *knew* had had direct contact with a blood prophet and might be able to give them more information about what they should do now.

Puddle, puddle, red red red.

Grass stained with blood where dogs had died the other day. She remembered it so easily, the ground soaking up the moisture.

Puddle, puddle, red red red.

How much blood would have to saturate the ground before it began to puddle?

She bolted up the short walk to her front door. "Call them, Virgil!"

Setting the magazine and picture book on the coffee table, she rushed to her room to retrieve her service weapon. Rushed back to the living room and fumbled with the latch on Rusty's crate.

"Sorry, girl. Sorry. You didn't do anything wrong. No, you didn't. Come on, now. We have to go. You can have a treat when we get to the office, okay?"

She was heading out just as Barb returned and handed her the paper with the cryptic clues. "Close up the house when you go, okay?"

Barb nodded. "Did you shut off the coffee?"

Jana shook her head. When she reached her vehicle, John was waiting for her and Kane was limping toward Maddie's house. She didn't see Virgil, but he might be running toward the town square and would get there before she did.

As soon as she got Rusty settled in the cargo area, she flung herself behind the wheel, hit the lights and siren, and stepped on the gas.

"Hey!" John grumbled.

Jana growled.

It didn't occur to her until they reached the office that nobody who could wear fur made a sound for the rest of the drive.

*   *   *

The howling vehicle pulled up in front of the sheriff's office.

"Nothing subtle about her this morning, is there?" Tolya asked, watching as Jana hustled the puppy out of the cargo area.

"Wolverine," Virgil growled softly. "Snapping orders as if . . ."

As if she were dominant, Tolya thought, finishing the sentence. "And you didn't correct her?"

Virgil's bared teeth were his only answer as he opened the office door.

John Wolfgard hurried into the office, then took up a position in the doorway that led to the back rooms, as if he wanted quick access to a number of rooms that had doors he could barricade against the human female.

Did this signal a temporary change in the pack hierarchy or something more serious that would require careful consideration by all the *terra indigene* running the town?

Rusty bolted for her crate. Safe ground. The pup's fear of the person she usually trusted said a great deal about Jana's state of mind—and explained Virgil's wariness.

Jana dropped a book and a magazine on her desk, gave the puppy a treat, and finally looked at all of them. She blew out a breath and said, "Maddie cut herself this morning. Cut her hands, multiple times." She held out a piece of paper to Tolya. "Virgil heard what she said. Barb wrote down the words. The children were looking at this book and magazine when everything . . . started. We need to figure out what Maddie saw that set her off, for her sake . . . and, I think, for ours."

Still wary of the female pack member, John came over to stand next to Tolya and read the words.

"Let me see the book," Virgil said, holding out a hand. He could have taken it from the desk, but he waited for Jana to hand it to him. A reassertion of dominance or prudence because none of them were certain of her right now?

"I can look at the magazine," John offered.

"It's time to ask Evan and Kenneth how long Maddie has been with them," Tolya said, watching Jana. "Time to ascertain if she had any formal training before becoming part of their family."

She nodded. "We need information from them—and we need to

know everything we can about the *cassandra sangue*." She looked at John. "You had experience living around a blood prophet."

"Jackson and Grace will know more," Virgil said as he turned the pages of the picture book. "They're raising the Hope pup and have experience with her cutting."

"I dealt with Meg when she came into the bookstore," John said. "Not when she . . ." He made a slicing motion across one forearm.

"There is a human female in this book," Virgil said. "The pups call her Grandma and she is walking a dog." He held up the book so they could all see the picture.

"Grandma hair," Tolya said grimly. "Jesse Walker has gray hair like the female in the picture, and she has a dog."

"I think I found the big water." John held up the copy of *Nature!* so they could all see the illustration of the Great Lakes that went across the top half of the center spread. "There's also an article about Thaisia's great rivers, but these lakes are the biggest water on the continent."

"Bumpy dark." Tolya looked at each of them. "Any thoughts about what that could mean?"

"Cave?" Virgil said.

<You don't believe that,> Tolya said to Virgil.

The Wolf looked at him. <No. Whatever it is, it will be bad. Not natural.>

"We're going to die, aren't we?" Jana whispered. She looked at Tolya. "Humans. Not the *terra indigene*. Something is going to happen somewhere in the Great Lakes area, and because it happens, we're all going to die."

Tolya had never seen a human who still had blood flowing through her veins look so alarmingly pale.

Virgil snapped, "Stop it. You're an enforcer, not some mewling, useless human."

"I—" Jana turned on the Wolf, then stopped.

Apparently the verbal nip by her boss was as effective as an actual bite to get her brain to start thinking again. A good thing for all of them to know about the human deputy.

"I will call Jesse Walker," Tolya said. "She may have some insights.

Virgil? If you could call Jackson Wolfgard and find out if Hope Wolf-song has been . . . itchy . . . this morning?"

"Should we alert the Lakeside Courtyard?" John asked.

"And tell them what?" Tolya replied. "An untested, and probably un-trained, sweet blood spoke prophecy this morning and one of the images might mean something will happen in or around the Great Lakes. That 'something' might happen in Lakeside or Shikago or any of the other human-controlled cities that still exist on the shores of those lakes—or even happen in one of the *terra indigene* communities around those lakes. Another clue seems pointed to a female who lives in Prairie Gold, which is here." He understood the need to do something, anything, but . . . "We don't know enough. Maddie is not Meg Corbyn or Hope Wolfsong. If we send out a warning without sufficient parameters, we could begin the very thing that will end in bloodshed. Deputy Jana is correct; if we stir up the *terra indigene*, which would include the Elementals and Elders, then humans will be the ones who will die."

"So we do nothing?" Jana asked.

"We keep watch," Virgil replied. "Tolya and I will make the phone calls; then I'll patrol the business district. You will take the vehicle and patrol the rest of the town, driving as if this was a normal activity, not howling down the streets."

Jana made a face at him.

<She shouldn't go out alone,> Tolya said to Virgil.

<Are we pretending everything is normal?> Virgil asked.

<Until it isn't.>

<Then John has to open the bookstore, and I want Kane to stay with the prophet pup to warn us if she does anything strange.>

<Agreed.> Turning to Jana, Tolya said, "Yuri is not on duty at the saloon today, so he will go on patrol with you, and Garnet Ravengard will answer the telephones as a substitute dispatcher."

"Why? Not why have Garnet—I agree it would be smart to have someone in the office, especially today—but why have Yuri go with me? He's not a cop."

"He is Sanguinati," Tolya said softly. "He is Other." He paused, then added, "He is a predator, Jana Paniccia, and if the trouble begins here, which is a possibility, you should not be driving close to the border of the wild country without a predator riding with you."

Tolya waited until Jana headed out to patrol and John left to open the bookstore.

"You're hoping the Maddie pup is wrong," Virgil said.

Tolya studied the Wolf. "Aren't you?"

A big mistake could cleanse all the humans from the continent of Thaisia—maybe even the whole world. But "all" would include the Becky girl . . . and Barb Debany . . . and the wolverine. Did he want that now?

"Should we warn Simon Wolfgard?" he asked.

"Let's talk to Jesse Walker and Jackson first," Tolya replied. "Let's see if either of them can provide some structure to vague images."

Tolya walked across the square at a brisk pace but not at a speed that would alarm the humans. As he walked, he gave his instructions to Yuri Sanguinati—and made his request to Garnet Ravengard, who was delighted to have the opportunity to answer the telephone and hear information before anyone else.

When he reached his office, he closed the door and made his call to Jesse Walker.

Jesse said nothing while Tolya explained the reason for the early morning call. She said nothing after he stopped talking. When a minute of silence filled the phone line, Tolya asked, "What are you feeling?"

Good question.

Whatever was going to happen, it wasn't going to happen in Prairie Gold. Not initially. Which meant this wasn't where she needed to be.

"I'll be there as soon as I can," she said.

"You're coming to Bennett?" Tolya sounded surprised. "I can call you with updates."

"No. I need to be there." The certainty settled around her. He didn't realize it yet—and she couldn't explain it—but she had a strong feeling that Tolya would need her in Bennett today.

"I will ask Anya to reserve a room for you."

"Tell her I'm bringing the puppy."

A sound that might have been a laugh. "If any guests protest about having a pet in the hotel, we'll tell them the puppy is *terra indigene*. Most humans wouldn't know the difference, and that will end any discussion."

Was he trying to lighten the mood or could he laugh about a puppy while watching a potential disaster take shape on the horizon?

"I'll be there." Jesse hung up. Throwing a shawl over the tank top she wore at night, she selected a white flag from the umbrella stand near her back door. Stepping outside far enough to be easily seen, she waved the flag.

Tobias had told her about the instruction to send up a flare if help was needed. This was a similar system that she had already worked out with the *terra indigene* living in the Prairie Gold settlement. A red flag meant danger, trouble, attack. White meant she needed to get a message to the settlement or, specifically, to Morgan and Chase. Or sometimes Rachel Wolfgard since she couldn't call the girl if something changed at the store.

The Hawk seemed to drop out of the sky and land a few feet away.

"Could you take a message to Rachel Wolfgard?" Jesse asked. "Tell her to stay home today. I'm not going to open the store. I have to go to Bennett." She thought of the one thing that might have the juvenile Wolf ignoring her instructions. "And tell Rachel that I took Cory-Cutie with me."

She gave the puppy a handful of kibble to gobble while she got dressed and packed a bag for the puppy, an overnight bag for herself, and everything else she thought she might need.

The third time she reached for the phone, she gave in and called the ranch. Tobias was already out with the men, which she expected.

"Ellen, it's Jesse."

A hesitation. "Yes?"

The hesitation told Jesse that Ellen felt something too—something too subtle to put into words. Yet. "Be watchful today."

"Of anything particular?"

Anything. Everything. "I don't know. I'm on my way to Bennett. I closed the store." The only time she closed the store was for an emergency.

"I see." Ellen, being another Intuit and a friend, would understand the messages under the words. "Call me when you get to Bennett. Tobias will worry."

Jesse snorted. Ellen always said that when *she* was worried. "I'll call."

After settling the puppy in the traveling crate, Jesse stopped at the gas station to fill her tank and then headed to Bennett at a reckless speed.

"Jackson and Grace are out hunting with the pack," the male voice said. "Should we find him?"

Virgil hesitated. "Where is the Hope pup?"

"Probably still at the den. She will be going to her lessons soon."

"She'll be watched? Will be with someone who will recognize . . . signs?"

"You think there will be signs?"

"Yes." Maybe. Bennett's prophet pup was untrained and untested. All her cutting had told them was that *something* was going to happen *somewhere*.

The male sucked in a breath. "We'll make sure she is watched. And we'll tell Jackson. The pack may need to hunt without him."

Virgil hesitated again. Couldn't depend on the warning given by the Maddie pup but couldn't ignore it either. "No reason to summon Jackson unless the Hope pup starts drawing pictures."

"We'll keep watch."

Virgil hung up.

We are here, he thought. *We are here.*

But where was the danger? And would any of them recognize it in time?

Barb fed the dogs and cats and birds. She waved at people and gave everyone a big, big smile as she walked around the town square, stopping at Move 'Em Out to buy a book she didn't want, lingering over a cold coffee and a breakfast sandwich at the diner. She wasn't fooling anyone. She saw that truth in the rictus smiles the Intuits offered in response to hers. They didn't know that a blood prophet had cut herself that morning, didn't understand feeling weighed down by a storm on the horizon, but they knew something was up when none of the *terra indigene* except the Sanguinati reported for work. The Others were flying around as they monitored the town, paying special attention to the roads and the railway station in a way that made the humans realize how easily the town could become a prison.

But Barb, who knew a little more than anyone else, walked around the square and smiled, and the people she saw pretended it was a normal day while they watched the Others, looked toward the Elder Hills—and waited for something they couldn't see.

A fter dropping her bags in her hotel room, Jesse headed for the mayor's office to meet with Tolya. When she first stepped out of the hotel, no one noticed her and Cory beyond a smile for the puppy and a "Good morning" to her—words that held too much anxiety to be sincere. Then . . .

She told herself there was no reason to feel embarrassed when all the people walking within sight of them froze in place because Cory started yapping at the Wolf who approached them. Having the puppy's butt parked on her boot while doing all the yapping? That qualified as ridiculous.

"Stop," Jesse said firmly. Like that was going to have an effect. She couldn't even make the "no cookies" threat she used to use on Tobias when he wouldn't settle down, because all the puppy would hear was "cookie" and that would provoke a different kind of frenzied excitement.

Why did children, regardless of species, learn the word "cookie" before words like "stop" and "no"?

After listening to the yapping for a minute, Virgil simply lifted his head and *howled*.

The bus and a couple of cars pulled to the curb as if responding to a siren.

Jesse sighed. Acting victorious, Cory pranced over to sniff Virgil, who gave the pup licks of praise. Or was he trying to smooth down some sticky-up fur? Who knew?

Glad Tobias wasn't there to make some smart comment about the similarities between Wolves and mothers when it came to sticky-up hair, Jesse said, "I'm on my way to talk to Tolya."

No warning. Virgil lunged at her, his teeth closing on the leash inches below her hand. He looked at her and growled softly.

Jesse let go of the leash. "I guess you're taking Cory for a walk."

"*Roo.*"

She watched Wolf and puppy trot across the street and into the grass on the square.

"She gets tired quickly," she called after them.

"She'll be fine," Tolya said, coming up beside Jesse.

"I know." As she looked at him, her right hand closed over her left wrist. Couldn't stop it.

He closed his hand over her arm. "Let's go up to my office."

"We need to help," she whispered. "If we help, we won't die."

"Come with me."

As they reached Tolya's office, he released her arm in order to rush to answer the phone.

"Tolya Sanguinati."

Jesse watched his face, watched the veneer of humanity fall away until there was nothing but a predator who could pass for human long enough to get within striking distance of prey.

"I understand," Tolya said. "I'll stay right here until I receive it." He hung up the phone and turned on his computer.

"What is it?" Jesse asked.

He fiddled with the mouse, with other objects on his desk, instead of looking at her. "Hope Wolfsong just finished one of her prophecy drawings."

There was more. She waited because she had a feeling he would tell her. *Needed* to tell her.

"Something about the drawing upsets you," Jesse said.

Tolya shook his head. "I haven't seen it yet. But Jackson Wolfgard *has* seen it." He finally looked at her. "And Jackson is afraid."

"Slow down," Yuri snapped.

"Why?" Jana snapped back. "Are you afraid I'll crash the car and we'll die?"

"I won't die. I'll shift to smoke in the moment before the crash and flow out of the hole you make in the windshield."

It wasn't that visual that made her take her foot off the accelerator. It was wondering if the Sanguinati knew the human saying about waste not, want not, and would consider it a waste of a fresh meal to let the remaining blood of a seriously injured human leak out onto the road.

"It will take time to scan the picture and send the e-mail," Yuri said. "And then it will take more time for the picture to download once Tolya receives it."

And if Tolya and Jackson Wolfgard hadn't received special permission from the Elders to have a phone line connecting Bennett and Sweetwater, a warning like a prophet drawing might come several hours too late.

"Besides," Yuri added, "we're not supposed to scare the humans until we know what's going on."

What am I, chopped liver? Jana thought. Another human saying best left unspoken in case it prompted questions about why livers should be chopped instead of just ripped out of a body and chewed.

It took every ounce of self-control to park the vehicle properly and walk up to Tolya's office. People stopped to watch her, then continued with their own business, satisfied by her behavior that they didn't need to be in emergency mode—yet.

Tolya's office felt crowded, stifling, even though there weren't that many bodies in the room. Still, two Wolves in human form took up more space than regular humans, if for no other reason than humans didn't want to get within biting distance of them.

Yuri shifted to smoke and drifted along the ceiling, shifting back to human form when he reached the rest of the Sanguinati, who were standing around Tolya's desk, effectively blocking anyone else's attempt to see the picture as it downloaded.

"Jesse." Jana nodded at the other woman.

"Deputy." Jesse eyed the Sanguinati, then looked at Jana. "I gather our puppies are having a playdate."

"Are they?" Jana focused on Virgil. "I hope Cowboy Bob didn't forget the rule—and the consequences—when it comes to giving out unauthorized treats."

"Cowboy Bob?" Jesse looked from human to Wolf. "Tobias used to watch a TV show about a doll named Cowboy Bob that could—"

"That's the one," Jana said, her attention still focused on Virgil.

He showed his fangs before looking away.

Busted, she thought. Virgil wouldn't have looked away first if he hadn't broken the rule.

"John." Tolya stared at the computer screen. The Sanguinati made room for the Wolf to slip around the desk and stand behind Tolya's chair.

"Blessed Thaisia," John whined. "That's Meg Corbyn."

Jana leaped toward the desk. Virgil hauled her back and growled, "Wait."

The printer began chugging, printing out a copy of Hope Wolfsong's prophecy drawing. As soon as it finished, Virgil snatched it out of the printer and held it so that Jana and Jesse could see it.

"Bumpy dark," Jana whispered. The picture was of Meg Corbyn in the trunk of a car. Alive? Dead? Hard to say. Definitely wounded.

They need you to think like a cop now. Think! "The license plate is clearly rendered. Would it be accurate?"

Virgil nodded.

Jana looked at the clock on the wall. "It's a little past noon in the Northeast Region. We have to send that information to as many police departments as we can."

"Just one," Tolya countered. "We send this picture on to Lakeside."

"Not to Lakeside," Jesse said firmly. "We send it to Ferryman's Landing."

Tolya began writing the e-mail to Simon Wolfgard and Vlad Sanguinati when Jesse Walker evaded Virgil and flung herself on his desk, slapping a hand over his.

"Tolya, *listen* to me."

Virgil yanked her off the desk with no regard to her gender or her age. Before the Wolf could throw Jesse out of the room, Tolya said, "Sending it to Ferryman's Landing would cause a delay."

"No," Jesse said.

He looked at Virgil. <Let her go.>

She returned to the desk, shaken, her right hand clamped over her left wrist. "This is why I needed to be here today. This. Right now."

"Then, speak." *And I will listen.* He didn't complete the words usually spoken to a blood prophet, but everyone in the room would have filled in what he hadn't said.

"By the time anyone in the Northeast receives a copy of that drawing, Lakeside will be in turmoil," Jesse said. "No one is going to be sitting at a desk waiting for an e-mail they don't know is coming. They'll be out trying to find Meg Corbyn, will be coordinating with the Lakeside police. And it would be cruel to show that picture to Meg's loved ones."

Would Vlad consider himself a loved one? Simon?

"We have to warn them," Virgil growled.

"Yes, we do," Jesse agreed. "That's why you should send it to Steve Ferryman. Someone will be answering the phone at the mayor's office."

Tolya looked pointedly at his own phone, a reminder that his phone wasn't always answered.

"It's an Intuit village. Someone will be answering the phone during business hours. And they'll have some kind of police force who can run the license plate just as easily as the police in Lakeside and get that part of the investigation moving. And Steve has contact with all the Intuit communities in the Northeast and can send out an alert. Another source of help, Tolya."

"They'll be one step removed," Jana said. "That doesn't mean they won't be concerned, but they won't be in the middle of the crisis."

Tolya started to ask John his opinion, but the Wolf who had lived in the Lakeside Courtyard and had known Meg Corbyn looked too devastated to offer anything right now—which made him realize Jesse Walker was right. Someone had to bring this information to the Lakeside Courtyard in person.

"Suggestions?"

"Let Jesse Walker call the communications cabin that sends our messages to the Northeast," Stazia Sanguinati said. "She is Intuit; so are the humans who work at that cabin. She will know what to say to them to convey the urgency of sending this picture to Ferryman's Landing."

He wasn't sure that Jesse Walker could express herself better than he could, but he would allow her to make the call. "Anything else?"

"The trains should be stopped," Nicolai said. "It's unlikely that the enemy has had time to reach the border, but I think the trains should be held at the stations and searched."

"The railroads will be reluctant to stop the trains without an explanation," Jana said.

Nicolai smiled, showing his fangs. It wasn't in any way a pleasant smile. "I will e-mail them and tell them the *terra indigene* are hunting a human enemy, and no train will be permitted to stop at the Bennett station until the enemy is found. Then each station will have a choice."

"That message doesn't tell them much," Jana protested.

"It tells them everything," Jesse replied, looking at Nicolai. "His name alone will tell the other station masters everything they need to know."

Tolya gave Nicolai a nod. "Send your message."

"Maybe it hasn't happened yet," Jana said. "Maybe we have time to stop it. Sometimes prophecies don't happen because they were seen and people acted on the information. Right?"

"You can't always act fast enough." Jesse Walker met Tolya's eyes. The grief and regret of what had happened to Joe Wolfgard and the rest of the Prairie Gold pack was still fresh for both of them. "Do you have Steve's e-mail address?"

"Yes," he said. "Make the phone call, Jesse Walker. Impress upon the humans working at the cabin that this message is more than urgent. It truly is a matter of life and death—for all of you."

If we help, we won't die. The words she had whispered such a short time ago seemed to echo in the room. He wondered if she argued to have Steve Ferryman involved in order to save the Intuits or if she had a feeling that involving the Intuits would make the difference in preventing the death that could become the trigger for so many more.

J esse's hands shook as she placed the call to the communications cabin. "Hello?" A male voice filled with tension, like he'd already seen too much. Already knew too much.

"This is Jesse Walker. I'm calling on behalf of Tolya Sanguinati, in Bennett. Your counterpart in the Northeast cabin needs to make an urgent call to Steve Ferryman at the mayor's office in Ferryman's Landing." Jesse stopped. Thought. "No. Your counterpart needs to make an *emergency call* and inform Steve that Tolya Sanguinati is sending him a prophet drawing via e-mail. Steve needs to get it to the right people as fast as he can. He'll know who they are."

"When is Tolya Sanguinati sending this e-mail?"

"As I speak. But Steve needs to know it's coming, even if he gets the phone message a minute ahead of the e-mail."

A weighty silence. "What kind of emergency?"

"Life or death for all of us." Her words weren't an exaggeration; they were the painful, terrifying truth.

Some commotion suddenly in the background. Raised voices. The man said, "Hold on a minute."

Jesse listened to the voices, then looked at Jana. "Something's wrong there."

"Are they under attack?" Jana asked.

"You there?" The man sounded spooked. Since he was an Intuit, that wasn't good.

"I'm here," Jesse replied.

"You said Steve Ferryman at Ferryman's Landing. That's the Intuit village on Great Island, near Lakeside and Talulah Falls. Is that right?"

"Yes." Definitely something wrong.

"A rider from the other cabin just came in with a printout of an e-mail that was sent from Ferryman's Landing to a long list of Intuit villages as well as the Northeast communications cabin. It's asking everyone to be on the lookout." He hesitated. "Does that picture you're sending have anything to do with the Lakeside Courtyard?"

"Why?"

"Because the Lakeside Courtyard's Human Liaison was abducted a short while ago by a man named Cyrus James Montgomery."

Jesse felt her stomach roll. Fighting against the nausea, she said, "Then let's all hope that what we're sending will help them find her in time."

Parlan had done his duty, flirting with his business partners' wives enough to make them feel good without flirting so much that the husbands might feel a flicker of jealousy—if they could take their eyes off the prettier, younger women who were traveling on the train. Now he wanted to go back to his private car before the train left the station—and before one of the women invited herself to join him.

"If you ladies will excuse me . . ." He pushed his chair back.

"It's outrageous," a man said as he and a companion entered the car and took the table on the opposite side of the aisle. "And no explanation!"

"There's a problem on the tracks?" Parlan suddenly felt uneasy in the same way he did when a game turned sour. "My apologies for intruding on your conversation, but what you just said sounds alarming."

"Alarming?" The man huffed. "Damned inconvenient, that's what it is. The station in Bennett is closed, so now *all* the trains are being held at whatever station is their nearest stop until . . . Well, that's the point. No one will tell us *why* the Bennett station closed, so no one can tell us when we'll get moving again."

"There was that robbery at the way station the other day," the man's companion said. "Maybe the authorities are closing in on the robber. He shot one of the people working at that station, didn't he?"

"If that was the case, you'd think they'd want the trains moving instead of being sitting targets. Might as well put up a big sign that says, 'We're stuck here, come rob us.'"

Spotting the conductor as the man entered the car, Parlan raised a hand, a quiet command that received more attention than the men who, also spotting the conductor, were loudly demanding answers.

"Gentlemen," Parlan said sternly. "We'd all like to hear what the conductor has to tell us, so be quiet now."

They wanted to argue—oh, how they wanted to argue—but they looked in his eyes and saw a hint of why he was the leader of the Blackstone Clan, why he, who seldom got his hands dirty, had influence over a man like Judd McCall.

"If you could tell us what you know," Parlan said quietly, shifting his gaze back to the conductor.

"Station master at Bennett said the Others are hunting for a human enemy, and he was closing his station until further notice. No trains allowed in and nothing going out. Every station master who received the message is holding the trains."

"Why? Surely a problem at one station shouldn't put a freeze on the trains throughout the Midwest."

The conductor gave him a strange smile. "One of the Sanguinati is the station master in Bennett. If he's giving the warning . . . Well, you're all free to disembark and find another way to where you're going, but stations have been designated safe ground as long as no one starts any trouble, so you won't find any man who works for the railroad, from engineer to porter, who is going to leave a station until we get a message that the trouble is past."

The conductor took a step toward the next car, then looked at the two men who had been making all the ruckus. "Don't usually tell passengers this because it would scare them too much, but there are *terra indigene* out there that like to chase the trains for the fun of it. And some of them can outrun a train, they're that fast and that big. Not that you actually see anything. It's more an impression that you're being chased. And sometimes the fun turns into a hunt. Everyone who works on the lines has seen what happens to a train when the Others attack—and what happens to the people inside the cars. We're not going to die today so that you can make a profit."

The conductor walked to the next car to inform the passengers of the delay.

Parlan shuffled the cards. He could try to call Judd and Lawry and find out if they'd heard anything—and if they hadn't, he needed to warn them that the Others were hunting a human enemy. Unless Sweeney Cooke and Charlie Webb had somehow gotten far enough ahead of Judd to have reached Bennett already, they weren't the cause of this lockdown of the trains.

If he went to his private car, he'd have the solitude he wanted but he wouldn't hear the news as it drifted through the public cars, wouldn't have a sense of what the Blackstone Clan's next move should be.

"If you ladies will excuse me for a minute," Parlan said. "I need to stretch my legs."

Gentlemen stretched their legs. Ladies powdered their noses. Human euphemisms for needing the toilet—and not using those phrases was one of the small ways a *terra indigene* who could otherwise pass for human revealed what it was.

"When I return, perhaps you'd like to play another game to pass the time?" The women fluttered like schoolgirls, their sagging middle-aged bosoms encased in garments that didn't invite a man's fingers to touch, didn't intrigue him into wanting to reveal what the garments hid. Parlan had a feeling their husbands' fingers were exploring nubile flesh right now, and being discovered by hurt, outraged wives would cast a shadow on his plans. So he squelched his desire for solitude and took just enough time to step outside and place the calls, leaving messages for Judd and Lawry. Then he stretched his legs before rejoining the women and keeping them occupied until dinner.

Jana rode Mel around the business district's side streets and up and down the residential streets, looking for any sign that the Elders were, once again, coming down from the hills to unleash their fury on the residents of Bennett—innocent people who had nothing to do with whatever was happening in the Northeast. Not that being innocent would make any difference.

Was ignorance better than knowledge? She and Jesse Walker were the only humans in Bennett who had seen the drawing of Meg Corbyn in the trunk of that car. They were the only ones who knew the name of Meg's abductor—Cyrus James Montgomery. They were the only ones who knew the problem wasn't something anyone here could fix, that it was happening hundreds of miles from here.

But every human here would pay in flesh and blood if the drawing Tolya had sent didn't arrive in time to help save Meg Corbyn. And she wondered, as she'd wondered throughout the day, what made this one woman so important to the *terra indigene* that her loss might unleash a flood of hate toward the rest of the humans on the continent.

She'd probably never know the answer, so she rode around the town square and the nearby streets where other businesses were located. People watched her, taking some comfort in the knowledge that she was there to serve and protect—just as she took comfort whenever she heard a Wolf howl.

We are here.

She wondered if that would be true tomorrow.

*   *   *

Virgil leaned in the doorway of the sheriff's office, conserving energy for when it was needed, and checked in with his brother. <Kane?>

<The Maddie pup is sleeping again. The human bodywalker gave the dads medicine that would make her sleepy. Her hands are bandaged, so we are watching movies since she can't play with the other youngsters today.>

Virgil smiled. <If she is sleeping, who is watching the movies?>

Since it was obvious who was requiring the adults to put a new movie into the disc player when the previous one finished, Kane ignored Virgil's question and asked one of his own. <Any news?>

<No.> He wished John hadn't told him and Kane stories about Broomstick Girl. He wished he hadn't begun to think of her as part of the Lakeside Wolves' pack, hadn't felt amusement mixed with sympathy for Simon's frustration in dealing with a female who was like an innocent, and somewhat clumsy, force of nature in her own small way.

He wished he'd seen a happy picture of Meg Corbyn before he'd seen *that* picture.

He watched Deputy Jana walk down the street from the livery stable.

How much of his tolerance for humans, and for dealing with the wolverine, was due to the stories about Broomstick Girl? And how much tolerance for humans would die throughout Thaisia if Simon didn't find Lakeside's sweet blood?

"You are done riding the horse who is not meat?" he asked when Jana reached the office.

"His name is Mel."

He shrugged because he knew it would annoy her. Right now, he preferred dealing with the wolverine.

The phone rang.

They looked at each other as the phone rang a second time. Then Virgil rushed to answer it. While he listened to the person on the phone, Jana would have been breathing down his neck if she'd been tall enough to reach it.

He hung up and dodged around her in order to head outside.

"Darn it, Virgil." Jana grabbed the back of his shirt and tried to stop him. Couldn't do it, of course, but she tried. He heard a couple of seams rip before he reached the sidewalk.

He'd decide later if he was annoyed or amused. Right now . . .

"*Arrrrroooooo!*"

Everyone around the square stopped moving, stopped working, maybe even stopped breathing.

<Simon Wolfgard found Broomstick Girl. She is hurt but alive. They are going back to Lakeside.>

"What?" Jana said. "Who was on the phone? What did they say?"

"They found her. Simon found her." Something hot and heavy filled his chest. Relief? He wasn't sure. Tonight he would shift to Wolf and run and run until that feeling eased.

"Alive?"

The wolverine smelled of fear. For herself or for the girl in the Lakeside Courtyard that she might have met in passing?

"Alive," he confirmed. "Hurt, but alive."

"Thank the gods," she whispered. Her voice shook but she stood straight.

"What do humans do when you receive news like this?"

"Laugh, cry, gather and hug each other. Become giddy enough to be a little stupid."

"Humans are always a little stupid."

She laughed. "I guess we are." Then she sobered. "The man. Cyrus James Montgomery. Are the police still looking for him?"

"No." Virgil met her eyes. "The Elders found him."

He was glad she didn't understand what that meant. Dead, yes. She understood that much. But not the rest.

He did understand what it meant—and he was glad.

Scythe watched the humans who filled the Bird Cage Saloon. They crowded all the tables and stood three-deep at the bar. Even Candice Caravelli and Lila Gold were behaving oddly. Excited and fluttery, like Yellow Bird when she gave it fresh food and water.

"This behavior is normal?" she asked Don Miller. Yuri Sanguinati was at the other end of the bar, filling drink orders as fast as he could. "They don't even know what happened."

"We don't know the specifics, but enough of us had a feeling that something bad was happening, something the sheriff and the mayor wouldn't—or couldn't—share with the rest of us. And now there's a feeling that the crisis is over, that things are okay again." Don looked at the customers. "So, yeah, this behavior is normal. Everyone wants to celebrate."

Scythe considered his words and nodded. "I will walk among the customers and smile at them."

"Which is exactly what the owner of a frontier saloon should do."

Pleased that she had correctly interpreted her role in this situation, she was about to step away from Don when she saw the look on his face. Sharp. Almost predatory.

<Yuri,> she said.

The Sanguinati looked up, looked over. Focused on Don. Then focused on what had caught the Intuit's attention.

So did Scythe, but all she saw was Jesse Walker elbow her way up to the bar.

"Jesse?" Don said.

"Bottle of whiskey. I'll take it with me."

Don hesitated, then selected an unopened bottle and handed it to Jesse. "I'll walk you out."

"Not necessary," Jesse snapped.

But Don was already moving to the open end of the bar—and Scythe moved with him, scanning the area of the saloon where Jesse had been. All these happy humans, and suddenly one who was important to the town was unhappy. In her saloon. Why?

As Don escorted Jesse to the door and Yuri kept watch, Scythe moved through the mass of human bodies who were laughing and singing poorly compared to Yellow Bird—a hunter moving through oblivious prey.

There was a male over there who looked angry, but the look disappeared when Garnet Ravengard walked by and stopped when the man spoke to her.

Perhaps she'd been mistaken. Perhaps he wasn't angry, just disappointed that he wasn't talking to a female.

But Jesse Walker. That was a problem someone else needed to fix.

*　*　*

"So we're okay?" Tobias asked.

Jana tightened her hold on the mobile phone as if it were a lifeline. She'd told him enough for him to appreciate how close they had come to disaster today. "We're okay. Didn't think of what it must have been like for the cops in Lakeside when the scariest forms of *terra indigene* declared war on humans and swept through the cities. The cops knew enough to understand what was going to happen—and there was nothing they could do to stop it. Nothing I could have done here to help anyone if things had gone the other way back East. Feels pretty helpless."

"You weren't helpless, Jana. You were out there doing your job. Keeping the peace. Providing vigilant protection."

"I wish you were here." *I wish you were kissing me and helping me forget what could have happened today.*

"Have you and your housemate worked out a system for when you need privacy, or is everyone okay with a closed bedroom door?"

"What?" She felt her face heat and wondered if Tobias had somehow sensed her thoughts or was just letting her know he'd like to explore the spark that was between them.

Tobias laughed. "You can give me an answer the next time I'm in town."

A Wolf howled nearby.

"Have to go," Jana said. "I'm still officially on duty."

"Long day."

"Yeah. But once the saloon closes and we make sure everyone who was celebrating is still sober enough to find their way home, Rusty and I will be heading home too."

"Good night, Deputy."

"Good night, Rancher."

As she ended the call, Jana wondered why those two words, deputy and rancher, made her feel a little sad.

Tolya knocked softly on Jesse Walker's hotel room door. He heard movement inside the room, but he didn't hear footsteps approaching the door.

All Scythe could tell him was there was something wrong with Jesse, that she was unhappy and upset when all the other humans seemed excessively happy, and that she had bought a bottle of whiskey to take back to her room. Yuri couldn't tell him much more than that.

He knocked again, louder this time in case Jesse hadn't heard the first request to enter.

More sounds in the room. How much had she drunk? Surely not enough in the time between Scythe's and Yuri's reports and his standing here to have done herself some harm. Easy enough to shift to smoke and flow under the door and . . .

The rattle of the security chain before the door opened with a jerk.

They stared at each other. Tolya was surprised at the stiff body and the anger on Jesse's face. Then the anger faded and the stiffness eased.

"Oh." Jesse opened the door wider and stepped to one side. "Tolya. Come in."

He came in and closed the door behind him. Put on the security chain. Then he moved closer, studying her. "You expected someone else." Not a guess; a certainty. Just as he was certain the other visitor would have been unwelcome.

She poured a double shot of whiskey in a water glass and downed it. "I may not be some fresh young thing anymore, but after waiting through this day to find out if we were going to survive, I just wanted to kick up my heels and have a little adult fun with a like-minded man. And no matter what anyone says, I am not lonely, and by all the gods, I'm not so old and so desperate for male company that I need to accept a pity fuck." She grabbed the bottle and poured another double shot. As she raised the glass, she looked at him. "You probably don't know what that means."

"I know what a pity fuck is, but I don't understand why someone would offer one to you."

She laughed, a bitter sound that troubled him—and angered him when he realized she had misunderstood what he'd meant.

Humans had sex without wanting to have a mate or young, so Jesse's age wasn't relevant, and despite being human, she was an interesting, intelligent female. Such a female would never be desperate for male company *if* she wanted company. But whatever words were said had hurt her, and he valued her too much to let her wallow in that hurt when there was something he could do.

"Who made such an offer to you?" he asked.

She shook her head. "Doesn't matter."

"It made you unhappy, so it does matter."

Jesse sipped the whiskey and eyed him. "It doesn't matter enough for me to identify the fool. He bruised my ego, hurt my feelings. I'll get over it."

Will you?

"It's just . . . I thought there would be enough single men here that one of them would want a skin-to-skin celebration. That's all I was looking for, some company tonight and, hopefully, some halfway-decent sex. But the man who approached me made it clear he would be doing me a favor, which is all I could expect, and I don't want that kind of company."

"There will be many having sex tonight?" Tolya asked.

"Oh, yes. It's a very human way of confirming that you're still alive."

Tolya walked over to Jesse and took the glass from her hand. "Enough."

"Why? If I can't have sex, I might as well get drunk."

"You are going to have sex, and I don't want to get drunk."

"How . . . ?" Her eyes widened when she realized what he meant.

"Not a pity fuck—and not a pity feed. A mutual give-and-take be-tween friends to celebrate being alive. Is that acceptable?"

She said nothing. She just studied him. Finally she nodded. "That's acceptable."

She looked away, and he was charmed to see her blush.

"Is it different with your kind?" she asked.

Tolya smiled. "In this form, I believe the mechanics are the same. The rest?" He shrugged. "You can tell me after."

As he kissed her, touched her, undressed her, he couldn't say if it was different for her, but it was different for him. This wasn't an impersonal hunt where sex was the bait. This wasn't a stranger's body to feed on and leave. This also wasn't romance as portrayed in human stories. This wasn't love, and it wouldn't be forever. Someday he and a Sanguinati fe-male would become a mated pair and would raise their young. But for tonight at least, he could touch and taste and kiss a woman's flesh in ways that pleased her. When he moved inside her and she moved beneath him, he told her without words that she mattered.

And when she guided his mouth to her neck in order to feed while passion fired her blood, she told him in her own way that he mattered too.

CHAPTER 26

Firesday, Messis 24

The words traveled swiftly.

They were carried on a wind howling out of the east—a wind that held enough heat to swiftly dry out grass and leave it vulnerable to a dropped match . . . or lightning's fatal kiss.

They were snarled in the rapids of creeks and streams and rivers. They were screamed down waterfalls.

They were shouted within the rumble of rockslides.

The teaching story with all its lessons would come later. But for now, the Elders and Elementals in the Northeast sent this message to every part of Thaisia:

Cyrus humans are a threat to the sweet blood. They are a threat to all of us.

Whenever a Cyrus human is found . . . destroy him.

Pawing the bedside table in the dark, Jana finally located her mobile phone and wondered who would call her before dawn.

"Jana? It's Tobias."

"Is this my wake-up call?" She rubbed sleep from her eyes and wasn't sure if she sounded flirtatious or grumpy—and didn't care. Then his tone reached her brain. "Is everything all right?"

"Something . . ."

Alert now, she waited as he worked out the words that might come close to describing what he was feeling.

"The cattle are restless," Tobias said. "The horses are uneasy."

"The weather?" It was Messis, so it was hot. And dry. She'd been so busy since she'd arrived in Bennett, she hadn't paid much attention beyond heeding everyone's advice and making sure she carried water in her vehicle or saddlebags.

"I think it's more than weather." He said it quietly, like he was afraid of being overheard. "If you're riding Mel today, be careful. Stay sharp. And pay attention to what he's telling you."

Restless animals. Something more than weather.

"I'll stay sharp," she promised.

"I have to go."

"Me too. I think Jesse is still in town. Anything you want me to tell her if I see her?"

He was silent for so long she wondered if he'd ended the call. "If she's going to be in town another day, have her call me. Otherwise I'll see her when she gets home."

"Okay." The next words came out in a rush. "Take care of yourself."

"Always."

She heard the smile in his voice as she ended the call. Then she sighed and turned off her alarm. No point trying for a few more minutes of sleep.

She padded through the house, let Rusty out for her morning piddle, started the coffee, put fresh water and some kibble in Rusty's bowls. Once the pup was back inside, Jana took a quick shower and returned to the kitchen wearing a long T-shirt and a towel wrapped around her head.

She found Barb, heavy-eyed and rumpled, staring into the open refrigerator.

"You have a case of refrigerator blindness this morning?" Jana asked as she took two mugs out of the cupboard and poured coffee into them.

"Poop on you," Barb muttered.

Amused—and wondering if her housemate was actually awake—

Jana steered Barb to the counter. "Drink coffee. Find your words. And your brain. And your bounce."

Barb made an unspellable sound but shifted her focus to staring at the mug of coffee instead of the inside of the refrigerator.

Jana made scrambled eggs and toast and watched Barb come back to life as they ate breakfast.

"Long night?" she asked.

"Long," Barb agreed.

"Do we need to have a talk about the birds and the bees?"

Barb stared. Then blushed. "No. Absolutely not. No."

"If I promise not to tell your brother the cop?"

Hesitation. "Maybe."

Oh, gods. Well, she'd brought it up, hadn't she?

She glanced at the clock and realized she didn't have time to find out more. Kane had stayed in the office last night with Cory, so she didn't have to drive him to work today, but that didn't mean Virgil wouldn't be standing by the police car waiting for her. Or he could be trotting to work on his own, marking territory as he went.

But she didn't think that would be the case this morning. If Tobias felt uneasy when everything should have been fine again, it was a good bet that Virgil knew why.

Jesse woke slowly, feeling ripe and deliciously languid. Used in the best sort of way.

Maybe she would stay in bed all morning. She could order a meal and have it delivered to the room and spend a few hours nibbling and reading. She always had a book tucked in her overnight case, even if she didn't expect to have time to read more than a chapter. This morning she could indulge herself and . . .

"*Arroo!*"

"Cory!" Jesse jackknifed to a sitting position and looked at the empty crate. Virgil had taken the puppy yesterday, and except for checking now and then to make sure Cory was all right, she'd left the pup in the sheriff's office and stayed focused on whatever she could do to suppress the panic that had built in people who didn't know what was going on but knew they had nowhere to run if the *terra indigene* turned against them. Then the news, brief as it was, that Meg Corbyn had been found alive.

Despite the majority of residents not knowing why the crisis was over, only that it *was* over, fear and stress had morphed into manic relief that left people—and she was among them—entertaining foolish ideas. And doing things that, perhaps, hadn't been wise. Except, gods, it had been a long time since a man had pleasured her the way she'd been pleasured last night. And if this languidness was caused by the amount of blood Tolya had taken, it was a small price to pay for feeling so incredible.

As she swung her legs over the side of the bed, Jesse noticed the note anchored under the book she'd set on the bedside table.

Jesse,

Your puppy is at the sheriff's office playing with Rusty. She is fine. You should eat a hearty breakfast this morning. Meat is recommended.

Tolya

P.S. You might want to wear a scarf if you are going to see your son later today.

"Scarf?" Jesse muttered. "In this heat?"

She scrambled out of bed and stared at her reflection in the full-length mirror. The bruises on her inner left thigh and the inside of her right elbow were dark but easily covered. The bruises on her neck . . . She hadn't had hickeys like that since her schooldays, when the mark was confirmation of being desirable. At least, that was the myth that swirled around in the sticky mess of adolescent hormones. Being desirable enough to be marked, claimed. And becoming more desirable because of that marking, that claiming. Other young men noticed girls who wore that particular badge—or hid it beneath a scarf.

Other men.

As she showered and dressed, Jesse considered how much Tolya might understand about human sex. Not the physical act. He knew plenty about that. Gods, did he ever know about *that*. But the emotions? Was the bruise just a result of his feeding or had he deliberately made it to serve as bait for the man who had hurt her feelings last night? Would such a man, seeing that bruise, approach her today and renew his offer of a pity fuck? And if he did, who would be watching?

Not Tolya. He was too intelligent for that, too subtle. But there were so many eyes always watching the humans. Crows, Hawks, Ravens. Was the puff of air just air, or the Elemental Air coming to stand beside you? Didn't matter who watched or who listened. She wasn't sure if the idiot man from last night was someone waiting for an interview that would decide if he would become a resident of Bennett or if he was passing through. She just hoped she didn't see him again and he was on the first train out of town.

She dressed in a blue T-shirt and jeans, willing to let people see the bruises rather than suffer from heatstroke by being overdressed. But she left her hair loose around her neck—and she did tie a bandanna around her throat. Since Tobias was on the ranch, she didn't care about shocking any of the men and, if she was honest, was a little bit curious about how someone like Virgil Wolfgard would respond to seeing that kind of bruise. But the girls—Barb Debany and Lila Gold and even Jana Paniccia? No, she didn't want to shock them by advertising that she'd had hot, steamy sex last night.

Looking out the window, she spotted Tolya talking to a female. Not a woman in the strictest sense, and not a shifter who couldn't quite get the human form right. Nothing wrong with that one's form, except you would never mistake it for a human.

"Elemental," Jesse whispered.

The female looked up, as if she could hear even a whisper once sound met air.

Jesse grabbed her room key and hurried down to the street.

The female was gone by the time she got outside, but Tolya was there, waiting for her.

"You look pale, Jesse. You haven't eaten yet." Despite being said courteously, the words sounded like a scold—but a scold that held affection.

How much should she read into him calling her Jesse instead of Jesse

Walker? She had a feeling that last night had changed something between them, that courteous formality had yielded to something warmer.

"No, not yet. But I will. Hearty breakfast, with meat." She studied him. "Any news about Meg Corbyn?"

"Let's go to the sheriff's office. Virgil, Kane, and Jana should hear this too."

They walked across the square in companionable silence.

Virgil stared at her neck for a long moment, then grunted, his sole opinion. Kane didn't seem to notice, but he was still in Wolf form so that might account for the lack of interest. Jana glanced at her, then Tolya—and then she blushed.

Jesse figured it wasn't the hickey that caused the blush; it was seeing it on Tobias's mother that threw Jana off stride.

"No need to tell him," Jesse said with a smile.

"I'm so with you on that," Jana replied.

"Human females," Virgil growled. "Even when you speak ordinary words, you speak a different language." Then his eyes met Tolya's, and a kind of electric tension filled the office.

"Air heard from her kin in the east. Meg Corbyn is alive, but there is . . . concern . . . about her mind," Tolya said.

Jana sucked in a breath. Jesse felt her heart pound.

"The cuts that Cyrus human made were not done properly," he continued. "As a result, Meg Corbyn is seeing too much."

"Will she recover?" Jesse asked.

"I don't know," Tolya replied. "That is all the information about her that traveled last night. But Simon, Vlad, and the rest of the Courtyard will help her."

"What else?" Virgil asked.

Tolya looked at the Wolf. "We have all received instructions from Namid's teeth and claws. We are to inform the Elders if a Cyrus human comes to Bennett—or Prairie Gold."

Virgil nodded. Jana looked uneasy.

Jesse felt chilled. "What's a Cyrus human?"

"Someone like Cyrus James Montgomery, the man who abducted Meg Corbyn," Jana replied, eyeing Virgil and Tolya.

She knew the name. After all, she was the one who relayed the message from the communications cabin. No, she'd been asking for a definition.

Meeting Jesse's eyes, Jana nodded to acknowledge that she would do whatever she could to get the term defined.

"Jesse, I will escort you back to the hotel, and you will eat," Tolya said.

Since she was hungry and feeling a little weak, Jesse didn't argue. Besides, she had a feeling that Jana would have an easier time getting some agreement on the term if other humans weren't around when she talked to Virgil.

"How much blood did you consume?" she asked quietly as she and Tolya retraced their steps across the square.

"Enough that you should be sensible and eat—but not so much that what was taken would put you in any danger."

"It never occurred to me that I might be in danger. Not with you."

He stopped walking and stared at her, and that made her smile. No, she wasn't forgetting that he was a predator who could easily snap her neck, or tear out her throat—or drain her of blood. But she trusted him.

"This isn't like the stories," she said. "We're not in love or fated to be together forever."

"That is true." He sounded wary.

"But I did enjoy being with you last night and would be happy to spend time that way again. Humans sometimes refer to such arrangements as 'friends with benefits.'"

"I have heard this phrase." He hesitated. "That kind of arrangement would be . . . sufficient . . . for you?"

She thought about the man in the Bird Cage Saloon—and she thought about the pleasure she'd felt with Tolya.

"I'm old enough not to let hormones overwhelm sense. And I'm clear-sighted enough to understand what this is—and what it isn't. So, yes, Tolya. This arrangement would be sufficient. If that changes, I will tell you."

"Very well, Jesse." He looked baffled but he smiled. "Go eat."

Relieved that she wasn't the one who had to define actions that amounted to a specific kind of crime, she walked into the hotel and ate a very hearty breakfast.

* * *

*D*arn *it,* Jana thought when Virgil turned on her, effectively pinning her against her own desk. *I have to remember how easily he can do that, even in human form.*

"Would you recognize a Cyrus human if one came to Bennett?" Virgil asked.

"It's not that simple."

"How is it not simple?" He leaned closer and bared his teeth, revealing the too-long-to-be-human fangs. "He *stole* the sweet blood from the Lakeside Courtyard and hurt her. He stole her *from the Wolves.*"

And that, more than all the rest, was what Virgil considered unforgivable.

She had to create a tightrope of words and get to the other side of this chasm that had opened beneath her. If she didn't get his agreement on the specifics of what made someone a Cyrus human, how many men would die just for being an asshat after one drink too many?

"I would be reluctant to accuse anyone of being such a person without some proof . . ."

"You would wait until he harms someone?" Virgil's eyes flickered with the red of anger. "Our Maddie is still a pup. She would not survive what was done to Meg Corbyn. But you would wait until she is bleeding?"

"That's not what I said." She put enough snap into her voice to have his eyes narrowing. "You can't accuse someone of a crime before the crime is committed."

He snorted.

"Can we agree that a Cyrus human is a man, or a woman, who abducts another individual, who takes someone against his or her will?"

He stared at her and said nothing.

"That's what Cyrus Montgomery did—he stole Meg Corbyn. Abducted her. That is the specific crime he committed that put her in danger. That is what makes—made—him a Cyrus human."

He still said nothing.

"Some behaviors are indicators that a person *might* behave badly, *might* be a danger to one of our citizens."

"You would recognize these indicators and howl a warning?"

"A warning that someone should be watched? Yes." She didn't want the Others to condemn some fool as a Cyrus human when he was actually guilty of some other kind of assault. Not that an attack of any kind was acceptable, but getting killed would be an extreme punishment when a person should spend time in jail for a crime. And the idea that the Elders might get involved scared her enough that she wanted to be very careful about making accusations.

"Watched if you're not sure," Virgil agreed. "But if someone is identified as a Cyrus human, then we will act."

Jana nodded. What else could she do? She *had* seen the picture of Meg Corbyn in the trunk of that car. And imagining little Maddie in the same situation . . . No.

Bark, bark. Yap, yap. The Me Time cell had been converted into a puppy pen, with Rusty and Cory having some social time.

"I hope they didn't find a stinkbug," Virgil said, sounding mildly concerned.

"Well, yeah."

"I will take the puppies for a walk. You should ride the horse that is not meat."

"His name is Mel." Since Virgil was already heading for the cells, she looked at Kane. "My horse's name is Mel. He *knows* that."

Kane just looked back at her.

"You're no help." She settled her gunbelt around her hips and checked her saddlebags to see if she needed to replace any supplies. "Howl if you need me. Or you can call. I have my mobile phone." Like either Wolf would use a phone when their howls carried from one end of the town to the other.

As she rode out to patrol the residential streets, one thought circled in her head.

Cyrus human. Cyrus human. What would the Others do to a Cyrus human?

May the gods help her, she hoped she never found out.

*   *   *

"It's a gods-damned mess," Parlan told Judd McCall when the man finally answered his phone. "Apparently, the station masters got the all clear, but with every train in the region piled up in whatever station they could reach, it could be a day—or longer—before trains on the secondary and tertiary lines are able to go on to their destinations." He heard a faint something that sounded like a reply. "Say that again. The signal faded out." Damn mobile phones. They worked well except when they didn't.

"Be glad your engineer got you into a holding," Judd repeated. "I'm in a small town. Not even enough people here to call it a town. They pretty much cleaned out the general store yesterday as soon as someone heard that the trains were being held and the supply run would be delayed. The only place I could buy food or water was the diner, and they were already crossing things off the menu by yesterday evening."

"And nothing happened."

"Not around here. But the cops who were traveling the roads and checking these pimples on a map were edgy, like they knew something, were looking for someone."

"Us?"

"No."

"Have you heard from my brother?"

"He's fine. So is his nephew."

Which meant the cops hadn't found Dalton yet despite the Wanted posters. And the roundabout phrasing either meant Judd thought he might be overheard or he had a feeling he needed to be cautious about making a direct connection between Parlan and Dalton by saying "your son."

"What about the boys?" Parlan asked, meaning Sweeney Cooke and Charlie Webb.

"Haven't heard from them. But I think one of them has anemia. Don't know which one."

So one of them had been shot when they pulled that half-assed job at that ranch. "Anemia" meant the blood loss was significant.

Parlan didn't ask how Judd had found out that much. Judd had a way of finding out about such things.

"You still planning on talking to officials about that business proposal?"

"As soon as we can get to Bennett and my business associates can set up a meeting." He hesitated. "Have you seen a newspaper lately?" The train picked up newspapers from every town that still had one, and what he'd read in the latest one seemed to confirm his decision to have the family run the respectable con for a while. "There was an article about outlaws becoming extinct in the new frontier."

"Didn't see it, but I heard of three robberies that should have been in and out and easy," Judd replied. "And they were easy. No resistance, no lawmen. The men robbed the bank and got out of town. But the towns aren't human controlled anymore, and that means humans weren't stealing just from humans anymore. According to the reports, the men barely made it past the town line before they were killed. I recognized the names of the recently deceased. I have a feeling those reports are going to convince quite a few of the boys that it's time to retire and find a more settled way to make a living."

Like we're planning to do, Parlan thought. *Problem is, there's no point trying to settle into a town that's dying, so more and more of those men will be coming to the towns that are stable—or being revived. Like Bennett. We need to get there first, need to become a strong presence in the town.*

"I'll get a stake in the town as soon as I can," he said.

"Unless I find something interesting, I shouldn't be more than a day or two behind you," Judd said.

Finished with the call, Parlan poured himself a large whiskey.

One way or another, Sweeney Cooke and Charlie Webb would cease to be a threat to the clan. One way or another, the person who identified Dalton and put his name on a Wanted poster would be found and also cease to be a threat.

One way or another, he'd deal the winning hand that would get the clan established in Bennett.

CHAPTER 27

Watersday, Messis 25

With the last animal fed and the last cage cleaned, Barb realized she had a free afternoon. She could go to the bookstore and browse—and visit with Joshua. But she didn't feel as comfortable being around him since the dog fight. She'd seen a side of him that scared her. Worse, he seemed to know that he scared her and was okay with that.

Since the dog fight, it had slowly occurred to her that whoever had named him had understood he would never conduct himself like someone who had grown up among humans. Whoever had named him had known that "painter" was another name for "panther."

Wondering if writing to her brother and asking for advice was really just asking for trouble, Barb headed for the saloon. She wanted a cold soda and some time to sit at a table and chat with one of the girls.

One look at Lila Gold told her this wasn't a day for chatting.

"What's wrong?" Barb asked. "Where is everyone?"

"Yuri and Freddie are working the later shift. Madam Scythe is doing paperwork in her office, and Don is in the back, doing inventory and fetching supplies. Candice is upstairs, changing into her work clothes, and Garnet and Pearl are coming in later."

"But what's wrong with you?"

Lila made a face. "Cramps. It's okay. It's quiet in here today, and all I have to do is mind the bar for an hour."

"Well, I can do that."

"Oh, no . . ."

Barb edged close to the door of Scythe's office. "Madam Scythe?"

A moment later, Scythe stood in the office doorway and smiled. "Barbara Ellen. Have you come to visit Yellow Bird? I feed him as you taught me, and he sings every day."

"I'm glad he sings, but I really came in for a cold drink."

Scythe turned her black eyes on Lila. "You can do this."

"That's the thing," Barb said. "Lila isn't feeling well. It's a human female thing, and it would be kind to let her lie down for an hour. I could stand behind the bar and pour drinks if anyone comes in."

"You are not dressed for the work, Barbara Ellen."

"We're about the same size," Lila said. "Barb could wear my other costume."

Barb beamed at Scythe. "It would be fun. And it would be a kindness."

"I would need to pay you," Scythe said. "That is a rule. I would need to fill out forms for an employee."

"You could pay me in free soda this afternoon. Then we could skip the paperwork because free soda isn't the same as money. And it's only for an hour."

Barb held her breath, waiting to see if Scythe's gold hair would change color.

No. The thin streaks of blue didn't widen, and no red or black—the danger colors—appeared.

"Very well," Scythe said. "You will work behind the bar for one hour so that Don Miller can do his other work and I can do mine. Tell Candice that she must come down in an hour and take your place."

"Yes, ma'am."

Barb and Lila went upstairs, knocked on Candice's door to tell her that her shift would start in one hour, then went to Lila's room so that Lila could get out of her costume and Barb could dress in the alternate one.

She had no more desire to work in a frontier saloon than in a regular bar, but she'd wanted to try on one of the costumes since the Bird Cage opened and she saw how the girls got to play dress-up.

"A corset?" She wrinkled her nose when Lila held it up. "Really?"

"Just enough of one to help the dress's shape and push your boobs up."

The corset wasn't tight, didn't restrict her breathing, but . . .

"Wow. I *do* have boobs."

Lila laughed. "I went out with a guy last week. He wasn't invited to stay and become a resident. Don't know why. But he seemed really interested in me and suggested we go out in order to get better acquainted. I didn't get any odd feelings about him, so I agreed."

"Not much to do around here yet unless you went to the diner or the bookstore."

"It didn't take long for us to get acquainted," Lila continued. "After the third time I caught him staring at my chest and looking disappointed, because my chest isn't as interesting without the corset doing what it does, he made some sorry excuse about forgetting that he needed to make an important phone call and we'd have to get together another time."

"Better off without him."

"Absolutely."

Scythe was behind the bar when Barb came back downstairs. She gave her temporary employee a long look.

"Stay behind the bar," Scythe said. "If men touch you, it will upset Virgil—and Tolya."

Not if the touching upsets you first, Barb thought.

Being a substitute saloon girl was fun. Craig and Dawn Werner came in for a cold drink, and they chatted about their puppy, their work as land agents, and when they expected to reopen the movie theater and start showing movies on the weekends.

She served one of the Simple Life men who now worked on the Skye Ranch and had come into town with Truman Skye to pick up the mail and some supplies. They had what Barb figured was meant to be an interesting conversation about manure.

Her hour was almost up, and she toyed with the idea of going into Scythe's office and offering to substitute for one of the girls during the quiet hours whenever someone needed time off.

Then the stranger walked in. He had the look of a man who had been on the road for a few days or had been working outside—not offensively dirty but not clean either.

"Good afternoon," Barb said when he reached the bar and stood facing her. He had a weird gleam in his eyes that made her uneasy, but she told herself she was safe enough with the bar between them and Scythe nearby. "What can I get you?"

"Girl who works in a place like this has got game."

What did that mean? She was just supposed to pour drinks. Besides, Freddie was the only one who ran the blackjack table and dealt hands for poker.

Then the man looked at her chest in a way that made her want to grab a shawl and cover up. There was looking and there was *looking*.

She was certain now he was more than just an asshat. There was something very *wrong* about him.

"You got game, girl?" He smiled—and Barb shivered.

"Stop." She tried to sound firm; she could barely make a sound.

"Maybe you like it dog style." He grabbed her hand and squeezed until she felt bone grinding against bone.

"No." She pulled and pulled, but she couldn't break his hold on her hand. She needed to yell, cause a fuss and catch Scythe's attention. But he scared her so much she just couldn't draw in enough breath to do that.

He leaned closer. "Or maybe I should come around to that side of the bar and . . ."

"Hey!" Candice shouted as she rushed down the last couple of stairs. "Let go of her, you son of a bitch!"

He released her hand. Barb stumbled back and hit the shelves behind the bar. A bottle fell and shattered on the floor.

Suddenly Candice disappeared from view. Don swung himself over the bar. He glanced past Barb's shoulder, then snapped his fingers and pointed at the floor before looking down.

Even scared past thinking, she remembered Lila telling her that was the warning to look away.

Barb turned her head and focused on Don's hand as a harsh female voice snarled, "Human."

The man made a choking sound before he stumbled out of the saloon.

Movement on her left. The swish of a skirt. The sound of Scythe's office door closing.

A different kind of signal because suddenly Don was beside her, muttering that he'd had a feeling there was something wrong. Candice was there too, and the two of them started guiding her to a table.

"I'm going to be sick," Barb gasped. "I'm . . ."

They hustled her to the women's toilet and got her inside before she vomited. When she was finished, she rinsed her mouth with water and opened the restroom door—and wondered if her legs would hold her long enough to get home.

Candice stood outside the door. She slipped an arm around Barb's waist.

"I broke a bottle."

"Don's cleaning it up," Candice said. "Don't worry about it."

"I've never had someone say bad things to me," Barb said as Candice steered her to a table that had a bottle of ginger ale and two glasses. "Not things like that."

"Then you've been lucky." Candice poured the ginger ale. She set a glass in front of Barb before taking a sip from the second glass.

Don was still behind the bar cleaning up the glass and spilled liquor when Virgil stormed into the saloon at the same moment the office door opened and Scythe stepped out.

Barb didn't look until Scythe passed their table. Then she risked a glance. Red hair—the color of anger—with thin streaks of black and blue. She wasn't sure if that color combination was within a safe range when dealing with a Harvester, but she noticed that Virgil wasn't shy about looking at Scythe. Then Harvester and Wolf looked at the floor— and Scythe snarled.

"That bunghole bugger peed on my floor!"

Candice choked, then whispered, "Gods. Don't you wonder how she knows words like that?"

There wasn't time to wonder about words because Virgil strode over to their table, slapped his fur-covered hands on the wood, and snarled, revealing Wolf fangs.

"That male. Was he a Cyrus human?"

She leaned away from him. She couldn't think, didn't even know what he meant. But she'd had enough of scary males, and she desperately wanted to give whatever answer would make Virgil go away.

The Wolf turned to Candice. His eyes were almost solid red with fury. "Was he a Cyrus human? *Was he?*"

"Yes!" Candice's voice cracked. "Yes, he was."

Virgil stepped away from the table and stripped off his clothes. Shifting to Wolf, he sniffed the stranger's pee, then ran out of the saloon.

Candice tried to take a sip of ginger ale, but her hands shook too much to hold the glass. "Gods, he's scary."

He was. He surely was. But as Barb sat there shaking, she realized she wasn't as afraid of Virgil's savagery as she had been of the weird gleam in the stranger's eyes.

Jana had finished a circuit of mounted patrol when she saw Virgil, in human form, rush into the Bird Cage Saloon. He wasn't howling for backup, so it probably wasn't serious. Might not even be official business. Might just be . . .

Virgil leaped out of the saloon in Wolf form, sniffed the ground, and ran north, heading for the train station and livestock pens.

Not good. Kane couldn't run yet, so the only reason Virgil wouldn't want his other deputy around was because he didn't want any human interference.

"Come on, Mel."

She aimed the gelding toward the hitching post across from the saloon. After tossing a rein over the post, she ran into the saloon and saw Barb and Candice huddled at a table, Don behind the bar, and Scythe staring at a small puddle.

"What happened?" When no one answered, she looked at Barb and Candice and put some bite into her voice. "What happened?"

"A Cyrus human came into the saloon," Scythe said. "He upset Barbara Ellen."

Jana felt the floor dip and swell for a moment. "A what? How could you tell?"

"Candice knew."

She hurried to the table. Barb looked pale. Sick. Frightened. "Barb?"

"He . . . said things. And he grabbed me." Barb held out her hand. "I was scared." The last words were whispered.

"Did you think he was going to abduct you?"

Barb gave her a blank look.

Jana looked at Candice. "Why did you say the man was a Cyrus human?"

"Because Virgil came charging in here, and the way he asked if the man was a Cyrus human, I was afraid to say no," Candice replied.

Gods, gods, gods. No question the man's behavior was out of line. The way Barb shivered told her that much. But out of line wasn't the same as trying to abduct her.

"I'll get a full report later." She ran out of the saloon and across the street. Flinging herself on Mel's back, she galloped north.

She had to catch up to Virgil. Had to stop him before . . .

Had it been trash talk that warranted a strong suggestion that the man leave town—or even warranted a bite from Virgil—or had it been more, a real threat that could have ended in rape or abduction? As law officers, they needed to determine that. And she needed Virgil to agree that *they* had to agree that someone was a Cyrus human before they acted. He couldn't go around scaring people into giving him an answer that would end up involving the Elders.

Galloping, galloping. She and Mel whipped past the town's new border—where human law ended. Mel dropped back to a lope while Jana looked for some sign of a man or Wolf as they approached the original town boundaries.

A scattering of buildings on the right, and a road leading to what the maps in the land agent's office had indicated was the newest developed area, which included a new building for the sheriff's department—a facility she'd never see, let alone use. Nothing on the left now but open land—and Virgil running in the middle of the road up ahead. But there were tire tracks and skid marks to the left, indicating that a vehicle had gone off the road and continued overland. He'd missed those.

She didn't hesitate. She followed the tracks, followed the miscreant. Technically she was out of her jurisdiction, but she'd worry about that later. First she'd arrest the fool and get him back within the town boundaries, and then . . .

Jana spotted the car. Not moving. Car door open but looking odd.

She spotted the birds circling high above the car. Circling and circling, as if waiting.

Mel stopped so abruptly she almost went flying over his head. He snorted and backed away. Tried to turn and run.

"Easy, boy. Easy."

She tried to coax him forward. He wasn't having it.

Then she remembered what Tobias said about paying attention to what the horse was trying to tell her.

Stopped car. Circling birds. She was probably too late to do anything more than report a death, but . . . Maybe Virgil *was* on the trail of the man who had been in the saloon, and that's why he'd ignored these tire tracks. Maybe this car belonged to someone who had been squatting in one of the houses and got spooked by something and tried to go overland instead of staying on the road. Maybe someone was injured and needed help. Being foolish shouldn't be a death sentence.

It was her *duty* to find out if someone needed help, her job to bring them back to town and human law. She hadn't gone back the other day to find out what happened to those people who had been poking around the houses. She was a cop. She should have gone back. How could she believe she could do the job if she walked away again?

"Okay, boy." Jana dismounted and ground tied the gelding. It wouldn't keep him with her if something more spooked him or he smelled a predator, but if there *was* something nearby, she wanted him to be able to get away.

She scanned the land around the car, looking for what Mel had sensed. She didn't see anything except some cloth fluttering near the car, didn't hear anything. She hesitated; then she approached the car, debating with herself every step of the way. Should she draw her weapon now or wait? Were the birds circling above *terra indigene* or regular ravens or vultures or whatever else was up there? She needed to . . .

Needed . . .

As she reached the car, the wind changed direction and smelled of death.

The lower jaw lay next to the left front tire. The rest of the head was caught in the smashed windshield.

Jana swallowed hard to keep her stomach down and looked at the fluttering cloth.

They hadn't eaten the body. Not all of it. Maybe there hadn't been time. After all, Virgil had been in pursuit minutes after the man left the saloon, and she'd been minutes behind Virgil.

She didn't see any legs, and the torso had been cracked open, all the richest organs scooped out and consumed—or carried off. But enough of the body had been left for the circling birds, for . . .

A shimmer in the air, like heat rising. But the rumbling snarl that was too close, too close, oh, much too close, wasn't a sound made by heat.

Her hand twitched, moved toward her gun.

Teeth clamped on her wrist, causing her to gasp because she was suddenly too scared to scream. Then the breath of a growl on her skin.

She hadn't worked for him that long, but she'd recognize Virgil's annoyed growl anywhere.

He tugged. She stepped back. He tugged. She stepped back.

Step by step they retreated from that shimmer in the air until Virgil swung her around so that she was facing Mel. Her legs were stiff with the effort to walk toward the horse instead of running.

Mel didn't have that problem. He'd held on to courage and loyalty as long as he could, but the moment she mounted and gathered the reins he whirled around and ran toward the town, which looked incredibly far away.

Had to get to the acknowledged border. Had to . . .

Virgil ran beside Mel. Ran and ran. Then the Wolf slowed to a lope— and Mel matched the pace, as if understanding that they needed to keep moving, yes, but the danger was behind them.

They slowed to a jog. Finally, when they crossed the line on a map that now separated Bennett from the wild country, Jana reined in the gelding and slid off his back. She took a couple of steps away before she bent over and threw up. She'd barely finished when Virgil grabbed her by the back of the shirt and hauled her a few feet away from the puke.

"Stupid human," he snarled. "Didn't you learn how to follow a pack leader?"

His shoulders and chest were thickly furred. His face was recognizably Virgil but wasn't fully the human form. She kept her eyes focused above his waist so she wouldn't find out what else wasn't fully human.

"You missed the tire tracks." The moment she said it, she knew it was the wrong thing to say.

"Missed them? I *missed* them?" The words came out as an outraged howl. "Even a puppy couldn't have missed them. You saw me. *You* were supposed to follow *me*."

He'd known the message about the Cyrus human had gone out to the rest of the *terra indigene* because he'd sent it. He'd known the Elders had found the man before she'd had a chance to catch up to him and tell him the man might not be that particular kind of enemy.

He'd known and had tried to lead her away from what she had found. But, like a rookie, she'd followed a trail that couldn't be missed and then justified approaching a potentially dangerous scene without backup. It could have been a trap, an ambush.

She'd been lucky today.

Virgil stepped back and let out a gusty sigh. "The hunt is exciting. The chase is exciting. It's easy for inexperienced hunters to forget that prey can be dangerous—or that a larger predator has already found the prey and made the kill. Even when you're focused on the prey, you should never forget about the other predators."

She nodded since there was nothing to say. She *was* an inexperienced hunter. This had been her first high-speed chase, in a manner of speaking.

"We should check the glove box in the car for some identification," she said. "There might be a wallet in the grass near . . . the remains."

"I'll go back and look for those things."

"We should arrange to have the car towed. Don't want gasoline or oil leaking into the ground."

"Tomorrow."

Jana hesitated, but it had to be said. "He wasn't a Cyrus human. He was a bad man who might have done bad things, but by our agreed-upon definition, he wasn't a Cyrus human."

Virgil studied her. She wondered if he had studied juveniles in his pack the same way.

"Did you smell Barbara Ellen's fear?" he asked. "Should a human female be that afraid of a human male?"

"No, she shouldn't." Jana realized she would be the one taking Barb's official statement, which would include exactly what was said and done. "Why did he go off the road like that? He might have gotten away if he'd stayed on the road." Mel couldn't outrun a car. Neither could Virgil.

"He looked at Scythe and it did something to his brain," Virgil replied. "He was already confused and dying before the Elders found him. Wounded animal trying to find a place to hide."

She wanted to believe the man was already dying before the Elders found him.

"Take Mel to the stable," Virgil said. "Then you need to talk to Barbara Ellen."

She nodded and turned toward the horse. Then she hesitated because one other person would need an answer today. "Are you sure he was already dying?"

"Why does it matter?"

"It will matter to Candice. If he was already mortally wounded before he left the saloon, then her telling you the man was a Cyrus human, whether he was or not, wasn't the reason he died. That will matter, Virgil."

A long look. "Tell her he was already dying."

She'd also sit down with everyone who worked at the Bird Cage Saloon and explain how the Bennett Sheriff's Department defined "Cyrus human" so that any other wrongdoer who came into the saloon could be arrested according to human law instead of facing the Elders' form of justice.

She mounted Mel and headed into town. But she looked back once and saw Virgil, in Wolf form, trotting back to the car—and the Elders who might be waiting there.

CHAPTER 28

Earthday, Messis 26

Despite this being the day of the week when *no one* was supposed to be at work or cause any trouble, the phone in the sheriff's office rang. And rang. And rang.

Virgil bared his teeth at it, but it was just a stupid machine that didn't know the pack member who would normally respond to its howl wasn't in the office yet.

Why wasn't the wolverine in the office yet? She had said Barbara Ellen was all right, and the human bodywalker had said nothing was broken in the hand that *bad male* had squeezed. They wouldn't have lied to him. They wouldn't have dared lie to him. But he knew from the teaching stories about humans that there were degrees of untruth between an actual lie and true speaking. Was Jana late because Barbara Ellen had other injuries and needed help and the females didn't want to tell him?

He'd make it clear to both those females that there would be no not-telling. They could whine about that all they wanted, but he'd make it clear that . . .

"What?" he snarled as he grabbed the phone that wouldn't stop ringing because it didn't know enough to be cowed by the dominant Wolf.

"Sheriff?" Male voice. Adult. Upset but not whining, not sounding weak.

"Yes."

"It's Zeke."

He didn't know the human well enough that he would recognize the man's scent, but he knew the name, knew Zeke was the leader of a business pack that was clearing out houses. "Yes?"

"We found a body. You need to come."

Parlan Blackstone looked around the private railcar that served as his home as well as a discreet place where he ran high-stakes card games and entertained women when he wanted female company. Moving from town to town had been essential to the clan. Even the wealthiest marks could be squeezed for only so long. Always better to move on and be welcomed back by those eager for a chance to get even than be seen as the embodiment of vices that had ruined a family's fortune.

Now he was gambling that he could gain a strong enough foothold in Bennett to secure a living for all of them—at least until travel restrictions relaxed and they could make their way back to the West Coast and settle down in one of the civilized cities still under human control.

Dalton would stay in Bennett with him. The boy would have to keep a low profile for a while, maybe even change his looks and go by another last name. Wouldn't be the first time they'd played that game. And Lawry would be there. Judd? Yes, Judd would stay with him, even if he had to put aside his preferred line of work.

They would streamline their operations back to the original clan. Bringing in Sweeney Cooke and Charlie Webb as muscle had been a mistake. Neither of them understood subtlety or the need to put aside their own gratification in order to do a job. They had smeared the clan with the shit of their behavior, and because of that, his boy's face and name were tacked to train station and post office walls all over the region.

One way or another, Sweeney Cooke and Charlie Webb had to go before the clan could establish itself in Bennett.

Unfortunately, Parlan didn't have a feeling about their success or failure. What he did have was the feeling that he'd dealt himself a bad hand, that coming into the Midwest had been a mistake, that he should have made the decision to play the respectable con before they'd left the Northeast. Or they should have gone to the Southeast Region and set themselves up in a virgin town—a place they hadn't plied their trade before.

Parlan wandered around the car, idly shuffling a deck of cards. That action always soothed him, helped him think, helped him sharpen his focus. He'd always been that way, even as a boy. He'd known when he could cheat—and how much—and when he needed to play it straight. His father had loved gambling but hadn't had the knack. Not with cards, not with dice, not with life. And his mother, who might have been a vibrant woman if she'd married a different man, had used her Intuit abilities to find the weakness in other people and inflict wounds, knowing just what to say to cause the most harm. It would have been a useful ability if she'd understood how to properly exploit it, but she'd inflicted one wound too many on him, and he'd walked away without a second thought, taking Lawry with him.

He'd had the knack, the knowing, the skill for gambling, that his father had lacked, and with Lawry's quick fingers and skill at con games, they had done very well for themselves. They were a clan now, a family-run business, even if one of their branches handled darker projects that were always lucrative in one way or another.

His mobile phone rang.

"Hello?"

"Found one of our boys," Judd McCall said. "We had a sharp reunion."

"And the other?"

"His gear is here. I'll find a place nearby to wait."

"You'll be able to make the meeting?"

"I'm on the outskirts, so meeting up with you won't be a problem."

"I'll be on the westbound train tomorrow. Should arrive in time for my business associates to set up an appointment with the town officials."

"I'll see you there."

Parlan ended the call and went back to shuffling the deck as he considered how to manipulate the straw-men businessmen partners into saying the right things to Bennett's mayor.

Walking over to the card table, he dealt four cards faceup.

Two black eights. Two black aces.

Parlan stared at the cards and wondered why they made him uneasy.

Jana had hoped Virgil would be off somewhere doing a sniff-and-pee patrol when she reached the office. No such luck. Not only was he there, but it was obvious he was waiting for her since he was standing outside. Worse, the backpack that held her crime scene kit was at his feet.

"What happened?" she asked when he opened the back of the vehicle.

Virgil picked up Rusty. "I'll put her inside. Wait here."

The pup was stowed in her office crate—or maybe was given the run of the Me Time cell. Either way, Virgil returned fast enough that Jana didn't think Rusty had been given a scritch or a treat. He set the backpack in the cargo area, closed up the back, and got in the passenger seat.

"What happened?" she asked again.

He gave her an address and then stared at her.

"I should have called and told you I might be a little late." It was tempting to point out that she wasn't actually late since this was her day off and she was just supposed to be coming in sometime that morning to check the e-mail from yesterday. But Virgil didn't look like he was in the mood to have her point out anything. "Barb decided her hand was sore enough that she needed some help feeding the animals, so Abby and I went with her. After I dropped the two of them back home, I came here."

Since he still didn't say anything, she headed for the northern road that would take her to the address.

Finally, he said, "A pack member who is injured shouldn't run with a hunt. If she can't keep up, she will fall behind, be alone. She can't dodge if prey turns unexpectedly. She should stay close to the den until she heals. A pack leader should be told these things. If he can't trust that he will be told, he will demand submission in order to find out for himself."

She could picture Virgil forcing a female Wolf into a submissive position so that he could sniff her and decide things for himself. Doing that to human females would be a violation, an assault. He wouldn't see it that way, but she knew how she would feel if he forced her down. Something to explain to him when he wasn't angry with her.

"Having me and Abby help her today . . . Friends were taking care of a friend. That's what we do."

She felt the weight of his stare before he growled, "And I'm not a friend?"

Friend? She wasn't sure. Pack leader? Oh, yeah.

She glanced at him and hoped her smile looked genuine. "I didn't need to bring out the big guns—or the big teeth—to convince Barb to do the smart thing. If I'd needed that kind of help, I would have hollered for you to come and deal with her."

He grunted and looked away, ending their little snarl-fest. Jana felt like she could breathe again.

"I brought your crime kit," he said.

It was tempting to remind him that it was called a crime *scene* kit, but . . .

Don't correct the big, big Wolf with the big, big teeth when he's still annoyed with you, even if he makes it sound like you're about to indulge in a bit of larceny.

"So we're investigating a crime?" She felt her shoulders tighten when they approached the spot where the man accused of being a Cyrus human had left the road and tried to go overland. Had he been heading for the place they were going to now and turned the wrong way?

"Dead body," Virgil replied. "The Zeke pack and the Fagen pack had gathered to scavenge what they could from the houses on that street."

"Salvage," Jana corrected. "They're salvage companies, not scavengers."

He shrugged, making her wonder if he saw any distinction. Making her wonder about something else. "Why are they working on Earthday? And why are they working so far out? There are still a lot of houses—whole neighborhoods—closer to the town line that haven't been cleared. Why work at houses that far into the wild country?"

Virgil watched the land, watched the sky, maybe watched something she couldn't sense or see. Finally he said, "Zeke said he and Fagen looked at the map, and they both had a feeling that they needed to check those houses today. They found the body in the first house they entered."

"So the Elders killed someone else?"

"No. A human did."

*   *   *

Tolya gestured to the table in his office that he used for meetings when the big conference table in another room wasn't needed. He waited for Judith and Melanie Dixon to take seats before sitting across from them.

Stewart Dixon had returned to his ranch, but the women had remained in town. The reason offered was that they wanted to keep an eye on the ranch hand who had been stabbed while trying to protect Melanie. He didn't doubt there was some truth in that, but he suspected they were staying at the hotel because the girl was afraid to go home.

"Do you have some news?" Judith Dixon reached for her daughter's hand.

"Perhaps," Tolya replied. "A man talked about doing . . . bad things . . . to one of the young women who live here. His words sounded similar to what your daughter described when the man came into your house."

"He's here?" Melanie Dixon lost all the color in her face.

"We don't know if it was the same man. The man who was in town is dead. Killed by the Elders." Tolya tried to assess the strength of these women. "I have a photo that was taken where he was found. The photo shows part of his head. We found no identity card. Nothing in the car or in his pockets showed a picture of him." He focused on Melanie Dixon. "I can't tell you if this is the same man who threatened you. That is something you would have to tell me."

The women stared at the folder under his hand.

"I want to see it," Melanie Dixon said.

"The Elders were angry." Tolya pressed his hand against the folder, as if the girl had tried to take it. "He doesn't look the same as a living man."

"I need to see, need to know . . ."

Want was one thing. You could live without things that were wanted. Need was something else. Need was about survival.

He removed the photo from the folder and placed it on the table.

"Gods above and below," Judith Dixon whispered. She covered the lower half of her face with her hand, as if imitating what she saw.

John Wolfgard knew how to work the camera the police used to document crimes, so he'd gone out to take pictures of the body since it wasn't safe for any human to be out there. He'd taken pictures of the head as it had been found—caught in the windshield—and then posed it in a way that could be sent to police in other towns. Tolya thought this posed picture looked more benign than the other photos since it showed the head sitting on the hood of the car. The lower jar was still on the ground and out of sight, which created the odd impression that the head was rising out of the car.

"That's him." Melanie Dixon shuddered. "I'm sure it's him."

"Then he is no longer a threat to any of you," Tolya said quietly.

"What about the men who were with him?" Judith Dixon asked.

"We'll find out who he is—and we'll find the other men." He smiled, showing a hint of fang. "That's a promise."

He escorted the women out of the building and watched them walk back to the hotel.

<Virgil?> he called.

<Jana and I are sniffing around a body. I'll talk to you later.>

Another body? It was tempting to demand details, but Virgil was the sheriff, and he was doing his job. Besides, what Tolya had learned from his brief observations of Vlad working with Simon Wolfgard was that you got along better with a dominant Wolf by asking rather than demanding.

Tolya strolled down the street. Time to do another part of *his* job and listen to the reports from the rest of the Sanguinati.

Virgil studied the meat with considerable regret. The *body*. There were humans around, so he had to remember to call it a *body* instead of almost-fresh meat. Good thing Tolya hadn't come with them. The Sanguinati would have regretted the waste of blood even more than he regretted not being able to have a quick snack. After all, *this* human didn't need his liver anymore, did he? Or any of the meat on the legs?

"Is this how humans usually kill each other?" he asked as Jana gingerly moved closer to the . . . body . . . while trying to avoid stepping in the blood. Sensible, that. Lots of *terra indigene* would follow a blood trail, even a small one, thinking they were following injured prey.

And that's what this reminded him of: injured prey. Run it down and hamstring it, then follow it as it bled and became weak enough to kill.

"Looks like he was already shot." She raised her camera and began taking pictures. "But all that blood . . . It's not from the gunshot wound." She looked toward the doorway at the human male who had reported finding the body. "Zeke, your crew and Fagen's will have to work another house for the next few days. Wait. You walked through the house already, right?"

"Most of it," Zeke said. "Fagen was checking the kitchen and cupboards, and I was taking a look in the other rooms. We stopped as soon as I found . . ." He nodded toward the body. "I didn't look in the other bedrooms."

"Okay."

"We'll work next door for a while, stay nearby."

"Thanks." Jana waited until Zeke left. Then she raised the camera again and took pictures of the lower half of the body. "To answer your question, no, this isn't how humans usually kill each other. They shoot each other, or stab each other, or they strangle with their bare hands or with some kind of ligature, or they hang each other, or poison each other. What they don't usually do is . . ."

"Hamstring them?" When Jana looked at him, he shrugged. "If his legs still worked, wouldn't he have tried to escape, even if he was weak?"

"I guess one of our town doctors is also going to be our medical examiner, so he'll have to give us the full list of injuries, but . . ." Jana pulled back the man's shirt, revealing one shoulder. "I think more than his legs were cut. I don't think he could move his arms to fight off his attacker. Once he was helpless, whoever did this cut the arteries. But the throat wasn't cut. That would have been a swift death compared to bleeding out."

"Two-legged predator. Maybe brain sick."

"Why do you say that? Don't Wolves go for the legs?"

Virgil nodded. "But we don't do it to make the prey suffer. And we don't stand back and watch it bleed unless the prey is too strong and we have to wait until it weakens before we can move in. This human doesn't look strong." He walked to the door. "I'm going to sniff around."

Returning to their vehicle, he stripped off his clothes, tossed them on the passenger seat, and shifted to Wolf.

"Yes," Jana said to whoever was on the phone, "we need the ambulance to pick up a body at this address. No sirens. No need to alarm everyone." She tucked the mobile phone back in her duty belt.

He caught a scent. Caught another. Not Zeke, not Fagen. But one of those scents . . .

Virgil leaped in front of Jana and snarled.

"What?" Jana snapped. "I'm just going to check out the rest of the house."

Me first.

He roamed through the house, keeping ahead of her. Old scents in these bedrooms. One fresher scent in this room. Not on the bed but under it.

He tried to squeeze under the bed to reach what he could smell, but he was too big.

Jana nudged his hip. "Get out of there before you get stuck. I'm smaller. Let me try."

He worked his way out from under the bed, yelping when he ripped out a bit of fur that got caught in the bedsprings.

Jana took the flashlight out of her belt and went down on her belly. "That backpack? That's what you want?"

"*Roo.*"

She squirmed and wiggled her way under the bed. "Got it."

When the squirming and wiggling didn't seem to work to get her back out, Virgil closed his teeth over her boot and pulled.

She let out a startled yip. As soon as he saw all of her, he let go of her boot and grabbed for one of the straps on the backpack, pulling it into the center of the room.

Yes. It had been covered by death smells and the scents of Elders marking territory by the time he'd returned with John Wolfgard to take pictures of what little meat was left, but he recognized the scent of the male who had hurt Barbara Ellen's hand.

So easy to shift paws into hands and open the zippers, but he scratched at the backpack and waited for Jana to finish brushing herself off.

"Darn dusty under there," she muttered. Then she looked at the back-pack. "But that's not dusty."

She opened each compartment. One held very stinky clothes. Another held money. Since Jana whistled when she saw it, Virgil assumed that meant it was a lot of money. Finally . . .

"This would be easier if you didn't keep sticking your head inside the pack."

It would be easier if she just pulled everything out so they could look at it instead of doing this dainty kind of pawing. The human was dead. And not just dead. He was already part of somebody's poop. He wasn't going to howl about her touching his stinky clothes.

"Identity card," Jana said as she pulled several items out of an inside pocket. "Several of them. And . . . a driver's license. I don't recognize the name of the town listed as his address, but I bet it's not in the Midwest. Sweeney Cooke." She sat back on her heels. "You think he was trying to get back here after the incident in the Bird Cage Saloon?"

Wounded animal going to ground. Made sense.

"Do you think he killed that other man?"

No. There was that other scent in the meat's room. He returned to that room, sniffing under the bed and in the closet. He sniffed around the rest of the house, following the scent out the door to a big stink that stung his nose and made him sneeze.

Gone. Lost.

He shifted back to human form and got dressed. A minute later the ambulance pulled up. Letting Jana deal with packing up the meat, he walked over to the next house and found Zeke and Fagen.

He stared at the Intuits. "The human who killed that man is still out there. He could be hiding in any of these houses. Or he could have moved on to another territory."

Zeke and Fagen exchanged a look. "When we saw that body, we had a feeling that the killing was personal, that the killer had followed that man here," Zeke said.

"Not a lot of places to go, so this would have been a good choice," Fagen added. "We've seen signs of squatters in other houses. Some places were searched and valuables were taken. Money, jewelry. And food."

"No one should be living out here," Virgil said. "Anyone who is might be dangerous. Might even be the two-legged predator who kills his own kind. If you see any sign of humans out here who aren't part of your pack, you run away and call us."

"Will do."

He returned to the sheriff's vehicle. Jana was still inside the house doing . . . something. He didn't need to see anything more.

He looked up and watched the Eagles riding the thermals while searching for prey.

No, he didn't need to see anything more. From now on, all the *terra indigene* around Bennett would be watching for signs of unwanted humans.

"Thanks for helping out today," Barb said.

"It's a change from mopping floors." Abigail worked up a smile she didn't feel. She rinsed out Rusty's water bowl and filled it with fresh water from the kitchen faucet.

She didn't want a dog. She didn't want something that would depend on her so much. But sweet Abigail might adopt one of the kittens in order to have a little fuzzy company now that Kelley had moved out.

Barb looked uncomfortable. "I saw Kelley this morning."

"A lot of people saw Kelley this morning." Saw him walking out of the hotel with that bitch Dina. Saw them talking and holding hands.

"I'm sorry, Abby."

"Me too." She put on a brave face but made sure her lip trembled. Had Kelley taken a room there, or had he and Dina met at the hotel for a meal? It didn't matter now that she had a plan.

While Barb and Jana had been busy feeding the cats that morning, Abigail had followed the susurrus to a closed room that held a desk and a wall of books. A study or office? Didn't matter what it was. Didn't matter who had lived there. What mattered was the small wide bowl that held the stones.

Obsidian. Onyx. Hematite. Jet. Black stones. Protection stones.

Abigail had held one hand over the bowl.

They hadn't protected the person who had used this room from anything. And they wouldn't protect anyone else. Even properly cleansed, these black stones had absorbed too much anger. They would remain dissonant and draw the dark things instead of repelling them.

She'd read her cards that morning, and she knew the black stones were coming. Her father, her uncle, her brother, Judd McCall. She'd run from them, but there was no place to run anymore. There was, however, a way to sour things for them once they arrived.

Obsidian. Onyx. Hematite. Jet.

She would offer to help the girls who cleaned the hotel rooms, and she would hide these stones in the rooms that were reserved for guests who were passing through.

Let her father and the rest of the Blackstone Clan experience a run of ill fortune and see how *they* liked it.

"Why do you think she'll know?" Virgil asked when Jana finished the call asking Candice Caravelli to meet her at the sheriff's office.

"I don't know if she'll recognize our victim," Jana replied. "But we didn't find anything in the house or the other backpack we found that would identify him. Everyone carries an identity card, even if it's a fake. Everyone carries a ration card, even when they're traveling."

"There is still plenty of food in Bennett."

"Supplies are more restricted in the Northeast and, I imagine, the other regions too. We're lucky that we have pantries and freezers of food available." Of course, eggs were becoming scarce and whatever milk Fagen's team found in the houses now had spoiled. She'd never thought she would look at a glass of milk as a luxury.

"My point is that I doubt anyone who came from Lakeside would recognize this man, which means we need to ask everyone who lives in Bennett who didn't come from Lakeside."

"Didn't you howl to other police?"

"I sent a picture of the man to every police department I could reach. I even sent it to the communications cabin to send on to the police in Lakeside, Great Island, and Talulah Falls just in case I'm wrong about him coming from that area of the Northeast."

"Sweetwater too?" Virgil asked. "There is a human town near there."

She'd thought Sweetwater was too far out of the way and too far west, but in frontier stories, outlaws often chose places that were out of the way and overlooked. So Virgil had a point. The human town near Sweetwater was called Endurance. If that wasn't a name for a hole-in-the-wall place, she didn't know what was.

"I'll send the picture to Jackson Wolfgard." Jana looked over as Candice walked into the office.

"Sheriff," Candice said warily.

Virgil stared at Candice, then pointed at Jana. "Talk to her." He walked into his office and closed the door.

"Am I in trouble?" Candice asked. "I didn't mean for that man to get killed. It's just, *he*"—she waved a hand in the direction of Virgil's office—"scared me."

"He tends to do that."

Candice gave her a wobbly smile. "I bet his bark is worse than his bite."

"You'd lose that bet," Jana said quietly. "Look, we found another body. We think it was one of the men who were at the Dixon ranch. Some things you said about your ex got me thinking, so . . ." She pulled out the crime scene photo she had cropped to just a head shot.

"That's Charlie," Candice said after a moment. "Charlie Webb. I guess he came hunting for me after all."

"I don't think he knew you were in Bennett. He was with three other men when he hit the ranch. Was he strong enough to be the leader of a gang?"

"No. After I'd known him for a while, I had the impression that he talked big but he was afraid of whoever was giving the orders. I think that's why he was rough with me; he needed to prove he was a scary son of a bitch because he was afraid."

He had reason to be afraid, Jana thought. *Whoever caught up to him isn't just a scary son of a bitch; whoever is out there enjoys inflicting pain as much as he enjoys killing.*

"Did Charlie mention any names?" Jana asked.

Candice shook her head. "He was always careful about that, even when he was bragging." She frowned. "A couple of times early on he said things about the people he was working with. Called one the Gambler and called another one the Knife. Then one night he came over and he was really scared. That was the first time he hit me. But he never used even those code names after that night."

"Okay, thanks."

Candice had barely closed the outer door when Virgil walked out of his office.

"This Charlie Webb ran with a pack," Virgil said.

"Sounds like it."

"You think he ran from the pack enforcer called the Knife?"

According to Abby, the Blackstone Clan was a family of gamblers and swindlers. Dalton Blackstone, Abby's brother, had been at the Dixon ranch when another man attacked Melanie Dixon. Charlie Webb had been recovering from a gunshot wound before someone had found him and killed him. Odds were good he had been shot while driving away from the ranch, and that connected him with Dalton Blackstone.

She'd have to ask Abby if her father was known as the Gambler. If he was, then someone else in that group was called the Knife—and was nearby.

"Before you came to Bennett, you were the dominant enforcer for your pack, right?" Jana asked.

She looked into his eyes and wondered if Wolves suffered from survivor guilt.

"Yes," Virgil replied, a warning growl beneath the word.

"If the actions of a member of the pack had put the rest of the pack in danger, what would you have done? I don't mean making a mistake, but a deliberate act."

"The enforcers would drive that Wolf out of the pack. But if that Wolf continued to be a threat, I would hunt it down and tear out its throat."

Not so different from the Knife, then. Once you were accepted, you didn't betray the pack. And since most packs were usually made up of family members . . .

Gods! What if they realized Abby was here and had been the one who identified Dalton Blackstone?

"We need to tell Tolya about this."

Virgil nodded. "He's expecting us."

Of course he was. She kept thinking that Virgil was as new to police work as she was, but that wasn't true. The human elements of the job were new to him, but he'd had plenty of experience protecting a pack.

She looked at him, stunned she hadn't seen it until now.

He *was* experienced. And that's why he'd realized this morning that a human enforcer for the outlaw clan was now encroaching on his territory.

CHAPTER 29

Moonsday, Messis 27

Tolya listened to the four businessmen spew nonsense about saloons being places where men could "cut loose" after a hard day's work, and how *they* were the ones who would be able to bring such entertainment to Bennett and do it up right. Whatever that meant.

He wasn't a stranger to business deals that involved humans—he'd handled agreements between the *terra indigene* and humans when he had lived in the Toland Courtyard. But Bennett was a different kind of place with particular needs and very strict rules, and if these strangers really had been "savvy" businessmen, they would have known that. Which meant there was something off about these men and their talk of business opportunities in the Midwest. The only opportunities these men could provide in most of the Midwest towns were easy meals for the *terra indigene* who were occupying those places.

Still, he listened because it gave him time to study the other predator in the room: Parlan Blackstone. The man had said nothing after the introductions were made, and gave the appearance of being an associate, an *employee*, of the other four men. He wasn't. Tolya wasn't sure yet how or why he was connected to the businessmen, but he was sure Blackstone wasn't the one taking orders. Not from those men.

Tolya waited until the men finally stopped talking, having said the same things a couple of times, proving they had no understanding of how Bennett worked or whom they would be dealing with.

The four men looked at each other, then at him.

"What do you think, Mr. Sanguinati?" Jowly Man asked. "We could sweeten the pot a bit. Help fund your next mayoral campaign and make sure you get reelected, if you get my meaning."

"There is no need for whatever you mean since there are no elections," Tolya replied. "I am the leader of this town."

"What if someone doesn't agree with your policies and wants a chance to run things?" Skinny Man asked.

"Then there would be a fight for dominance." He smiled, showing a hint of fang to remind them that they weren't dealing with another human. "But it is unlikely that there would be such a fight. The Sanguinati are here at my invitation and are in charge of the businesses that are of most interest to each of them."

"So the Sanguinati are in charge of . . . ?" Parlan Blackstone asked.

"The bank, the train station, the post office, the hotel, and"—Tolya raised a hand to indicate the conference room and the rest of the building—"the government."

"And the sheriff?"

"Wolfgard. He prefers biting humans to talking to them, which makes him excellent at enforcing the town's laws." Tolya leaned back in his chair. "Gentlemen, it's clear you're under some misunderstanding about how permission is granted to reopen a business or start up a new endeavor. Simply, in order to run a business here, you must live here. You must work in the business you have chosen. Everyone here has a purpose. No one is idle. If you have mates and older offspring, they will be expected to work in their trained professions, or, if those professions are already fully staffed, we will find another kind of work for them that matches their skills in some way. As part of the resettlement package, you are given the business property and its current assets as well as a house. You can choose from any that are within the town's new boundaries and are not presently occupied. You will sign a contract and agree to reside in Bennett for five years—assuming you do not break any serious laws and end up being killed or eaten. If you must leave to attend to other businesses in other cities, you will inform my office of your destination and when you expect to return. Your family does not go with you unless you are leaving Bennett for good. If you do not return by the expected date, your claim to the business and residence are forfeit and you will not be allowed to return."

Tolya watched the men turn pale or sweat. Only Parlan Blackstone looked calm and mildly interested.

"This isn't a human-controlled town," he said with a softness that made them all flinch—even Blackstone. "This is a mixed community ruled by the *terra indigene*. The predators you can see are the most genial of the ones who will keep watch over what you do. But even we will kill you without hesitation if we consider you a threat to the town or its other residents." He waited a beat. "Would you like to talk it over and give me your answer tomorrow? Visitors can stay for up to five days. If your business here requires more time, you can apply for an extension."

"What?" Jowly Man blustered. "You would just throw us out of the hotel?"

"We would dispose of whatever wasn't consumed, yes."

He was glad neither Stavros nor Vlad was around to hear him talking like some vampire gangster in a human-made movie, threatening his would-be victims. Vlad might be appalled. Stavros probably would laugh himself silly before applauding. Then again, Stavros had often played to the vampire stereotype found in human books and movies as a way to deflect prey from realizing what his being called the Toland Courtyard's problem solver actually meant.

The four businessmen hustled out of the room, and Tolya expected them to be on the next train out of Bennett.

Parlan Blackstone gave him a measuring look and remained seated.

Feeling a hum of anticipation, Tolya waited.

I played the wrong hand, Parlan thought. *Should have come in on my own, playing the first respectability card, instead of using those blowhards as straw men. Now the deal might be soured past saving.*

A clan of Intuit gamblers and outlaws had every reason to avoid dealing with the *terra indigene*. Too much danger with little or no profit. So he'd never met any of the Sanguinati. Had heard plenty of whispers, sure. But that wasn't the same as looking across the table and having the chance to judge your opponent.

"You had a question, Mr. Blackstone?" Tolya asked.

Parlan met Tolya's eyes. If he were sitting across the poker table from this . . . man . . . could he bluff his way to a winning hand or would he acknowledge a dangerous adversary and fold? He had a strong feeling that it wouldn't take more than a hand or two for the vampire to be able to spot the most subtle kinds of creative dealing—and he suspected that the response to anyone caught cheating would be lethal.

He should call Judd and Lawry and arrange another place for a rendezvous. But, damn it, this was the only viable town in the whole area that had access to the railroad as well as highways. It was one of the few towns in the northern Midwest Region that had a growing population and opportunities to own a business without any capital required. It was the *only* place he'd seen lately where he felt they had a chance to disappear into the rest of the population for a while—after they found the person who had connected Dalton with Cooke and Webb and was responsible for his name being on that damn poster.

"You've traveled around the Midwest, Mr. Blackstone?" Tolya asked.

"A professional gambler is like a professional entertainer," Parlan said with a smile. "Moving around is part of the business. Was part of the business. I'm looking to settle down now, have my own place."

"Running it with those other men?"

"Running it with my family. Those men were looking for an investment. I didn't have the cash to purchase a business, so . . ." Parlan shrugged. "But it sounds like it's elbow grease that's needed, not cash."

Tolya nodded. "I understand."

Did he? Parlan wasn't sure what the vampire understood.

"We're trying to identify two men who came to Bennett recently," Tolya said. "Would you be willing to look at pictures? Perhaps you've crossed paths with one or both of them during your travels and could supply a name."

"I'll give you what help I can."

Tolya opened a slim leather case and removed a folder. "These are police photos. You understand?"

Parlan nodded. Had Judd anticipated the body would be found this soon?

"There is this one." Tolya took one photo from the folder and set it on the table in front of Parlan.

Charlie Webb. Just a head shot, so there was no way to tell how he died, but that had to be Judd's work.

"Don't recognize him. Sorry."

"Then there is this one. We know he attacked the daughter of a rancher who lives north of Bennett. He also threatened a young woman who lives in town."

Parlan prided himself in having no tells—at least none a mark could detect—but he couldn't stop himself from sucking in a breath when Tolya put the other photo on the table. The half a head positioned on the hood of the car spoke of a savagery even Judd couldn't match.

"Do you know him?" Tolya asked.

"No." Parlan swallowed hard. "What happened to him?"

"Namid's teeth and claws found him."

"What was he doing that far away from the town?"

"He wasn't that far away. He was still within the town's old boundaries but outside of the new boundaries. Here, you can cross into the wild country simply by crossing the street. And as soon as you cross that line, you're prey." Tolya tucked the photos back in the folder. "Of course, even within the town, where human law does apply to some extent, humans who misbehave are seen as prey."

It was said so casually, Parlan wondered if Tolya Sanguinati knew who he was and was hoping he'd slip and indicate in some way that he knew Cooke and Webb—because if he knew those men, he would also know Dalton Blackstone.

Blackstone wasn't a common name, but if forced, he could admit to some distant kin named Dalton Blackstone—someone who was a decade older and had a son named after him. But that meant his own son definitely needed to change his looks and arrive in town using an alias.

He needed time to get a feel for this place, to get a sense of what he should do. He needed to find out if Dalton was in danger of being hunted by whatever had killed Cooke.

"I'd like to take a look around and think about reopening one of the saloons on my own," Parlan said. "I noticed the Bird Cage Saloon was open for business, so am I right in thinking you don't object to the business itself?"

"You are correct." Tolya said nothing else for a moment. "You're still considering relocating to Bennett, Mr. Blackstone?"

"I am. Thaisia has changed, and, as I said, it's time to settle down. As a professional gambler, I can make sure games of chance in my saloon are run clean, and my brother can handle the bar."

"Would you like to see the saloons that are available?"

Parlan shook his head. "First I'd like to spend a little time in the saloon that's already up and running, get a feel for the kind of entertainment the town is looking for."

"Our entertainment will seem quite small to you."

He forced himself to smile. "Perhaps. Then again, small can still be profitable for everyone."

"I understand you have your own railroad car."

"Yes. The men on the train moved it to a siding before the train went on to the next station, but no one working at this station knows anything about pumping out the waste tank or filling the clean-water tank." *Or so they said.* Then again, he'd seen only two people working in the station—one dealing with the deliveries and the other handling the ticket counter and the little shop. "I'd like to rent a room at the hotel, if that's all right."

"I'll inform the hotel's manager that you'll be checking in." Tolya pushed back his chair and stood, a clear signal that the meeting was over. "Did you leave your luggage at the station? Nicolai will bring it to the hotel for you."

"Thank you," Parlan said as he followed Tolya's lead.

Maybe this was for the best. The blowhard businessmen—to say nothing of their wives—would have become tiresome very quickly. If they hadn't already bolted back to the train station, trying to buy tickets on the next train to anywhere, he'd sever their business arrangement by forgiving their debt as long as they left town. Then he would spend a few days considering the possibilities while he got acquainted with the town and its officials.

He'd consider other things too. After all, there weren't many places for someone to run anymore.

"Is there a jeweler in town?" Parlan asked.

"There is," Tolya replied. "His store is down the street, next to the bookstore."

"Glad to hear it. I have a couple of family pieces I'd like evaluated."

"It's good to evaluate family pieces from time to time."

As Parlan walked down the street to the Bird Cage Saloon, he had the uneasy feeling that Tolya hadn't been talking about jewelry.

Tolya stared out the window, thinking of this latest group of ill-informed humans. How could they understand so little and still manage to survive? Or had they understood so little about Bennett because the deal wasn't of interest to them to begin with? Was the plan to grease the right palms, make the deal, and then disappear, leaving their "associate" to run the saloon?

Might have worked if they'd been dealing with another human.

A fight for dominance. He'd seen that flash of interest in Parlan Blackstone's eyes when that was mentioned. If Blackstone really intended to settle in Bennett, it wouldn't take long before he chafed at the town's restrictions and began to think, as humans so often did, that he could change things to suit himself and his pack.

If someone believed that a human form meant thinking like a human, if someone didn't understand what would happen to this town if the Sanguinati and Wolfgard *didn't* rule here . . .

It would be simple enough to eliminate Blackstone. The Sanguinati could slip into his room tonight and feast while he slept. But this was the adversary they could see. The other members of the pack might be harder to find once the leader was killed. And if they killed one member of that pack, they needed to kill them all.

<Yuri?> Tolya called. <A human named Parlan Blackstone has come to town. He'll be visiting the saloon.>

<I'll keep watch,> Yuri replied.

Tolya thought for a moment. <Is Lila Gold working at the saloon today?>

<She is.>

<Ask if any of her books or papers talk about fights for dominance in frontier towns.>

<Virgil, a Blackstone human has come to town,> Tolya said. <Not the one identified from Hope Wolfsong's drawing. This is an older male. Maybe the dominant male of that pack. Certainly a predator.>

<Is he the Knife?> Virgil struggled to keep his fangs from lengthening to Wolf size since Becky Gott was telling him about buttons and he didn't want to scare her.

<No, I think this is the Gambler. He denied knowing them, but I could tell by the change in his scent that he recognized the two males who were killed—and the one killed by a human didn't surprise him.>

<So we still have to find the Knife. Plenty of unclaimed places where a human predator could hide—as long as he stays hidden.> Spotting Jacob Gott heading toward them, Virgil turned and walked away. Human pup or Wolf pup, the solution was the same: when an adult got tired of playing with a puppy, he walked away. <Where is the Gambler now?>

<He asked about Kelley's shop and the Bird Cage Saloon. I suspect he'll be heading for one or the other.>

<I'll check the shop. Are you going to tell Scythe?>

<I told Yuri. He'll watch our visitor. But someone needs to keep Abigail Burch away from the town square and our visitor. And close watch needs to be kept on our prophet pup.>

<Kane's been staying close to the Maddie pup. I'll tell Jana to check on Abigail and Barbara Ellen.>

<You'll *tell* Jana?>

The humor in Tolya's voice made Virgil growl. <She works for me.> And she was third in the police pack. *Third.*

But the wolverine *was* the dominant female in their pack.

Virgil sighed. Mixed-species packs were harder to handle than Wolves.

He stopped at the sheriff's office and took Rusty across the street to her piddle spot. When he brought her back to her crate and the pup looked at him with sad eyes, he gave her a scritch. "You and I will go out on the square and have a good run before your mom takes you home."

The office door opened. Rusty tried to rush past him to welcome the person standing in the doorway.

"I took her out," he said, holding the pup. He heard boots moving across the floor, and he felt her at his back. The wolverine walked quietly for a human—except when she didn't, and that, he suspected, was deliberate. "She should have a good run. Been in the den too much lately."

The wolverine sighed and crouched to give pats and accept licks. "I know. I wish I could take her with me when I ride Mel."

"Why don't you? The horse that is not meat wouldn't fear a puppy."

She looked like she was going to argue with him about the horse, but she didn't. A passive wolverine? Should that worry him?

"You think she would be okay, would be safe, off the leash? There isn't that much traffic on the square, but there are the buses and taxis and some personal vehicles."

"Pups follow the adults. That's how they learn." Virgil shrugged. "You ride. She and I will run. And she'll learn."

Jana nodded. "Okay." She nudged Rusty back into the crate and closed the door. "The person who killed the man we found the other day . . ."

"Is nearby. So is the Blackstone called the Gambler."

"The Blackstones are Abby's family."

Virgil nodded. "She needs to hide."

Jana looked at her watch. "I'll call Barb and see if she knows where Abby is working this afternoon. But if someone spots her before I find her and follows her back to her house . . ."

"Kane is watching the Maddie pup. If a stranger appears on the street, he'll howl for us."

Virgil waited a minute after Jana left. Then he walked across the square to the jewelry store to see if he could flush out his prey.

Heart racing, Abigail ducked around the corner and pressed her back against the wall.

Oh gods, oh gods, he was already here. Her father was at the registration desk, checking into the hotel.

It had been so easy to talk the young man who had been assigned to clean the transient guest rooms into letting her help. He usually did other kinds of maintenance in the hotel, but they were short staffed today because two of the girls had called in sick. One girl really was sick and had been at the doctor's office when Anya had called to confirm there was actual illness. The other girl hadn't wanted to come in that day and was now scrambling to find some other employment before she was put on a train heading for an arbitrary destination.

The young man told her this in a voice filled with hushed awe. What had seemed like a harmless fib to have an extra day off had become a hard lesson in how the *terra indigene* differed from human employers.

Abigail made sympathetic noises, but she wondered how many times the girl had played the "I'm sick" card to get out of work. It sounded like it had been one time too many if Anya was calling the doctors to check on employee health.

The cleaning service she worked for was run by a human, and a good worker would be given some leeway, mainly because there were more jobs than workers right now. Still, sweet Abigail wouldn't shrug off her job unless a friend needed help.

Six rooms. Six stones. While the young man took care of the bathrooms, Abigail used a penknife to slit each mattress near the headboard and shove one of the black stones into the slit before making up each bed. The dissonance in the stones would wrap around the person as he slept, and even something that looked like good fortune would have a sting.

They had finished up and she had been about to leave when she saw her father.

So close. A few minutes earlier and he might have seen her coming out of one of the rooms. Now . . .

Her mobile phone buzzed. She pulled it out of the pouch she used for personal items—a shapeless embroidered thing that suited sweet Abigail.

"Hello?" she whispered.

"Abby? It's Jana. Where are you?"

Where was she supposed to be this afternoon? And where could she say she was now? "I'm . . . I'm at the coin-operated laundry near the hotel."

A moment of puzzled silence on Jana's end of the line, but it was the only place nearby that Parlan Blackstone wouldn't visit and Abigail could hide.

"Stay there," Jana said. "And stay out of sight. I'm coming to get you."

So the wannabe deputy knew Parlan was in town and he meant danger. She could work with that.

After all, she didn't have to fake being afraid.

The jewelry store looked more like a pawnshop that specialized in glass being passed off as real gemstones and baubles that no self-respecting thief would bother to take. Oh, pretty enough for women who couldn't tell the difference, but a disappointment to him. Still, if that's what they were selling in Bennett, Lawry wouldn't even have to run a con in order to swap junk for high-end pieces of jewelry.

Parlan studied the man who stood behind the back counter—the one place that had a few decent pieces with actual gemstones. Early thirties, thinning blond hair, carrying a bit too much weight for his frame. A soft man.

But in other hands, the store could be a useful way to move jewelry and jewels that were acquired by less than legal means. Lawry might prefer that to working in a saloon, and it would be a place to stash goods for associates. Yes, that might be better than all of them working in the same business. Diversify to establish roots quickly.

"Do you sell pieces on commission?" Parlan asked.

"Those two cases all have jewelry that was brought in by the salvage company. They get a percentage from the sales."

"Costume jewelry. Trinkets." It took effort not to sneer at the junk. "They don't bring in anything with gems?"

A hesitation. Something in the eyes.

Parlan swore silently. The jeweler was a fucking Intuit. And wary of him asking questions.

"Anything that is deemed valuable is held for possible heirs. But not here."

Not even being subtle about telling him there wasn't anything there to steal.

"I didn't realize Intuits were living in this town," Parlan said, sounding casual but meaning it as a threat. Intuits who lived in a human town could often be very accommodating in exchange for someone keeping their secret. But there was no reaction from the jeweler. No wariness. That meant the Intuits weren't hiding that extra sense that had been the reason for generations of persecution. Damn it!

"This is a mixed community," the jeweler replied. "Plenty of Intuits have settled here."

Not what he wanted to hear. He'd always avoided Intuit communities because they were bad for business. But . . . "Have you ever heard of an Intuit who could match a stone to a person? Not just that a garnet, for example, would be a good stone for a person but picking the one garnet out of a pile of stones that resonated with the person in exactly the right way? A person like that might have a strong reaction to stones that were supposedly dissonant with whoever handled them."

"I've never heard of a jeweler who could make that precise a match between stone and customer. Must be a rare ability—if it isn't just a brag to boost business."

Because of his own ability, Parlan knew when someone was bluffing—or lying—and the jeweler had just revealed his hand. Abigail, the deceitful, faithless bitch, was in town. Somewhere. "Well, you know how it is. People exaggerate Intuit abilities to justify their own mistakes."

The bell over the door jingled. The jeweler looked relieved.

Parlan turned away from the counter and faced the newcomer.

The gray in the hair was too well blended into the black to be caused by age, especially when combined with the face and body of a man in his prime. The amber eyes that were fixed on him held unnerving focus. Casual clothes—jeans, shoes, checked shirt. And a star pinned to the shirt pocket.

"You must be Sheriff Wolfgard," Parlan said, expecting the Other to be surprised that he would know.

"You must be Blackstone," Wolfgard replied. "The Gambler."

By all the dark gods, how had he known *that*? Had Charlie Webb been in town shooting off his mouth before Judd found him? Or had the mayor identified him that way, knowing he was a professional gambler? Either way, here was the sheriff rushing over to get a look at the stranger who had come to his town.

He met the Wolf's eyes. He'd stared down plenty of men—especially the ones foolish enough to call him a cheat. But this was different. The amber eyes didn't look away; the lips pulled back, revealing teeth that weren't human; and the sound coming from that throat . . .

Parlan looked away, acknowledging the Wolf's dominance.

"If you'll excuse me, Sheriff?"

He waited until the Wolf stepped aside. It bothered him that he wanted to hurry, wanted to run.

The fucking beast made his skin crawl.

Parlan headed for the saloon. He wanted, *needed*, a drink. And he wanted time to consider what the clan would need to do in order to stake a claim in Bennett.

"Sheriff?"

Virgil looked at Kelley. The fear smell had been in the shop before he'd entered, so he knew he wasn't the cause. "What?"

Kelley wiped a hand across his forehead. "That man said a couple of things that made me think he was fishing for information about Abby."

Virgil growled. "He said her name?"

"No." Kelley shifted from one foot to the other. "But he said some things that reminded me of how Abby had acted around some gemstones just before we moved to Bennett. It . . . caused some trouble between us.

Made me see things differently. Just because our marriage is over doesn't mean I want her to get hurt."

"He's trying to sniff her out."

"Yes, I think so."

"Then we'll have to sniff out the rest of his pack before he finds her."

Two men were sitting at a table, drinking beer and playing checkers. Two other men, dressed almost identically in what Parlan considered a work uniform, stood on either side of the bar. The bartender had black hair, dark eyes, and olive skin.

Sanguinati. Gods, weren't any of them blond-haired and blue-eyed? Or had they bred any other coloring out of their species?

The other man had medium brown hair, green eyes, and an easy smile. Young, with that first real-job eagerness. Watching him shuffle a deck of cards and add a bit of flash to the hand work before he dealt out two hands of cards, Parlan smiled.

The Sanguinati looked at him. "Can I get you something from the bar?"

"Whiskey from your best bottle."

While the vampire retrieved the bottle and a glass, Parlan moved closer to the other man. "You work here too?"

"I'm the saloon's professional gambler."

You're hardly that. Takes more than a few fancy moves to be a professional.

He indicated the cards on the bar. "Is this a closed game?" He'd learn more by playing a couple of hands—and losing so they would be eager to have him come back—than he would by asking questions.

"No, we can add another player. I'm Freddie, and that's Yuri." Freddie scooped up the cards he'd just dealt and shuffled again to include Parlan.

Yuri set the glass of whiskey in front of Parlan and set the bottle on the bar just out of reach of Parlan helping himself. Then he reached under the bar and retrieved a metal cake tin. He set it on the bar, opened it, and . . .

"Do you usually stake your customers?" Parlan asked as Yuri placed stacks of quarters in front of each of them.

"I'm still learning this game, so this is just for practice," Yuri replied. "At the end of it, all the coin goes back in the box."

Were they kidding? Apparently not.

"All right, gents, ante up. We're playing five-card stud." Freddie dealt the cards.

Parlan looked at a pair of nines. Nothing else to work with, but he put a quarter in the pot.

Freddie barely looked at his cards before pointing a finger at the vampire and laughing. "Raised eyebrows is a tell, my friend. Signals that you've been dealt a good hand—maybe a *very* good hand."

"Or, knowing that a human would think that, it could be a bluff and I'm trying to fool you into thinking I have a very good hand when I have nothing," Yuri replied with a little smile.

Freddie studied the vampire. "I can't get a feel for if you're bluffing."

"Maybe because I'm not. I'll call your quarter and raise another." Yuri tossed two quarters into the pot.

"Huh. We'll see." Freddie looked at Parlan. "You in?"

"I'm in." Parlan matched the bet and swore silently. Freddie was another Intuit gambler—one who would recognize someone else with his particular skill.

"And the dealer is in. Cards?"

The boy was good with his hands, clever with his patter—and didn't cheat. Of course, it was pointless to cheat when you were playing for quarters, which was ludicrous. The saloon wasn't going to make any money, and a gambler wasn't going to make enough for the time invested.

His place would be for the serious gamblers, not these chickenshit children playing at being men with their penny-ante games.

They played a few hands. The vampire had no feel for the game, and his decision to bet or fold seemed to have no connection to the cards he held since he folded a couple of times when he had the winning hand—something Freddie explained when he turned over his friend's cards.

Freddie, on the other hand, had decent skills at poker and was equally

good as a blackjack dealer. At least, that was the sense Parlan had from
the banter between the two males.

From their talk, he gleaned that the place had another bartender and
a few girls who gave customers something pretty to look at. Neither of
them mentioned the person who actually ran the saloon, which he found
interesting.

"Last hand," Yuri said. "Looks like we're starting to get customers."

Freddie didn't move, just held the cards in a white-knuckled grip before setting the deck on the bar. "No. We're done." He took a step back.
"We're done."

"Freddie?"

Parlan saw the vampire change from genial bartender to predator in
a heartbeat.

Freddie shook his head. "I don't want to deal this hand. We're done."
He hurried away, heading toward the toilets, if the sign on the back wall
was accurate.

Curious about what had spooked the boy, Parlan reached for the
cards. That's when *something* walked out of the office next to the bar.
Female, with gold hair streaked with blue and red—and black eyes that,
when he met them, produced a moment of dizziness.

What *was* that thing?

"Ma'am." Parlan turned away. Keeping his hand on the bar, he waited
for the dizziness to pass before he walked out of the saloon.

They didn't water the whiskey; that was all. Had there been some
kind of scent in the place that affected him, something that he hadn't
noticed? Since he felt fine within moments of being outside, Parlan dismissed the dizziness and strolled around the square, taking a good look
at the main business district as he considered possibilities.

Scythe watched the stranger leave the saloon, his steps a little hesitant.
"Maybe you took too much?" Yuri commented as he, too, watched
the man.

"Barely a sip of his life energy. Just enough to encourage him to leave."
She looked toward the toilets. "Freddie is upset. Why?"

Yuri shook his head. "The Blackstone man didn't do anything suspicious or try to cheat. After Tolya warned me to be on the lookout for the man, Freddie and I decided on a signal if he sensed anything. But he didn't say the words."

"Something made him uneasy." *And it wasn't me.*

"The cards."

"But he didn't see them."

Yuri stared at the deck. "No, he didn't. And yet . . ." He dealt the cards as Freddie would have, turning them faceup so they could see each hand. "I would have had four hearts. I think, if I'd discarded the Jack of Spades and drawn another heart, I would have had a good hand. Maybe a winning hand."

"Better than Freddie's? He had three females."

"I play to be congenial and because it seems to be an expected part of a male working in a frontier saloon, but I don't pay that much attention to what wins and what doesn't, so I can't say if my hand would have beat his." Yuri tapped a finger on the last hand. "So this must be the reason Freddie got spooked."

Scythe frowned at the black cards—two eights and two aces. "Why?"

"I don't know. But I wonder how Mr. Blackstone would have reacted if he'd seen those cards."

Parlan stopped in the shops and talked to the people who worked there, giving his same spiel over and over—he was thinking of resettling in Bennett, had heard it was a place that held adventure as well as opportunities, even for an old gambler like himself who had loved frontier stories when he was a boy. The shopkeepers looked frazzled and a little panicked, but all of them had big smiles. Adventure? Yes. Opportunities? Definitely. A lot of work? More than could be packed into the hours in a day, every day.

He went to the diner and ordered coffee and a meal so that he would have a reason to sit for a while without anyone thinking anything about it.

Bennett was like a boomtown from the frontier days, when a lot of people converged on a place and businesses sprouted like weeds. Most of the people hadn't been in town—or even in this region of Thaisia—a month ago, and new people arrived every day, looking for work, looking for a place to settle, looking for a buffer between them and the *terra indigene*. Those looking for a buffer usually took the next train out after meeting the mayor and seeing the sheriff. The rest were busy getting businesses back up and running, taking over places that existed. No need to pay the previous owners. They were dead and gone, replaced by sheep who would do what the dominant predators wanted them to do.

He spent the day looking around. He spent the evening in his hotel room thinking.

The respectable con wasn't going to be enough. This place was going to be a magnet for opportunists and outlaws who, like himself, needed someplace to shelter for a while. They would arrive, all swagger and attitude like they would have done a year ago. But too much had changed, and what they might have gotten away with before would cause terrible trouble now. They wouldn't see it, wouldn't accept it, and as sure as all the dark gods smiled on shady endeavors, they would never back down for a sheriff that got furry and howled at the moon. Instead of growing and prospering, the town would break apart—unless the people controlling the town were known to the opportunists and outlaws, unless those people already had reputations and were feared.

It was just like in the frontier stories, when the outlaws were squeezed out, were corralled by lawmen and rules until the only places they could live were places not fit for humans.

He had a feeling there was only one way the clan would prosper in Bennett.

He called his brother Lawry.

"We need to take the town," he said quietly.

"Are you drunk or crazy?" Lawry also spoke quietly, but that didn't dilute his astonishment. "The HFL tried eliminating the Others, and look what happened."

"They tried to destroy the Wolves and pulled all the *terra indigene* into the fight. We're going to play by their rules—and win."

"How?"

"A fight for dominance." He'd thought for hours about Tolya Sanguinati's comment about how leadership could change. "We challenge the existing leaders to see who will control the town. When we win, we become the rulers. We don't mess with the smaller shifters. They can stay. And we don't mess with what lives in the wild country. By my reckoning, there are a handful of Sanguinati and a couple of Wolves controlling the town. If we defeat them, we win." He'd even considered how to present his argument so that Tolya Sanguinati would help make that happen.

"Until we find Sweeney Cooke and Charlie Webb, we can't take on that many opponents, even with Judd's skills."

"Cooke and Webb are out of the picture. Dead. I know that for a fact. But I have a feeling that plenty of other associates will be here soon, and we'll invite a few of them to stand with us to form a new government."

"What do you want me to do? The boy and I are shacked up in a piss hole almost on the border that divides the north and south Midwest Regions."

Parlan frowned. "Why are you that far south? We're supposed to be meeting here."

"No choice. The closest place south of Bennett is a village called Prairie Gold. Damn place is a nest of Intuits. Couldn't sneak our boy into the truck-stop motel, and I couldn't buy supplies for two people because the bitch in the general store was looking at me too hard, seeing too much likeness between me and something she'd seen somewhere."

The damn Wanted poster. A family resemblance would be enough to give some Intuits a feeling about Lawry that could lead to Dalton's capture.

"You want us to head your way now?" Lawry asked.

"Yes. And give me any news you hear about anyone of interest heading this way."

"I heard Sleight-of-Hand Slim is riding the trains," Lawry said. "But I also heard a couple of passengers were pulled off a train recently and eaten, so I don't think he'll be riding the trains much longer."

Ending that call, Parlan called Judd next and told him the plan.

"The HFL proved that Wolves weren't immune to bullets, but the vampires might be harder to kill," Judd said.

"Harder, but not impossible," Parlan replied. "In human form, they should die like anything else." He wasn't sure about that, but it sounded reasonable. "Besides, a fight for dominance doesn't have to be a fight to the death. If I put this to the mayor the right way, we could pull this off with some bluster and a couple of shots fired in the air to show our superior weapons and let them surrender the field and leave town. They don't need Bennett. Humans do."

"And after this mock fight?"

"I become Mayor Blackstone and you become Sheriff McCall, and we keep our fine town safe from anyone who would take advantage of the smaller shifters and the humans who sank everything they had into getting here and now have nowhere to go. So we'll look after them and put a sharp edge on the law in case they forget to be grateful."

Judd laughed softly, a chilling sound. "I can get behind that."

Of course he would. Judd was so good with knives because he enjoyed using them. But he was equally efficient with a gun when the work called for it.

"I can reach out to Frank and Eli Bonney," Judd said. "Last I heard, they weren't far from here. Same with Durango Jones."

"Do I know him?"

"You know him by another name. He changes names more often than he changes his underwear."

"Ah, yes. Him." Swaggering fool with too much love for the bottle— and an equal love for making trouble—but damn good with a gun despite his flaws. The sort of man who would need to feel the sharp edge of the law once they had taken the town.

"Tell them I intend to be the next mayor, so they should all come to town as upstanding citizens. We've got a five-day window before visitors have to commit to working in the town. They can play tourist without anyone asking too many questions."

"I'll pass the word."

Parlan waited, sensing that the other man had more to say.

"They found the damn body too fast," Judd said. "Don't know what those crews were doing so far out from the main town, but they found the body too fast."

"I know. The mayor showed me a photo from the crime scene."

"Bastard."

"Showed me another photo of a problem solved."

Judd understood. "What took him out?"

"Nothing human." Parlan thought for a moment. If the sheriff knew he was the Gambler, then . . . "I have a feeling the sheriff knows you're called the Knife. Be careful."

"There are eyes everywhere. I can feel them. But there are a few squatters living in empty houses. They're sufficient camouflage. Easy enough for me to slip out at night and raid nearby houses for supplies, same as they're doing. They don't stay more than a few nights in any one area. Then they move a couple of blocks away and set up again. Just have to watch out for those crews coming in to strip the places."

"I'll call when the rest of the clan, and any associates, reach town."

"Looking forward to it."

Yes, Judd McCall would look forward to it. And so would he.

L ater that night, when the town was quiet, Tolya went to Yuri's house. "Did Lila Gold have any information?" he asked.

"I told her you were interested in reading about dominance fights in frontier towns." Yuri hesitated.

"And?" Tolya prompted.

"She said she had a feeling that you should talk to Jana, that what you were looking for had to do with perception rather than historical truth."

An interesting distinction. Did Parlan Blackstone make the same distinction?

Tolya went to the front door and looked across the street. Lights were still on at Jana and Barbara Ellen's house, so someone was still awake.

"I'd better pay our deputy a visit," Tolya said.

"Are you staying here tonight?" Yuri asked.

"Yes." Unlike the humans in the town, he didn't need to worry about crossing paths with one of the Elders, but he wanted to look at any information he could gather as soon as possible.

He strolled across the street. He'd seen Virgil at the end of block, and Virgil had seen him. The Wolf made no comment about him visiting the two females, and he offered no explanation.

Then Virgil howled, alerting the entire street and probably waking up half the humans who lived there. And then Rusty howled, responding to her pack leader and ignoring Jana's command to hush.

And then something in the Elder Hills howled—and *that* sound made Tolya shiver.

Up and down the street, he heard doors that had been open to let in the cooler night air quietly close.

"Mr. Sanguinati?"

Jana stood at the door, looking at him through the screen.

Tolya smiled. "I apologize for showing up at your home, but Lila Gold suggested I talk to you about frontier stories."

"Oh." Grabbing Rusty's collar, she opened the door. "I'm not a scholar like Lila, but I have some novels set during the frontier days."

Entering the house, Tolya allowed the puppy to sniff him while he greeted Barbara Ellen, who blushed—a reaction he decided had more to do with her sparse amount of clothing than with him.

"You were preparing for sleep?" he asked when Jana led him to another room and turned on the overhead light.

"Why do you ask?"

"Barbara Ellen's clothing." *And yours.*

Jana nodded. "We weren't expecting company." She waved a hand at the bookcase. "What were you looking for?"

So they were going to pretend she was wearing her deputy clothes. He could do that. "A fight for dominance in a frontier town."

"A fight that's in a 'this town ain't big enough for the both of us' kind of story or something else?"

"A fight between two packs." Tolya watched the rapid beating of her pulse. Knew exactly where to place his mouth on her neck to drink deep.

Outside the window, he heard a soft growl. Virgil would never consider taking a human for a mate, but that didn't mean he wouldn't protect a member of his pack even if she wasn't *terra indigene.*

Jana hesitated, then selected a book and handed it to him. The cover was dominated by a badge and what humans called a six-gun. The background was land dominated by hills.

"This is the one." She sounded unnerved for reasons he didn't understand.

"Why?"

"The elements on the cover were part of a cryptic message that led me to Lakeside and the job fair. My foster father read this particular story a lot. It's about a fight for control of a town. It wasn't his favorite frontier story, but he thought it held an important lesson, especially for a girl who wanted to be a police officer."

Tolya thought he knew what a father would tell a girl child. He smiled. "Justice prevails? The good guys win?"

Jana didn't return the smile. "No. The lesson was that sometimes the good guys don't win—or survive."

CHAPTER 30

Windsday, Messis 29

Tobias looked at the dead cattle and swore fiercely until he remembered that the ranch hand who was riding with him today was a girl. Not that "Ed" Tilman would appreciate the label, but what he'd learned from his mother about what was proper when around the female sex wasn't shrugged off just because Ed wanted to be one of the boys.

"Think the Elders did this?" Ed asked in an excited whisper.

"The Elders don't use or need guns to bring down anything that lives out here or anywhere else," Tobias replied, then added silently, *including us.*

Ed frowned at the two dozen carcasses. "Why would someone shoot cattle and then leave them?"

"Meanness or just wanting to cause trouble." Or maybe the intention had been to rustle the cattle until the thieves realized there was nowhere to go with them. All the cattle bore the Prairie Gold brand, so taking them up to Bennett to sell would be futile. A phone call to the sheriff would keep the cattle out of the stock cars connected to any outbound train. The rustlers couldn't sell them to neighboring ranches because the people on those spreads all knew each other. Gods, the Skye Ranch was the next closest ranch, and Truman had worked for him until a couple of weeks ago.

And moving a herd through the wild country without at least one of the *terra indigene* in the crew? There wouldn't be a cow, horse, or man left by the time the nearest town came in sight.

So whoever had stolen the cattle had killed the animals out of spite because stealing was unprofitable, if not downright dangerous.

Tobias looked up and spotted a hawk overhead. Not sure if he was looking at a hawk or one of the Hawkgard, he removed his hat, held it above his head, and waved it in a wide arc a couple of times. He waited a few seconds, then waved the hat again.

The hawk paid no attention. Either it was a *terra indigene* who had decided to ignore him, or it was just a plain old hawk.

Tobias settled the hat on his head. It had been worth a try.

The *thump* of something large hitting the ground behind him had the horses jumping forward, wanting to run.

Wheeling his horse around, Tobias reached for his revolver, then jerked his hand away from his weapon and stared at the Eagle, who stared back at him before shifting into a human male. The head still had feathers instead of hair, and the legs were almost human-shaped but were supported by human-size Eagle feet that had *very* large talons.

"Mercy," Ed whispered, looking at her saddle instead of the naked male in front of them.

"Morning," Tobias said, ignoring his young, blushing ranch hand.

"Yes," the Eagle replied. "It is morning." A pause. "That is a greeting?"

"It is." He smiled. "But it's also the time of day."

Humans make everything complicated.

The words weren't spoken, but the Eagle made his opinion plain to see. Then he pointed at the cattle. "They are dead."

Tobias nodded. "Shot. Probably last night or very early this morning. Have the *terra indigene* seen any strangers around here?"

"I saw some earlier, but not live ones. They are not far from here." The Eagle thought for a moment. "Not far for me."

Tobias glanced at Ed, who had gone pale. It was all a grand adventure until a person made a mistake. Not wanting to sour the girl, he didn't ask how many strangers were now being eaten or if someone needed to deal with a vehicle or horses.

He pushed his hat back. "Well, maybe you could pass the word along that there's meat here for the taking."

"You don't want it for your own . . . flock?" the Eagle asked.

"Normally, I'd see about hauling some of the meat to the ranch or getting some of it to town, but I have other concerns right now."

"Defending territory."

"Yeah. And checking on family." And warning the other ranches that there might be more cattle rustlers or horse thieves in the area.

"I will tell the rest of the *terra indigene* about the meat," the Eagle said.

"If you notice any more strangers near the ranch or the town, I'd appreciate a warning. Or warn my mother."

"The Jesse who teaches Rachel Wolfgard."

"Yes."

The Eagle raised his arms as if to pump wings and fly. Then he stopped. "All strangers are enemies?"

Careful. "No. Some are just people passing through or stopping because they have some business in Prairie Gold. But some could be a danger to another human." *Or even to some of you.* Which wasn't something he would say right now. He'd heard what happened to the man who had been called a Cyrus human and didn't want to be responsible for someone else dying that way.

The male shifted back to his Eagle form and flew off.

Tobias waited a minute, then glanced at Ed again. "You okay?"

"I've never seen one of them looking like that." She blew out a breath. "Guess you get used to it."

"After a while, you do." He scanned the land—and saw nothing. But he had the feeling something very large, something he just couldn't see, was moving toward them. "Come on. There's nothing we can do here, and I need to get back to the ranch."

As they rode back to the ranch house, Tobias wondered how many birds riding the thermals were keeping an eye on him.

Armed with the slim directory she'd found in Kane's desk and the list Anya Sanguinati had provided from the hotel register, Jana spent a couple of hours calling police departments and sheriff's offices located in towns throughout the Midwest Region, trying to find out if any of the men who had recently checked into the hotel had been known associates of Sweeney Cooke or Charlie Webb. What she discovered was how few of those towns still had any human residents. The beings who had answered the phones growled or howled or screeched at her as they tried to form human words. She couldn't understand any of them, but she gave them all the same message: if they needed help, they could call the sheriff's office in Bennett. She wasn't sure what assistance she or Virgil could give, but maybe, if someone was trying to be the law in those towns, just having someone talk them through procedure would be enough— assuming they could understand her better than she could understand them.

She made notes about the towns that still had a human population and humans upholding the law. When she finished her calls, she opened the map of the Midwest Region and circled those towns in red.

So few.

The men on the other end of the line had been relieved to get a call from Bennett and have confirmation that the town was coming back— and humans were coming back with it. The men were surprised when they learned that she wasn't a dispatcher or secretary but an actual deputy calling on behalf of the sheriff. And she was surprised when she realized those men no longer cared about the gender of a police officer as long as the person who wore the badge was human and knew how to uphold the law—and had some ability to deal with the Others.

Namid's teeth and claws had been viciously thorough about thinning the human herds in this part of Thaisia.

Still, those lawmen recognized the names of some of the visitors who had checked into the hotel yesterday and gave her a list of others who couldn't be considered upstanding citizens.

The names and "occupations" made her think of the frontier stories she loved to read. In fact, she was certain that some of those names *had* been borrowed from frontier history. Sleight-of-Hand Slim was a card-sharp; Frank and Eli Bonney robbed banks, gas stations, and just about anything else for fun and profit and often had a handful of men riding with them; Durango Jones was often a gun for hire; William and Wallace Parker were cattle rustlers and horse thieves who might be more interested in horses than cattle right now since horses could travel where cars could not. And then there was the Blackstone Clan, who were suspected of a lot of things but had never been charged with anything.

Don't go messing with Judd McCall. He likes his work too much.

Half the men who mentioned the Blackstone Clan had told her that. Deal with the clan if you must, but steer clear of McCall.

Would Abby be able to tell her something about the man?

When the phone rang, Jana answered it, still focused on the list.

"It's Tobias. Do you have a minute?"

"For you, I have two." Did that sound like she was flirting? She hoped not. She wasn't in a flirting frame of mind.

"Lost some cattle last night or early this morning," Tobias said. "I suspect rustlers tried to make off with some of the herd and then shot the animals when they realized there wasn't anywhere they could go."

"You already lost some of the herd during the HFL attacks, didn't you? What will this do to Prairie Gold?"

"We'll be all right. We've got plenty of bison in the freezers from—"

Jana heard shouting, people yelling for Tobias.

"Darlin', I have to call you back."

She let Rusty out of the crate so the pup could wander around the office, sniffing for Virgil and Kane. When she heard Rusty barking, the sound rising to a frustrated, agitated note, she abandoned the phone for a minute to find out what was in the cell area—and wondered who had locked Cowboy Bob in the Me Time cell, leaving the stuffie propped against the wall.

"Okay, okay, I'll spring him," she muttered, heading back to the hook that held the keys. But the phone rang again, and she rushed to answer it just as Virgil walked into the office. "Tobias?"

"Everything is fine here," Tobias said.

"Except for the dead cattle."

"Except for that. But I invited the *terra indigene* to make use of the meat. The Elders have been neighborly about not hunting and eating the cattle, so I wanted them all to know these cattle could be taken. I guess *they* decided to be neighborly too, because something just dropped one of those steers outside the ranch house. You like steak?"

"Yes, I like steak." A sound had her glancing over her shoulder. Virgil was licking his lips in a way that was so not human. "So does Virgil."

"I'll bring you some beef next time I come to visit."

"Do you need someone to come down there and investigate?" She hadn't been to Prairie Gold and was curious about what an Intuit town looked like. Then again, she'd only been in Bennett a couple of weeks and so much had happened, she hadn't had a chance to unpack all her books yet, so visiting someplace new wasn't high on her list at the moment.

"No need. The people who did this won't be doing it again."

It was the flat way he said it that told her why they wouldn't be doing it again.

She stared at her desk, trying to think of something to say, and noticed two names on the list she'd compiled of less-than-upstanding men who practiced dubious professions. "Those people might not have been the whole gang, and there might be other . . . professionals . . . passing through your town."

"That's not good news. I left a message for my mother about the rustlers. She'll spread the word around Prairie Gold. And I've been calling the other ranches that have been resettled. I'll call them again with an update."

"If anyone sees anything, let us know."

"Will do. Have to go, darlin'. Have to do something with that beef before Ellen tries to do it on her own. I'll try to call tonight."

"Okay." She wanted to talk to him, wanted to see him. Wanted him to be safe.

"What?" Virgil growled as soon as she hung up.

She relayed Tobias's message, as well as the information she'd received from the towns with human lawmen.

"Freddie Kaye is a gambler." He eyed the list she'd made.

Jana wondered what he would do if she had some business cards made for him as a joke that said "Have Teeth, Will Bite."

Nah. She didn't have to wonder what he'd do.

"Being a gambler doesn't equal being a bad person," she replied. "Freddie helps create the ambiance of a frontier saloon, and his running the games keeps them within the boundaries of entertainment instead of the real lose-your-paycheck kind of gambling."

"Blackstone wants the real kind of gambling."

"There will always be humans who want to gamble for high stakes. I guess we can't force the people here to be prudent if Blackstone opens one of the other saloons and offers high-stakes games."

"Why can't we force them? We're the enforcers. It's our job to discipline the pack members."

"You can't stop someone from doing something stupid if they aren't also breaking the law."

"Huh."

That grunt of disagreement made her suspect that Virgil had already supplied some citizens with a few sharp reasons to follow *his* rules.

Of course, when it came to following *her* rules . . . "Why did you lock Cowboy Bob in the Me Time cell?"

"He gave the puppy an unauthorized treat."

He said that with a straight face, so she looked him in the eyes and said, "Huh."

*M*om, *some cattle were shot last night. The men responsible are dead, but there could be others around. Be careful.*

Jesse ignored her aching left wrist as she watched the two strangers who had come into her shop a few minutes after the phone call from Tobias. She'd had time to empty the cash drawer of half the money, take Cory-Cutie into the back room, and tell Rachel to stay with the puppy no matter what.

"I counted the money in the drawer," Rachel said as Jesse stuffed the bills into a drawer in her desk. "Twice." She whined softly. "I did it wrong? Is that why I have to stay back here?"

"No, honey, you did it just fine, but you need to do what I say today. Exactly what I say."

Rachel looked at Jesse's wrist. "You have feelings? About me and Cutie?"

So easy for some people to think of something as expendable because it wore fur. "Yes. I think it will be better right now if you stay back here and stay quiet. And don't answer the phone. All right?"

"But if I'm back here, who will help you protect our territory?"

It was tempting to grab the shotgun she had tucked under the counter on a shelf her grandfather had built for that purpose decades ago, but she wasn't sensing that kind of threat from the two men. In fact, she wasn't sensing *any* threat from them. They'd been polite from the moment they'd walked into her store, had been impressed by the amount of goods she still had on her shelves, and had taken two of the boxes she had indicated were available for people to use to pack up their shopping.

"Lotta work for one person, running a place like this," one of them said as he placed boxes of ammunition on the counter. Two boxes were the caliber that fit the revolvers both men wore. The other box of ammunition held the same rounds she used for her own rifle.

"I have part-time help, and friends help out with some of the heavy lifting," Jesse replied.

"That's everything," the second man said, bringing a box to the counter. He looked sheepish when the first man stared at the two bags of chocolates and the bag of caramels resting on top of the box. "Got a sweet tooth," he told Jesse. "Haven't seen bags like this in a while. Hope you don't mind."

"Better to have someone buy them and enjoy them than have them go stale," Jesse replied. She rang up the purchases and hoped Rachel would stay quiet in the back room a little while longer.

"Noticed you have a bank, but it wasn't open," the first man said.

"It opens late on Windsdays," Jesse replied. In truth, she had no idea why the bank wasn't open.

He removed a money clip from the front pocket of his jeans and handed her a hundred-dollar bill. "Keep the change."

"Then my cash drawer won't balance."

He shrugged. "Then put it in a charity jar as thanks for satisfying my cousin's sweet tooth."

Jesse hesitated, then nodded. "All right. I'll do that. Appreciate it."

The phone rang.

He looked at her, waiting. The cousin with the sweet tooth also waited.

"You take care, ma'am," the first one said. He lifted the second box, and the men walked out.

Jesse grabbed the phone. "Walker's General Store, Jesse speaking."

"Mom? You okay?"

Tobias. "Had a couple of visitors just now."

"Are you okay? Is Rachel?"

"We're fine. Well, I told Rachel to stay in the back and be quiet, and she and the puppy are a little *too* quiet—"

A low growl told her Rachel's opinion of *that*.

"But they're fine." She looked back at the young Wolf, who was standing to one side of the doorway, peering at her with one eye. Jesse pictured Rachel peering from behind a rock or tree in much the same way as she watched her prey.

As she listened to her son relay the information he'd received from Jana, she tucked the phone against her shoulder and watched, as if it were connected to someone else, her right hand close over her left wrist.

You take care, ma'am.

It had sounded like something anyone would say when leaving, but it had been a warning—and Jesse suddenly knew why the bank wasn't open. Stanley Weeks, who ran Prairie Gold's tiny bank, must have had a feeling that the bank needed to be closed today.

And she had a sudden feeling that . . .

"Tobias, we have to go."

"Mom?"

"Rachel and I have to leave the store. Right now. I'll call as soon as I can."

She hung up, grabbed the shotgun, and put out the Back in 10 Minutes sign on the counter. Small town like this, it wouldn't look strange for the store to be empty when the lone person running it needed to take a break.

"Rachel, honey, we have to go. Put Cory on her leash. We'll go out the back." Jesse went into the back room, grabbed her daypack, then hesitated, inexplicably resistant to leaving when she *knew* they needed to go.

She opened her gun safe and swapped the shotgun for her rifle—and felt the resistance vanish. Closing the gun safe, she headed out the back door, grabbing the red flag out of the umbrella stand as she left.

Rachel followed at her heels, carrying the puppy.

She walked swiftly, holding up the red flag—the signal to the *terra indigene* that there was trouble in Prairie Gold.

"Should I howl for Morgan and Chase?" Rachel whispered.

Wolves. Men with guns.

Jesse shook her head and wished Tolya was there. She didn't know if the Sanguinati were impervious to bullets, but she thought there wasn't much that could hurt one in his smoke form.

She dropped the red flag, chambered a round in the rifle, and looked at Rachel. "I'm going to take a look around. If the street is clear, we're going to cross to the other side and run into the library." She doubted whoever was producing this feeling would be interested in walking off with a bag of books.

She heard the car before she reached the front of the building. She heard it slow down and swore at herself for not paying attention. She'd crept up along the side of the damn bank! But after that moment's hesitation, the car continued a few more yards and stopped in front of her store.

Made sense. Money was all well and good, but even bank robbers needed to eat, and supplies were now a different kind of wealth.

Jesse risked a look around the corner. Car still running for a quick getaway. She was about to retreat and tell Rachel to stay put when she spotted Phil Mailer—and he spotted her. Before he could raise a hand or shout a greeting, she shook her head and put a finger to her lips.

Phil looked at her, then looked at her store. He retreated inside the post office. She hoped he was calling other businesses to tell folks to stay inside and not trying to gather a posse.

Maybe it was because Rachel sensed something. More likely, it was because the memory of what had happened the last time human enemies had come to Prairie Gold was still too sharp, too raw. Whatever the reason, the young Wolf howled. Jesse didn't know if it was a warning or a cry for help. Either way, whoever was inside her store and waiting in the car had to have heard it. They might ignore a single howl, might not react with alarm—or something worse.

Then they all heard a howl that couldn't have come from anything as small as a *terra indigene* Wolf—a deep, savage sound that was much too close for comfort. That howl raised the hair on her arms and the back of her neck—and taught her what the word "bloodcurdling" meant.

Peering around the corner again, she watched a man run out of her store and race around the hood of the car to the passenger side. He yanked the door open, threw a sack on the floor—and looked up. Smiling fiercely, he drew his revolver, aimed skyward, and shot twice. Then he jumped into the car and the driver burned rubber as the car raced down the street, heading out of town.

The Eagle fell out of the sky and hit the street right in front of her.

"No!" Jesse shouted as she rushed over to help. Falling to her knees, she dropped her rifle in order to reach for the bird, knowing it was too late.

"Jesse?" Phil Mailer crouched beside her. "Is it . . . ?"

"Dead? Yes. Fetch one of the flat bedsheets from the store."

As soon as Phil hurried to the store, Rachel, in Wolf form, rushed to her side and licked her face. Jesse thought the gesture was as much to receive reassurance as to offer it.

Had the Eagle been flying over the town for a reason, or had this been plain old bad luck? Would the man have taken those shots if the howl of something that was so much more—and worse—than a Wolf hadn't given him a reason to flee at just that moment?

"Rachel, honey, I'd like you to call for Morgan and Chase so they can tell me what needs to be done now."

Rachel howled again. Jesse didn't know if a Wolf howling in Prairie Gold could be heard in the *terra indigene* settlement, or how far the Others could communicate using their special form of communication. She just hoped that Morgan and Chase would respond so that other forms of *terra indigene* wouldn't.

When Phil returned, she wrapped the Eagle in the bedsheet, took it back to the store, and set it in a laundry basket. Phil picked up her rifle and followed her, sucking in a breath when he saw the store. It wasn't the open register and empty cash drawer that had him swearing. It wasn't seeing how many boxes of ammunition were missing that had her own temper simmering. It was the gratuitous destruction of supplies. The thief had taken what he'd wanted; then he'd thrown bags of flour and rice and noodles on the floor, breaking the packages open by stomping on them, leaving a mess for her to clean up. Leaving the people of the town with a little less to eat.

She had plenty stored in the back room. She'd bought supplies because she'd had a feeling the town would need them—and Tolya had bankrolled those expenditures because he'd agreed with her. But that meant . . .

Jesse hurried behind the counter, jerking to a stop when she saw the box of kitchen matches on top of a wad of paper towels from the roll she kept near the counter to wipe up spills of all kinds. She stared at three spent matches and the partially burned towels.

"The paper towels and the rest of the matches didn't burn," she said softly. They should have. A burning building would have distracted everyone on the street from paying any attention to the strangers who had robbed the store.

"Did you want it to burn?"

Phil cried out and staggered into a shelf, knocking over a jar of dill pickles.

Jesse stared at the male whose red hair was tipped with yellow and blue. She knew about the Elementals. She had seen Air. So she understood that the creature standing on the other side of the counter was far more dangerous than a man with a gun.

"Did you . . . quiet . . . the fire?" she asked.

"Yes. Should I have let it burn?"

"No. Saving the store was a kindness to all of us, and I thank you for doing that."

Fire looked around the store. "You have many things that can burn."

"That is true." What else could she say? There wasn't much in the store that *wouldn't* burn. "I should call Sheriff Wolfgard and tell him about this."

"Why?"

"Because those men are probably on their way to Bennett."

Fire smiled—and Jesse's bowels turned to water. It took every drop of courage to stay on her feet and not mess herself. She'd faced down an Elder when she'd taken the young humans and *terra indigene* into the hills to hide them from the men who belonged to the Humans First and Last movement, but she hadn't been as terrified of that unseen threat as she was right now.

"We know what the car looks like." Fire turned away from the counter. Just before he vanished, he said, "Cars can burn too."

* * *

Jana deleted an e-mail advertising a product that promised to increase the size of her penis and wondered how whoever had sent *that* out had survived when so many legitimate businesses hadn't. Then she deleted an e-mail for a special cream that would plump up and firm your breasts to your partner's delight.

Gods, it was tempting to print that one out and give it to Virgil.

Nothing urgent in the rest of the e-mails. Some of the sheriffs in other towns had sent her additional information about the men they considered outlaws even if the law had no proof of wrongdoing that would hold up in court. She, in turn, promised to keep them updated when those men left town—and what direction they were heading.

As she closed the e-mail program, her phone rang. "Sheriff's office."

"We need help. Please, we need help."

"Who is this? Where are you?"

"Truman Skye. Skye Ranch. We saw the fire and went to investigate. Found the woman. She's in a bad way."

"Burned?"

"No." Truman hesitated before whispering, "I think the Elders killed her husband. Please come."

"We'll be there as soon as we can." Jana hung up and rushed to the office door. If she was going to have to holler every time she needed Virgil, she was going to find a megaphone. Then she spotted something better—a Hawk perched on the hitching post across the street from the office.

She ran across the street and said, "There's trouble at the Skye Ranch. I need Virgil right now." She stared at the Hawk. She had no idea where Virgil was patrolling since he was trying to cover the whole town on his own. Kane was still watching Maddie, partly to keep the blood prophet safe from questionable humans and also because he was still healing and didn't have the speed or stamina yet to be out patrolling. And she was in the office and patrolling the town square so that one of them would be near the hotel and bank and the other businesses that might be vulnerable to this swarm of strangers who had been arriving over the past couple of days.

Realizing they both couldn't leave, she said, "Never mind. I'll call in when I can."

She ran inside, closed Rusty in the crate, and called one of the doctors. "Someone at the Skye Ranch needs immediate attention. I'm heading there now. You might need the ambulance for this one."

She grabbed her gear, jumped in her vehicle—and almost screamed when she saw the Hawk settled in the cargo area.

"By all the gods, what are you doing back there?" And how had he gotten inside when the windows were closed?

Being in Hawk form, he didn't bother to reply. He also made no effort to leave.

"I don't have time to argue." She headed south, pushing for as much speed as she could get as soon as she was away from the town square— and almost drove off the road when smoke suddenly flowed up from beneath the passenger seat and shifted into Yuri Sanguinati.

"Gods!" Jana screamed. "Are you *trying* to scare me into heart failure?"

"You didn't wait for Virgil," Yuri replied. "I—" He looked back at the Hawk. "We were available to assist you." He paused before adding, "You are not the kind of hunter who should go out alone."

Because she was human? Because she was female? Because cops in human cities usually had a partner when they responded to a call?

She slowed to a sensibly fast speed while she fumbled to get the mobile phone out of its holder on her belt. She handed it to Yuri. "I didn't lock the office. Someone should be there. We still have a storeroom full of uncataloged weapons, and we have some newcomers in town who would love to help themselves to that kind of loot, if we believe everything I was told about them."

She drove while Yuri made the call. Based on his side of the conversation, she guessed he was talking to Tolya.

"I'll tell her," Yuri said just before he ended the call.

"Tell me what?"

"Virgil is . . . upset . . . with you for running off without him."

"Virgil can kiss my furless ass," Jana snapped. "The information I was given indicated we needed to respond ASAP. He wasn't available, so I used my initiative."

When Yuri said nothing, she took her eyes off the road for just a second. "What?"

"I don't think kissing is what he has in mind. And I don't think you want his teeth anywhere near your furless ass."

"Are you laughing at me?"

"Yes." Yuri nodded. "Yes, we are."

Darn it! She'd forgotten about the Hawk riding in the back, listening to everything.

Silence filled the vehicle for the rest of the trip, giving her time to gather herself for whatever she would find at the Skye Ranch.

When she and Yuri walked into the ranch house's kitchen, leaving the Hawk to find the location of the fire, Jana knew something more—and worse—had happened since Truman Skye made the call asking for help.

"The doctor and ambulance will be along soon," she said.

"Don't need them anymore," Truman replied. "Not for her." He stood up and swayed as if drunk. Then he found his balance. "This way. She left a note."

Oh gods.

"I never thought." The Simple Life woman Jana figured to be the cook and housekeeper looked devastated. "She was grieving, yes, and what happened was terrible, but I never thought . . ."

"We'll get to that." Jana focused on Truman. "Show me."

Two open bottles of pills on the bedside table. Apparently more than enough to do the job.

"We brought her in here to rest until you arrived," Truman said. "She . . ."

Jana picked up the note that was on the floor beside the bed. Simple. Cryptic. Chilling.

I saw what killed my husband. It's out there, watching us. Always watching us.

She looked at Truman. "Did she say anything to you? Anything about what happened?"

"Can we . . . ?" He walked out of the room. Jana and Yuri followed him back to the kitchen.

The Simple Life woman wasn't there, but there was a plate of biscuits on the table, along with butter and a berry jam, all under mesh covers to keep away the flies. Jana wasn't interested in food, but she recognized the custom of providing sustenance so that survivors could continue.

"She and her husband were trying to find a way to reach their daughter, who lives in a small town in the Southwest Region," Truman began. "I don't know how long they'd been traveling or where they started from, but they were at a crossroads—the one that would head up to Bennett or down to Prairie Gold—when they were forced to stop by a car blocking the road. Two men with guns. They stole the couple's car and left them with the other car. The car had gasoline and it started, so they decided to head north to Bennett to report the incident and turn the car over to the police.

"The attack was so sudden, the woman didn't know what was happening. One moment they were driving along, with nothing of their own except her big purse, which the gunmen had tossed out of her car, and the next thing they knew, something knocked them off the road and they were pulled from the car. Her husband tried to tell the Others that it wasn't their car, that they hadn't been involved in whatever had happened, but . . ." Truman swallowed hard. "They ripped her husband apart right in front of her. Then a red-haired man riding a brown horse appeared out of nowhere. The moment he touched the car it started to burn. Once the car started burning, they let the woman go and just . . . disappeared.

"We saw the smoke. When we drove out to investigate, we found her staggering down the middle of the road. We brought her back here, and I called you."

"Did she have the pills on her?" Jana asked.

"Don't know. She wasn't carrying anything when we found her, so she might have found the pills in the drawer. We're still getting everything sorted and settled. We didn't check the drawers, didn't think she'd . . ." Truman rubbed his face with his hands. "That woman. Her husband. They didn't hurt anyone."

"You think her mate was killed by mistake," Yuri said.

Truman gave Jana and Yuri a bleak look and nodded. "Do you think that will be a comfort to their daughter if you can find her?"

"It is regrettable, but mistakes happen," Tolya said. Who had called Jesse to tell her about these humans, and why?

"Mistakes happen?" Jesse's voice held cold condemnation. "Two innocent people died, and that's all you can say?"

"Isn't that what humans say when they do something similar?" Tolya snapped. "Namid's teeth and claws have had little exposure to humans except when killing is required. The vehicle that was spotted was the same vehicle being driven by the humans who you sensed were a danger, who you hid from, *who tried to burn down your store.*"

"The vehicle was the same; the people were not. They were victims, Tolya, more so than me. The Elders killed that man right in front of his wife."

"And humans have never done such a thing."

He was angry—with her, with the Elders, and especially with the men who had caused this sudden schism between human allies and the *terra indigene.*

"You're not going to see anyone's side but your own, are you?" Jesse said.

"I could say the same about you." He hung up on her, partly because her naïveté annoyed him. Having lived in an isolated town her whole life, she should have a better understanding of what lived just out of sight—except for those last moments when it appeared right in front of you. But the other reason for ending the call was Jana and Virgil walking into his office, both looking grim.

"They were innocent people," Jana said. "Victims."

"An ally had been threatened," Tolya countered. "The Elders and Elementals responded to eliminate the threat."

"Nobody was threatened by that man and his wife! They didn't do anything wrong, and now they're dead."

"Look around you, Deputy," Tolya said coldly. "You live in a town that was full of people who 'didn't do anything wrong' and still ended up dead." Having used up his patience talking to Jesse, he turned on Jana. "What should the *terra indigene* have done? Decline to track the vehicle that held humans who posed a threat? Should Fire have stood back and watched Jesse's store burn?"

"No, but they didn't have to kill those people! They could have apprehended them and waited for us to arrive."

"They killed an Eagle," Virgil snarled. "They had guns."

"They, they, they!" Jana snarled back. "The *they* who killed the Eagle and tried to burn Jesse's store were armed robbers, *not* two middle-aged people who were trying to find their daughter. I would think even the Elders could tell the difference."

"Be careful, *human*," Virgil said.

"Yes! I'm human. Sorry I don't have fangs and fur."

"Not half as sorry as we are."

She took a step back and looked at the Wolf as if he'd just delivered a wound that would prove fatal.

And Tolya, too angry at her species to deny his predatory instinct, went in for the verbal kill. "Do you know why the Sanguinati don't mind living around humans? Because you're our preferred prey. But the Elders look at you and see a blight, a disease that spoils the world. They consider proximity to humans as a contamination, but some of them have to be contaminated now because too many of the shifters that used to watch your kind were killed by the Humans First and Last movement, so the choice, as the Elders see it, is to be close enough for some forced inter-action or to eliminate all of you."

"The only good human is a dead human," Virgil growled.

"The Elders did what they understood to be right. But perhaps you have a point, Deputy Paniccia, and only humans should deal with human-against-human conflicts in whatever way you see fit, and the *terra indigene* will deal with anything that is a threat to us."

"But . . . ," Jana began.

"Works for me," Virgil said.

"And me." Tolya stared at Jana. "That will be all, Deputy."

He watched her stagger out of his office. Then he looked at Virgil.

"What about the prophet pup?" Virgil asked. "She can be used against us. If we don't protect her, we have to destroy her."

"She's Namid's creation, both wondrous and terrible. We'll protect her."

"She's still a human."

"She's not like the rest of them." He heard the relief in Virgil's sigh. "What are you going to do about Jana?"

"She is still a deputy working for the town, but she and the pup will have to be their own pack. As you said, she has to deal with human troubles and we will deal with the rest."

Now that his anger had faded, Tolya considered the strangers who had arrived recently. Too many of them were coming into town since Parlan Blackstone showed up, and none of them seemed interested in finding work. Which meant they were here for another reason. "If she's killed by a human? What then?"

Virgil stared at him with those amber eyes. "Then we go back to killing all the problems without anyone whining about us making mistakes. Truth, Tolya? It's never a mistake to bring down an enemy—or bring down prey. If we had killed more of the humans when they were talking about causing trouble instead of waiting until they did cause trouble, there would have been a lot less humans in this part of Thaisia and more of the shifters would have survived."

Tolya studied the Wolf. "You don't believe the story. That's why you're angry with Jana. You don't believe those humans were innocent."

"They weren't the ones who stole from Jesse Walker or tried to burn her store, but the Elders wouldn't have killed the human male the way we were told they did unless they had smelled something on him or heard something that wasn't right."

"And the female?"

"You know what form of Elder she saw."

"Yes, I know." He'd seen it the night the Elders had set the final boundaries for the town. It was a very old form—a nightmare that walked on two legs.

"Did she choose to kill herself just because she saw that form of *terra indigene*? Or did she choose a human way to die because she knew the Elders would have a reason to come hunting for her and now had her scent?"

"Are you going to say that to Jana?"

Virgil smiled grimly. "What for? Until she accepts what it means to live in this part of Thaisia, she won't listen."

"Darlin', I don't want to argue with you," Tobias said.

Jana held the phone so hard her hand hurt. "You're agreeing with Virgil and Tolya?"

Silence.

"Tobias?"

"I've already done this dance with my mother, who was shaken up enough that she isn't thinking straight. And neither are you."

"So it's all right for the Elders to kill someone because that person was in the wrong car?"

"Jana, the Elders kill humans all the time." Tobias's voice was ripe with impatience. "They went to war against the humans and eliminated the population of entire towns. They and the Elementals have flung passenger trains off the tracks and killed anyone who survived the crash. People get in a car and head out for another town and are never heard from again. Maybe it's different in towns back East where you don't have to look the truth in the eyes every day, or maybe I learned a lot from Joe Wolfgard in the short time I knew him. Bottom line? They killed those people, and maybe that's a sorrow."

"Maybe? How can it be anything but a tragedy?"

"You find any identification?"

"The woman's purse was still in the car when it burned. But she and her husband were forced to change cars with the robbers!"

"That's the story she told." Tobias huffed out a breath. "You're a cop, darlin'. I know this hit you hard, but you need to start thinking like a cop who works out here."

"Meaning what?"

"Truman told you the story as it was told to him before that woman took her own life. Right?"

"Right," Jana snapped.

"Who was with you when you went to the ranch?"

"Yuri Sanguinati and one of the Hawks. I can't tell them apart." She could almost feel Tobias wince. Obviously an Intuit with a feel for animals knew the feathered Others all by name, along with the names of their mates and the chicks still in the shell.

And I'm being a bitch because I'm tired and scared and feeling very alone right now.

"Did you ask any of the *terra indigene* if any of them saw the exchange of cars? They might not have understood everything they were seeing, but they would know the difference between an aggressive act and cooperation."

Exchange of cars. The words made her think of a handoff.

"You think it could have been a staged meeting?" she asked.

"They were in the wild country, Jana. Believe me when I tell you that when you're out there, there is nothing a human does that isn't observed by someone. Not anymore. My guess? The Elders watched whatever happened between the two men who robbed my mother's store and the middle-aged couple who died and concluded they were a single pack. And having decided that, they attacked the stationary target."

"They were driving to Bennett," Jana argued, but there was no longer any conviction in her words.

"Did you go out to look at the car?"

"Yes. It was . . . at the crossroads." She'd heard the words when Truman told the story but hadn't absorbed the meaning at the time. "If they'd been stopped at the crossroads by the robbers and were driving to Bennett when the Elders attacked, why were they still at the crossroads?" And what had been said when they thought no one was around to listen?

Exhausted, Jana sank into a chair. "They weren't innocent."

"If there really are outlaws gathering in Bennett, I think it's more important to make amends with Virgil than to argue the guilt or innocence of people who are already gone."

Later that evening, as Jana heard the Wolves howling, she wondered how a female Wolf apologized to a pack leader and how much groveling a human female would have to do to be accepted back into the police pack.

CHAPTER 31

Thaisday, Messis 30

"Bennett is Virgil's territory." Morgan Wolfgard glanced at the small cooler tucked behind the seats. "Why do I have to come with you?"

"I need to get this meat to Jana before she goes to work, which means being on the road before daylight," Tobias replied. "You're here to tell the Elders why I'm bending the rule about only traveling during daylight."

"Why does she need meat from you? Don't they have meat in Bennett?"

"She and Virgil had a fight. This fresh meat is her way of saying she's sorry."

"Huh." Another glance at the cooler. "So you risk being eaten in order to bring Virgil some meat so he won't eat the human female?"

"She works for him, so he won't eat her." *Gods, I hope he's not angry enough to start thinking that way.*

"Is it good meat?"

"A cow's liver and a good-size roast." Seeing the wistful look, Tobias fought to keep a straight face. "I wrapped up the heart for you as a thank-you for coming with me."

Morgan licked his lips and turned back to watch the road.

I guess he doesn't need to watch the cooler now that he knows he'll get his share of the meat. Which was good because Tobias really wanted Morgan's attention on whatever might be watching the car and deciding to attack them.

They passed the crossroads. The burned-out car was two car lengths away from the road. Most likely, that was where it had landed when it had been struck by whatever Elder had first attacked the vehicle.

Morgan sat up straighter. "These humans, the outers."

"Outlaws," Tobias corrected.

"They are a breed of human, like Cyrus humans?"

The question chilled him. "I don't rightly know. What did the Cyrus human do?" He'd heard what had happened to the man in Bennett, but he still didn't know exactly what the first "Cyrus human" had done to deserve being killed that way.

"He stole Broomstick Girl—and he hurt her," Morgan replied. "Cyrus humans are enemies of the *cassandra sangue* and the *terra indigene.* The teaching story hasn't traveled this far yet, so that is all I know." The Wolf stared at Tobias and added softly, "That is all we need to know."

Tobias drove for a few minutes, thinking it over. "Why is this girl so important?" When Morgan growled, he said hastily, "I'm not saying she shouldn't be, I'm asking why. I'd like to understand."

"She saw the danger. She tried to warn all the Wolfgard. Many didn't hear the warning in time and were killed, but many escaped the HFL humans because she bled . . . and she saw."

Blood prophet. Through his mother, and because of some things Jesse had told him in strictest confidence, he knew the locations of the two *cassandra sangue* whose vision had saved not only some of the Wolfgard but Prairie Gold as well. "Does Broomstick Girl live in Sweetwater or Lakeside?"

A soft growl of warning before Morgan said, "Lakeside."

Gods, what had the *terra indigene* heard? "Would it be permitted for a human to hear the teaching story about the Cyrus human?"

Morgan cocked his head. "Why would you need to hear our story? Don't you have teaching stories of your own?"

"We do, but I'm not sure our teaching story about Broomstick Girl and the Cyrus human would travel this far from Lakeside."

"It is an important story."

He didn't dare tell Morgan that a young woman being abducted might not be considered important news if the abduction took place in another region.

"It's a very important story for my people as well as yours. But news doesn't always travel between regions anymore." Not quite true, since the Elders hadn't eliminated the means for radio and television programs to span the continent of Thaisia. But lately there had been too much—and nothing—to say, especially when humans finally understood that the Others also listened to what was said on the radio and television.

"When I have learned the story, I will tell you," Morgan said.

"Thank you." Thinking it would be easier to walk through a nest of rattlesnakes, Tobias answered Morgan's first question—and hoped he wasn't simplifying things too much. "When someone talks about outlaws, I think of the frontier stories. Outlaws were the humans who robbed banks or stores. They stole cattle and horses. And the sheriff and deputies would catch those humans and put them in jail because they broke human law." He thought for a moment. "If the *terra indigene* see someone they think is an outlaw, they should capture him and howl for the sheriff and let the sheriff take that human to jail."

Morgan nodded. "Outlaws we capture." He thought for a moment before adding, "But if they attack us, we will eat them."

Jana walked into Virgil's office, set a small roasting pan on his desk, and lifted the lid. When the Wolf said nothing and did nothing except stare at the contents of the pan, she said, "It's an apology."

"It looks like meat."

"It is meat. I figured you would like that more than chocolates or flowers."

"I do." Now, finally, he looked at her. "Why are you apologizing?"

"This is my first job as a deputy. I'm going to make mistakes."

He nodded. "The meat is an apology for which mistake?"

She'd made more than one? Darn it! "The woman's death upset me."

"But not the male's death?"

"Yes, but I didn't see him. I did see her. And because she killed herself, I accepted her version of events as she related them to Mr. Skye. I should have asked if any of the *terra indigene* had seen anything. I should have been more respectful when I tried to explain why I felt those people should have been apprehended rather than killed. I was thinking with my feelings instead of my head."

Her last statement seemed to confuse him until he took a deep breath. Then he focused on the meat sitting right in front of him and licked his lips.

"You want to rejoin the police pack?" he asked.

"Yes. Sir. Yes, sir."

He stared at her. "All right. You can rejoin the pack. Just remember that there are enemies among the humans living in this town."

"I'll remember." She kept her eyes focused on the desk. Submissive. Offering no challenge.

"Get to work," Virgil said.

Jana dashed for the door. Before she crossed the threshold, he added, "Tobias Walker might want to kiss your furless ass, but if you challenge me again, I will discipline you like any other member of the pack and you will feel my teeth. Understand?"

"Yes, sir."

Back at her own desk, she turned on the computer and set the pen and pad of paper beside the phone to take the day's messages—and noticed how her hands shook. With relief. Yes. Her hands shook with relief that she didn't have to handle human conflicts on her own.

She would keep telling herself that until she believed it. But that other thing?

Kiss her furless ass. Right. She should have known Yuri or the Hawk would tell Virgil what she'd said. And, if asked, because one of them was bound to ask, she could tell them that Tobias *hadn't* kissed her ass.

Of course, this morning he might have gotten around to doing more than kissing her senseless if Barb hadn't wandered into the kitchen half asleep and screamed the whole street awake when she flipped on the lights and found a strange Wolf munching on a large heart.

That sure had gotten the blood pumping in a different kind of way.

Barb had tried to apologize for screaming, tried to say she *knew* the Wolf had to be a friend of Virgil's and she'd only screamed because she was sleepy and startled and she hadn't meant to disturb him while he was eating his breakfast, but the Wolf just snarled at her. It might have been a nasty standoff if Tobias hadn't unlocked the back door and held it open so the Wolf could grab the rest of the heart and enjoy his meal in the backyard.

After Tobias explained who Morgan was and why he'd been in the kitchen, there hadn't been time for her to do more than thank him before she hurried to get ready for work.

But thinking about the kiss they'd shared in her bedroom before all the hoo-haw in the kitchen had her feeling fluttery in a *good* way.

She called the number for Tobias's mobile phone. "I've been accepted back in the police pack."

"Good for you."

She could hear the smile in his voice. "You have any errands you can run while you're here?"

"I might have one or two. Why?"

"I wasn't sure how things would work out with Virgil, so I left Rusty at home. I was going to take an early lunch break to let her out. And Barb will still be working."

"You don't say. Well, maybe I could come by, drop off some lunch."

Jana smiled. "Maybe you could. I'll call when I'm heading to the house."

When Virgil came out of his office, she gave him her best and brightest smile. He gave her that Wolf stare for a moment or two, then walked out without saying a word.

Parlan checked the labels on the bottles behind the bar. Then he looked around again.

Neighborhood bar. Local watering hole. Almost everything on the very short menu he'd found was food cooked in grease. A quick look in the preparation area had him backing away from the rotted or moldy food. The salvage company either had missed this place or hadn't reached this street.

Parlan selected a bottle of whiskey, used a clean handkerchief to wipe the dust off a glass, and poured himself a healthy measure. Not rotgut but not the best. This wasn't the kind of place that would serve the finest blends.

There was a separate room for parties or meetings. High-stakes
games could be conducted back there. But . . .

Parlan sipped the whiskey and thought he still tasted the dust until he
looked at the floor. Maybe it was the smell of mouse turds that interfered
with the taste of the whiskey.

It would take a lot of work to make this place presentable—more
work than he wanted to put in, especially when there was that saloon on
the town square that was already up and running and had exactly the
kind of ambiance he wanted, and his persona of a frontier gambler would
slide right into that place. Of course, once he challenged Tolya and won
the fight for control of the town, he'd have to keep the gambling low
profile in public and he might have to find someone to manage the place
along with Lawry. Not that Other with the strange hair. She had to go.
And he might need to make other changes in personnel.

The door opened. Two men swaggered up to the bar.

The taller one said, "Set 'em up, barkeep."

"Frank." Parlan took two glasses from under the bar and didn't
bother to wipe them off before pouring the whiskey. He set a glass
in front of Frank and the other in front of the shorter, younger man.
"Eli."

Frank and Eli Bonney were outlaws in the truest frontier sense of the
word. They loved to steal. They weren't Intuits, didn't have that special
sense, but they were damn good at their work. They were also just a
touch crazy, which made them too impulsive for subtle jobs. Since there
wasn't going to be anything subtle about taking over leadership of the
town, and since killing things was the boys' second-favorite activity, Parlan had agreed with Judd about dealing them in for this takeover. If the
impulsiveness and the touch of crazy made them difficult to handle later,
then Judd would take care of them.

"You planning to set up here, Parlan?" Frank downed the whiskey
and looked around. "I would have thought you'd be aiming for that fancy
place in the center of town."

"I am. But I have to appear to be looking at what is available so that
nobody thinks too much about me staying around."

"That fancy place have any girls?" Eli asked.

"Teases," Parlan replied. "None that do more than that. And don't go thinking you can use any sharp persuasion to get one to oblige you. Last man didn't do more than talk that game and still ended up dead."

"Whorehouse?" Frank asked.

Parlan shook his head. "A handful of Sanguinati and a couple of Wolves run this town, and they don't appreciate why that's a necessary business."

"Ma can get one set up quick and do it right," Eli said. "She has a knack for that sort of thing."

"Where are you boys staying?" Parlan asked.

"Set up in a house on the south side of town," Frank replied. "McCall said there are plenty of empty houses that still have food, and we should lay low until everyone arrives. Speaking of arrivals, Ma and Daddy should have been here by now. You hear anything?"

"No." Parlan poured them all another whiskey. "You arranged to meet?"

"Had some business a ways south of here. Met up at a crossroads and did a car swap. They should have been a couple of hours behind us unless the car crapped out on them."

"Shouldn't have," Eli said. "And they should have enough gas in the tank to get here."

Parlan's hands suddenly felt cold, his tell when something wasn't right. "Let's head over to the Bird Cage Saloon. It's one of the best places in town to pick up gossip. If your folks had to stop at a ranch for any reason, one of the bartenders would know."

I love doing crochet. It's a calming activity, and you end up with something pretty and useful. I could teach you.

Scythe stared at the instructions Lila Gold had so helpfully left on her desk. If bouncy Lila was the end result of a calming activity, Scythe didn't see the point. Besides, she *was* calm. Mostly. She hadn't harvested anyone since she arrived. Sipped, yes, but she hadn't feasted. Even the Sanguinati discreetly fed on the humans who lived in the town.

Then again, performing a human activity and discussing that activity would help her blend in. Perhaps she would accept Lila's offer and go with her to the store where the yarn was sold. If nothing else, visiting the store would be an excuse for prowling the streets. There were strangers in town that Tolya and Virgil didn't trust. And a human who wasn't trusted was really nothing more than prey.

She removed a file folder from a desk drawer, opened it, and reviewed the work schedule for the rest of the week to confirm when Lila would be working. Slipping the folder back in the drawer, she left her office to talk to Yuri, who was working behind the bar. As the owner of the saloon, she felt it was important to talk to the other predators who worked there. Since she didn't think Yuri would be interested in crochet and he'd already inquired about Yellow Bird when he came in that morning, she couldn't think of anything else to talk about except the work schedule.

She'd gone behind the bar, and Yuri had turned toward her when Virgil walked in. They could both talk to Virgil, and then she wouldn't appear foolish asking Yuri about schedules.

"Did you let Deputy Jana rejoin the police pack?" Yuri asked.

"She brought good meat as an apology," Virgil growled.

Yuri grinned, showing his fangs. "And by letting her rejoin the pack, you get to play with the puppy again."

Virgil bared his teeth and showed *his* fangs.

Scythe tensed.

Yuri looked at her hair and said, "This is banter, teasing. Showing fangs is not always a threat."

Scythe looked in the mirror behind the bar. Blue hair with broad streaks of red, starting to curl. So many things she struggled to understand. But the Harvester who lived in the Lakeside Courtyard had had to learn these things too.

"Showing fangs when someone is . . . teasing . . . is not a threat?" she asked, wanting clarification.

"Not between us." Yuri made a circle with one hand that included her as well as Virgil. "If those words were said by someone who was not considered a friend . . ."

"My teeth would have been on his throat," Virgil finished.

"Ah." Scythe relaxed.

"The wolverine did wrong and needed to learn," Virgil said.

"Being excluded from her pack was gentle punishment," Yuri added.

"Being excluded does not always feel gentle," Scythe said quietly.

They looked at her; then they looked at each other.

"I guess it doesn't when it goes on too long." Yuri looked toward the door. "We have customers."

"I'm not dressed for work." Scythe took a step back, intending to go up to her suite and change into one of her costumes. Then she saw their customers and stayed behind the bar.

Virgil didn't recognize the two men who came in with Parlan Blackstone and couldn't catch their scent. Not that it mattered. They moved like predators.

<Morgan?> he called.

<What?>

<Where are you?> He knew Morgan wasn't in town to challenge him, so why did the other Wolf sound uneasy?

<I am at the bookstore. Tobias Walker is helping me buy a book for Rachel.>

Huh. Well, bringing a gift to a potential mate made sense. But why did Morgan sound uneasy? John wasn't dominant enough to be a rival, and he . . . No, he wouldn't consider having another mate while he lived so close to humans. Never again. <Did you sniff around Jesse Walker's store after the bad humans killed the Eagle?>

<Yes.>

<Come to the saloon. See if you recognize the scent of the human males who just came in.>

<Where is this place?>

<Tobias Walker will know.>

Parlan Blackstone approached the bar and nodded at Yuri. "Barkeep."

"Mr. Blackstone," Yuri replied. "What would you like?" He smiled, deliberately showing a hint of fang.

"Whiskeys all round from your best bottle," Blackstone said. He looked at Virgil. "Buy you a drink, Sheriff?"

"I'll have my usual," Virgil said.

Yuri poured three whiskeys before setting a shot glass with a golden liquid in front of Virgil.

"What is that?" Parlan asked.

"My usual." He saw no reason to tell a potential enemy that he liked apple juice. Humans were too fond of poisons.

"Nice place," Taller Stranger said as he looked around.

"My place," Scythe said.

She sounded mildly territorial, and anyone who didn't know the warning signs—the curling hair now equally divided between broad red and blue streaks with a few threads of black—wouldn't realize she was a long way from calm.

She, too, recognized other predators, regardless of species.

"I was telling Frank and Eli how I'm looking to open one of the neighborhood bars and hope to fix it up even half as nice as this saloon." Parlan looked at Scythe but didn't look her in the eyes. "You must have put a fair piece of work into this place when you acquired it."

"Yes." She offered nothing more. She looked past all of them.

Tobias Walker entered with Truman Skye, followed by Morgan.

Tobias glanced toward the men at the bar, then put an arm around Truman's shoulders and tried to hustle the other human to a table near the back of the saloon.

"Couldn't sleep last night," Truman said. "I kept seeing that car, kept thinking about—"

"Nothing you could have done," Tobias said loudly, his hand tightening on Truman's shoulder so hard the man whimpered.

<I'll keep him quiet.> Scythe grabbed a bottle and glasses and strode over to the table.

<If you harvest a little too much, I can put him in the Me Time cell,> Virgil said. <I don't think any of the females will annoy me enough today to need it.>

"What's this about a car?" Parlan Blackstone asked, looking concerned.

"Car went off the road near the Skye Ranch," Yuri replied. "Caught on fire. Some of the ranch hands rushed to the site to try to help, but they were too late."

"What about the people in the car?" the taller one, Frank, asked.

"They died."

Virgil watched Morgan brush by the two strangers, taking a sniff as he passed. The humans looked like they'd been kicked in the head and didn't even notice the other Wolf.

<Their scent was around Jesse Walker's store,> Morgan said. <They killed the Eagle.>

<Scent isn't enough to satisfy human law,> Yuri reminded them.

<They killed one of the Eaglegard, not another human,> Morgan snarled. Then he hesitated. <But there were the scents of more than these two strangers in the store.>

<If we kill the wrong pair of humans, we might start a stampede,> Virgil said.

Something felt wrong about these humans—more wrong than the other strangers who had come into town. He wanted to tear out their throats and be done with it. Unfortunately, he knew how the wolverine would react to that. She'd say something snippy like "Nobody makes 'Sorry I Killed You By Mistake' sympathy cards," and then he'd have to bite her. And then she wouldn't let him play with the puppy. And he couldn't blame Cowboy Bob for the bite because Cowboy Bob didn't have any teeth.

Reaching that conclusion made him feel sufficiently hostile to humans in general and these males in particular, so he focused on the problem. <We wait. As soon as other humans see them breaking the rules, we kill them.>

<Tobias Walker says that humans who break rules are called outlaws and are supposed to be captured and put in jail,> Morgan said.

Why? There wasn't any mess to clean up if you killed them outside, and a cell wasn't large enough for all the predators who would want to feed on the available meat.

To the men, he said, "You finish your drinks, then come across to the sheriff's office to turn in your weapons."

"Give up our guns?" the smaller one, Eli, said. "Fuck you."

Frank clamped a hand on Eli's right arm. "Why?" he asked Virgil.

"No firearms are allowed within the town's limits," Virgil replied. "Turn them in or get out."

Parlan Blackstone looked pointedly at Tobias Walker. "I don't see you telling him about that rule."

"He has special permission to carry a gun." Virgil didn't offer an explanation.

Blackstone put money on the bar. "I guess we should go over now, if someone is in the office."

"I'll take you over."

"All by yourself?" Eli shook off Frank's restraining hand. "Three against one? Those odds don't worry you?"

Before Virgil could decide how to answer, since humans with guns *were* a reason to worry, Yuri laughed and said, "Virgil might be the only one you see, but he won't be the only one escorting you." Any pretense of humor left the Sanguinati's face. "If something should happen to Virgil and one of *them* took offense . . ." He reached under the bar, then held up a book of matches. With deliberate movements, his dark eyes fixed on the humans, he lit one match and used it to light the rest of the matches in the book.

Burning. Burning. Burning.

Looking at the men, Yuri smiled.

I t took all the subtle intimidation Parlan could bring to bear and not so subtle manhandling by Frank to keep Eli in check long enough for them to hand over the guns and get away from the part of town that had too damn many *things* watching them.

They returned to the neighborhood bar where they'd met up. Parlan would have preferred going to the hotel but realized that anything Eli said that was overheard could end his bid to take over leadership of the town and establish the clan in Bennett.

"They killed Ma and Daddy," Eli shouted. "That fanged bastard all but said that the car had been torched deliberately and they died."

But the Others didn't say the two people had been killed in the fire, Parlan thought. He had a feeling that Frank had heard what hadn't been said, but Eli was too shocked to understand that he and Frank had been at least partly to blame. They had swapped cars with their parents. The Others had traced the car and didn't know or didn't care that it was being driven by different humans.

He didn't believe for a moment that the car had been torched because the boys had robbed a store. But killing the Eagle?

Which one had pulled the trigger? And what would the other one do once he understood that killing the Eagle was the reason the elder Bonneys had died?

He had no illusions that the guns they handed over to Wolfgard were the only ones they had with them. He had to make his move soon and challenge Tolya Sanguinati before the men who were gathering to fight the Others began turning on each other.

CHAPTER 32

Firesday, Messis 31

Dina drove beyond the town's new boundaries to a street that wasn't marked for salvage. Zeke had a feeling they needed to stay inside the town for a while, ignoring the fact that a lot of those houses had already been picked over by new residents or squatters who pocketed any cash they could find, and that included raiding the piggy banks in children's rooms. Not that she blamed them, exactly, but she'd gotten in the habit of supplementing her pay by stuffing a few large bills in the back pocket of her jeans when she was going through a house.

Was that why Zeke had been so mean, so *insulting*, this morning? Because he was pissed that she took a tiny cut off the top? As if they didn't all do that!

"What the fuck are you doing, Dina?" Zeke had said. "You got your man, lured him away from his wife."

"Didn't take much luring." She'd taken a deep breath so that her quite impressive breasts became even more impressive. Not that it had any effect on Zeke. He'd taken her on as part of his crew because she had a knack for finding secret stashes as well as the gold jewelry, and at first she'd thought of him as more than a job opportunity, but his initial interest had faded, all because she'd flirted one evening with Fagen just to test the waters.

"You were there to help Kelley make the decision, weren't you? But now you're looking to do a lap dance with Larry when you couldn't be bothered with him before? Why? Because he asked Sarah Gott to go to the movies with him this weekend? The moment he's interested in someone else you're hot to have him?"

"That's crude, Zeke."

"You're damn right it is. Did you play the 'how married is he?' game where you were from? Well, you don't play that game if you want to work for me. We don't need any trouble here, and I don't want to work with someone who wants to see if she can get past the zipper of every married man in town. And don't think I'm not aware of how much you've been taking out of the houses on the sly."

She'd given him her "I'm not a vanilla-sex kind of girl" smile. "But you haven't told anyone."

He'd looked angry and sad and, so much worse, disappointed. "Yeah, Dina, I have. I gave Tolya Sanguinati a list of the houses you've worked in case the attorneys reviewing the inventories of valuables report something missing that we should have turned in."

Fucking bastard. It was tempting to start a rumor that the only reason Zeke and Fagen weren't interested in sleeping with her was because they were banging each other, but Fagen was interested in Lila Gold and not keeping it a secret, and there were too many other Intuits in town who would contradict her and accuse her of trying to start trouble.

But if she had to turn in *everything* on the official jobs, she needed to boost her income at the houses Zeke wasn't touching.

She turned into a driveway, got out of the car, and surveyed the house.

She liked Kelley. She did. He was a nice guy. It wasn't her fault that he thought adding a little chocolate sauce to vanilla sex was totally adventurous while she liked a little rough and just a touch of mean. Since she wasn't going to get that from Kelley, why couldn't she scratch that itch with someone else? It was only sex, after all. And hadn't he strayed with her, so what was the difference?

Taking two banker's boxes out of the backseat, Dina studied the house again. Then she looked at the house across the street and two doors down—and knew that's where she'd find what she was looking for.

* * *

Hearing a car pull into a driveway nearby, Judd went to the front window and eased the curtain aside. Recognizing the logo painted on the front doors, he swore quietly. Salvagers. He'd chosen this location because he'd had a strong feeling that the salvagers wouldn't stray this far after finding Charlie Webb's body, but it looked like he'd been wrong this time.

He watched the woman—*one* woman—get out of the car. Watched her retrieve boxes from the backseat. Watched her look at the house he'd chosen—and head his way.

No other cars. No other people. Dumb thing to do, coming out here on her own.

But even dumb people knew things. Besides, too many eyes could spot him during the day, and there were a lot of hours before nightfall.

He could think of a few ways she could entertain him. Afterward, he'd take the car and choose another house a couple of streets away. The car, with its logo, would provide him with camouflage and help him slip into town unseen when Parlan challenged the vampire for leadership of Bennett.

This fight for dominance was a risk, sure, but Judd had worked with Parlan long enough to know the man had considered the odds, had calculated the best approach that would give them the winning hand.

Besides, they were stacking the deck with every outlaw gang they knew who could reach Bennett in time for the showdown.

As he heard the woman working on the front door's lock, Judd looked around the room to make sure he'd been careful. Nothing out of order, nothing to disturb the dust and alert anyone that someone was staying there.

He moved silently, returning to the kitchen and taking out the supplies he'd need from the drawer where he'd stashed them. Plenty of rope. A gag he'd made by threading a thin collar through a small ball that must have been a dog's toy. A corkscrew. A knife. A lighter and a fork. He put them on the kitchen table, then took up position in the exact spot that would keep her blind to his presence until it was too late.

The front door opened and closed. Stealthy movements, which meant she wasn't supposed to be here. Wasn't that perfect? If she wasn't sup-posed to be here, no one would think to look for her here.

When she came within range, he moved, striking fast and just hard enough to stun her, just hard enough to keep her confused while he dragged her into the kitchen and secured her to the kitchen table's legs. The moment she tried to scream, he shoved the ball gag into her mouth and secured it behind her head.

Grabbing her hair, he turned her head so that she could see him over her shoulder. "Are you clean?"

She stared at him, terrified.

"I'm going to play with you for a while. There are plenty of things I can use besides my cock if you have any diseases. So I'll ask you once more. Are . . . you . . . clean?"

She nodded.

"Good." Judd ran a gentle hand from her shoulder to her hip. "It's been a long while since I've had a chance to indulge like this. A long while."

Dina didn't know how much time had passed. A few minutes? Hours? He'd done . . . things . . . to her. Terrible things. She had a feeling that places inside her were broken now, maybe forever.

She heard him return to the kitchen. She wanted to wail, wanted to scream out the fear. But she knew better than to make a sound, knew what he'd do. What he'd done.

She heard him move to the sink. Heard water running.

His hand came in sight, and in his hand . . .

"Want it?" he asked.

Water. A dog's bowl filled with water.

He let her lap some water before setting the bowl on the floor, just out of reach. Another kind of torment.

"Time for us to talk."

She said nothing.

He laughed softly. "Good girl. I'll ask questions. You have permission to answer. You raise your voice . . . Well, you won't be as valuable to me without your tongue, will you? You understand?"

Dina nodded.

"Say 'Yes, sir.'"

"Yes, sir." Her voice cracked.

She barely held on to the questions long enough to give him answers. Couldn't remember what she'd said a moment later. But she told him everything she knew about the Sanguinati and the Wolfgard and that female deputy.

"Anything you want to say?" he asked. "This is your chance."

Odd how she hadn't remembered the rose quartz and turquoise pendant until that moment, hadn't noticed the chain, which now felt like it was slicing into her neck.

"Abby was right," she whispered.

He leaned toward her. "Say it again."

"Abby was right. She said this pendant would draw dark things to me."

He sighed, a sound so filled with satisfaction she hoped—oh, how she hoped—that he was done with her, that he would let her go so that she could find help because there were things inside her that were broken.

"Tell me everything you know about Abigail," he said. "Everything."

As his hands performed tiny tortures, she told him everything she knew about Abigail Burch. When she couldn't think of anything else, he gagged her. Just before he left the kitchen, she felt a sharp pinch on the inside of her thigh. She heard the shower as she watched a red puddle slowly form under her.

He came back and crouched beside her, careful to avoid the puddle. "Still here?" He sounded . . . cheerful. "You know, I have a feeling that, except for the last cut, if this had been your idea instead of mine, you would have enjoyed it."

A door opened and closed. A car started.

The light faded.

"I wondered when I would hear from you," Parlan said, struggling to strip any hint of impatience or anger from his voice. No one scolded Judd McCall.

"Had things to do today," Judd replied. "Found a reliable source that confirmed the law consists of two Wolves and a female deputy. One of the Wolves was injured in a fight not too long ago and is still gimpy. And most of the human residents think the female deputy is a joke, but my source didn't like the deputy, so that opinion might be skewed."

"So we have the three cops of sorts and six Sanguinati." That tallied with what he'd observed.

"There's also a Panther and a feral boy who might join the fight. And a Wolf runs the bookstore."

And there was that creature running the saloon. "You think the Panther and bookworm Wolf will be a problem?"

"I think they'll need to be eliminated to make sure you stay in power," Judd replied. "Most of the people living here have never handled a gun, let alone know how to use one. If they didn't object to a bloodsucker running the town, they won't rebel against you."

"Well, I know you'll keep everyone in line, Sheriff McCall."

"That I will. When do we go?"

"Tomorrow. Lawry is here with my boy, staying out of sight in one of the abandoned houses. And the Bonney boys are here and looking to inflict some hurt on anything that gets in their way."

"Who else came in?"

"Sleight-of-Hand Slim and Durango Jones have taken rooms at the hotel. William and Wallace Parker are also here. Jones brought some of his men. They're gathered north of town. The Parkers were supposed to meet up with their men, but the men never showed."

"Parkers' men may not have shown up, but there are plenty of others who have, and they'll join us. Settling down for a while is looking better and better for most of these boys. So the numbers are in our favor."

The numbers were in their favor. So why did he feel like someone else was dealing the cards? Nothing he could do except play the hand he was dealt.

"We're going to treat this like a human election with a lot of chest beating and bluster, only nobody gets to vote. The Others wave their weapons; we show ours; they back down because they've learned what guns can do—and we take the pot."

Judd snorted. "They aren't going to yield."

"Probably not. But we'll be seen as issuing a fair challenge and giving the Others a chance to leave town. Whatever happens after that is their fault, not ours."

"Well then. Sounds like we'll be sleeping in our own town tomorrow night."

"Yes, we will."

Abigail left the office building with the rest of the cleaning crew. After seeing her father at the hotel, she'd heeded Jana's advice to stay away from the town square, but she didn't like cleaning the houses, and there weren't that many open businesses that weren't on the square or on the streets just off the square. Since she didn't want everyone knowing she was Parlan Blackstone's daughter, she couldn't explain why she couldn't work in the buildings she'd specifically asked for when she'd joined the cleaning company. The woman who ran the company was an Intuit and had started giving her funny looks, as if the sweet Abigail persona was starting to unravel.

She'd spent the past few days cleansing and renewing her protection stones and prosperity stones until they were strong again. Until she felt shielded again from all dissonance.

Today she'd reported for work and gave vague answers about what she'd been doing, implying that the injury Barb Debany had received when she'd been accosted by that man had been more serious than she'd let on, and she'd needed a great deal more help than anyone had realized. Being her friend, Abigail had, of course, stepped in to help.

That might have satisfied Abigail's boss for a day or two longer if Barb hadn't been seen riding Rowan around the town square yesterday. So Abigail was back to work with the usual crew, holding her breath every time a door opened.

At quitting time, she walked out of the office building with the rest of the men and women—and almost walked right into her father as he dodged two women who were too busy gossiping to get out of the way.

He looked her right in the eyes, touched two fingers to the brim of his black hat, said, "Ma'am," and kept going.

Abigail stood rooted to the sidewalk until someone jostled her while trying to reach the bus that would take the first wave of workers home.

Her legs shook as she climbed the stairs and almost gave out before she found a seat.

He hadn't recognized her. She'd known him the moment she saw him, but he hadn't recognized her. Had she changed that much in three years?

Abigail let out a huge sigh of relief. He wouldn't stay long in a town like Bennett, and once he left, she'd really be safe.

Parlan kept walking up the street for his meeting with Tolya Sanguinati. He tipped his hat to the Simple Life women who were waiting for the bus; smiled at the blond girl who sat in a rocker outside the saloon, fanning herself; and wondered who owned the ponies grazing in the square—ponies that didn't look like any breed he'd seen before.

No movement, no look, no gesture, betrayed his rage. But as he walked and smiled, a single thought filled him: *Found you, bitch.*

"The Eagles and Hawks have told me that two packs of humans are hiding in the houses just beyond the town borders," Virgil said. "One to the north and one to the south. Big packs." He looked at Tolya, who was leaning against the mayor's desk, then at Air. "I think they are being squeezed between us and the Elders, just like the bad dogs were squeezed and then hunted."

"You think those humans are going to attack the town?" Tolya asked.

"Not the town. Us. They're going to attack us, and we can't survive packs of humans with guns. Once we're gone, the town will be their territory."

"It won't be theirs," Air said. "Never theirs. The Elders and Elementals won't allow it."

"But we'll still be dead," Virgil growled.

Tolya thought about the book Jana had loaned him, the book now sitting in his desk drawer. The good guys hadn't won—and most hadn't survived—because the villains had been sneaky, had made promises that were nothing more than lies.

Was Parlan Blackstone part of this, or were his arrival and the arrival of these human packs so soon afterward two separate things? He would know soon enough.

"Do the Elders know about these packs of humans?" Tolya aimed the question at Virgil but looked at Air.

Virgil shrugged, but Air said, "They know."

And have done nothing. After seeing some of the Elders who lived in the hills, he wasn't sure he wanted them to do anything, but he also didn't want to see Virgil, Kane, and John dying the way Joe Wolfgard had died.

"Those humans haven't crossed into our territory," Virgil said. "Not yet."

"But they've sent scouts." Tolya held up the list of hotel guests that Anya had provided. Two of them claimed to be in the cattle business and were in Bennett looking to buy some stock. One was a gambler who didn't sneer at the betting limits that had been set for play in the Bird Cage Saloon, and for some reason, that made Freddie Kaye very uneasy. Another who had spent time in the saloon didn't seem to have a profession, but Yuri believed the human was a predator waiting for his chosen prey. "And then there is Parlan Blackstone, who seems to be here without the rest of his pack."

"They'll be coming if they're not already here and hiding," Virgil said.

Tolya nodded. "Blackstone asked for a meeting and should be here at any moment." He looked at Air. "Could you stay, quietly?"

"And then tell the Elders what is said?" she asked.

"Yes."

"You don't need me here," Virgil said. It wasn't a question.

"No," Tolya agreed. "But depending on what Blackstone says, you should prepare for a fight."

Virgil gave him an odd look. "I'll prepare for a fight no matter what he says. But I'll tell you now, if the humans start a fight, I'll keep killing them until they take my last breath."

Parlan had thought about how to approach Tolya, how to play this hand. Should he go in as the tough leader who had the force behind him to take control or the man who would have preferred a quiet life but felt he had to stand up for his people?

He couldn't read the damn Sanguinati, but remembering the last time he'd met Tolya in this office, he decided to go in soft.

"Appreciate you seeing me," Parlan said as he settled in the visitors' chair.

"Have you decided which saloon you would like to run?" Tolya pulled a yellow legal pad to the center of his desk and picked up a pen.

"Ah. Well. That might not be happening for some time."

"Oh?" Tolya set the pen on the pad.

"You've got a problem, Mr. Sanguinati. The town has a problem. Nothing that can't be sorted out, but some changes need to be made."

"Oh?"

He wished he could get a sense of what this vampire was thinking. "People—humans—need a place to live."

"Which is why we have allowed some humans to return to Bennett," Tolya replied.

"And humans need to be governed by other humans," Parlan said, watching the vampire. "We can get a little crazy when we start feeling like cattle in a pen."

"But you are cattle in a pen, Mr. Blackstone," Tolya said pleasantly. "Bennett may be a large pen without any visible fences, but it is still a pen that provides some shelter from the wild country. That is true of all towns in Thaisia. It's even true of the cities. It has always been true. Humans who think otherwise are foolish or delusional."

"We can't view ourselves as prey animals," Parlan replied sharply. "We *aren't* prey animals to be slaughtered on a whim."

Silence except for a clock ticking somewhere nearby.

"What did you come to tell me?" Tolya asked.

"Humans have been pushed out of so many places in the Midwest, there's nowhere else for them to go. So they're coming here. But they need to live in a human town governed by humans." Parlan took a deep breath and let it out in a sigh. "I've talked to some of these men, listened to the citizens who are setting up homes and businesses. Something has to change, or things will get ugly. That's why, Mr. Sanguinati, I and some like-minded men are going to challenge you and the other town leaders to a fight for dominance."

Tolya blinked. "I beg your pardon?"

"My former business associates must have been talking after they left Bennett about how humans could take control from the Sanguinati." Parlan doubted the blowhards had remembered the comment, let alone said anything, but they were long gone, so he could claim they'd said whatever he wanted them to say. "And, somehow, men who have been coming into town lately are thinking that I'm going to be the next mayor, that humans will uphold human law in Bennett."

"So the packs of men who have gathered in houses just beyond the town boundaries are here because they believe you can participate in a fight for dominance and win?" Tolya sat back in his chair. "That is . . . unfortunate. Quite regrettable."

"What do you mean?" Parlan's hands were cold. "You said . . ."

Tolya sat forward, his folded hands resting on the pen and legal pad. "My dear Mr. Blackstone, those men misunderstood."

Cold, cold, cold. So cold his fingers almost couldn't bend. "It sounded clear enough to me."

"When I said a fight for dominance was the only way leadership would change, I meant between one group of *terra indigene* and another. Humans can't challenge us for dominance."

"Why not?"

Tolya gave him a sympathetic smile. "It can't happen because the Elders allowed humans to return to Bennett and resettle the town on the condition that the town was under the control of leaders who were *terra indigene*. The day that is no longer true, the town will cease to exist. The train station will close because trains will not be allowed to reach the town. Nothing will come in—and nothing will go out. Nothing. Anyone living here will not be allowed to travel through the wild country. That is the Elders' territory, and to them, you really are nothing but prey."

So cold. So fucking cold. How had his luck changed so much and so fast?

A thought occurred to him—and rage warmed him just enough to consider how to get out of this mess.

He wouldn't be able to save all the men who had gathered on the outskirts, but he might still save the clan.

"There's no stopping it," Parlan said regretfully. "There's going to be a fight. But we can keep it to a display of strength, at which point I and my people will concede and withdraw our challenge."

"In exchange for what?"

"For me and my family being allowed to remain and open our saloon and become citizens of Bennett." Parlan leaned forward. "Look, I didn't ask to represent this group of people, but I have enough of a reputation that I have some influence over them. If I and my delegation meet you and yours, and we are seen to concede after acknowledging that you're the stronger leaders, the other men will have to agree or leave. And, frankly, it will prevent a slaughter on both sides."

Tolya hesitated.

Gotcha.

"So this challenge will be made without you using human weapons? This will be done without a single shot being fired?" Tolya stared at him. "You do understand what will happen if I agree to this and a single *terra indigene* is injured or killed? One shot, Mr. Blackstone, and you all die."

"I understand." If he had to sell out the rest of the men who had come here in order to keep his family alive, so be it.

"I must take advice and will get back to you this evening with a decision."

"Take advice? You're the leader."

Tolya studied him. "I am amazed by the human ability to be willfully blind. How can you come to a place like this and not understand what's out there?" He stood. "I'll have a decision this evening about your faux challenge. In the meantime, perhaps you should encourage the men you can influence to get as far away from here as possible before nightfall."

Parlan smiled grimly. "Leave so they don't die?"

"Oh, they're still going to die. But they won't be here to fire the shot that will kill you and your family."

CHAPTER 33

Firesday, Messis 31

Air rode Thunder deep into the Elder Hills, the steed's hooves drumming the earth, a herald for the oncoming storm. She rode until she reached the place where Namid's teeth and claws met with Elementals when a decision was required.

The Elders were already there, waiting for her.

<A human pack is going to challenge the Sanguinati and Wolfgard for control of Bennett,> Air said.

<That is foolish,> a female Elder said. <We allowed humans to return because the Sanguinati and Wolfgard rule that place.>

<The male who is the human leader claims he didn't know humans couldn't participate in a fight for dominance.> Air looked at the Elders. <Packs of humans have gathered for this fight. They have the kind of weapons that killed the Wolfgard before.> She hesitated. <I don't know if the Sanguinati can survive so many enemies. The Wolfgard know they cannot.>

Air waited while the Elders considered what was about to happen in the town that bordered their home.

Elementals had their own connection to the world and took care of the world in their own way. They seldom interfered, for good or ill, with the creatures that lived in the world, and were usually indifferent to the help or harm they caused the smaller species—except when they or the Elders were needed to reshape a piece of the world. Then they worked with Namid's teeth and claws to thin out herds that had grown unchecked—or to eliminate a species that had become too much of a threat to the rest of Namid's creations.

They had joined with the Elders across the world to eliminate a certain breed of human, so Air waited now for the message she would take back to Tolya—and then share with the rest of her kin.

<Why didn't the Sanguinati eliminate the enemy when this human first arrived?> The female Elder sounded troubled.

<The human caused no trouble, offered no challenge,> Air replied. <He was no different from the other humans who have talked to Tolya about living in the Sanguinati's territory.>

<Until now.>

<Until now,> Air agreed. <The human promised to challenge and then yield, acknowledging the Sanguinati's dominance and control of Bennett. He promised the human weapons that kill would not be used.>

<Should we believe this human?> a male Elder asked.

<No,> another male voice answered.

Air felt the change in the rest of the Elders. This one hadn't taken on a two-legged shape recently, when the decision had been made to assume a humanlike form in order to hunt down the humans who used to live in Bennett. Whatever its true form, this Elder's shape stood on two legs but there was nothing humanlike about it. It was an ancient form, fanged and furred and terrible in its making—and, Air noticed, feared by the rest of the Elders.

That he was here, now, was a choice she found interesting. But she could afford to find this Elder interesting. She and her steed were the only beings here that he couldn't harm.

<The human packs are not the same kind of humans as the ones who are living among the *terra indigene*,> he said. <The humans in the packs prey on other humans. And they will prey on the smaller shifters. They have done this in some of the empty places the smaller shifters reclaimed, and we killed enough of them to drive them away.>

<Now they are here,> the female said.

<Now they are prey to be destroyed.>

Air understood now. The Elders who had gathered to thin the human herds were scattered again, hunting and moving within their territories as prey moved to feed. But here, in these hills, there were many Elders—more than enough to destroy this particular kind of human.

What had Tolya told the Blackstone man? Cattle in a pen. Yes. Knowing there were many Elders here, these humans who preyed on their own kind had been herded toward Bennett. Toward this one Elder in particular.

<Humans who were allowed in the Wolfgard territory are not our fight,> the terrible one said. <If the human leader and his small pack challenge the Sanguinati and then yield and leave the Sanguinati's territory, that is not our fight. As long as no *terra indigene* is injured or killed, we will stay in our territory. But if any human in the Wolfgard territory uses the *bang* that killed the Wolves, then this challenge becomes our fight, and we will thin the human herds again.>

<My kin and I will help if we are asked,> Air said. <Otherwise, we will not interfere.>

It was settled, then—or as settled as anything could be when humans were involved. The Elders and Elementals would keep the human packs currently in the wild country from entering the fight, and Tolya would allow the Blackstone man to challenge and yield in order to prevent a fight that would kill the Wolfgard in Bennett.

As she rode back to Bennett to give Tolya the Elders' decision and then meet with her kin, Air wondered if the Blackstone man would keep his word. And she wondered which human was going to break the rules and get them all killed.

Parlan searched his hotel room, then searched it again. During the third search, he finally found the slit in the mattress—and the black stone that had been placed inside.

Fucking bitch, trying to sour his luck with one of her fucking stones! But when had she slipped into his room? Or would he find a similar stone in other rooms at the hotel? Who else's fortune had Abigail soured? Not the people who were looking to stay in Bennett. She wouldn't need to play that con with them, not at first. But there were a limited number of rooms available for transient guests. Had the bitch put a dissonant stone in each of those rooms? If she had . . .

William and Wallace Parker. Sleight-of-Hand Slim. Durango Jones. They were all staying at the hotel.

Despite being an Intuit himself, Judd didn't believe that gemstones could bring a person good fortune or sour a person's luck. He didn't believe Abigail's claim to recognize which stone could alter a person's fate. He'd always said she was playing a con within a con while doing her spiel with Lawry.

But Parlan believed there had to be something real about her ability—and that's why he began to sweat as he studied the black stone now sitting on the bedside table.

Now he knew why his meetings with the vampire had been going sour. His bitch of a daughter had set him up to fail even before he arrived.

Parlan twitched when the phone rang. "Hello?"

"This is the front desk," a female voice said. "Mr. Sanguinati would like to see you at your earliest convenience."

"Thank you." He hung up. A couple of minutes later, he left the hotel and walked to the building next door.

"I thought you were going to take advice," Parlan said when he entered Tolya's office.

Tolya smiled. "I did."

"That was fast." And made him wonder if the vampire had tried to play him.

"Sometimes it is." Tolya stood in front of the desk. "Your proposal to challenge and then yield has been accepted. You and your delegation and I with mine will meet in the town square. Once the challenge is concluded, as long as no weapon is fired and no *terra indigene* are injured, you will be allowed to leave town by car or train."

"We agreed I could take over one of the saloons," Parlan protested.

"We did, but the Elders overruled that agreement," Tolya said softly. "If you remain in Bennett, you will not survive very long. Your family will not survive."

"Is that a threat?"

"No, that is a statement. Now I must go. I have other business to attend to this evening."

Parlan walked out of the government building, Tolya beside him.

A Wolf howled, somewhere nearby. Then another howled a few blocks away. Then a third.

And then something else howled. Something that made Parlan's skin crawl just from the sound of it.

"What is that?" he whispered.

Tolya Sanguinati shuddered. "That, Mr. Blackstone, is a warning."

S tanding outside her house, Jana shivered, frozen by the sound of that last howl. The one that didn't belong to a Wolf.

Barb stood just inside the screen door, looking at the street. "What do you think it means?"

Nothing good. "I'm going to check on the neighbors."

"But dinner is almost ready."

"I won't be long."

Jana jogged across the street to the Gotts' house. They were home and dinner was on the table. She declined an invitation to join them, then hesitated. She wasn't an Intuit, but she was learning to be a cop and trust her instincts.

"Stay home tomorrow," she told Hannah. "All of you. Stay away from the town square."

"Trouble?" Hannah asked, looking toward the Elder Hills.

"Maybe."

She went up the street to Maddie's house and talked to Evan, asking that he and Kenneth stay home with the children tomorrow.

That *something* howled again and reached inside her past the place of rational thinking. But she wouldn't—*couldn't*—allow herself to be too afraid to think.

The Ravengard had reported sightings of strangers moving into houses within the town's borders, but Craig and Dawn Werner, as the town's land agents, had issued no paperwork for houses on that street. When she told Virgil, he wouldn't let her check it out and threatened to lock her in the Me Time cell if she defied him.

This had something to do with outlaws, with the men coming into town these past few days. But until someone broke the law, she didn't know what to do about it.

Parlan bought a bottle of whiskey at the saloon and returned to the hotel. He needed to eat, but first he needed a couple of stiff drinks to settle himself.

"Parlan."

He turned and waited for Sleight-of-Hand Slim, Durango Jones, and the Parkers to join him. "I think we could rustle up a few more glasses if you want to come up and join me for a drink."

William Parker went to the hotel's dining room and returned with a tray of glasses.

Parlan didn't want the company, didn't want any of them in his room, and hoped none of them noticed the stone he'd found in the mattress, which he'd left in plain sight.

"I saw you at the poker table," he said as he poured a glass for Slim.

"Cards weren't with me at all tonight," Slim replied. "Made me glad they were playing for small stakes. If I didn't know better, I'd say I was jinxed."

Parlan's hand shook a little as he poured Durango's drink.

"We set for the showdown?" Durango asked. "Tomorrow, isn't it? Judd called and told me he'd moved some merchandise to a couple of houses just north of the tracks. At that location, the goods will have easy access to the train station and other places on that side of the square."

Damn it! More men inside the town meant more chances of someone getting itchy and making a mistake.

He poured drinks for William and Wallace Parker, and finally one for himself.

He saw it in their eyes. If he told them he was going to challenge the Sanguinati just to back down, they would kill him now and go in his place, not knowing what would happen when the first shot was fired. Even if he told them what would happen, they would still go into the fight with guns blazing. Outlaws were becoming an extinct breed of human who couldn't survive in any environment except human-controlled towns, and they were being driven out of those places too. These men *needed* Bennett, and they weren't going to walk away.

But he might be able to convince them that they had a chance, and keep them believing it long enough for *him* to get away.

"We call out the mayor and the sheriff tomorrow," he said, raising his glass. "To new beginnings."

They toasted, they drank, they talked—but Parlan had the feeling none of them trusted him quite enough anymore.

CHAPTER 34

Watersday, Frais 1

Startled awake, Jesse grabbed for the phone on her bedside table. "Hullo?"

"Jesse Walker?" A young female voice. Shaky.

"Rachel?" She knew it wasn't Rachel but couldn't think who else would call her at that hour of the morning.

"No, it's Hope. Hope Wolfsong."

Jesse sat up, her heart suddenly pounding. "Hope? Did something happen in Sweetwater?"

"We're safe here."

That didn't actually answer her question.

Turning on the light, Jesse looked at the clock. "Honey, where are you?"

"At the *terra indigene*'s communications cabin. Amy Wolfgard is with me. Please listen. I don't think there's much time before . . ."

Jesse heard Amy's sharp, anxious whine and took a guess at why there wasn't much time. "Jackson doesn't know you left the Wolfgard cabin?"

"No, but that doesn't matter. You have to listen."

A chill went through Jesse. "You drew a picture."

"I was teaching Amy how to draw, but we fell asleep, and Amy said

I got out of bed and started drawing." A suppressed sob. "Something bad is going to happen."

"Can you send me the drawing in an e-mail?" Jesse asked.

"There isn't time."

She swung her legs over the side of the bed. "Tell me."

"I drew a picture of two towns. One town is seen from a hilltop or maybe high up like a Hawk or Eagle would see. It has a long rectangle in the center with trees and grass and a pond."

"That sounds like Bennett."

"A red shadow is creeping through the town, consuming it piece by piece. Amy says I cut a finger to make the red. That's why . . ." A hesitation. "The other town looks abandoned. A sign above one building says Walker's General Store. The windows are broken, and there is debris in the street, like there's no one left to clean it up."

Another chill went through Jesse. "Hope, honey, where is Jackson?"

"He and Grace went out for a run. They'll be upset when they come back and—" Hope sucked in a breath.

Jesse hadn't heard the howl, but another sharp whine from Amy told her that Jackson had found the drawing—and was now calling the Wolf-gard to find their missing blood prophet.

"Jackson needs to talk to Bennett's mayor, needs to send that drawing to him."

"No!" Panicked breathing. "If Jackson sends the drawing, the man will know about me. That's why I called *you*!"

Something wasn't right. "Honey, Tolya Sanguinati already knows about you. He's received drawings from Jackson before."

"But he won't be the only one who sees it!"

Jesse's left wrist throbbed. "Who else would see the drawing?"

"The man made of black stones."

"Don't brush this off, Tolya," Jackson snapped. "Hope drew this picture. It's not an idle warning."

Tolya rubbed his forehead, then felt disgust at having acquired that human gesture. "I'm not brushing it off, Jackson, or dismissing what

Hope saw. I just don't know what to do about it. The Elders and Elementals will deal with the enemy in their territory, but there aren't enough Sanguinati and Wolves to win a fight with Blackstone and his allies if we really fight."

"You trust him to keep his word?"

"Of course not. He's a human who cheats his own kind. He's not going to be honest with us."

Silence. Then Jackson said, "What can I do?"

"Don't let the Hope pup send any drawings or call anyone until you hear from me or from someone in Prairie Gold. I'm going to destroy everything you've sent me that might tell someone like Blackstone what she is and where to find her." And he'd have to figure out what to do with their own prophet pup.

"Be careful," Jackson said. "Humans are sneaky."

In Jana's book, the good guys don't win—and most don't survive—because they believed the bargain they had made with the villains. "I'll call you."

As soon as he hung up the phone, Tolya reached out to Yuri, using the *terra indigene*'s form of communication. <Go to Maddie's house. Make sure everything is quiet there.>

<Nothing's quiet,> Yuri replied. <I'm heading there now. So are Jana, Barbara Ellen, and the Wolves. Maddie is . . . upset.>

<Bleeding?>

<Don't know. Kenneth woke Jana, asking for help. She called me and Virgil.> A beat of silence. <I see Jana. She's wearing her gunbelt and gun over sleeping clothes.>

<We're going to fight the Blackstone Clan for control of the town. Meet me and the rest of the Sanguinati at the mayor's office once you've helped Jana and Virgil.> He thought for a moment, then added, <The Wolves need to be at this meeting too.>

As he turned away from his desk to look out the window, the phone rang again. "Hello?"

"Why were you on the phone so long?" Jesse demanded.

"Business," Tolya replied. "Why are you calling so early?"

"You're in trouble. Tobias is picking me up. We'll get there as soon as we can."

"No. Stay away from Bennett today."

"Can't." Heavy breathing. "Hope Wolfsong called me."

Jackson hadn't mentioned that—probably because Hope had "forgotten" to tell him about the phone call. "This isn't your fight, Jesse."

"Yes, it is. I have a feeling that I'm the wild card. Your adversary has no reason to think Prairie Gold has that much of a stake in what happens in Bennett."

"I believe my adversary is an Intuit, so he might sense more than you think. And there can be no wild cards in this fight." He didn't want her there, didn't want one more friend anywhere near this place if they really had to fight.

Silence. Then Jesse said, "Tolya? I'm counting on you and your people winning this fight. But know this: if you should lose, the new leader won't hold the town for long, because I will put a bullet through his brain."

Tolya stiffened, alarmed by her words. "His pack would kill you."

"Yes. But he'll still be gone, and my people will be safer for it."

"Speak, prophet, and we will listen," Jana said for the sixth time. She wasn't sure Maddie heard her words or if the girl *was* speaking the prophecy to the best of her ability.

Maddie raised her shaking arm, her hand shaped like a gun. Pointing at Kane, she wailed, "Bang! Bang!" The hand moved to point at Virgil. "Bang!" Then to Jana. "Bang! Bang!" Then to the rest of them—Barb, Yuri, Kenneth, Evan, even her brother Mace. "Bang! Bang!"

"The doctor gave us an oral sedative for her," Evan said. "It's supposed to calm her down enough to break the cycle when she's like this. Should I . . . ?"

Jana nodded. The girl hadn't cut herself and therefore didn't have the veil of euphoria to protect her mind from the visions. Maddie was being tortured by whatever she was seeing, and Jana didn't think the girl would be able to make herself understood any better than this.

She closed her hands over the girl's. "We understand, Maddie. We heard you, and we understand."

Maybe her words had gotten through the terror. Or maybe Maddie's body couldn't take anymore. Either way, Maddie collapsed so suddenly, Jana barely had time to catch her before the girl's head hit the floor.

Leaving Evan and Kenneth to deal with Maddie and the rest of their children, Jana walked out of the house with Virgil, Kane, and Yuri.

"We're going to fight the Blackstone Clan for control of the town," Yuri said.

"When?" Virgil asked.

"Today. Tolya wants the Sanguinati and Wolfgard to meet at the mayor's office as soon as we're done here."

Virgil looked at Jana. "Put on your deputy clothes. You're coming too."

She didn't bother to tell him she hadn't taken a shower yet. Most likely, he could smell the difference.

Not important. Not today.

She ran across the street to her house, almost tripping over Rusty when she went inside.

"I know, pup." She let Rusty out in the backyard, then headed for her bedroom to get dressed, hesitating when she heard the phone ring.

"I'll get it," Barb called out.

A minute later, Barb tapped on the bedroom door and opened it partway. "That was Zeke. Kelley called him a few minutes ago. Dina didn't come home last night and Kelley is worried. Zeke thinks she's catting around, if you know what I mean, but he didn't want to say that to Kelley. And Zeke is more ticked off that she took a vehicle out yesterday and didn't log where she was going."

Jana buttoned her shirt and tucked it into her jeans. "Did he give you the license plate number of the vehicle Dina took out?"

"Yes. I wrote it down for you." Barb waited a beat. "What can I do?"

"Let Rusty back in and feed her. And if any of our feathered neighbors are home and available, ask them to contact me if they spot the vehicle." Jana slipped past Barb and went into the bathroom to brush her teeth. "You should stay away from the town square today," she said as she brushed and rinsed.

"But I have to feed the animals!"

"They'll have to go hungry today. Stay home, okay?" Jana looked at her friend. It all came down to choices. "I'm not an Intuit. I don't get feelings that way. But there's going to be a fight, and you need to be ready. Pack a go bag for yourself. Food and water for you, Rusty, and Buddy. Convince Evan and Kenneth that they need to pack go bags for themselves and the kids *right now*. I suspect this won't be the first time they've needed to leave in a hurry. If there's any indication that we'll lose this fight, you all pile in their car and get as far away from Bennett as you can."

"And go where?"

Only one place they could go. "Into the hills. Drive as far in as you can, then go on foot. Tell whatever stops you that Maddie is a sweet blood and you need to get her to Jackson Wolfgard's settlement in Sweetwater." Before Barb could protest, Jana said, "Maddie can't stay here. The Blackstone Clan and some of the other men who have come into town in the past couple of days are dangerous. Can you imagine what they would do with, and to, a blood prophet, even one as young as Maddie?"

Barb swallowed hard. "I'll do my best."

"Your best will be great." Jana made sure she had everything she needed before she headed out the door.

Don't want to be late to my first gunfight.

But she wondered if Maddie's pointing finger had already revealed the outcome of that fight.

After listening to Tolya's recap of his "agreement" with Parlan Blackstone and then the description of the Hope pup's drawing, Virgil eyed his *human* deputy. Jana smelled a bit musky, which was actually pleasant, but the pale face and sour-sweat smell that was also on her skin made him wonder if she was ill.

"So we're all going to meet the Blackstone Clan and their allies?" Jana asked. "A show of strength, a couple of snarls, and they raise their hands and surrender because they promised to do that?"

Some other message passed between the wolverine and Tolya. Virgil growled softly at being excluded. She was *his* deputy and shouldn't have secrets. Not from him.

"Not all of us," Tolya replied after a moment. "Nicolai will remain at the train station. Stazia will guard the bank, Anya will stay at the hotel, and Isobel will keep watch on the other side of the square. So will Joshua Painter. The delegation meeting the Blackstones will consist of Yuri, Virgil, and me."

"Where I am positioned?" Jana growled.

"You're going to be available if someone calls for help," Virgil replied. "Make sure the police howler is parked away from the square so the enemy doesn't see you drive away."

"You're excluding me?" Jana stared at him. "Why? Because I'm *human*?" She looked at Tolya. "Three of you are going to stand up against . . . how many?"

"Four of us," Saul Panthergard growled.

Virgil wondered who had told Saul about the meeting, then decided it didn't matter. They needed all the big predators living in Bennett.

"Fine," the wolverine snapped. "Four. Against how many?"

"Numbers don't matter," Tolya said. "Human weapons can't be used, and Blackstone already agreed to yield."

"And when something goes wrong?" she persisted.

"Then we'll kill as many humans as we can," Virgil replied.

"Before you die."

"Yes."

She looked upset about something he'd already accepted.

"You're not being excluded," Tolya said. "You're the next line of defense. So are Anya, Stazia, Isobel, and John. Kane will protect the Maddie pup, but he'll need help if she has to run away and hide."

"I already took care of that," Jana said. "Barb will help Evan and Kenneth take the kids to safety."

They didn't have time for the wolverine to keep arguing, so Virgil stepped on her foot and growled, "When we hunt, I decide your position, and I've told you what I decided."

"They're going to cheat." Her hands balled into fists.

"So are we."

Virgil met Tolya's eyes. The Sanguinati understood perfectly why he didn't want the human deputy around to see the fight. In their Wolf form, the Wolfgard were big. In their true *terra indigene* form, they were even bigger—and could not be seen by human eyes. They could be shot—and killed—in their true form, but they would kill a lot more of the enemy before that happened.

Virgil looked at Saul. "You sure about being in the fight?"

Saul gave Virgil a feline stare. "Joshua woke up early this morning, dreaming of metal, jagged-toothed traps disguised as rabbits. The boy and I will fight."

"I'm still hoping Parlan Blackstone has as much influence on the other outlaws as he believes and can convince them to back away from this fight and leave town," Tolya said. "But no matter what happens, the outlaw humans won't take the town." He smiled at Jana. "Our last defense will see to that."

"Me?" She sounded squeaky.

"No," Virgil said. "The Harvester is our last defense. There are good reasons why Plague Rider is another name for Scythe's form of *terra indigene.*"

CHAPTER 35

Watersday, Frais 1

Jana found two more speed loaders in the storeroom. The darn room still held enough weapons to hold off an army—or supply an army—and she didn't know what to do about that. She carried the speed loaders and two boxes of ammunition to her desk, then went back for a shotgun and a box of shells.

She hadn't found any vests. Either they weren't standard issue here or the cops who had lived in Bennett had been wearing them when the Elders swept in and killed everyone. Either way, she hadn't found anything she could use as protection in a gunfight.

When she headed for the storeroom again, Virgil said, "How can you run fast if you're carrying all those things? And how can you use any of them when you're carrying all of them?"

"I thought I could hide a couple of them or . . . something." Jana closed her eyes. The idea of having hidden stashes of guns had been alluring—and more like a frontier-story shootout—until she considered the one thing that had never been in those stories. "Some of the men we're going to be fighting are Intuits and experienced fighters. If they 'sense' things in a fight, they might have a feeling of where they could find extra weapons."

"Yes." Virgil studied the weapons that filled the top of her desk. He pointed at the boxes of ammunition. "These are the danger. Without them, this"—he pointed at the shotgun—"is a metal club. It can hurt, even kill, but the enemy has to be close enough to hit with it or throw it. And if the enemy is that close, he's close enough for fangs and claws to kill *him*." He considered the weapons for another minute. "You should have a knife."

She reached down, pulled the switchblade out of her boot, and held it up for him to see. "I've got one."

She couldn't tell what he was thinking, but she could guess. "I know this is my first fight, but I won't let you down. I'm not going to choke or freeze or . . . whatever."

Virgil smiled. "I don't care what Tolya says, *I* still think one of your ancestors mated with a Wolverine and somehow had some young."

She wasn't sure if that was meant as an insult or a compliment.

His smile faded. "Once John and I shift to Wolf form, we won't be able to talk to you."

She nodded. The Wolves would be able to communicate with each other and the rest of the *terra indigene*, reporting the enemies' positions. None of them would be carrying mobile phones—and none of them would be able to afford the seconds needed to shift into a form that could talk to her.

A sudden breeze ruffled Virgil's hair.

"I can deliver messages to Deputy Jana," Air said, taking shape near the office door. "The Elementals agreed to help if we're asked."

"Then I'm asking." Virgil turned to Jana. "If you need to tell us anything, you call for Air. And if I need you to go somewhere, she'll tell you. Understood?"

As soon as Jana nodded, Air disappeared—or was no longer visible.

"We need to hide the ammunition," Jana said. "You're right that, without bullets, the long guns are nothing more than metal clubs and the handguns can't do any more damage than a rock."

Virgil started to say something, then shook his head. "No time. The Blackstone humans are gathering in the square to challenge Tolya." He stripped out of his clothes and shifted so fast she had a weird flash image of his naked human body that left her unsure of having actually seen him.

She tucked two of the speed loaders in the special pouch on her duty belt, picked up the shotgun and a handful of shells, then followed Virgil out the door.

"Mom, I'll say it again. I don't feel easy about you being in a gunfight."

Jesse glanced at Tobias, who had been driving at a recklessly high speed ever since he picked her up at her house. "Son, I'm not easy about you being in this fight either, but we have just as much at stake as the people living in Bennett." *And you're not driving this fast to protect the Sanguinati or the Wolves.*

"You think our two guns will make a difference?"

Not their guns, but their presence, would alter the fight. She could feel it.

Jesse closed her eyes as her right hand closed over her left wrist. "Yes. We'll make a difference."

Parlan settled the two revolvers into their holsters before he loaded the derringer with its single round. It might carry only one bullet, but that bullet could bring down a horse or blow the leg off a man—or a Wolf. Of course, all the weapons were for show, but he couldn't issue the challenge without them.

He studied Judd McCall, who seemed oddly elated.

He'd had to tell Judd and Lawry about the deal he'd made with Tolya Sanguinati. Lawry had fretted about what would happen down the road if other associates heard that Parlan had double-crossed the men who had come to Bennett to help him secure the town. And Judd? It was like Judd had expected it, had been waiting for the day when Parlan's luck ran out and he'd betray everyone to save his own skin.

Still, Judd slid a look at Durango Jones as he loaded his guns—silent confirmation that he would take care of Durango if Parlan kept the deal with the vampire and got the clan safely out of Bennett. Parlan and Lawry would handle the Parkers if required.

"Where is Sleight-of-Hand Slim?" he asked.

"He'll take up a position inside the saloon doors to ambush whoever tries to use the place for cover," Judd said.

Of course, in order to do that, Slim would need to kill the thing that ran the saloon. And that would queer the deal—assuming Slim got off a shot before the thing killed him.

Why hadn't Judd killed Slim quick and quiet? Or had he, and this was just a way to explain the other man's absence? No way to tell, and no time to ask.

"My men will take over the train station and shoot any of the Others who are still in there," Durango said.

Parlan's hands went cold. Taking over the station wasn't part of the plan. Not his plan, anyway. "And the Bonney boys?"

The other men looked at each other and shrugged.

"Taking care of their own business, I guess," William Parker said.

"We've got enough men, whether Frank and Eli show up or not." Judd gave Parlan a cold smile, as if he'd already set payback in motion for the anticipated double-cross.

Parlan remembered the one other person who wasn't in the room. "Where's Dalton?"

"Probably going round to have a talk with his bitch sister," Judd replied. "I found out she was in town and where she lived."

"And you told him?" He'd told no one that he'd seen Abigail in town because he hadn't wanted anyone in the family distracted by that news.

Judd smiled. "I did. Figured she owed him more than she owed me."

Parlan bit back his anger. "It could have waited until after the fight."

Judd's smile turned mocking. "We've got enough men for this fight. We'll win it without him."

Durango Jones and the Parkers were watching this byplay with growing suspicion. If Judd McCall was turning on Parlan Blackstone just before a fight, something was very wrong.

Trying to regain the upper hand, Parlan said, "You have a feeling we're going to win?"

Judd's smile sharpened. "Don't you?"

*   *   *

Even Rusty's wild barking couldn't compete with the pounding on the screen door's frame.

Running to the front of the house, Barb grabbed the pup's collar and stared at Kenneth Stone, who stood there wringing his hands.

"Maddie?" she asked, hoping he said *no*. She was still putting together emergency supplies. She wasn't ready to flee if that's what Kenneth had come to tell her.

"No." Kenneth hesitated. "I have a feeling the doctors need to be at the hospital today. It's a very strong feeling."

"We've barely got the hospital open and only for emergencies," Barb protested.

"There's going to be an emergency." His eyes pleaded with her. "Evan says you should call because Jana is your housemate. The doc will think I'm overreacting, but he'll listen to you. Please."

Intuits were sure there was going to be an emergency. Oh gods.

"I'll call. Are you packed in case . . . ?"

"Almost, but Kane is uneasy about something and keeps getting in the way. Almost bit me when I came over to talk to you. Didn't want me leaving the house."

"Go home. Stay inside. I'll make the call."

Looking out the door of the land agent's office, Jana couldn't see the other side of the square, didn't know when the men would walk out and do the posturing that, hopefully, wouldn't end in a real fight.

"Anything we should do?" Dawn Werner asked as she cuddled her puppy to keep it quiet.

"Stay inside and stay away from the windows until you get the all clear," Jana replied.

She felt a puff of air against her neck a moment before Dawn gasped.

"Deputy Jana, a Hawk says there is a stranger sniffing around the Maddie's house," Air said. "The stranger has a gun. Kane is staying inside to protect the sweet blood."

Which left everyone else on the street unprotected. "Tell Virgil I'm heading to Maddie's house to back up Kane."

Jana went out the back door of the land agent's office and ran to her vehicle. She'd parked on the street instead of in the parking lot behind the sheriff's office. Now she was glad of the extra precaution since she could drive away without anyone in the town square being the wiser.

"I'm coming, Kane," she whispered. "Hold on."

A bigail stuffed a dress and two sets of underwear into a small carry-all. She added her prosperity and protection stones and all the money she could find around the house—including the stash she'd found in an envelope taped to the underside of the drawer in her bedside table.

She had the feeling that she had to get out, had to get away, had to leave *now*.

She stuffed a large bottle of water, a jar of peanut butter, a sleeve of crackers, and a spoon into the carryall.

She dashed out the front door—and froze when a voice said, "You bitch. You're the reason my name is on a Wanted poster."

B arb listened to the doctor tell her with growing impatience that he wasn't going to the hospital today, that he had *office hours* today, that there was no reason . . .

"Doc, are you an Intuit?" Barb interrupted.

A weighted silence. "Yes. I am."

"Then you understand that some things shouldn't be dismissed."

"You're not an Intuit, Ms. Debany."

"No, but I was asked to tell you that it was important—*vital*—that you work at the hospital today." She swallowed hard, remembering little Maddie's hand pointing at all of them like a gun. "Something bad is going to happen. You need to go to the hospital now or you won't be able to get there and help the people who need you."

Heavy breathing. Then the doctor said, "I'll make some calls and get to the hospital as soon as I can."

"Thank you."

She hung up and started to call Jana. Before she finished dialing, she heard someone outside say in a loud voice, "You bitch. You're the reason my name is on a Wanted poster."

* * *

Tolya walked out of the government building, Yuri beside him. Virgil, in Wolf form, was waiting for him in the square. John was also in the square near the spring, keeping watch for any humans who might be doing something sneaky. The other Sanguinati were in position, as was Scythe.

<Someone is sneaking around the Maddie's house,> Virgil said. <The wolverine is heading there to help Kane.>

That either took Jana out of the fight or put her in a confrontation on her own, since Kane would protect Maddie.

Parlan Blackstone walked out of the hotel, flanked by two men and followed by three more.

Virgil focused on the man standing to Parlan's left. <That's the dominant enforcer. That's the one called the Knife. I know his scent from the house where that male was killed.>

<The biggest threat?> Tolya asked.

<Yes.>

A flurry of reports from the *terra indigene* who were keeping watch. Humans sneaking around the back of the bank and saloon. Humans sneaking up to the train station. More humans sneaking toward the Universal Temple and the community center.

Too many humans sneaking around if Parlan Blackstone had intended to keep his word.

Ravens gathered in the trees from one end of the square to the other, acting as sentries and reporting on the humans' movements. Hawks and Eagles flew overhead, circling the square, ready to attack. Coyotes were keeping watch at the side streets. Saul was somewhere in the square, in his true form, moving silently toward Blackstone's pack.

Tolya smiled, showing a hint of fang. "Mr. Blackstone. Is there something you want to say to me?"

Their footsteps filled the land with an odd and terrible silence as they moved along the wide, flat trails the humans had built. It didn't matter if these Outlaw humans hid inside the dens or tried to run away in the metal boxes that rolled on these flat trails. The enemy would be hunted down and destroyed.

They quickened their steps, salivating at the thought of the coming feast.

Parlan studied the Sanguinati. Did the vampire *want* him to look like a fool? How was he supposed to yield to a stronger force when Tolya had brought one other vampire and a Wolf and was so clearly outnumbered?

He didn't like Judd being on his left, didn't like the knife hand being in position for a strike to the back or ribs. He didn't like a lot of things about this deal, and he wondered exactly when this game had gotten away from him.

And he wondered if Judd McCall was working for himself these days or had gone into business with someone else.

For now he had to play this hand and do his best to win.

"I think this town would be better served by having a human mayor and a human sheriff," Parlan said, raising his voice to be heard by any people listening at the hotel doorway or hiding in the other nearby stores. "In frontier parlance, I'm calling you out, Mr. Mayor, but I'm doing so in the manner *you* said was required for a change in government. I'm challenging you for dominance, and the human residents of Bennett are behind me."

Tolya looked at the men with Parlan. "I don't see any residents, Mr. Blackstone. I see strangers who have come into town over the past couple of days. Drifters. Outlaws."

"Humans looking for a fresh start," Parlan countered.

"Humans who have made no effort to come to my office and ask about available jobs."

Call and raise, Parlan thought. "Humans who will take their place in Bennett society as soon as there is a human government."

"There will not be a human government," Tolya said. "This town exists with the Elders' permission, and it will continue to exist only as long as it is ruled by the *terra indigene*. If you manage to form a human government, you condemn all the humans living here—including you and your delegation."

What to do? Parlan felt the tension in Lawry, had a feeling the men behind him no longer had his back.

Tolya studied him. "You can't win. Your only choice is—"

Hearing a familiar female voice coming from the direction of the bank's back entrance, Stazia Sanguinati flowed over the counter and shifted to human form from the waist up.

"I don't think they're open." The woman sounded breathless—and frightened. "I don't think . . . Oh. Hello."

One of the cleaners who worked with Abigail Burch. A timid woman who came in every Firesday to cash her paycheck and put a small amount in a savings account. Usually she came in alone. Today, when she shouldn't be here, she came in with two men. The taller one had a hand wrapped around the woman's skinny arm.

"The bank is closed today," Stazia said—and wondered how they'd gotten in when she was certain she'd locked the front and back doors.

"That's all right," the taller one said. "We're not customers."

As the shorter one raised his weapon and fired, Stazia shifted her upper body to her smoke form. That shift could be done in moments.

But this time, she wasn't quite fast enough.

Gunshot. Across the street. One shot.

The humans looked toward the bank.

That moment when the Knife looked away instead of watching him, Virgil shifted to his true form and ran. A bullet whizzed under his tail, but the Knife couldn't see him, no longer had any idea of his size or his speed.

Blackstone and the other enemies shooting now at anything. Everything.

Virgil hit one of the men at full speed, knocking the enemy to the ground. He tore at the hand, the wrist. Tore at the face and throat. Then he leaped away as other enemies shot their own companions while trying to shoot him. But he was gone again, running, charging, slashing.

More enemies entered the square, shooting at everything. Blood and feathers on the ground as other *terra indigene* entered the fight. A Coyote screamed in pain.

He didn't think about Tolya or Yuri. He didn't think about Kane or the wolverine. Couldn't. Too many enemies now, and he was fighting alone, separated from his pack.

But he would keep on fighting, keeping on killing, until the enemy took his last breath.

"They tricked me!" Abby cried. "They tricked me into telling them your name."

Barb dropped the phone and ran to the front door, forgetting what her brother had told her about finding cover in dangerous situations—only thinking about helping a friend who was in trouble.

As she reached the screen door, she hesitated and saw the next few moments as a nightmarish montage.

Bang! Abby falling, a bloom of red spreading over the front of her dress.

Kane bursting through of the screen door of Maddie's house so fast the man didn't have time to turn and fire before the Wolf's teeth closed on an arm and pulled the man down.

Bang! The gun went off as the man fell.

Kane savaging the man, closing his teeth on the man's throat at the same time the man got his hand under the Wolf's belly, and—

Bang! Bang!

Silence.

Silence and . . .

There was a hole in the screen door big enough to let in the flies. Why was there a hole in . . .

The moment he heard the gunshot, Tolya knew what would happen. What had to happen.

He and Yuri shifted to smoke and raced to the nearest tree a heartbeat before Parlan and the other men started shooting.

A Raven flew toward them. <Humans are hiding with the hor—>

A shot from the direction of the livery stable. The Raven fell.

Gunshots at the far end of the square, where Saul and Joshua had been keeping watch. More of the enemy must have slipped into town and would surround them.

He didn't call to the other Sanguinati. Some of them wouldn't answer, and he didn't want to know. But he felt a hatred for humans that ran deeper and blacker than anything he'd ever felt before.

Staying close to the ground, he and Yuri raced across the street and wove through the low-growing plants that dotted the area between the stable and the blacksmith's. Reaching the stable, they flowed around the building and over the sill of an open window in the back wall.

The two men with rifles who were using the stable doors for cover never realized the Sanguinati were there until Tolya and Yuri shifted to human form from the waist up and tore out the humans' throats.

Scythe heard the first gunshot and abandoned the napkins she'd been folding—a useless human activity that Candice Caravelli had assured her would give the impression that she was occupied by a necessary task if someone should come into the saloon. After ordering Candice to go to her dressing room and stay there, Scythe had taken up a position at the end of the bar.

Now, underneath the sound of gunshots in the square, she heard the faint sound of a boot on the wooden floor, coming from the saloon's rear exit.

Her hair turned solid black and coiled as she silently moved into position.

The gun and gun hand entered the main room first. Then the arm. Finally the rest of the man came into view—and he caught sight of her.

She looked him in the eyes and absorbed every drop of his life energy before he hit the floor.

Dead. Completely harvested. Still . . .

Remembering how it was done in frontier stories, Scythe stepped on his gun and moved it out of reach.

She was sated—a sensation she hadn't enjoyed in a long time. It felt delicious, but . . . Maybe she was a little too sated? If more prey crossed her path, she wouldn't be able to absorb enough life energy to do more than a little damage, and there were many enemies out there fighting with the Wolves and Sanguinati.

She looked at the gun. Six-shooter just like in the frontier stories. She pulled back the hammer, aimed at the already dead man, and fired.

The sound hurt her ears, but the action was simple enough.

As she moved to the front doors of the saloon, her black hair gained a few threads of red. She was too full to be instantly lethal if someone looked at her, but she could still take enough life energy to confuse her enemy—and the gun would do the rest.

J ana turned onto her street and hit the brakes as Kane burst through the door of Maddie's house and attacked the armed man.

Bang!

Bang! Bang!

Throwing the gearshift into park, Jana scrambled out of the vehicle and used the car door for cover as she drew her own weapon and shouted, "Police!"

No sound. No movement. Nothing.

Abby was on the ground too, but Jana ran to Kane and the man, needing to disarm the assailant in case he was wounded but still alive.

Maybe her presence was perceived as a signal that it was all right to come out. Or maybe so little time had passed that people were just now shaking off fear-freeze. Either way, by the time she reached Kane and saw that the assailant had bled out from a torn throat, Hannah and Sarah Gott were running toward her, and Evan and Kenneth were rushing to check on Abby.

Holstering her own weapon, Jana touched the Wolf's shoulder as she looked into unseeing eyes. "Kane?"

Already gone.

He went down in the line of duty. She wasn't sure that would be any comfort to anyone—and it occurred to her that the first time she had to notify next of kin, she'd be telling Virgil that his brother was dead.

After pulling Kane off the man far enough to secure the weapon, she looked at Evan and Kenneth. "Abby?"

Evan shook his head.

Something wasn't right. More than the three dead bodies. Something . . .

Rusty's frantic barking finally got through to her. "Barb?" she shouted. "Barb!"

How many shots had been fired?

Jana ran to her own house, pulled open the screen door, and . . . *"Barb!"*

Arriving just behind Jana, Hannah pulled off her apron, swiftly folded it, and crouched beside Jana, saying, "Use this for the wound. It's freshly washed."

She pressed the fabric against the wound. "We have to get Barb to the doctor's." Except the medical building was on the town square, smack in the middle of the fight.

Evan rushed up. "We had a feeling, so Barb called the doctor just before all this . . . At least one of the doctors will be at the hospital today."

The dead would have to wait. "Help me load her into my vehicle. We can't wait for the ambulance."

Evan and Kenneth carried Barb while Jana kept pressure on the wound as best she could.

"I'll go with you," Hannah said. "Sarah will take your pup and the bird to our house, and clean up . . ."

"Anything we can do?" Evan asked after he and Kenneth got Barb settled in the back with Hannah now applying pressure on the wound while Jana wiped her hands on her jeans, smearing them with blood before she got behind the wheel.

"Call the neighbors and make sure nobody else was hurt," Jana said, putting the vehicle in drive. "And stay inside until this is over—unless you have to run."

Then she put the vehicle in park again and stepped out shouting, "Air! Air, I need you to send a message!"

Air appeared. She looked at the Wolf in the street. "Virgil is fighting."

"You don't need to tell Virgil anything." Jana pointed toward the Elder Hills. "Can you get a message to *them*?"

"Yes. But they are dealing with humans who are in their territory. They are not fighting inside the town boundaries."

"You tell them . . ." Jana struggled to breathe past a sudden flood of anger at beings who ignored boundaries whenever it suited them but couldn't be bothered now? "You tell them if they don't want the rest of the Wolves to die, they'd better . . . fffffffuck the boundaries and get in the fight!"

She jumped in her vehicle and drove off.

Oh gods, oh gods, oh gods. Did she really say that? Well, the Elders wouldn't know the *F* word, right? And what difference did it make if they did? They needed to stop sniffing their own tails and *do* something!

As she raced to the hospital, Jana realized Virgil wasn't the only notification she would have to make that day. She'd have to tell Kelley about Abby. And as she drove, she prayed she wouldn't have to send that kind of message to Lakeside police officer Michael Debany.

T heir footsteps filled the street with an odd and terrible silence as they moved unseen toward the bodies, Wolfgard and human.

They hadn't needed Air to deliver a message. They had been close enough to hear the howling of that . . . *female* . . . who *dared* to challenge Namid's teeth and claws. They didn't understand all the words, but they understood the tone.

The female didn't want boundaries? Then there would be no boundaries. And the first human they would deal with . . .

The terrible one sniffed around the bodies and breathed in that female's scent. They didn't need to follow the trail of the metal box, so they would join the fight in the center of the Sanguinati and Wolfgard territory. Sooner or later that female would come to the watering hole—and he would find her.

"W e've got company." Tobias took his foot off the gas and tapped the brake.

"We don't have time for this," Jesse snapped. Then she saw what Tobias must have sensed moments before—the horse and rider in the middle of the road.

"We make time for him." He stopped the truck and rolled down his window.

Yes, Jesse thought as she watched Fire and a brown horse with a storm-gray mane and tail move up alongside the truck.

Fire leaned down to look at both of them. "You don't want to go to Bennett today."

Jesse leaned across Tobias. "We have to. A fight is going to happen today."

"It has already started."

Oh gods. How much of Hope Wolfsong's drawing is going to come true?

"Where are the other humans coming from?" Tobias asked. "Which direction? North or south?"

"Both. The Sanguinati and Wolfgard are too few to fight so many humans."

Jesse studied the Elemental. "Can't you help?"

Fire met her eyes. "If we are asked, we will help. That was our agreement with the Elders."

This was about saving Prairie Gold—not just the town but the ranch and the farms that were part of it. It was about saving Bennett and the friends who lived there. It was about making a choice that would claw at her heart and shred her sleep for years, if not forever.

"A red flare means we need help," she said quietly. "That's correct, isn't it?"

Fire nodded. His steed moved to the side of the road to let them pass.

"Why did you ask him about the flare?" Tobias asked a minute later as he turned down a street that was a couple of blocks away from the Universal Temple, then parked in front of a house. "Mom? What are you thinking?"

Jesse said nothing, just loaded the red flare before slipping the flare gun into her daypack. Then she picked up her rifle and got out of the truck.

Giving her a worried look, Tobias chambered a round in his own rifle as soon as he joined her.

"We have to stop the reinforcements from reaching the town square," she said.

The briefest hesitation. "Then we'd better get moving."

He headed for the temple, and Jesse wondered if her boy knew what she was about to do.

Tolya flowed along the branches of the trees, searching for Parlan Blackstone. The humans had scattered, hiding in doorways and along the sides of buildings, firing their guns at random at every furred or feathered being. Ravens, Hawks, and Eagles had been turned into bloody mist and feathers. At least one Coyote was dead near the pond.

And the outlaws kept coming.

He didn't know where Virgil was, or Saul, but he'd seen some humans trying to crawl away from the square with their bellies torn open or their hamstrings sliced by sharp teeth. He didn't know where Yuri was either. Nicolai wasn't answering him. Neither was Stazia. Dead? Or too focused on the hunt to respond?

Spotting one of the males who had stood with Parlan Blackstone when the human had made the challenge, Tolya flowed down the shadow side of the tree trunk nearest his enemy. Then he hesitated. Why would an enemy simply stand there unless . . .

Reversing direction, Tolya flowed back up the tree—and saw one of the other humans waiting for one of the *terra indigene* to try for the man acting as bait. The human with the rifle was so focused on shooting whatever came for the bait that he didn't notice the smoke at the base of a tree, didn't notice it moving up his leg—moving into a long tear in the man's jeans.

The human didn't notice anything until he staggered from rapid blood loss.

That was the moment Tolya flowed down the tree, formed solid hands and forearms, and snapped the bait's neck.

A shot. A sting.

Tolya released the body and rushed up the tree to take cover in the branches—and saw part of his finger lying in the grass below.

*F*ucking vampires, Parlan thought as odd pockets of fog began filling the square, turning a fight that had gone on longer than it should have into a bullet-filled game of hide and seek. They had to finish this, had to take control of the town. All they needed to do was kill the mayor and the sheriff—and he couldn't find either one of them.

And they needed to end this fight before they became so befuddled by the fog that they started shooting each other by mistake.

Jana drove away from the hospital. Both doctors were there, as well as the nurse/midwife. There had been other cars in the parking lot, along with a van that belonged to Fagen.

She hoped those cars didn't belong to people who had been injured. She hoped Barb wouldn't need more help than the doctors could provide.

Then she stopped hoping about things she couldn't influence and put all her energy into getting to the town square in time to help Virgil.

Tobias ducked behind an abandoned car and opened and closed his hand four times.

Twenty men in the parking lot behind the Universal Temple and the community center, ready to move out and join the fight in the town square.

Twenty men. Twenty lives against the fate of two towns—and all the other humans who depended on those towns existing.

Jesse took the flare gun out of her daypack.

"Mom?" Tobias whispered. "What are you . . . ?"

Her son was a good man. She didn't want this on his conscience, and she didn't want him to stop her. This is why they were here. This is what would make the difference.

She popped to her feet, aimed the flare gun at the community center—and fired the red flare that was a call for help.

She dropped to the ground as some of the men started shooting at her. Then they stopped shooting because . . .

"Get down, Tobias. Get down!"

Jesse pressed herself to the ground and held her son's hand. She wept as they listened to men scream.

As they listened to men burn.

Leaving the car near the stable, Jana raced to the town square. Sporadic gunfire meant either there weren't many of the outlaws left in the fight or they were hesitating because the drifts of fog that were concentrated in the square made it difficult to tell friend from foe.

Was that a familiar snarl? Drawing her weapon, Jana moved toward the sound.

As he ripped and tore the enemies' flesh, the terrible one caught the scent of *that* female. A faint scent, but not one he would forget.

Tossing aside the meat, he entered the town square.

Finally—*finally*—he'd cornered the challenger, the reason for all this misery.

Snarling, Virgil shifted to his Wolf form because he wanted this enemy to see what would tear out a throat. He approached Parlan Blackstone, who dropped his guns and backed away.

John approached on Virgil's right, and the two Wolves focused on pushing the enemy back and back and back.

Then the wind shifted, bringing the scent of an enemy behind them.

Trap! <Run!> he snarled at John, leaping to one side as Parlan pulled out a little gun and fired.

Virgil circled tight around a tree and ran straight at the short man who had been in the saloon with Blackstone and had howled about giving up his guns. He hit the man with such speed and force, when his jaws closed on an arm and he used his own weight to throw the prey to the ground, he felt the prey's shoulder tear.

Two guns fired in rapid succession. One bullet hit the ground right next to his right front paw. The other . . .

He saw another enemy fall, heard Jana shout his name.

And heard another shot.

That little derringer could blow the leg off a horse—or a Wolf. Parlan watched the Wolf struggle to get up on its remaining three legs.

He was out of ammunition, but the fight was over. Had to be over.

Then he saw that fucking sheriff bring down Eli Bonney, saw Frank Bonney's shot miss the Wolf as Frank took a bullet in the chest.

Then he saw the smoke, caught a whiff of something that made him think of country fairs when those huge grills were fired up to cook up loads of meat.

Parlan knew then. He had to get out of this fucking town.

He turned, intending to run to the car rental place next to the train station—and stared into the black eyes of a female with coiling black hair that held thin streaks of red. Then a sudden exhaustion brought him to his knees.

Jana saw Virgil knock a man to the ground. Saw another man aim at the Wolf.

As she raised her weapon and fired at the man, she shouted, "Virgil!"

Something hit her in the side, knocked her off her feet. Knocked the gun out of her hand.

She tried to reach for her gun, but her body wouldn't move right. Gasping, she looked at the man who approached her with a smile on his face and a gun aimed at her heart.

The air behind him shimmered, like heat. Then . . .

He must have sensed it, tried to turn and fire. But it was too fast—*so fast*—and it grabbed him by his torso and thighs, lifted him as if a grown man weighed nothing and . . .

When she was a girl, she had a set of pop beads—colored beads that could be put together and taken apart to make many combinations of necklaces and bracelets, and when you pulled them apart they made a distinct popping sound.

She heard that sound now as a man's spine popped, as his body ripped in half.

Blood flooded out of that body, forming a puddle. Red red red.

The Elder that took a visible form stood on two legs—furred and fanged and clawed and huge. A nightmare humans were never meant to see. It stared at her as it held the two halves of the man.

This is what that woman saw when it killed her husband, Jana thought. *This is why she killed herself.*

It bared its teeth, and she felt its snarl rumble in the ground beneath her.

It took a step toward her, still holding its prey.

Then Virgil was there, standing over her, snarling in challenge as he faced down the Elder.

"Virgil," she whispered. "Run." She couldn't help him, and she couldn't escape. The best thing he could do for the rest of the shifters was get away from a predator that could break him as easily as it broke the man. "Run."

Of course Virgil, being Virgil, didn't run. He just snarled louder.

Stupid Wolf.

The last thing she saw before her vision faded was Virgil's foot too close to her face—and that terrible Elder walking away with its prey.

CHAPTER 36

Watersday, Frais 1

"Stupid female. You think you're a big predator who can ignore guns and challenge Namid's teeth and claws. But you're not a big predator. You're a *small* predator puffed up with attitude."

Oh, goody, Jana thought as she became aware of sounds—and pain—again. *Virgil's on a rant.*

". . . puffed up with attitude."

Worse, the rant seemed to be on a continual loop.

"What happened?" she asked, barely able to hear her own words.

Virgil's face was suddenly close to hers, red flickers of anger in his amber eyes. "You. Got. Shot."

She remembered that. Remembered the pain, the man who was going to finish killing her, and the furred nightmare that walked on two legs.

"I licked the wound clean," Virgil said.

Okay, she wasn't going to think about that, especially since she could feel herself fading. Failing. "Through and through?"

"What?"

"Did the bullet go through me?"

"No. It was stuck in you. I got it out."

"How?" Why were the last thoughts in her life going to be fueled by morbid curiosity?

"With. My. Teeth."

She stared at him as he bared his teeth. He had something caught between two teeth, like a bit of greens. Except it wasn't lettuce or spinach or anything that benign. It looked like meat. Flesh.

Her.

"Jana!" Virgil snapped her name and waited, watching.

His pack sister was gone again. Gone.

He leaned closer. Felt the shallow breath on his face.

"Jana!" Another voice calling her name.

He looked up and saw Tobias running toward them.

The man dropped to his knees, bent his face close to Jana's. It hurt to see the look of relief on the human's face.

"She's still with us," Tobias said, looking around.

"Most of the Wolfgard were dead when Kane and I got back to the den after the attack by the HFL humans," Virgil said softly. "The pups were dead. My mate . . . I licked her wound clean, but it didn't help. I couldn't fix my mate. All I could do was stay with her until she wasn't there anymore." He looked at Jana. "I can't fix my pack sister either, but I will stay with her until she isn't here anymore."

"*Virgil.*"

Virgil looked at the man. "Kane doesn't answer when I call."

"Virgil, Jana isn't a Wolf." Urgency filled Tobias's voice. "Jana is human, and the *human* bodywalker is at the hospital right now fixing up people who got hurt in the fight. Help me save her, Virgil. Help me save Jana."

They could save her?

Virgil sprang to his feet and ran to the edge of the street to look around. The horse that was not meat would be able to run fast to the human bodywalker's den, but . . .

Seeing the van coming toward him, he stepped into the street. The van screeched to a stop. The driver lifted himself halfway out the window.

"Gods, Virgil," Zeke shouted. "What the . . . ?"

Before Virgil could snarl a command—or bite the humans who had looked past him—past *him*—and now were foolishly scrambling out of the van—he heard movement behind him and turned to meet the threat.

Not a threat. It was Tobias, carrying Jana.

"Zeke, I'll get the doors," Larry said.

Zeke dodged around Virgil—who allowed him to dodge—and ran to Tobias.

"Oh gods," Zeke said, looking at Jana.

"Can't wait for the ambulance," Tobias said.

"Come on. Larry! Spread some of those bedsheets we picked up yesterday."

As Tobias and Zeke lifted her into the van, Jana groaned in pain.

Snarling, Virgil shifted to Wolf, ready to deal with any human who hurt the wolverine.

Then Zeke jumped out of the back of the van and Tobias said, "Virgil? You coming?"

He hesitated. <Kane?> No answer. <John?> No answer.

<Virgil!> Yuri called. <Candice Caravelli found a car with keys inside. We're taking John to the vet. One leg is gone. We don't know . . . I'll protect him.>

<Then I will help protect the wolverine while she is here.>

<Jana's . . . ?>

He didn't want to say more, didn't want to think. He leaped into the back of the van, careful not to step on Rusty's human mom, who was bleeding again.

Zeke closed the doors. A moment later, the van jolted forward, almost throwing Virgil off his feet. He lay down on the other side of Jana, giving her the only things he could—warmth and companionship.

Jesse approached the station platform. She hadn't seen Tolya as she and Tobias made their way from the southern end of Bennett's town square to the northern end. Tobias had headed off to help Jana. She continued on her own to the train station.

How many *terra indigene* had fought here? She stepped around dead men, automatically moving weapons out of easy reach as she went. She didn't think all these kills had been made by Elders. The bodies were too intact to be the work of Namid's teeth and claws.

Someone groaned inside the part of the station that stored packages and other freight.

Judging by the smashed boxes, a part of the fight had happened here, and the fighting had been fierce.

She found Hawks, Crows, and Ravens. Some were in their feathered form. Others were mostly human in shape—if you didn't look at the heads with beaks or the feet that had talons large enough to gut a man. All were dead from gunshot wounds.

Then she found Nicolai Sanguinati. One side of his face was masked by blood, and his breathing was harsh. He stared at her and slowly bared his teeth, revealing a fang that had broken at some point.

"Nicolai." Jesse kept her voice firm, just as she had the time Tobias had tried to ride a green colt and ended up with a broken leg. "It's Jesse Walker. Do you remember me?"

Could a Sanguinati have a concussion? Or brain damage? Nicolai looked like he'd taken a terrible blow to the head, but he could be paralyzed from some injury that she couldn't see. And what she could see of him would haunt her dreams for a very long time.

"I . . . remember." Every syllable took effort.

"Good. I'm going to step outside for a minute and find help. Then I'll come back and stay with you."

A quick look around confirmed that the telephone that had been on the counter had been smashed and the cord had been pulled out of the wall. Jesse took a couple of steps toward the passenger side of the station, then shook her head. Even if the phone worked, she had a feeling that there wouldn't be anyone answering phones today.

Standing outside the station, she whistled—the loud, sharp sound she'd mastered years ago to call a boy to supper.

Birds circled above her. Ravengard maybe. Vultures, more likely. But the vultures were ordinary birds, not *terra indigene*, and nothing responded to her whistle until . . .

She didn't recognize the man and woman who approached her cautiously. No visible wounds, but she figured the majority of the folks in

Bennett weren't used to handling guns and would have stayed out of the fight. Not like in the frontier stories where citizens grabbed shovels and pitchforks to help defend their town. But the hard truth was that any human who had picked up a weapon today would have been seen as an enemy.

"Who are you?" she asked.

"Craig and Dawn Werner," the man replied.

"You hurt?"

They shook their heads as they stared at all the bodies on the platform.

"I need you to find one of the Sanguinati. Any one of them will do. Try the hotel, the mayor's office, or the saloon. If you can't find one of them in those places, keep looking. Tell them Nicolai is at the train station and needs a little help." Nicolai needed a lot of help, but she was certain Tolya would prefer having injuries downplayed.

"Okay," Dawn said. "Is there anything we can bring back for you?"

"Water."

They hurried away, and Jesse hurried back to Nicolai.

Not knowing what was wrong with him, she stayed out of his reach. But she also stayed within sight so he would know he wasn't alone.

A few minutes later, Tolya walked in.

Jesse felt a moment of relief, even joy, at seeing him before she registered what she was seeing—or not seeing in his dark eyes.

This was a Sanguinati male without any pretense of humanity. Oh, the shape was still human enough, but it was a predator who stared at her.

"Nicolai needs your help," she said.

He dipped his head in the slightest acknowledgment, his eyes never leaving her face, never losing awareness of her hands—and the rifle she held.

Keeping the gun pointed at the ground, she moved slowly toward the door. He turned with her, keeping her in sight, his attention never wavering.

Predator. Other.

And she was human, one of the distrusted.

It surprised her how much that hurt.

She didn't want to believe he and the rest of the *terra indigene* had become enemies of the humans living in Bennett and Prairie Gold, but she wasn't sure that was true.

What had it cost the *terra indigene* to win this fight—and what had the humans lost?

Virgil left the hospital. Stinky place. Kept making him sneeze.

He could have helped keep the wound clean, but the human bodywalker wouldn't let him inside the fixing room, said he had to wait.

He would have shredded the fool's leg if the bodywalker hadn't made Tobias wait outside the room too.

He started to call for his brother, then stopped, already knowing there would be no answer. And John? A Wolf with three legs couldn't survive in the wild country, even with the pack's help. He wasn't sure John could survive in this human place either.

Something howled. A deep sound. Distant.

Virgil shuddered. Even shifters didn't want to approach *that* form of Elder. But he wasn't going to let that howl go unanswered because the wolverine had *challenged* the terrible one, had been the reason the Elders had attacked the enemy inside the town's boundaries. If he didn't answer now, Namid's teeth and claws would come back down from the hills— and after all the humans were dead, all the *terra indigene* would go back to the wild country and leave this place to the carrion eaters.

All the humans, including his pack sister. That he would not allow. *"Arroo!"* I am here. *"Arroo!"*

I am here. I am here. I am here.

Alone.

"Come on, darlin'. Time to wake up." Tobias's voice, warm and coaxing.

"Stupid female thinks she's a big predator . . . *small* predator . . . puffed up with attitude." Virgil. Still on a rant.

Jana tried to move. Big mistake. "Hurt," she whispered.

"Of course you hurt!" Virgil said from somewhere she couldn't see. "You. Got. Shot."

Tobias looked toward the door. "Not helping, Virgil."

Virgil just snarled.

Shot. Yes. She remembered. She'd been fading. Failing. Now? "How bad?"

"Well, Deputy, it was a little more than a flesh wound." Tobias said the words lightly, but now that she could focus enough to see his face, she could tell the effort to keep it light was costing him, because it didn't last. "You lost a lot of blood. But the doc patched you up and said the bullet didn't hit anything vital. You'll be in here for a day or two so that the doc can keep an eye on you, and then you'll be on desk duty for a while once you go back to work." He paused. "One thing about living around Intuits. Plenty of people showed up at the hospital, saying they had a feeling the doctors needed help and patients needed blood."

Tobias reached for something on the bed tray positioned over her knees. "There might have been concerns about the blood that the hospital had stocked, but look what Fagen and his food salvage crew found to assist patients in their recovery." He held up a container full of a green substance.

"No one raided the kitchens here and took the green gelatin?"

"Nope. The hospital has its full complement of the stuff."

"Goody." Light banter. An effort to say nothing important. "Barb?"

"Neither doc here is a surgeon, but they got the bullet out. Barb might have some trouble with that arm and shoulder, but the doc expects she'll heal up fine otherwise."

"Frontier surgery."

"Wasn't quite that bad. Modern facility—or as modern as a place like Bennett could afford to have—and plenty of people to help. She'll be all right. So will you."

"Her family lives in Lakeside. Someone should tell them."

"Tolya will take care of that."

They heard Virgil snarl, a sound ramped up several times from his usual unfriendly greeting. And they heard someone say, "It's time for her pain medicine, so move your furry rump."

Jana looked at Tobias. Tobias looked at her. They both looked toward the door as Sarah Gott walked into the room.

"Honestly," Sarah said as she approached the bed. "He won't come in, he won't stay out. He just blocks the doorway and scares everyone."

Jana drifted in and out for the rest of the day and night. Whenever she surfaced, Tobias was there to talk, to hold her hand, to read to her until she drifted back to sleep. And Virgil was there, blocking the doorway and making a nuisance of himself.

But when she woke shortly before dawn, she felt something under her hand and realized Virgil must have come into the room at some point. And at some point, someone must have explained to him about germs and keeping things clean in a hospital, because what she found under her hand was Cowboy Bob carefully wrapped in a plastic bag.

CHAPTER 37

Earthday, Frais 2

Jesse tapped on the doorframe of the mayor's office.

"Jesse Walker," Tolya said, his voice cold and precise. "Come in."

"I guess I started this by pushing you to let Bennett be a viable town again. I'm sorry for that."

"Those humans, the outlaws, would have come sooner or later."

"Yes, they would have." *But you would have killed them the moment they arrived instead of leaving yourself open to a threat.* "How is Nicolai? Does he need blood? Do you?"

"No." Sharp. Almost cutting.

"Is there anything I can do to help?"

Softer now. "No. Thank you. A Sanguinati bodywalker is coming to assess what can be done for Nicolai. Until then . . ." He left it unsaid.

"And you?" Jesse asked.

He held up his right hand, showing her that the first joint of the ring finger was missing. "A small but valuable lesson."

She wondered how humans were going to survive that lesson. She saw the predator, devoid of any feelings for anything but his own kind. But she had a feeling that, given time, some measure of friendship might be accepted again.

"I'm going to talk to Kelley. I heard Dina's body was found."

"Yes. She was killed by a human."

More than killed. Tortured. Raped.

There was nothing more to say, so she turned to leave.

"Jesse."

She looked back.

Tolya studied her with those cold, inhuman eyes that maybe—*maybe*—held the tiniest bit of remembered warmth. "Fire told me what you did to help us."

"To help all of us. My people and yours."

"That choice will have weight in whatever we decide to do about Bennett."

Jesse nodded and left. She had been shaped by the wild country just as much as the *terra indigene* who lived in the Elder Hills, and she could be just as fierce and as ruthless when it came to protecting her own.

Nothing she could do about the dead—not Dina or the men who'd burned—so she would do what she could for the living.

Tolya stood behind his desk in the mayor's office and faced Yuri, Isobel, and Anya. "We are the keystone form of *terra indigene* here. We're the form most adapted to human places." *Urban places, not places like this.* "If we leave, no other form wants to take over the leadership of this town. If we leave, most of the *terra indigene* will abandon the town as well."

"Will Scythe leave?" Yuri asked.

"This will become her hunting ground."

"You're deciding this without asking Grandfather Erebus?" Isobel asked.

"I was given the task of securing the town so that the railroad station wouldn't be taken over by humans who were enemies of the *terra indigene*. The only way to do that was to bring in more Sanguinati and other forms of *terra indigene*—and particular humans. But I was too indulgent, allowed too many humans to come in too quickly. And I waited instead of killing Parlan Blackstone when he first arrived. We paid dearly for my mistakes."

They didn't disagree with him. They'd lost Stazia. They would never know what had compelled her to partially take on a form vulnerable to human weapons, but she hadn't been able to shift fully to smoke before being struck by a bullet and damaged beyond saving.

They had taken her into the Elder Hills and buried her in a secret place—and had agreed that they would not acknowledge to *any* human that a Sanguinati had been killed in the fight because humans might be able to figure out how it had been done and try to do it to the rest of them. If anyone asked, Stazia had left Bennett.

Nicolai, on the other hand . . . Jesse Walker was the only human still alive who had seen Nicolai, was the only one who knew how badly humans could damage one of the Sanguinati. Nicolai had fought hard, had killed so many, but at least one of the enemy had delivered a crippling blow. One side of his face looked crushed, but he couldn't shift it out of its human form. He also couldn't shift one arm and most of his torso. And the parts that were smoke sometimes almost shifted to human or, usually, shifted to the Sanguinati's true form.

With the help of a Sanguinati bodywalker, Nicolai would find his way back to a single form or he wouldn't. If he couldn't, he, too, would have to leave Bennett.

"If we stay, there must be changes," Yuri said.

"If we stay, the humans who are here now will be under our protection," Tolya said. "Strangers who come to Bennett will be prey. Humans like Parlan Blackstone and his clan will not be allowed to survive long enough to become a threat."

"If the Elders now consider 'outlaws' as a dangerous form of human who act in a particular way, there won't be many of them who live long enough to reach Bennett," Yuri said.

"There will still be prey." Tolya said, knowing that even among the humans who would have their protection, very few of them would *not* be considered prey. Not anymore. He made a small hand gesture to indicate Yuri. "You'll take over the train station?"

Yuri shook his head. "I'll stay at the saloon. Saul Panthergard said he'd handle the station until Nicolai is well. And Joshua will stay at the bookstore and help John."

A three-legged Wolf had no chance of surviving in the wild country, but a man who had lost an arm could still do work and provide himself with food and shelter.

Tolya looked at the Sanguinati. Anya, Isobel, and Yuri met his eyes and nodded.

"We stay," he said.

As they turned to leave, Anya said, "Parlan Blackstone survived. Where is he?"

Tolya's lips curved in a grim smile. "He's with Scythe."

Parlan had a bad feeling that the rope around his chest was the only reason he was still able to sit in the chair. His arms and hands weren't bound. Neither were his legs. It didn't matter. They'd stopped working. His heart labored to keep pumping. His lungs labored to draw in each breath.

"Where's my son?" he gasped, barely recognizing the weak, quavery voice as his own. "My brother?"

"Dead," the *thing* replied. "All dead."

"I issued a challenge, all right and proper."

"Nothing about your challenge was right or proper," she said. "You knew what would happen if any of the outlaws killed one of the *terra indigene*. And yet you thought you could stack the deck, that you could cheat in your dealings with us and somehow win."

"Not true," he gasped, fighting to breathe. Of course it was true. It should have worked, but it all went wrong. "If I've done wrong, then I should stand trial."

"There is no need for such human things here. Besides, Virgil and Tolya already decided what to do with you." She brushed close to him and suddenly leaned down, her face right in front of him, giving him no time to look away. "They gave you to me."

He didn't look at her for more than a wavering heartbeat.

As she walked away, her black hair coiling, he felt the strangest sensation.

He felt it start to rain inside his skull.

CHAPTER 38

Thaisday, Frais 6

"Easy, now." Tobias opened the truck door and held out his hand. "Let me help you."

Jana didn't argue about receiving help. After two days in the hospital and two days at home, she was glad to be back to work, even if it was desk duty.

She was glad to be alive.

Standing on the wooden sidewalk, she studied the new sign in the window of the sheriff's office. "Did you do that?"

Tobias shook his head. "Virgil did. He called you his pack sister, when he thought you were . . . Well, you know."

She blinked back the sharp sting of tears. Pack sister? Really? Ah, geez.

Ignoring her quiet sniffle, Tobias said, "He's missed you. He hasn't forgiven you for thinking you were big enough to stop a bullet, but he's missed you. He even filled the little fridge in the office with containers of green gelatin because someone at the hospital told him it was a food humans liked when they were injured and needed to get well."

"Oh gods," Jana groaned. "Now I'm going to have to eat it."

"Yep."

Jana thought about that. "Barb is going stir-crazy at home, and she still needs plenty of help doing things. And I'm going to need to take breaks and little naps throughout the day."

"Darlin', why does that sound like you're about to pull Virgil's tail?"

"Because you're getting to know me?" And if she gave Virgil a reason to snarl at her, he would know she was getting better.

Tobias laughed.

Before they went into the office, Jana took another look at the sign and smiled.

HE HAS TEETH.

SHE HAS A GUN.

THEY ARE THE LAW.

Virgil stared at Jana's desk. Her *empty* desk. His pack sister was supposed to come back today. Why didn't she come back? No, her scent was here and fresh. A little different because there was stinky human medicine smell mixed with it, but no wolverine sitting at the desk. Didn't she want to be police pack anymore?

He heard muffled voices coming from the cells in the back. Female voices.

He hurried back there, then stopped at the Me Time cell. Just stopped.

"Tobias Walker, what are you doing?" he demanded.

Tobias stepped down from a stool and raised his hands. "Hey, I'm just a guy. I'm doing what I'm told."

"We decided to fix up the Me Time cell so that Barb and I can rest when we need to," Jana said brightly. "And Tobias put up the curtains for us so that we could have privacy."

Virgil eyed the changes. Curtains long enough to almost brush the floor. The rods were secured to the bars with barely a paw of space between rod and ceiling. They covered the two sides of the cell that weren't walls.

The cot, which had had a thin mattress that was supposed to be un-comfortable to encourage good behavior, now had a thick mattress and a big pillow with arms that looked like the top half of a puffy chair.

Barb sat in a rocking chair that also had cushions and pillows, her feet up on an ottoman, and one arm in a sling.

He pointed at the chair. "That's dangerous. The puppy might get her tail caught under it."

"There's plenty of room for her," Barb said, pointing at the space un-der the cot. "See?"

Rusty poked her head out and gave him a welcoming yip, but she didn't come over to greet him. No, she stayed right next to her mom's leg. *Traitor.*

Who had remembered to bring her food and take her out to piddle? Who had taken her for runs that, they had agreed, were not going to be mentioned to her mom?

Who had gone back to the stinky hospital to rescue Cowboy Bob after Jana didn't need the stuffie anymore?

"Thanks, Tobias," Jana said, slowly getting up from the cot.

"Anytime." He stepped out of the cell, taking the stool with him. "I'll leave you ladies to get settled in, and I'll be back in a bit with some vict-uals."

As Virgil watched, unsure what to do, Jana pulled the cell door part-way closed and pulled the curtain all the way across the bars, shutting him out.

Jana heard the slow click of nails on the floor—again. Then the hesi-tation and silent approach, followed by audible sniffing and a nose poking under the curtain.

When Virgil retreated—again—Jana got up and moved the big read-ing pillow to the other end of the cot, turning it so she could sit with her body supported and her feet on the floor.

She'd meant it as a joke, as just enough of a tail pull to annoy Virgil so that he would know she was okay. She'd thought he would respect a privacy curtain for about five minutes before pushing it aside and growling at her. But he hadn't done that. He was acting like that piece of fabric was a stone wall keeping him out, a barrier he could not cross.

Barb stirred and opened her eyes.

"You need anything?" Jana asked quietly.

"No."

The rapid click of nails. Had Virgil been standing at the door to the cells, waiting to hear one of them speak?

She looked at Barb. They waited.

The audible sniff. The nose poking under the curtain. And then . . . a whine.

He sounded so lonely. But he wouldn't enter the den made for her and Barb.

She pulled the curtain aside and looked at the big Wolf. "You can come in if you want to. We're just sitting here pretending we don't fall asleep every ten minutes."

She sat on the cot to give him room. Besides the rocking chair and ottoman, Tobias had added a narrow storage unit that allowed them to keep containers of water and juice on one shelf and a selection of books on another. It hadn't seemed crowded, but Virgil took up most of the available floor space when he lay down.

Rusty crawled out from under the cot, gently mouthing Cowboy Bob, and went over to greet the Wolf.

Watching them, Jana wondered if Virgil had become Rusty's favorite stuffie—and how many unauthorized activities those two had engaged in during the couple of days she'd been in the hospital.

And she wondered whether he'd slept at all since the fight, or if he'd been patrolling and letting certain Elders know that he was still there.

As his eyes closed, Jana felt him relax against her legs. He didn't even stir to challenge Tobias when the man returned, which told her how exhausted Virgil had to be. And it told her one other thing—that Virgil trusted her to stand guard when he couldn't.

Tobias looked at Barb, who was dozing again, then at Virgil and Rusty sprawled on the floor, sound asleep. He gave her a smile and a wink before quietly retreating. When the phone rang, she heard him answer it and tell someone that he would take a message.

As news about what happened in Bennett traveled to human towns,

Jana hoped a particular message would reach the Elders who ruled and protected the wild country.

We are here. We are different but we stand united to protect our home. We are different but we protect our families, whether they are families by blood or by heart. We are different but we are not alone. Never alone.

We are here.

GEOGRAPHY
AND OTHER INFORMATION

NAMID—THE WORLD

CONTINENTS/LANDMASSES

Afrikah
Australis
Brittania/Wild Brittania
Cel-Romano/Cel-Romano Alliance of Nations
Felidae
Fingerbone Islands
Storm Islands
Thaisia
Tokhar-Chin
Zelande

LAKES AND RIVERS IN THAISIA

Great Lakes—Superior, Tala, Honon, Etu, and Tahki
Feather Lakes/Finger Lakes
River—Talulah/Talulah Falls

MOUNTAINS

Addirondak
Rocky

CITIES AND VILLAGES MENTIONED IN THE STORY

Bennett, Endurance, Ferryman's Landing, Hubb NE (aka Hubbney),
    Lakeside, Prairie Gold, Ravendell, Shikago, Sparkletown,
    Sweetwater, Talulah Falls, Toland

CALENDAR

DAYS OF THE WEEK

Earthday (a spiritual day and a day of rest)
Moonsday
Sunsday
Windsday
Thaisday
Firesday
Watersday

MONTHS OF THE YEAR

Janius
Febros
Viridus
Aprillis
Maius
Juin
Sumor
Messis
Frais
Grau
Novembros
Dormente

CAST OF CHARACTERS

BENNETT

Air (Elemental)
Abigail Burch
Kelley Burch
Candice Caravelli
Zane Coyotegard
Barb (Barbara Ellen) Debany
Dina
Judith Dixon
Melanie Dixon
Stewart Dixon
Fagen
Fire (Elemental)
Fog (pony)
Larry
Lila Gold
Becky Gott
Hannah Gott
Jacob Gott
Sarah Gott
Charlee Hawkgard
Evan Hua
Freddie Kaye
Maddie (*cassandra sangue*)
Manuel
Don Miller
Pearl Owlgard

Joshua Painter
Jana Paniccia
Saul Panthergard
Garnet Ravengard
Anya Sanguinati
Isobel Sanguinati
Nicolai Sanguinati
Stazia Sanguinati
Tolya Sanguinati
Yuri Sanguinati
Scythe / Madam Scythe (Harvester, Plague Rider)
Kenneth Stone
Thunder (pony)
Twister (pony)
Craig Werner
Dawn Werner
John Wolfgard
Kane Wolfgard
Mason (Mace) Wolfgard
Virgil Wolfgard
Zeke

FERRYMAN'S LANDING

Officer Roger Czerneda
Steve Ferryman

LAKESIDE

Captain Douglas Burke
Meg Corbyn (*cassandra sangue*), aka Broomstick Girl
Jenni Crowgard
Officer Michael Debany

Nadine Fallacaro
Officer Karl Kowalski
Merri Lee
Lieutenant Crispin James Montgomery
Erebus Sanguinati, aka Grandfather Erebus
Vladimir (Vlad) Sanguinati
Tess
Simon Wolfgard

PRAIRIE GOLD

Wyatt Beargard
Shelley Bookman
Ellen Garcia
Tom Garcia
Phil Mailer
Truman Skye
Floyd Tanner
Edna (Ed) Tilman
Jesse Walker
Tobias Walker
Stanley Weeks
Chase Wolfgard
Morgan Wolfgard
Rachel Wolfgard

SWEETWATER

Amy Wolfgard
Grace Wolfgard
Jackson Wolfgard
Hope Wolfsong (*cassandra sangue*)

MISCELLANEOUS

Daniel Black
Martha Chase
Wilbur "Pops" Chase
Henry Hollis
Cyrus James Montgomery
Stavros Sanguinati
Joe Wolfgard

OUTLAWS

Dalton Blackstone
Lawry Blackstone
Parlan Blackstone, aka the Gambler
Daddy Bonney
Eli Bonney
Frank Bonney
Ma Bonney
Sweeney Cooke
Durango Jones
Judd McCall, aka the Knife
Wallace Parker
William Parker
Sleight-of-Hand Slim
Charlie Webb